DIGGING DEEPER

A NOVEL

BY

KATHLEEN HAUN

aventine press

Published by Aventine Press
55 East Emerson St.
Chula Vista CA 91911
www.aventinepress.com

ISBN: 978-1-59330-985-5

Printed in the United States of America
ALL RIGHTS RESERVED

OTHER NOVELS BY KATHLEEN HAUN

Dear Carrie
Letters from the Eastern Sierra, 1878-1899

Passing Storms

Moving On

No Trees For Shade
Bodie, California 1880

Chasing the Dream

Declining Fortunes

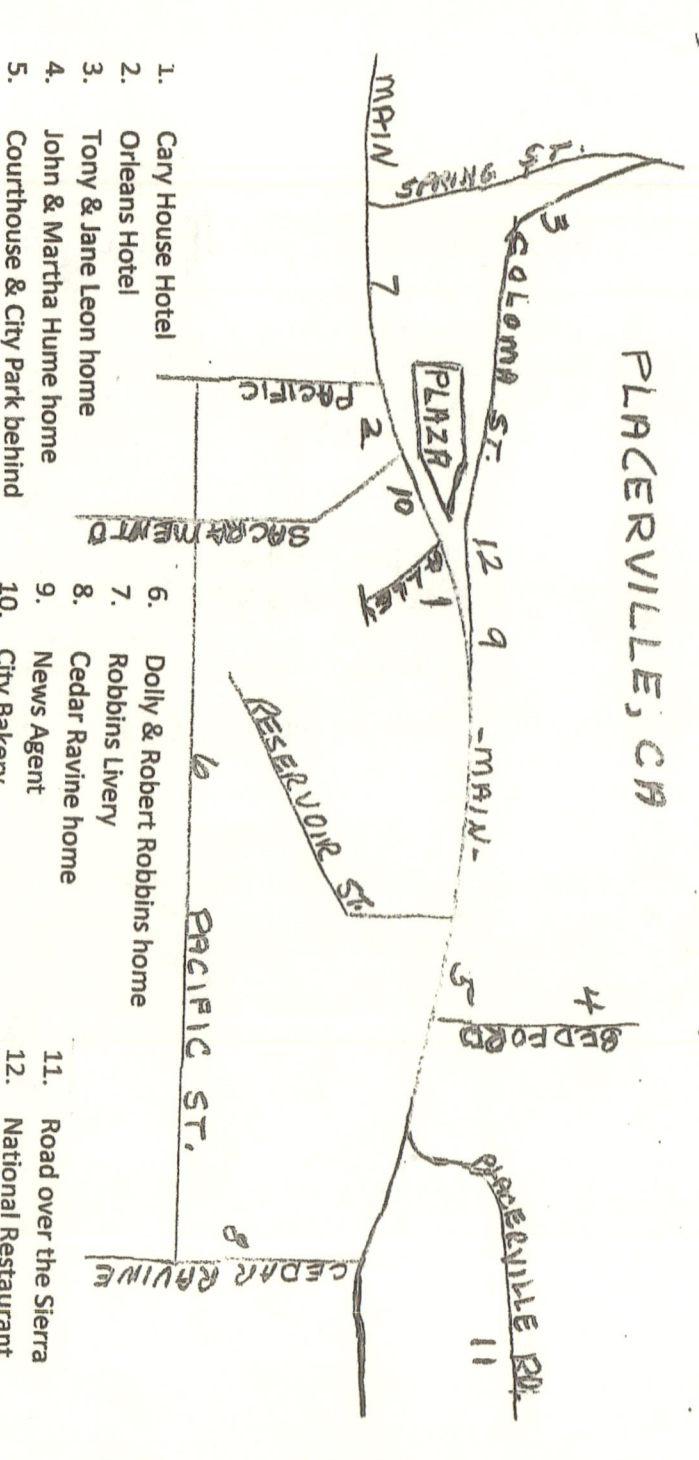

PLACERVILLE, CA

1. Cary House Hotel
2. Orleans Hotel
3. Tony & Jane Leon home
4. John & Martha Hume home
5. Courthouse & City Park behind

6. Dolly & Robert Robbins home
7. Robbins Livery
8. Cedar Ravine home
9. News Agent
10. City Bakery

11. Road over the Sierra
12. National Restaurant

FOREWORD

"Will you walk into my parlor?"
said a spider to a fly.
"'Tis the prettiest little parlor
that ever you did spy."
Mary Howitt, 1799 - 1888

Roger Murphy stood in front of the window of his mother's cozy house on "B" Street in Virginia City, Nevada, not far from his own home. It was the snowy part of the winter of 1886, and as he looked out at the street's light traffic, he thought of slogging to the Bucket of Blood Saloon to relieve his boredom. His wife was busy at home, and the day stretched before Roger without definition, having gotten the impression that his wife wanted him out of the house so she could expend energy in cleaning it. He sighed loudly.

"Roger, what's the problem?" Lucy Murphy looked up from where she was comfortably ensconced on the new satin sofa not far from the small parlor stove. His attractive mother had just celebrated her 50th birthday, but looked ten years younger and had the energy of a woman twenty years younger. She now inserted a leather book mark between the pages of the novel she was reading and laid it on the table next to her. "If you're not going into town to play poker, or some such entertainment, then why don't you sit down and read a book?"

Roger turned to his mother with a gleam in his eyes. "I'll tell you what I'd like to do."

"What's that?" Lucy smiled.

"I'd like to hear from you why we moved from Jamestown to Placerville during the Civil War, when I was almost six years old. All of it, details and all."

"Oh, that." Lucy was no longer smiling. "It was a combination of things."

"All I remember is a lot of strange, whispered conversations that stopped the minute I was anywhere near. I've always known it was something you weren't eager to talk about, so I've never asked you before. But I'm a grown man now." He couldn't hold back an impish grin. "I think I can handle whatever it was about, don't you?"

"Yes, of course. In fact, you're the same age now that I was when I went to Placerville in the summer of 1862."

Roger moved to one of the chairs across from the sofa and glanced up at the light scar on his mother's cheek. "Is it so unpleasant that it will upset you to relate it to me?"

She resisted the urge to roll her eyes. "In the first place, it has nothing to do with the scar." She looked at the tea tray in front of her, started to reach forward, and then stopped. "I got that a good number of years before the events of what you're asking about. But to answer your question, in 1862 when we were still in Jamestown, California, I was asked to come to Placerville."

"Who by?"

She sighed with resignation as she removed the tea cozy from the large china teapot before pouring amber liquid into her cup. "It's a rather long story, not to mention complicated, so you'd best get something to drink and make yourself comfortable. Even before I arrived in Placerville, a lot had taken place to disturb the population there." She glanced at her son with a silly smirk. "I only added to it."

Knowing his mother so well, Roger wasn't surprised at that admission. He poured himself a whiskey at the sideboard, diluted it with two pumps of seltzer from the glass dispenser, and returned to his chair. He was glad she couldn't hear his heart beating, because he was more excited than he wanted to admit. She was seldom willing to talk about her past, so he wanted nothing to disturb them until he got the entire episode laid before him. Of course, that wasn't realistic and it took parts of several days that week to get the whole story from her. But in the end, he finally knew. And he felt a greater pride of being her son than ever before.

CHAPTER 1

*"This Strange Adventure may lead, in a later chapter,
to the revealing of a mysterious crime."* The Londoner

May, 1862

The spring of 1862 closed out a winter season that those in the Sierra Nevada mining town of Placerville, California, were relieved to see come to an end. In fact, citizens throughout California were looking forward to a pleasant summer after a catastrophic, record-setting winter of heavy rain and flooding. The concept of *dry* was a very welcome one.

For those unfortunate people who have not had the pleasure of visiting Placerville, it is located on the western slope of the Sierra Nevada, and 50 miles east of the state capitol of Sacramento. Resting in a narrow, shallow valley at just under 1,200 feet in elevation, it is surrounded by the beauty of tree-covered rolling hills, rushing creeks, and miles of well-used trails. But this indicates nothing of its welcoming and friendly population, or its unique place in the history of the West. The latter may of course be researched, but the former can only be experienced in person.

This welcoming atmosphere was true of the town even in 1862, at which time it had been the County Seat of El Dorado County for only five years. Starting out as a gold rush camp fourteen years earlier, and having rebuilt itself after the fire of 1856, it was established as an important supply center for those crossing the Sierra on the Placerville Road. Due to the news of the fabulous wealth of mines, among which was the already famous Comstock Mine, most of those heading *east* through town were aiming for Virginia City in Nevada Territory, which had been carved out from Utah Territory a year earlier. Those heading *west* through Placerville were mostly those who had found out the hard way that the wealth of that fast-growing town was not obtainable by everyone. However, some of the western bound stages arrived in Placerville with bags of gold ore that were dumped on the porch of the Cary House Hotel where the Wells, Fargo & Company offices were located.

Placerville had mines of its own, but they were now mostly hard rock mines owned by big conglomerates rather than placers worked by prospectors with picks and pans. Of course, there were still those holdouts hunting for whatever fragments of gold that might remain in the creeks, but each year there were fewer of these hopeful searchers.

Although Placerville could not brag about the same kind of excitement brought on by the wealth rumored to be in Gold Canyon and Virginia City, it had something those Nevada Territory towns did not. It had a well-developed, civilized society and an organized government. It also had pride of place, being located amid giant pines, oaks, and fir trees that had not been completely stripped from the surrounding hillsides for heat and building material during *the rush* back in the early 1850's.

No longer a ramshackle mining camp of tents and log cabins without laws and little order, Placerville after more than a decade of growth was a town that had aspirations of becoming a major city. It had, after all, several churches, fraternal organizations with their own halls, and of course a fair number of saloons and gambling halls. Main Street was lined with shops that included bookstores, breweries, markets, bath houses, an iron foundry, and a soda works. Most of the Main Street sidewalks were covered, with posts every eight feet along the edge that held up these covers, most of wood but some of canvas. As County Seat of El Dorado County, it most notably had a fire department, a formidable brick courthouse flanked by law offices, a City Police Department, and the County Sheriff's Office.

The weather was warm in the summer, and usually entertained no more than a foot or two of snow in the winter. Hangtown Creek, the source of much early gold, ran north of the town, its source being at the foot of Smith's Flat about two miles east of the town, and fed by streams from several ravines adjacent to the town. Only after the three months ending in January of 1862, when 63 inches of rain had fallen in the area, had the creek for the first time looked more like a river.

Thankfully, there had been little damage to Placerville, especially when compared to the calamities that had occurred in Sacramento and other lower elevation California towns that winter. The creek was already lowering, its flow dumping into Weber Creek a mile and a half away, and that creek running into the South Fork of the American River which in turn flowed into the Sacramento River. Placerville's reputation as an easily traversable town remained intact.

The moderate temperatures of May meant the remaining snow was melting quickly on the narrow, twisting road across the Sierra that cut along sheer mountain walls while at some points also overhanging the American River rushing far below. This snow melt meant that the town could once again make money off those human hoards on their way to the wealth of the mining towns of the Eastern Sierra and into Nevada.

These men, and a very few women, took no notice of the tall, stately trees still on the hills curving around Placerville that were full of spring birds and their twittering song. Nor did they notice the colorful wildflowers that blossomed wherever the sun warmed the earth. For those in town and those traveling through, it was commerce that created excitement that spring. The dog-legged course of Main Street was lined with huge, lumbering freight wagons piled high with hay, fresh food, mining supplies and inventory for the shops and mines. The wagons' metal-rimmed wheels cut deep ruts into the mud of Main Street while the shouts of the freighters filled the air with oaths as they urged their mules, horses or oxen forward.

But no one in town complained, because it meant food and items to fill empty shelves, and even more importantly, money spent in local businesses. Although most of the freighters halted their wagon teams only briefly before continuing on over the mountain, it didn't matter. They had to eat, sleep, drink, visit the ladies not mentioned in polite society, and hopefully spend considerable time in a gambling hall. So, one way or another, the town benefitted.

One thing of importance Placerville lacked this spring of 1862 was the Pony Express Office at the east end of town, which had been shuttered and locked since October of the previous year. That eighteen-month, famous enterprise was no more. No longer would townspeople watch with hopeful expectation as a young rider raced down Main Street to the office to hand off part of what was in his saddlebags, then leap onto the saddle of a fresh horse, and immediately continue on westward. The thrilling memory of it, however, would linger far into the future.

While the streets were full of freight wagons and men on horseback trying to avoid them, as well as spring wagons full of local goods and even a few fancy black rigs, there were also people who filled the wooden plank sidewalks. Whether women in long dresses and carrying woven shopping bags, business men in suits and ties, or ranchers and miners in denim, they all stopped to visit with one another. As they talked each morning, they inhaled the bacon-scented smoke that rose from stoves inside comfortable wooden or stone houses, restaurants and an occasional saloon with a chop house inside. At the same time, the laughter of children going to school could be heard as they raced down the streets in answer to the clanging of the school bell in the distance.

Eventually, after the day's busy activities were completed, kerosene lamps would be lit in homes as traffic on the streets decreased and customers in the saloons increased. A few of the more prosperous establishments had gas lighting, fed by hard coal furnaces and channeled through iron pipes. But light at night was minimal, and everyone took for granted a night sky densely filled with stars. The wind might pick up during the night due to the area's close proximity to mountain canyons and rising peaks, but few nights would be interrupted by a gun shot. There might be some shouting during a disturbance of the peace, or a fist fight in a saloon, but the wildest of the old days was part of the town's past. Or so they hoped.

All in all, the casual observer that spring would have said that Placerville was an average California town going about the business of recovering from a wet winter while getting on with the chores and tasks of daily living. And for most people in the town, this was true. What many did not want to think about, and tried even less to speak of, was something unusual that had been taking place over the last month.

There was a subtle, underlying tension that was growing among a portion of the population. It was not yet in the nature of something that one might see published in the newspapers, or that would become part of historical content. But it was nevertheless worrisome and causing a disruption to the normal enjoyment of peaceful conviviality between townspeople, which until lately had been an accepted part of life.

Just outside the post office at the west end of town, a woman stopped on the sidewalk and looked around to see if anyone was near her. Jane Leon — Mrs. Tony Leon, that is — looked down at the few envelopes in her hand with a worried frown. She had ceased going through her mail inside the post office because she didn't want to expose it to prying eyes. This was especially true now that so many others in town had received the same type of letter and might recognize the block printing on an envelope. She slid her mail into her cloth shopping bag before pulling her shawl up around her shoulders and hurrying home.

Middle-aged at thirty-seven, Jane Leon was of average height, her mousy brown hair pulled back from her not unattractive face into a knot under her hat, which ladies referred to as a bonnet. This one was new, had pink silk flowers on one side, and she was very proud of it even if it was a little behind the latest fashion in the East. She would also be sure to hide it before her husband returned from his latest pack trip into the mountains.

Jane had trusting brown eyes, and fair skin lightly freckled from spending so much time on the back porch of her home while working at her spinning wheel. She was known for her warm and friendly personality, and was secretly proud of a figure that only needed a little assistance from a light corset. Her husband liked to say she needed no corset at all. It was the best of the few compliments she had ever gotten from him.

Her dress on this day was beige calico with a brown fleck. Drab would easily summarize a description of her wardrobe, although she did have a black dress kept for funerals, and a dress she kept aside for what she called *dressy occasions*. Although silk with velvet trim, it was an unremarkable gray with only one swag across the front of a skirt that allowed for only two petticoats to hold it out. She had once purchased fabric of a dark golden color, but Tony had said it was too bold and she had returned it to the store.

Jane had long ago accepted her nondescript appearance and her marriage to a judgmental husband who was critical of everyone he knew unless they were his drinking buddies. He hadn't always been this way, but over the last few years he seemed to have lost much of his sense of humor, at least around her. The men he drank with probably would have said otherwise. Nevertheless, because he was a packer gone for weeks at a time, she had taken over the running of the household and their finances. She often smiled to herself, smug with the knowledge that Tony didn't realize this meant she had also taken over control of much that he did when home. It was the reason she was content to wear whatever he preferred for her.

She was irritated now not because she wished for what was bright and flamboyant, but because she felt that no one so average as herself deserved to be singled out for unwarranted attention. She just couldn't understand what she had done to have stepped out of the shadows into the glare of someone's unwelcome criticism.

Once again at home, Jane went through the small stack of envelopes in her hands. She immediately felt the heavy beating of her heart calm as she realized that she didn't have another of *those* letters today. She prayed God that the two letters received over the past month would be the end of it. Thinking of the importance of people's opinions, she told herself, "I'm a respectable woman married these past eleven years, even if I've not had a child." What woman had she harmed so badly that they would choose to do something like this to her?

Unfortunately, she had a husband who because he spent long periods away from home, might believe the trash written in the letters. She wondered if he had heard about these anonymous letters being received by some of the Placerville citizens. He hadn't said anything about them the last time he had been home, even though he had spent considerable time in saloons where the letters must have been under discussion. However, she knew how reluctant men were to talk about anything they felt might cast a shadow of doubt onto their reputations. And the anonymous letters certainly might do that. On the other hand, she also knew how much men liked to talk about rumors, even if they decried such a thing as gossiping.

Tony Leon was an average looking man of forty-five with a thick, neatly trimmed beard, a muscled body that carried not one ounce of unnecessary fat, and shrewd brown eyes that nevertheless managed to look a little vacant much of the time. He had left his Scottish homeland as a young man where, in order to be given a job he wanted, he had declared himself a sheep man. That this hadn't been true might not have mattered, except that he had been raised in a seafaring village and knew absolutely nothing about caring for sheep. The tragedy of this had been demonstrated when he had sheared to the point of nakedness a small flock under his care in early October, and they had consequently died of exposure during the cold winter that followed. The townspeople in the village where he had made this mistake had taken extreme umbrage and he had thought it best to leave the area.

The story of his idiocy might not have followed him, what with a long sea voyage followed by a perilous crossing of the Isthmus of Panama between him and Scotland, but he had more than once when under the influence of alcohol repeated it to his fellows. As he explained it, he had ended up in San Francisco where he had met Jane, had settled down there for several years, and after once again displeasing an employer, had decided to work for himself. They had moved to Placerville just after the 1856 fire, and he had proved himself a hard worker among those rebuilding the town. He had thus gained the acceptance he had long sought for himself.

Jane had assumed that with Tony a respected packer, and always welcomed home by friends after being gone for weeks at a time, that they had found their ideal home. But after this latest letter, which falsely accused her of unspeakable things when she had been in San Francisco prior to meeting Tony, as well as licentious activities while he was gone on his trips, Jane was wondering if they would once again have to move.

Tony too had received a letter. It had been left on the front porch where Jane found it when she had gone out to sweep the porch one morning. She had ignored his name on the envelope, and had read the contents. The note had been pretty general about his "past mistakes", although it had hinted that more specifics might follow. Jane was aware of the rumor that her husband had a bit of a roving eye, although as far as Jane knew that was as far as it had ever gone. Nevertheless, because many people knew of his occasional, crudely inappropriate comments about women that were sometimes said too loudly in public, it might give bait to someone looking for claims they could make in an accusatory letter. She threw it into the stove fire and said nothing about it to Tony.

Of course, Jane had no doubt that Tony had "visited" one of the "local ladies" at one of the "boarding houses" in town. She preferred thinking about the subject in euphemisms because it made the topic more detached from the reality of the life she shared with her husband. Maybe, Jane thought, if her mother had not always referred to sex as "one's duty" she would have made herself "available" to her husband more frequently over the years. It might also have upped the odds for successful procreation.

But the pattern of their lives was set now, and she assured herself that Tony was content with their life together. She took pride in the fact that she was a very good housekeeper and cook, and assumed this was important to him, too. She also managed their money so that there was always plenty of food in the pantry, an amount put by for emergencies, and a little left over that she gave Tony for his amusements. Yes, she thought, Tony was a fortunate man because of her. And she made sure he knew it.

Over on a nearby street, Mrs. Jones had not been so lucky that day. She sat in her parlor reading again what she considered disgusting accusations aimed at her from some awful woman. She was just happy that her husband Joseph was at work.

Roberta Jones was basically happy with her life. When she looked in the mirror, she saw a pretty woman of thirty with caramel colored skin, glossy dark hair and bright green eyes. She never questioned whether or not men other than her husband considered her attractive, because the only thing that mattered to her was Joseph's opinion. And he assured her with both words and actions that she was still the love of his life. Her full figure might need the help of a corset to emphasize a waist, but she claimed that she was still working to get back her old figure after the birth of their child. This ignored the fact that the child had just celebrated his eighth birthday.

On this day, with Joseph still at work and her son in school, Roberta sat at the kitchen table and slowly sipped a cup of coffee. It was the fifth time that day that she had picked up the anonymous letter, about which Joseph knew nothing. Although what it said was a lie, the concept of such sexual behavior between men and women rather intrigued her.

Oh, not that she would ever have allowed a man to touch her in that way. No, not ever, even when she was a girl, as the note claimed she had done. Well, probably not. But it was a concept new to her and it aroused certain tingling sensations she had not felt since shortly after her marriage to her rigidly respectable, bank clerk husband. She had to admit that although he had advanced beyond being a clerk, his skill in bed had not advanced, more's the pity. She sighed heavily and hid the letter at the bottom of her jewelry box.

Women, however, were not the only ones receiving such a missive that day, or for that matter over the past month. Bert Caulfield was married with three small children, and a wife often unwell and confined to her bed. He knew this made him susceptible to some nasty woman accusing him of looking elsewhere for female companionship.

He had in fact visited one of the more respectable parlor houses in his off time as part of the construction crew building the new California Brewery for Mr. Jacob Zeisz, at the east end of town. The brothel he had chosen for his erotic escapade was known for employing discreet ladies, which made it a favored house by those most needing to protect their reputation. Now he wondered if someone had seen him entering or leaving.

Bill Coffey, who shared a room at the Cary House with two other men, read his letter and was tempted to laugh. "I should have such an exciting sex life," he thought to himself. He was a clerk for W. M. Donahue, a liquor dealer on the north side of Main Street, and he feared that was what he would be well into the foreseeable future. He was exceedingly average in appearance, not even capable of growing a decent beard as was the current fashion for men. So, unlike most people who received a letter, Bill wasn't opposed to its contents becoming known, or at least the knowledge that he had received one. That way, he could spice it up a bit in the retelling.

Bill Bland sat on a tree stump next to his cabin on the edge of town and read his letter. Some jokester once said that if his face had one additional red blotch, people might think Bill had the plague. But it was just years of skin damage from sun and wind, beginning with his efforts during the gold rush. The red of his nose, however, was due to his regular imbibing of strong drink. After having received two letters suggesting that there was much about which he should be ashamed, he was beginning to question what he might have done during those worrisome blackout periods while drunk. Whatever he had done, even if innocuous to most, his very proper wife would be sure to disapprove. And when she put her mind to it, she could make his life very unpleasant.

The other two men who received letters that day quickly destroyed them and never admitted to them. They were prominent personages, after all. They had no patience for some crazy woman's prank, for that was how they chose to think about the letters. With proper motivation, denial can be amazingly successful.

At first, most recipients thought they were the only one to receive such a letter. But over time, as people realized they weren't the only target, they became less frightened. Still, many were no longer comfortable meeting the eyes of those with whom they had in the past enjoyed almost daily conversation. And then, of course, they started wondering what the letter writer might have said about other people. Eventually, some townspeople concluded that "where there's smoke, there must be at least a little fire."

What had started as titillating gossip between women, and a ribald joke between men, had gradually become a common enough circumstance that people could no longer easily ignore it. Fortunately, enough people had not received a letter that it was still possible to deny having been a recipient and have it accepted as the truth.

On the day when Dolly Robbins received her first letter, she looked at the envelope inked with block letters inscribing her name and realized what it would be. But Dolly, half way into her twenties and with the wisdom gained from a harsh life, showed no fear or disgust at what she read via words cut from a newspaper. In fact, she laughed. What the sender accused the pretty blonde and curvaceous woman of doing was ridiculously mild compared to what the writer could have said.

When she stopped to consider, Dolly realized that the writer must not know about her time working in a Nevada City parlor house. Many in town did know, but accepted her anyway because of her marriage and her general comportment that prompted them to forget, or at least forgive. Therefore, she reasoned that if the writer had known about her past, they would have made that the core of the message.

Some towns wouldn't have been as accepting, something Dolly knew only too well, but thankfully this one was. She had always assumed it was because the town had for so long been known as *Hangtown* due to its early wild ways. Like so many towns that had originated during the California gold rush, those that had lasted through the 1850's had experienced enough drama and excitement that legends about them would never die.

Many of those legends were not based on events anyone wanted to brag about, but were nevertheless now accepted as part of the way things had been when survival and the finding of gold had taken precedence over everything else. And although society in general was always more forgiving of a man's missteps than those of a woman, when it came to anyone doing whatever had been necessary to sustain life during *the rush*, acceptance in California was more readily given.

Dolly's curiosity about the letter writer had grown as she had become aware of more of her friends receiving them. Dolly loved Placerville and the citizens who had been so kind to her, and she had a strong regard for what was honorable and right. When she discovered that both men and women of all classes, and regardless of marital status, were receiving these letters, she thought of the suffering caused by them and became increasingly angry.

One day, as Dolly beat rugs on the clothesline, her usually compassionate mind pictured a woman's smirking face on the rug before her and she commenced to beat it with gusto, sending more dust into the air than she ever had before. After noticing a bend in the wire of the cloverleaf-shaped rug beater, she laughed herself calm again.

Still, Dolly was saddened by the way people were looking at one another. Whether talking to an old friend or only a business acquaintance, the thought was always underlying that *this* person could be the traitor to the peace and comfort that everyone had taken for granted. Trust, even between long-time friends, was suddenly at a premium.

At supper one night, Dolly's husband, Robert, jokingly commented, "I wonder what Lucy Murphy would think about all that's going on."

Robert had for years worked in a livery stable in Nevada City, California, where he had met Dolly. Now he owned his own livery stable and blacksmith shop there in Placerville, albeit a small one. But he had a way with horses and mules that men in town appreciated, and some were willing to pay him beyond his normal fee when a valuable steed needed extra care.

Some of the town ladies thought Robert would have been *a catch* if he had been single, but it was obvious that he was still in love with his wife. One couldn't go so far as to call Robert Robbins handsome, although his clean-shaven features were regular and strong, and he exuded a charisma that attracted attention. Robert was well-muscled, in his early thirties, just a little over six feet, and he moved with confidence. He was also outgoing and dependable, and well-liked by just about everyone. He was not unaware of this opinion regarding himself; however, lately he had sensed a coolness from some of his normally talkative customers, and he didn't like it one bit.

Dolly was staring at him, thinking about his reference to Lucy Murphy. Finally, she spoke one word, but with such definite meaning that it conveyed to her husband all that she had in mind. "Indeed!"

"I was only joking." He put down his fork and looked at his wife, realizing that he had awakened an idea in her that he might later regret.

"I bet she'd be able to solve this mystery." Dolly chuckled as she added, "And get the busybody to mend her ways."

"Admittedly, Lucy is clever and persuasive, and she certainly loves Placerville. But..."

"And she's fearless." Dolly thought back to when she had met her friend Lucy, back when Lucy was unmarried and had for a short time been the cook in the parlor house where Dolly had worked as one of the girls on the line. "She's had a lot to face up to."

"Yes," he agreed, loath to think about those times. He didn't care about his wife's past, understanding why she had been forced to make some difficult choices when younger, and after all that's how he had met her. But he still didn't want to talk about those days when she had been a *soiled dove*, a term he thought especially appropriate for his gentle, soft-spoken wife.

"Mainly," Dolly continued, "Lucy is someone that we can all trust absolutely. Many people here know her from her visits, too." She looked at her husband, her dimpled smile showing her eagerness. "I'm going to write to her and ask her to come help us."

Robert nodded with good natured resignation. "The spare room is going to have your sister in it when she gets here, you know."

"Oh. Right. I almost forgot about Melanie's visit." She felt a stab of guilt that she immediately pushed away so she didn't have to analyze it. "Well then, we'll help pay for a room in a lodging house for Lucy if needs be."

"Huh!" Robert snorted. "She'd never allow anyone to pay for her visit. Besides, with the money her husband pulls in, they can afford to stay wherever they want."

"I doubt Jim will come with her."

"That's too bad." Robert couldn't hide his disappointment. "I like him, even if he is a professional gambler. Back in our Nevada City days he was known as a square dealer, and he still is."

"First things first," his practical wife declared. "I'll write to her tomorrow and see what kind of a response I get from her."

The next day, while Dolly was composing her carefully worded letter to Lucy, the widow Butterick was reading through the letter she had received two days before, a more threatening one than the first letter she had received. She had slept little since receiving this one, and had eaten barely at all. However, she had swallowed more whiskey than she had over the last few years combined. Consequently, she was in a state of mellow confusion. Still, it had not taken away the dread and terror of discovery.

How had the horrid letter writer found her out? How many other people now knew, or soon would? Unfortunately, because of the limited and mostly narrow-minded and hypercritical company Mrs. Butterick chose to keep, she was not aware that letters of vague innuendo were being sent to many other people in the town. The guilt that had haunted her the whole of her life gave the words such clear meaning that she assumed everyone would be able to deduce what these letters gave away about her. She didn't kid herself that the contents would not eventually be made public.

The first message she had received had just been a cutting from the *Mountain Democrat* Newspaper. Most people had probably thought it merely a bit of humorous but wise, three-line filler at the bottom of a column. *"A moment of passion sometimes gives occasion for a lifetime of repentance."* To Mrs. Butterick, however, it was a truth with which she had lived for the last thirty-five years. Her mind raced ahead with questions and conclusions.

Who could it be that had found out her secret? She had led an upright life except for that one slip, and that was so many years ago. She was a woman of fifty-five, and thought to be a widow, lending even more respectability to her life. She still had a good if somewhat generous figure and was proud of her thick, silver hair. Shouldn't she be able to have confidence that her past was buried and would never come to light, especially considering the exemplary life she had lived for so long? This was especially true of a past so damaging to a woman held in high esteem by the whole community, chief of which were the people in her church.

After all, it was Elsie Butterick who was called upon to read the Sunday lesson more often than anyone else. Her diction was so precise, and her love of God so obvious. Her familiarity with Bible phrases was often commented upon. And it was her advice that was often sought, although confidentially, by the assistant pastor when he was approached with a problem he felt beyond his ability. Some people even thought he might be considering courting her.

But some things could not be accepted as permissible. Not in a society that was critical of a woman showing a stockinged leg, more properly referred to as a *limb*, an inch above the top of a leather-clad ankle. When the contents of the letter became known, and surely it would, she would never be called upon again for anything. Not to speak at church, not even to arrange the flowers or to organize a fundraiser. Certainly, the pastor would never condone his assistant seeing her socially.

It also wouldn't matter that everyone had always thought her a sparkling hostess whose invitations to supper parties had for years been coveted. No one would dare accept an invitation to her home now, for any reason, not if they wanted to maintain their reputation. And when they passed her on the street, they would turn away from her. She had seen this happen to other women who had fallen from grace for less of an infraction of society's rules than the one she had broken. If the townswomen didn't treat her the same as the others they had ostracized, their integrity would become as suspect as hers. She would be alone and shunned for the rest of her life.

The depth of her despair and panic was something she could not have put into words, but was unfortunately so deep and so complete that she could feel nothing else. There was only one fact that resonated with her and that was the utter loss of everything that mattered to her, and all that made up the substance of her life.

After three days and much of each sleepless night running all of this through her mind, Elsie Butterick wrapped her shawl around her shoulders, took her beaded purse in hand and walked into town. Mr. Morrill, the druggist on the corner of the Plaza, thought it was a little soon for her to be purchasing more of the laudanum that she used from time to time for her rheumatism. However, she explained with great embarrassment that she had dropped the other bottle, almost full, into the kitchen wash water by accident. It never occurred to him to question such an upright lady and long-time customer. Besides, it was a common off-the-shelf purchase, especially by women. The arsenic in each tablet only amounted to .3 grains.

Back home again, she poured the two containers of laudanum tablets into her best crystal glass, usually used only for company, along with a large quantity of whiskey. She hoped it would cover the bitter taste of so many tablets while facilitating their dissolving, and also contribute to the potency of the concoction.

She placed the glass on the little table next to her chair facing the window, and spent a few minutes looking out at the street that was lined with cottonwood trees. She had watched them grow over the last five years, and briefly regretted not being able to see them at their full maturity. But at least the daffodils were blooming now and she could see them in the front yard of the sweet young couple across the street.

She next lit a match and watched the accusatory letter catch fire in a glass ashtray on the table. With one hand resting upon the Bible on her lap, with the other hand she reached for the glass. After only a moment of hesitation, with her eyes on the daffodils, she gulped its contents. She then placed the glass carefully back on the table, not wanting it to fall from her hand and break on the floor. The daily girl would arrive the next morning and would find her, and Mrs. Butterick didn't want the girl to get cut picking up the pieces. That wouldn't be nice.

Deep in thought a week later, Lucy Murphy looked out the parlor window of her house in the residential area of Jamestown, seventy-four miles south of Placerville. She rocked back and forth in her beloved rocking chair covered in petti-point roses across the back, and pondered how one's plans can sometimes change very unexpectedly. An unfamiliar horse and buggy passed down the street and she wondered if it might be visitors coming to see her friends. If so, she was happy the area was having such pleasant weather. At the same time, she had not forgotten the letter lying in her lap as though calling out for her attention.

Lucy caught Jim watching her from his chair on the other side of the table between them, where he was occasionally glancing around the newspaper he was holding up. Still, he didn't interrupt her train of thought. He knew his wife well, and realized that she would tell him what was in the letter from her best friend when she was ready. Or at least as much of it as she thought he needed to know.

Lucy was twenty-seven, with light brown hair that when not mounded becomingly on her head, hung down past her shoulders in thick waves. At five and a half feet she was taller than most women of her time, and although most of her life she had been willowy thin, she wasn't far from that now. This allowed her to reject the wearing of a corset much of the time. That she also did not wear multiple petticoats, especially those reinforced by metal, had by now been accepted by all who knew her. It was only part of why she was considered "bold". She was often more outspoken than most women dared to be, and was known to have strong opinions that she had the audacity to voice even in mixed company. She also had a husband who evidently was not moved to chastise her behavior. Nevertheless, she had many friends because she was always kind, compassionate and generous. And she could always be trusted to keep their secrets, after of course offering them advice.

Jim Murphy was several years older than his wife, his black hair offset by blue eyes that glittered like the waters of a deep lake whenever he was excited or gripped by humor. He was close to six feet tall, his shoulders broad and his legs long and muscular. Some thought he had more the look of an outdoorsman than a professional gambler, which served to confuse other gamblers trying to *read him*. Jim was very successful.

Just the night before, Lucy had overheard Jim talking to a friend of his as the two men sat on the front porch after dinner. Jim had told his friend that he was a contented man, married to an intelligent and exciting woman that had given him an unusually talented son. He had even admitted that the house was one Lucy had inherited from a kind old woman for whom she had worked just before they had married. This meant that he didn't need to worry about putting a roof over their heads, all the money he earned at the gambling tables going into purchasing whatever contributed to their comfort, as well as a possible higher education for his son. It wasn't one of the largest houses in town, but after the addition they had built onto it, it was adequate for the three of them and Freda.

Fortunately, Jim was fond of Freda, because she was so important to Lucy and young Roger. Freda had finished raising Lucy during the start of the 1848 California gold rush after Lucy's dying mother had indentured Lucy to her. After that, Freda and her husband, with Lucy's help, had fed the prospectors in the gold rush towns along the western edge of the Sierra. After Freda's husband had disappeared, Lucy and Freda's adventures had expanded far beyond California.

All they had endured together had drawn the two women together in a bond that brought Freda back to California from New York after Roger's birth. It allowed Jim and Lucy a degree of freedom most parents didn't have, and they were very grateful. But it also gave Freda a family beyond an unpleasant sister left behind in the East.

Being a professional gambler, Jim needed freedom to come and go. He seldom worked in Jamestown, a small town with only a few saloons, which allowed those who lived there to be familiar with his skills. It meant spending time in Sonora or Columbia, or even further north in those mining towns still functioning now that the rush for riches had turned from prospecting to hard rock mining. Occasionally, he ventured further west to Stockton or Sacramento, and once a year he spent two weeks in San Francisco.

But he enjoyed most those times when Lucy wanted to visit her friend Dolly in Placerville. It was an excuse to enjoy a number of saloons in a town where hundreds of people regularly passed through on their way to the famous riches in and around the rapidly growing mining town of Virginia City. But Jim also liked Dolly's husband Robert, so staying with them was a pleasure. Robert was the only man Jim could tolerate while spending whole days fishing, a pastime Robert loved but didn't like to do alone. Being an activity far outside Jim's normal routine, it gave him a complete and relaxing break.

The only thing that marred the Murphy family's life was the news of the war of succession that some called the Civil War, although it was anything but civil. Men were choosing sides between the Union and the Confederacy even there in California, and there had been a few clashes. It hadn't gotten too bad yet, but if the war continued much longer, Jim thought the few hot arguments that had turned to fights might increase.

It had been a little over a year since South Carolina had passed an ordinance of secession that declared that "the union heretofore existing between this State and the other States of North America is dissolved." Within the following few months, Mississippi, Florida, Alabama, Georgia, Louisiana and Texas had done the same thing, their representatives and senators withdrawing from Congress.

Many people had thought that the war was inevitable when considering the differences between the northern states and those in the south. One area was a trading economy and the other a planting economy, one free and the other slave-holding. President Buchanan's administration had seen the divide worsen, and soon after President Lincoln had assumed the reins of government, the war had indeed become inevitable. By the summer of 1861, North Carolina, Tennessee, Virginia and Arkansas had also seceded from the union. By this summer of 1862, 83,000 men had been ordered for the Federal army, and a blockade of the whole southern coast had been proclaimed.

The victory of Manassas in July of 1861 had rendered the South exultant and enraged the North. The Federal government had dedicated 500,000 men and five million dollars to the subjugation of the seceding states. The autumn and winter just past had been dedicated by General McClellan, the new Commander-in-chief of the Army, to organizing and training the raw recruits of his vast army.

By the time Placerville was bothered by anonymous letters, the war had progressed, and although news of the war was slow to reach all the way to California, it did reach them. This included the fact that Jefferson Davis had been inaugurated in February as the regular President of the Southern

Confederacy. The armies had been reorganized and a Conscription Act had been passed to fill up the confederacy's ranks. Now that the South was waging a defensive war, the enthusiasm of those men who early on had signed up was much reduced.

The more he read about the war in the newspapers, the guiltier Jim felt about his inability to participate. Caught between not wanting to leave Lucy, almost lost to him once already in his life, he was not eager to do so again.

"Jim?"

"Yes, dear?" He brought his mind back to the present. "Is Dolly's letter troubling?"

"Somewhat. She says the townspeople are receiving anonymous letters. And not nice ones."

"They never are, are they?" He tried not to smirk, but wasn't very successful. Then he saw Lucy's troubled frown and immediately sobered.

Taking his question as mere comment, she continued, "It's taken Dolly some tactful probing, and just a little eavesdropping, but she thinks most of the letters are bringing up secrets from people's pasts, or accusing them of illegal behavior in their current business dealings."

"Anonymous letters in Placerville? There aren't that many women there."

She looked at him as though he had said something risqué in mixed company. "What does that mean?"

Lucy resented any suggestion that women were not as intelligent or capable as men, and Jim had never been able to convince her that all women were not as sure of their self-sufficiency as she was. "Well, anonymous letters are usually written by women, aren't they? And addressed to other women? I mean, when they're trying to start trouble. Come on, now, admit it."

Reluctantly, Lucy had to agree that he was correct. "Dolly does say the tone of the few letters she has seen do sound like the taunts of some vile woman. The words or whole phrases are cut out from newspapers."

"Does she get specific about what kind of things the letters are accusing?"

"No, but she says some are more funny than scandalous, while others are preposterous in their claims and easily ignored. But some are presumed to be so disgraceful that those who have received them won't talk about their content."

"Or maybe what was said in *those* people's letters was so accurate that they couldn't afford to have what was said associated with them."

Lucy nodded and bit her lower lip. She had always been amazed at the various ways people could show malice. "Overall, very disturbing."

"And?" His smirk returned and this time he let it show.

"What do you mean?" She tried to sound innocently naïve, but was pretty sure he saw through her effort.

Jim grimaced. "I sense there's more you want to say."

"You know me too well," she laughed. However, before she could explain further, a dark-haired boy ran into the room and plopped down on the rug between their chairs with a deck of cards in his hands.

Roger had recently reminded them that he was now five *and a half* years old. He was a small version of his father, with the same brilliant blue eyes and black hair, and tall for his age. Roger proceeded to shuffle the cards with dexterity rare for a child of his age, aided by long, graceful fingers more often associated with an adult.

Roger had watched his father shuffle cards since birth, and had always been fascinated by the movement. It filled Lucy with joy to observe Jim as he watched his son, his face lit with warmth and affection. It was as though, even after almost six years, he couldn't quite believe he had fathered a little person that could engender in him such an intensity of complex feelings. Jim especially watched Roger closely when he played with the cards, waiting to further school his son if there was an opportunity to do so.

Looking up, Jim found Lucy watching him. He smiled and looked into the large hazel eyes that expressed so clearly whatever mood she was in at the moment, as well as a bit of caution while assessing each encounter as friendly, dangerous, or simply humorous. But she always looked at him with complete and utter trust, earned during shared experiences about which few people knew anything. When she saw his eyes wander briefly to the small, faded scar on her cheek, she knew he was hoping no one would ever know all that had happened in their lives back in the mid-1850's.

Jim returned his attention to his son and felt a surge of pride that almost choked him. Roger, who seemed naturally expert with cards, had learned to count to 100 at two years old, then how to add and subtract when three years old. After that, his abilities quickly extended beyond the mere shuffling of cards to include a basic understanding of poker.

Lucy looked down at the letter in her lap. "Dolly says people are getting edgy, looking at one another with suspicion. She says retrieving the mail each day is becoming an act of courage."

"Does the anonymous sender ever put the letters in places where people live or work, or are they always mailed?"

"All of those. I get your meaning, though. It makes a difference when trying to discover who might be sending them." Glancing back down at the letter, she told him, "The police seem to think the whole thing merely a prank and nothing to worry about, but I doubt they've gotten one or they'd be taking it more seriously."

"Sadly, you're probably right. But by then the fabric of the town's united spirit will be full of holes, and not easily mended."

Lucy looked at him with admiration. "My dear, that's practically poetic."

Jim simply shrugged, trying to hide his embarrassment by returning his attention to watching his son.

"Mr. Hume, the City Attorney, thinks that eventually the sender will get bored and stop. He's a smart man. We met him last fall when we were there."

"I remember. We met his brother James, too. Now there's a man who'll someday be somebody."

Lucy was still focused on the anonymous letters. "Dolly says the messages are getting nastier and more threatening. At least hers are, so she assumes the same for other people. And just before she posted this letter, she added a post script. One woman, a neighbor of theirs, was so shaken by whatever was in her letter, that she became unhinged and committed suicide. She had tried to burn the letter in an ashtray, but enough of it was left that Sheriff Hunter could tell what it was."

"Could he tell what the subject of it was?"

"She doesn't say. But the Coroner, Mr. Eichelroth, determined that she had taken an overdose of laudanum." Lucy pinched her lips together and frowned. "Nasty stuff! It's recommended to women for every complaint from cramps to arthritis."

After several moments of watching her read through the letter once more, Jim anticipated her. "Does Dolly want you to come to Placerville and help solve the mystery?"

This had indeed been the topic Lucy had been marshalling her courage to bring up. "Yes. Do you mind if I leave you on your own for a couple of weeks?"

"Of course not. If I have to leave too, Freda will take over."

"We're so lucky to have her here."

Lucy stood up from her chair and bent down to kiss her son on the top of his head. But she was already thinking about what she would pack. She was looking forward to once again being in Placerville, a favorite town she enjoyed visiting. It was always a pleasure to see Dolly, whom she had met in Nevada City six years earlier, and where Dolly and Robert had come to her aid when she had so desperately needed their friendship.

Those had been difficult days, when Lucy had cooked for the working girls in one of the better parlor houses. Both Lucy and Dolly had made their choices in order to simply survive, but it still wasn't something they wanted widely known. Lucy knew that it had been a difficult time for Jim, too. He had lost track of her for months while he searched through the mining camps of California just a few steps behind her after she had run away from the brothel in order to escape the law. It was a shared experience they never talked about with Dolly and Robert, but that nevertheless bonded them all together.

Now, in 1862, the old gold rush towns were no longer places where a man could pick chunks of gold out of crevices with his Bowie knife, such as had been possible in 1848 and '49. Back then, Placerville had first been known as Old Dry Diggings, followed by the self-explanatory name of Hangtown.

The town still had a Main Street that was a long road of tamped earth and crushed rock with several curves to it, but now there were many side streets branching north and south. There was even a sub-division called Upper Placerville at the eastern approach. In the heart of town was the Plaza, near where citizens hoped to build a bell tower in a few years. Of course, there were many saloons and dance houses, and even a few bawdy houses on the edge of town amid the young, second growth trees.

Lucy pictured the town's neat cottages shaded with cottonwood trees and covered with bowers of passion flower vines. The wood for these homes had come from a lumber mill not far from town, the timber utilized not only there but by the mines up on the surrounding hills.

The population was also different from that of the early 1850's. The town's original citizens had been composed of native Californians, pioneers from the East having crossed the country in a wagon, those having sailed around the horn from other countries, and deserters from the Army and Navy. Back then, all of them had one thing in common, and that was the finding of gold.

Placerville was now populated by people determined to put down roots and develop prosperous lives. They still hoped to find wealth, but it was as much from their businesses as the prospecting they did when there was time. Placerville was on the main route that connected the big coastal cities of Sacramento and San Francisco, as well as the agriculture of the San Joaquin Valley, with the new wealth on the eastern side of the Sierra. This meant the wealthy mines in Gold Canyon leading up to Virginia City and the Comstock Lode. It also included the mining town of Monoville in the Sierra foothills and the new discoveries in Aurora further east. Because of Placerville, people could avail themselves of supplies, rest, and recreation before setting out on their arduous trek across the Sierra.

A number of good women populated Placerville now, their number steadily growing since the days of the rush. These were not only wives and mothers, but also women who owned legitimate businesses such as dressmaking, book stores, laundries, and even a brewery. Of course, those women more "available" had always been there. At the same time of their arrival, the professional gamblers had shown up.

Two days after the arrival of Dolly's letter, Jim loaded Lucy's luggage into their rig and handed her a pouch of coins that surprised her with its weight. "Isn't this a lot more than I'll need?"

"Maybe. But I think you should stay at the Cary House instead of with Dolly and Robert."

"But..."

"You need to be seen as an impartial observer, simply visiting a town that you enjoy. After all, many people know you from your previous visits. Why not tell them that you're getting over an illness and your husband is treating you to some time away from home?"

"I see." She looked up at Jim and resisted the urge to throw her arms around him for one last embrace. "Dolly and Robert are of the town and are just as much under suspicion as anyone else."

"Right." He smiled as he reached out for her hand, his blue eyes sparkling with mirth. "And it's true that your husband wants to treat you. He won a big pot last week. Since you encouraged me to go to Columbia for that particular tournament, when I really didn't want to go, I think you deserve a cut of the winnings." Lucy laughed, but Jim was suddenly serious. "Promise me one thing. If there's trouble...if you feel in danger... Oh hell, if you want me to come there for any reason, just send a telegram. The telegraph office is on the northwest corner of Main and Coloma Streets, upstairs. You can trust George Shaw, the operator. He knows how to be discrete."

Appreciating that Jim didn't want to give the impression that he thought Lucy incapable of taking care of herself, she told him with mock meekness. "Yes, dear, I will."

"Oh, get in the rig," he laughed. "It's my burden to be married to an independent woman who's well aware of her abilities."

Jim drove Lucy to Sonora, and from there she took a coach of the Pioneer Stage Line that was heading north. Lucy looked out the side window as it moved forward, waving to Jim as he disappeared in the raised dust of the coach. She felt a lurch in the pit of her stomach that was not only from the sudden movement of the coach. Leaving Jim for even a few days was always difficult for her, but she had never told him how much this was true. But then, he had never told her that he felt much the same.

About the time the six passengers had adjusted to the sway and bounce of the stage, it swung around a curve at what Lucy thought was an unnecessarily fast speed. The two men to her right slid to their left, trapping her against the left door of the coach. As they righted themselves, Lucy looked at the three men dressed in suits that were sharing the seat across from her, their fear unmistakable. They were staring out the side windows and every muscle in their faces were drawn tight.

One of the men next to her, his dusty boots and denim pants giving evidence of having recently been on the trail, said, "I wonder if the driver spotted trouble ahead."

"Like what?" This was from a small man across from Lucy who squeaked when he spoke. "You mean like a holdup?"

"Could be. There's been some of that on this route."

"I haven't been in the West very long. I'm from Ohio. So it's true that bad men hold up stagecoaches?"

"Sometimes," the dusty man told him.

Lucy spoke up, hoping to be encouraging. "As long as the driver throws down the bank box, we'll be okay. That's all they want." All she received in return was a squeak of alarm.

The coach returned to a more sedate pace, although certainly nothing that could be called slow, and everyone visibly relaxed. As they passed a cluster of trees and rocks, Lucy looked out the window and saw the butt end of two horses moving away from the road. Evidently there had been men thinking of holding up the stage, but possibly the sight of an alert guard sitting next to the driver with a shotgun across his lap disinclined them of the effort.

Two miles before reaching the next station, one of the horses turned up lame, and the driver refused the urging of some of the passengers to proceed faster. Lucy was grateful that he was unwilling to permanently harm the horse, and was surprised that two of the men with the squeaky gentleman across from her had no such consideration.

"I could walk faster than this damn coach is moving," one of the peeved men claimed in a huff. It wasn't the first time he had complained about something as he flicked dust, both real and imagined, from his suit front. At the same time, he refused to wear a cotton duster over his clothes, even though it was supplied free of charge by the stage company. At every station at which they stopped the other passengers had hoped he would be leaving them. That he had not, only increased their irritation with him.

No one was more tired of him than Lucy. When he repeated his faster-walking claim once more, she told him, "Maybe you could walk faster, but then your backside wouldn't be resting in comfort while the horses do all the work."

Knowing this was an outspoken comment for a woman to make, she tried to soften it with a smile. She expected the other men to be affronted by such boldness, but they merely hid their smiles and looked out the window. The complainer fell silent.

After the teams were changed at stations almost every fifteen miles along the route, which took two full days, the stage finally arrived in Placerville in front of the Cary House. Lucy graciously thanked driver J. J. Crowder for safely getting them to their destination. It was the best compliment she could come up with, considering the rough travel, the threat of a holdup, a lame horse, and miserable food at most of the stations. Nevertheless, it had been a pretty typical journey.

Lucy took a moment to look up at the Cary House before ducking under the canvas shade across the front. The three-story brick building with its iron railings across the veranda fronting the second-floor rooms was impressive. Once inside, she smiled with satisfaction as she entered the large lobby with sofas and chairs arranged into seating areas under the glow of large crystal chandeliers. A row of large windows to her right allowed soft sunlight into the room that increased the sense of welcome.

After her luggage had been carried inside by James Derham, the porter, she approached the long mahogany counter to the left of the entrance. Mr. McClure, the clerk manning the desk, greeted her warmly. "Mrs. Murphy. How nice to see you again. We received your husband's telegram yesterday, and I've assigned you a nice room on the east side, second floor. It's been newly renovated and is now one of our best rooms, especially favored by the ladies." His smile wasn't exactly smarmy, but it came close. He started to touch his mustache to twirl the ends, but stopped himself just in time.

"How nice," she commented, hoping she sounded as pleased as he wanted her to be. He moved the glass and iron stand-lamp closer to the ledger as she dipped a pen in the ink well, and neatly wrote her name beneath those of so many others.

"I'm sure you'll find it quite comfortable." He lowered his voice. "It's only two doors down from the facilities."

"Thank you, Mr. McClure. I'm sure it'll be more than comfortable. How's the hotel doing?"

"Oh, splendidly," he boasted. "We're almost full. Of course, most of the Pioneer Stage Line drivers share a room. As do miners and others of the trades. But we have several men of distinction living here now, too. Such as Mr. Sloss, Mr. Hume's law partner, and Mr. Seeley, the jeweler on Main near the theater. Oh, and Tom Patten, the County Clerk, also lives here now."

"Quite an esteemed clientele."

"Oh, yes," he beamed. He then called out to a uniformed young man standing near the stairs to his left, "Mr. Lowell, please be so good as to take Mrs. Murphy to her room."

Taking the key from the clerk and glancing at the attached brass tag, the steward picked up Lucy's two suitcases and valise. The stage line had allowed her so much luggage only because they had not been hauling the full complement of passengers and she had kept the valise under her feet.

She followed Mr. Lowell up the stairs and into her assigned room. On the way, the steward told her about events in the town. "Miss Lizzie Gordon is appearing at Mr. O'Donnell's Theater this weekend."

"How nice." She was afraid of saying more, not wanting to encourage him in further conversation. She was tired, thirsty and eager to see for herself the hotel's modern *facilities*.

Mr. Lowell left happy, having received a nickel gratuity, something not everyone gave him. Not yet being an expected gift, it was still received with gratitude no matter the amount. A nickel would buy him a good cigar, and it would buy Lucy the steward's willingness to do her any needed favor in the future.   Lucy viewed with approval the room with its double bed covered with a white, islet bedspread and a dark blue comforter folded across the end of the bed. She eyed with approval the four pillows in crisp, freshly ironed linen cases stacked at the head of the bed, and wished she had time for a nap. An enclosed night stand stood on either side of the bed beneath lamps with tall glass chimneys, and she knew that in one of the night stands would be a lidded, porcelain chamber pot even with facilities down the hall. They had passed the dumbwaiter where these would be carried downstairs to be cleaned before returned to the appropriate room. After all, no woman could be seen walking the hallways in only a robe. Whereas later generations might talk about bodily functions, thanks to modern plumbing they wouldn't have to directly deal with the issue. Lucy's generation never discussed such a thing, but did have to deal with it.

After her sojourn down the hall, Lucy sat back in the blue velvet chair by the window on the far side of the room and took a moment to experience the pleasure of sitting somewhere quiet. She put her purse on the small, marble-topped table next to her and pulled off her gloves. Grateful that the room also had a larger table with two chairs, where she could enjoy room service meals, she was exceedingly pleased with the accommodations. The pitcher and bowl decorated with yellow roses at the end of a long, mahogany dresser was inviting, and she gratefully used some of the water in the pitcher to cleanse dust from her face. She dried off with a surprisingly soft, white towel lying next to the bowl.

After dusting her nose with a little rice powder, she pulled back the dark blue drapes at the window so they were all the way open. She found that her view below was of a small, tree-shaded brick courtyard between the hotel and the building next door. Noting the wicker chairs, she thought it a delightful retreat where she might read the local newspapers. Lifting the sash window, she could hear birds in the tree shading the chairs below, as well as piano music drifting in from a nearby saloon. A cool breeze quickly freshened the room, and she decided to leave the window open.

Returning to the lobby, she informed a new clerk at the desk that she would be back before dark. Lucy waved to chatty Mr. McClure working with the account books at the far end of the counter and walked briskly through the room. After turning left once outside on the sidewalk, she turned left again onto Sacramento Street and smiled as she heard strange music coming from the nearby Chinese District. Dolly and Robert lived on Pacific Street, which was the next street on her left, running parallel behind the hotel.

It was nice to be walking after so long on a cramped stage, and the steepness of Pacific Street's rise stretched her muscles. She passed Reservoir Street on her left and a number of tidy cottages shaded by newly planted trees that would someday be large and giving cooling shade.

Dolly and Robert's house was not far up from Sacramento Street, and although not one of the smallest, it was by no means grand. It looked to be recently painted, however, and she was impressed with freshly planted flower beds along the inside of the white picket fence. Lucy walked along the narrow, rock-edged path and climbed the steps up to the long porch hosting a scattering of wicker chairs. Shortly after she let fall the brass knocker on the front door, it opened to Dolly's joyously yelped greeting and unabashed embrace. It was all the welcome Lucy desired.

CHAPTER 2

*"Two kinds of gratitude: the sudden kind
we feel for what we take, the larger kind
we feel for what we give."* E. A. Robinson

Friday, May 30

Dolly told Lucy to relax on the sofa in the middle of the parlor. Since it faced the arched opening of the kitchen across the room, she could smell the day's baking. It reminded her of the hours she had so often spent with Freda in their kitchen, Roger usually playing nearby. A shock of longing hit her in the chest, and she was determined to find the perpetrator of the anonymous letters as quickly as possible so she could return home to her family.

As Dolly prepared the tea tray, Lucy sat and looked around her at the place she considered her home away from home. It was a pleasant room, bright because of the windows across the front and the reflected light that bounced off pale yellow walls. Through the windows Lucy could see the passion flower vines trailing from the white, wooden arch over the front walk at its mid-point. When arriving, she had been so eager to reach the front door that she hadn't paid it much notice. Most of the front yard was shaded by a large cottonwood tree, beneath which a bench awaited anyone desiring rest. From there, because the house was not far from the Chinese section to the west, one could sometimes hear the sounds of bells and wind chimes. And if the wind was right, even the smells of exotic cooking.

Lucy returned her attention to the parlor. The light brown sofa and the two matching overstuffed chairs had recently been reupholstered, and now had crocheted antimacassars draped over the backs to protect the fabric from men's hair oil. A large braided rug beneath the sofa and chairs acted like a staging area in blues and yellows against the dark wooden planks of the floor, and added to the cheeriness of the room. A dark mahogany sideboard shining with bee's wax, and draped in a fringed burgundy scarf, sat near the kitchen door. On it was a silver tray with several bottles of liquor and a seltzer bottle. Looking down on this inviting arrangement from the wall was a large oil painting of a mountain lake at sunset.

Paintings of mixed sizes were arranged on the other walls as well, most of mountain scenes reminiscent of the Sierra, and all painted by local artists. There were also pocket planters in the shape of birds between the paintings, each one filled with dried flowers. An embroidered sampler in a dark frame, embroidered by Dolly when a young girl, hung on the wall next to the door to the kitchen.

Lucy didn't have to turn around to see the large stone fireplace on the room's end wall that faced the back of the sofa. She had just last fall enjoyed it, although now it had been cleaned in anticipation of warmer weather. Still, there was a stack of firewood in the corner just in case the weather turned cold, which in spring was not unusual. Two chairs were arranged at an angle on either side of the fireplace so the occupants could feel the warmth while reading a book from the tall bookcase nearby. It was a room that cooled the spirit in the heat of summer and warmed the soul in the cold austerity of winter, and Lucy felt wondrously happy to be there.

Dolly came out of the kitchen sporting a big smile and carrying a tray that she placed on the table in front of the sofa. Lucy looked at the plate of small donuts Dolly had made that morning and felt her stomach roil with hunger.

After sipping their tea and helping themselves to a donut, all while assuring one another of the wellness of family, Lucy started in directly on the subject of her visit. "From what you told me in your letter, I think your concerns are well-founded. This is something that may have started just to make targeted people uncomfortable, maybe to get even with them over some imagined slight. Maybe so the sender could sit back and gloat at her handiwork. She probably thinks it amusing."

"But it isn't," Dolly practically exploded, a curl of her blonde hair falling loose over her ear. "It causes suspicion and distrust even between friends you thought you knew well. I hate thinking that some woman I know is so vindictive, or just plain hateful." Never one to turn down something sweet, Dolly took a second donut from the plate and bit into it with relish, releasing a sigh that seemed to purge her anger. "I haven't heard of anyone receiving a letter lately, though. Mrs. Butterick's suicide might have scared the sender. So maybe it's all over."

"We can only hope." She turned to her friend and asked as gently as she could, "Dolly, exactly how many of the letters did you receive?" It felt strange to be asking such a thing of a good friend, and she hoped Dolly didn't feel she was being interrogated. But Lucy knew better than most Dolly's past, and how it opened her up to accusations she would not want discussed in pubic.

Lucy realized her hesitancy was unwarranted when Dolly laughed. "Three letters. I guess my past isn't as unknown as I thought it was, although my close friends know and don't care. The first note didn't threaten me with anything, and frankly, it didn't sound as though the writer knew of my past. But the next two letters harped on the fact, using the worst of the words to describe a woman in the profession."

"You can't tell me that many of the women around here don't care." Lucy didn't try to hide her skepticism.

"Oh, well, some of course." She shrugged with a nonchalance that Lucy found surprising. "But remember that during the rush it wasn't unusual for people to arrive out West with their history changed. It was just accepted. Some of that still lingers, especially with the men who run the town. If I had lied about my past and then got found out, it would have been worse."

"And Robert is very well respected, isn't he?"

Dolly screwed up her mouth, which Lucy noted was lightly rouged, old habits sometimes being hard to change. "Well, yes, that's a good part of it. People don't want to offend him."

"My dear, we may not like it, but we're mostly considered just an extension of our husbands." Lucy took a sip of tea and reached for another donut. "Our reputation hinges more on theirs than on anything we have done in the past, or even do now. So if the men of the town like Robert, and their wives know it, you will be accepted at least outwardly."

Dolly looked steadily at Lucy. "You mean that privately they may not be as accepting as they appear to be when with me."

"I'm sorry. Was I too forthright?"

"Oh, Lucy, of course you were." But she said it with an affectionate smile. "Do you think I don't already know all that?" She reached for another donut. "I just don't care. As long as they're nice to my face, they can live with whatever nasty thoughts they harbor in their hearts. It'll be their digestion that'll be disturbed, not mine."

Lucy laughed, delighted to be once again with her always positive friend. "Well, I'm sure those who have taken the time to know you, truly do like you. How could they not?" She looked at the pretty young woman across from her, to whom she had always felt like an older sister, with a fondness that made Dolly blush with pleasure.

Feeling the need to change the subject, Dolly asked, "Did you bring a good dress?"

"I brought several, as well as money to have a seamstress fit me to any she might have on hand."

It was not the habit of stores in the West to carry ready-made dresses for women, although stores had plenty of men's and boy's pants, shirts, and suits. A woman made her own clothes or found a dressmaker to do it for her, and were fortunate if a seamstress offered partially made dresses that needed only to be fitted and hemmed. Of course, men far out-numbered women in most western towns, so this made sense for shopkeepers who had room and money for only a limited amount of inventory.

"Do you have an occasion in mind where I'll need a fancy dress?"

"There's a small gathering tonight at the home of the City Attorney, John Hume." Dolly smiled eagerly. "As you know, he lives among the better homes on Bedford Avenue. We were invited because Robert saved a prize horse of his. You'd think it was one of his children the way he carried on with his gratitude once it was eating well again. He found out that I had slept in the horse's stall when Robert had to be elsewhere one night, so Mr. Hume thinks even I'm laudable."

"Will they mind if I tag along? I only met Martha Hume once and that briefly."

"Thinking you might get here in time for the dinner party, I asked Mrs. Hume if she'd mind your coming with us. Since she met you on your last visit, she was sincerely pleased."

Dolly returned to the hotel with Lucy and they agreed that she had one dress with her that would be acceptable for the dinner party at the Hume residence. The full-skirted dress was midnight blue satin with a low neckline, short sleeves and a snug bodice, as was the fashion for evening gowns. With the full skirt having only one drape across the front, it allowed for the impression of its wearer as preferring simple elegance. Thankfully,

Lucy had brought with her appropriate jewelry, evening gloves, and a short cape that would not detract from the dress's tasteful lines.

Lucy gave the dress to one of the chambermaids so it could be pressed, and then treated Dolly to a light meal in the hotel's dining room. Waiter Bill Baldwin took their order and welcomed Lucy back to town. With her energy revived by once again being with her best friend and the anticipation of good food, Lucy thanked Bill for his attentiveness. Recalling why she always liked staying at the welcoming Cary House, she reached for her coffee cup with a sigh of contentment.

Lucy was pleased to note that Dolly had lost none of her enthusiasm for life that she had displayed when a favored lady in a quality parlor house in the town called Nevada, fifty miles north. It would be several years before the town would officially be named Nevada *City*, but some did call it that. Yes, Lucy thought, Dolly is still just as lovely and outgoing as she ever was, but thankfully a happy marriage has mellowed her natural exuberance and flirtatious mannerisms.

Lucy and Dolly didn't spend too much time over their food, so they could have plenty of time to prepare for that night, having eaten just enough to keep them from being too hungry at the supper party. A man might show a voracious appetite, but it would never do for a lady to be seen partaking of her food except in small bites sedately consumed. Consequently, dining in a large group was sometimes awkward. One didn't want to be the first finished, but also not the last. The first might get one criticized as gluttonous and the second as showing disdain for what had been served. Either one of these would put a lady in a bad light. It was always best to match the timing set by the hostess, even if the last of the vegetables had to be pushed beneath the garnish at the edge of the plate.

That night Robert borrowed a rig from his livery, and just before dark he and his two ladies turned off Main Street to head up Bedford Avenue. Dolly glowed in magenta satin and Robert kept sneaking glances at her, smiling with pride. As the two horses slowed at the effort to pull uphill on the narrow and steep road that led into one of the town's most elegant neighborhoods, Lucy felt her heart beat with anticipation.

Those houses nearest Main Street were somewhat modest, but they soon approached those that were larger, with gardens more colorful and better maintained. These were the homes belonging to the wealthiest and most influential of those running businesses and filling local government offices. They stopped in front of one such two-story house with red shutters bracketing windows on a white clapboard and red brick house. Lucy immediately noted multiple brick chimneys cutting the skyline above the peaked roof, along with several smaller black stovepipes further back from the street where the kitchen would be located. It was the first thing that told of the owner's prosperity.

Robert slowed the horses when he saw that another rig was already tied to the iron ring on the post in front of the house. Prepared for this, he tethered one of his horses to a heavy weight that he removed from the back of the carriage. The horses, knowing this meant they were going to be there awhile, let out their breath and relaxed. Lucy and Dolly picked up their skirts and with Robert's assistance, climbed up four rock-lined steps that brought them to the flat of the lawn and the path to the front door. Looking up at the house owned by John Hume and his wife Martha, Lucy was duly impressed.

An iron fence outlined the small, green lawn with a stone walkway cutting through it to a large, heavily carved front door. Decorative cornices and corbels accented the porch below a railed veranda off the second floor, flowerboxes overflowed with red geraniums, and large cottonwood trees graced the lawn on either side of the path. Dolly looked around her and frowned as she compared the yard to her own gardening efforts.

Realizing her friend was harshly judging herself, Lucy leaned in and murmured, "They probably have a gardener." She was rewarded by seeing Dolly's smile return.

Mr. Hume was the District Attorney for the County, the City Attorney, and also had his own law practice with partner George Shloss. Thirty-seven years old and a gentleman of distinction, Mr. Hume had a thick crop of black hair, dark eyes and a luxurious mustache. His elegant, dark-haired wife was thirteen years his junior, and had just given him a third son. Baby Robert Alexander and his brothers, two and five years old, were being cared for this night by Martha's seventeen-year old sister, Martha Tackaberry, who lived with them.

John's brother, James B. Hume, was the town's Deputy Tax Collector, but was soon to become the City Marshal. It was assumed by many that he would also be named as the town's Chief of Police. Lucy wondered why he had not been invited to the dinner, but Martha managed to work it into the early conversation that James had company of his own at his house on Piety Hill.

Martha Hume was a gracious hostess known for helping with charitable causes throughout the town, and Lucy had instantly warmed to her when they had met the previous fall. It was more than an honor to be invited to the Hume home, it was an enviable status symbol. For Dolly, it was a sign that she had been accepted in society, even if it was mostly because of Robert's standing.

The door was opened by a young houseman wearing a black suit whose roominess might have been because it had until recently belonged to his somewhat larger father. But he wore it proudly and was especially proud of his black bow tie because he had purchased it with money he had earned, along with the jar of pomade used to slick down his unruly brown hair. He stood at attention just like Mrs. Hume had trained him to do and took the guests' wraps without looking them in the eyes. He hung the coats and capes from one of several ornate metal arms on either side of the oval mirror of a large, mahogany hall tree and then led the way into the parlor to the left.

Although Dolly reached up and draped the long, thin chain of her small purse over her wrap, Lucy kept her beaded purse with her. It was small enough that it could be slipped into a hidden side seam of her skirt if necessary, and even with the compact derringer inside, it was light enough not to sag the fabric. The gun was a precaution Jim insisted upon whenever Lucy traveled away from home, and since she knew how to use guns effectively, she didn't object.

Lucy quickly took note of the interior of the large house. It displayed the typical luxuriousness of the era — burgundy satin-brocade sofas and chairs, dark wood furniture, ornate picture frames, and heavily carved banisters on the stairs leading to the bedrooms on the second floor. Heavy, dusky-rose drapes puddled on the floor on either side of the two large windows facing the street. The extra fabric at the bottom was sufficiently generous to declare the owners wealthy enough not to care about the excess cost, but not so much as to make visitors think them wasteful with their money. The presence of a small parlor stove in each of the bedrooms upstairs was a much greater extravagance.

Crystal chandeliers hung from the middle of each first-floor room's ceiling, enhanced in the parlor by oil lamps and in the dining room by wall sconces and silver candelabras on the table. Dolly had informed Lucy that most of this elegance had been freighted there from Sacramento or San Francisco, and had wished she could afford the freight charges alone.

However, for Dolly, the best thing about the house was that it had indoor plumbing. She looked forward to later that evening utilizing the facilities and being able to pull the chain on the gravity flow water box above the toilet. Robert had promised to have one installed for their house after he built on a room for it, but Dolly was resigned to a long wait.

Lucy was received with cordiality just this side of courtly grace, and was immediately reassured that her presence was indeed welcome. The young man who had greeted them at the door, not quite a butler but more than hired help, served them cocktails in the parlor. With one couple having already arrived, soon another couple joined them, making it nine at the table.

Lucy told Mrs. Hume, "I'm sorry to make an uneven number."

Martha Hume waved her hand. "Oh, think nothing of it. The table is huge. I'd be pleased if you'd sit next to me. I so enjoyed our visit the last time you were here."

Both Lucy and Dolly were hoping they would be given the opportunity to see the new baby, but neither knew how to make the request. They needn't have worried. Martha asked rather shyly, "Would you ladies like to see the baby later?"

"Oh, yes!" they answered in unison. All three women laughed, but it was Dolly who added, "I'm so hoping that I'll have one of my own someday. Your two other boys are so adorable, but I wasn't fortunate enough to see them when they were babies."

After that Martha visibly relaxed as she decided that she rather liked Dolly, who was after all closer to her own age than many of the wives of the men with whom John associated. She had met Dolly before, of course, but they had not had the opportunity to visit. Women were always civil to Dolly, and some even reluctantly admitted to enjoying her company, but few of them opened their homes to her. Martha decided she was going to change that whenever she could.

Lucy turned to meet Mr. and Mrs. Morrill. George was a druggist in town, his shop on the Plaza at the west end of town, while their house was on the south side of Washington Street. He not only compounded prescriptions, but also dedicated part of his store to paint along with what was needed to apply it. He had recently begun carrying window glass, something not all homes had at their windows, but which was greatly desired. Dolly had sometimes purchased her scent from his perfumery, along with her other feminine articles.

Mary Morrill was wearing a dress of the latest design, and Lucy suspicioned that it had not been made locally but had been purchased in San Francisco. It fit her lithe figure perfectly and its shade of blue highlighted blonde hair that lightened every summer after she spent time out of doors enjoying regular open-carriage rides.

Mr. and Mrs. Louis Landecker were the other couple, both in their late thirties. He was tall, thin and yet well-muscled, with a short beard that took the eye away from his thinning hair. He ran a wholesale and retail grocery on the southwest corner of Main and Sacramento Streets.

Sarah Landecker's beige dress with black velvet trim looked charming on her. It was showing a little wear at the back, and the hem had been inexpertly sponged, but the dress fit her petite frame well. Her dark brown ringlets cascaded to her shoulders and gave her an appearance of elegance. But Sarah's smile could easily distract anyone from such things, so charming was it. Nevertheless, although she had a soft manner of speaking that was engaging, she was also known for her lack of tolerance for those she considered not her social equal.

Once the introductions had been completed, everyone sipped a perfectly blended punch cocktail. Upon receiving compliments, Martha in turn gave the credit to Sarah Landecker. She in turn declared that the recipe had been obtained from a hostess in San Francisco during their last visit there. The integrity of the social discourse having been satisfied, Mrs. Hume was ready to change the subject.

"Thank you, Thomas," she told the young man. "Why don't you see if you can give assistance in the kitchen?"

"Yes, ma'am."

He left almost noiselessly, and again Lucy was impressed with how well trained he was. She turned her attention back to the room just in time to see Mr. Morrill, his back to the gathering, at the drinks table where he quickly helped himself to a second cocktail. Mrs. Hume saw this too, but of course being the perfect hostess, she pretended that she had not. After ten minutes of general conversation, Mrs. Hume ushered everyone into a large dining room before anyone could help themselves to another cocktail.

The long table was draped in a crisp white cloth, the tapered candles in tall silver candelabras reflecting their light onto place settings of fine off-white china, heavy cut-crystal goblets and perfectly aligned silver flatware. The guests were placed so that there were four on each side of the table, with Mr. Hume at the head, and thus leaving the other end of the table without a setting. Lucy wondered if this was to allow for an unexpected arrival.

A wide, low arrangement of mixed flowers and ivy ran down the middle of the table, a sign that the food would be served on pre-filled plates rather than at the table. It made for much less fuss, but also meant that portions might be too large, or worse, meager.

Immediately upon taking their places, a bowl of clear soup was set before them by two women. Mrs. Bates was in her middle thirties, and not only looked older but also showed her Irish roots with fair skin and red hair. The other woman was plain in the extreme and barely past being called a girl. Both wore high-necked, black bombazine dresses that rustled when they moved around the room. The starkness of the black was off-set by white ruffles at the neck and wrists, and a long, white pinafore apron that protected these expensive uniforms. The women were so competent, however, that the aprons would remain spotless throughout the meal.

When the soup bowls were removed, a small plate of poached fish in sauce took its place. As Lucy picked up her fish knife to cut into it, she hoped no one would find a bone and embarrass their hostess. At the same time, Thomas placed on the table three open-weave, silver-plated baskets lined with white cloths and holding buttery yeast rolls. He then poured white wine into one of several glasses above each place setting.

The highlight of the meal was when plates were brought in piled with sliced beef, roasted potatoes, fresh peas cooked with celery and drenched in butter, and the plate complimented by a peach half that had been stewed and spiced with cinnamon. Each served plate held just the appropriate portion for its recipient. Thomas again entered and this time filled a second glass with red wine.

Half an hour later a trifle bowl was brought in by Mrs. Bates and placed at the open end of the table. At the same time, the younger maid, the meek

Miss Hershel, began clearing the dinner plates. Thomas followed, carrying a tray of glass bowls and a bottle of brandy, which he placed next to the trifle bowl before completing the removal of dinner plates. Mrs. Bates poured a small amount of liquor over the top of the trifle and initiated a flambé moment, the occasion accompanied by the expected exclamations of amazement and pleasure. Mrs. Hume couldn't resist a smile of humble acknowledgement, if not a little relief. Mrs. Bates dished up bowls of the lady fingers layered with jelly and whipped cream while Miss Hershel delivered the filled bowls to the guests.

Thomas served the men port and the women a light sweet wine, and conversation lagged while the dessert was enthusiastically consumed. A moment after the last spoon was laid down, Mrs. Hume rose and suggested the men retire to the backyard while she and the ladies powdered their noses. As the guests made their way from the dining room, they passed a haughty Mrs. Bates, an uncomfortable Miss Hershel, and a proud Thomas as they stood by the door to the kitchen. They accepted compliments with a demure humility that pleased Mrs. Hume. It occurred to Lucy that the whole evening so far had been choreographed no less meticulously than would have a theatrical presentation, and possibly even more successfully.

Dolly had wondered what the new maid might look like, and was not surprised that she was extremely plain and hadn't smiled once. It had gotten around town that Mary Mahon, a maid who had been with the family for several years, had "gotten above herself" and decided to wear scent one day. She was promptly let go, and was currently working as a chambermaid at the Cary House, where she never smelled of anything stronger than soap. Miss Mahon considered it quite a come-down, and the other chambermaids were well aware that she was nursing a grudge.

The conversation during cocktails had been composed of typical small talk such as the weather, theatrical events, and new businesses in town. However, everyone had become more comfortable with one another through the hour and a half at supper. Consequently, the topics of conversation as they relaxed on the patio were gradually more specific to people and events familiar to them all. It had started with births, illnesses, and accidents, but then the subject had been raised about a few people recently leaving town.

Lucy's back ached from maintaining properly erect posture throughout the long meal, and she was relieved when they adjourned to the large porch at the back of the house shaded by mature trees. They relaxed onto wicker chairs with thick pads, arranged around a low wooden slab table that gleamed with a heavy coating of varnish. The garden surrounded them so that the scent of roses and honeysuckle filled the air, accompanied by the chirps of crickets and far in the distance the howl of coyotes.

Thomas wheeled out a cart carrying coffee in a large silver carafe and pieces of divinity fudge stacked on a tiered glass server. Next to the small china cups was a large bowl overflowing with chunks of white sugar alongside another of brown sugar, while a chilled silver pitcher was filled with fresh cream. Everyone generously partook of it all as soon as it was offered. Lucy almost broke out in giggles, thinking they must look like unrestrained children at a party.

To keep herself from such shameful behavior, she looked out at the garden and up at the fading light in what had been a clear blue sky. The cool evening breeze caused the leaves in the trees to rustle and gently brushed Lucy's warm cheeks while pushing the scent of the roses nearer. It was entrancing, and referring to an earlier topic, Lucy exclaimed, "I can't imagine anyone wanting to leave Placerville. They'd have to have a very good reason. It's hard to think of anything unpleasant happening here."

Mr. Morrill cocked a brow at Lucy as though reminded of something. Rendered less tactful after two cocktails, wine with supper, brandy on the trifle, and a glass of port, he said, "I wonder if Mr. Donahue is leaving so suddenly because he got a letter."

There was stunned silence for several confused moments. It wasn't because they were uncertain about the type of letter referenced. They just weren't sure if Mr. Morrill had made a lamentable social blunder, or simply a mild breach of etiquette they could conveniently ignore.

Mary Morrill, however, boldly decided to take the honesty bull by its sharp horns. "We'll never know, will we? I'm certainly not going to talk about the letter I got."

Everyone looked at her, surprised that she would admit such a thing. But Lucy mentally rubbed her hands together with glee, relieved that she now didn't have to think of some way to get this subject underway.

Having caused the desired reaction, Mrs. Morrill continued. "Of course, what it said was totally false, but it was so vividly stated that it was still embarrassing to read."

Mr. Hume shook his head. "This whole thing is most unpleasant. When did you receive your letter?"

"Just this morning." Her husband looked at her with a raised brow, obviously unaware of any of this until right then.

Again Mr. Hume shook his head. "I had hoped that after Mrs. Butterick's unfortunate demise that the letter writer wouldn't send more. I hadn't heard of anyone receiving one since that sad event. Now you get one today, so they must have started up again."

"If the pattern holds," Mr. Landecker announced, "there should be others arriving over the next week."

Mr. Morrill's scowl was formidable. "If we catch whoever is doing this, there's talk of forming a 601 to take care of the miscreant."

Mrs. Morrill refilled her husband's coffee cup and urged him to drink. Everyone had heard the same rumor, but it was best not to put it into spoken words. The only letter more dreaded than an anonymous one, was one signed "601".

A "601 Committee" was code for vigilante justice, wherein a group of local citizens banded together to seek justice when the law either refused to "do its job", or had not yet had the opportunity to try. Over the last decade, often a "601" was formed when justice in the form of public punishment was thought best, especially if there was no court anywhere near. However, they didn't always resort to hanging the guilty party. Sometimes they simply branded him on the face, lopped off a finger or ear, or administered a number of lashings across the back. The least they ever did was to banish the individual from the town or general area. If they dared to return, then they would receive one of the harsher punishments.

These anonymous committees also often sent out notices to surrounding towns about the upcoming punishment to be publicly dispensed. Such publicity helped to maintain the fear of a note received that was simply signed "601", informing the recipient that a certain behavior was to cease immediately *or else*. The origin of the number 601 has had various interpretations, but arguably the most impactful is "six feet down, zero trial, one rope".

"I realize that any discussion of these letters at an elegant social occasion such as this is a bit of a faux pas," Lucy said as innocently as she was capable of feigning, "but I imagine that the past couple of months have been so unpleasant that rules of etiquette have become less important than getting to the bottom of what has taken place."

Nodding, Mrs. Hume said, "I completely agree. Let's not have any false reticence about admitting what's been happening."

Dolly tactfully remained silent, feeling that she was the last person there who should comment on any subject deemed improper. She never quite forgot her nebulous standing within the scope of proper society.

It was Sarah Landecker, up to now having also remained silent, who added her support. "You're so right, Martha. I hesitated to say anything, but if you and Mrs. Murphy can be so bold, then so can I."

"Oh, please everyone. Please call me Lucy." She was met with smiles, the other women then feeling free to ask for the same familiarity of acquaintance. The men, however, did not join in, and in fact, were not expected to do so by any of the women.

But it wasn't the subject of names that caused the men to look a little sheepish. They were being forced to accept that it was the women who were showing the moral courage to confront the subject of the letters. Louis Landecker cleared his throat and muttered, "Indeed!" Having expressed his support while yet remaining uncommitted to what he really thought, he sat back and sipped the cold coffee in his cup.

John Hume's legal mind had not lost track of the fact that it had been Lucy who had encouraged the conversation in this awkward direction. He now turned to her. "Will you be staying long in town on this visit?"

Lucy was ready for him. "I'm not sure. I've been ill recently and my husband thought it would be best for me to get away for a rest. There always seems to be so much to force activity at home, even when one should be recovering."

Dolly spoke up. "And I promised to see to it that she gets plenty of rest balanced with exercise and good food."

Lucy laughed. "I can honestly say that I have never gotten a bad meal in Placerville. Your restaurants are more than adequate and your markets are full of things we don't often see in our Jamestown market, as well-stocked as it is."

Martha Hume admitted graciously, "Well, being a supply town helps. We can choose the best off the freight wagons before they move on over the mountain."

John cut in quickly. "Not that we take away from the supplies going to east side towns. But let's face it, being closer to Sacramento and the San Joaquin Valley, what we get on this side of the Sierra is bound to be fresher than after it has traveled all the way to the Eastern Sierra."

Her husband having clarified the town's integrity, Martha said, "Now that the weather is turning warmer, I hope we hear that the flood waters are receding faster in and around Sacramento."

Mr. Hume frowned. "Poor Mokelumne City was totally destroyed I hear. And part of Sonora and Nevada City were under water. But the rebuilding has started, and of course most brick or stone buildings survived. Still..." It wasn't necessary to say more about the hardships of so many starting over.

"Well, what do you expect," Mr. Landecker commented, "when the North Fork of the American River at Auburn rose thirty-five feet? Even our creeks here looked more like rivers for a short while. We can be thankful that we had so little damage from it."

"The floods this past winter were so momentous an occasion that I even wrote about them in my journal," Mr. Morrill commented. "And in more detail than I do about most things."

Robert nodded. "Same here. I usually write about the teamsters and their animals, along with the weather. But how can you address the weather without the floods?"

Not only did these and many other men and women write in their journals about the historic flood during the winter just past, some also described the flood in long letters sent back home in the States to friends and relatives. The newspapers that had not been flooded out also described the catastrophe as it occurred, and during the months following. Over the next century and a half, as scientists would gain more knowledge of weather events, there would be even more understanding of what had happened.

"The Great Flood" started in November of 1861 with rain that turned to snow in the mountains. This was then melted by warmer than usual rain, which was followed by more alternating days of snow and rain. In the central valley of the state, and all the way north into Oregon, it rained for almost 40 days straight. This weather action would someday become known as the movement of "atmospheric rivers", but this was the first time it had been experienced in the settled West. Eventually, water covered the whole of California from the Coast Range to the Sierra foothills.

The flooding that took place impacted the whole of California, but especially Sacramento, being situated at the confluence of the Sacramento and American Rivers, both of which were used as trade routes. Originally built sixteen feet above the low-water mark of the rivers, the city of Sacramento had been raised another four feet in 1853 by bringing in fill dirt. Nevertheless, people had still recognized that there was danger from the rivers over-flowing their banks, so a levee had been built *around* Sacramento to protect the city.

Unfortunately, this meant that when the rain water built up in the city past what the ground could absorb, the water had nowhere to drain, and the townspeople realized they had walled themselves in. Considerable devastation occurred before chain gangs were used to break through the levee walls, allowing the water to rush out. But as the rains continued, even this was of little help because it hadn't been done while the rivers were still low enough to carry the run-off as part of their flow. Once the rivers breached their banks, nothing could keep Sacramento dry. In fact, in January of 1862, the Capital was moved to San Francisco to protect records and services.

The agriculture of the central valley ranches and vineyards became submerged under water, and little of it recovered. Further south, the plains of Los Angeles County, being a marshy area scattered with small lakes and cut with meandering streams from the mountains, was able to absorb much of the twenty-eight inches of rain that fell there. But it could only do it for so long before the agriculture along the Los Angeles River was inundated, and nearby small farming settlements submerged.

The whole of the area formed a large lake system connected by streams and run-off. Those streams with the most powerful flow cut channels across the plain and carried water to the sea. The rains moved south, and in February of 1862 the Los Angeles River, the San Gabriel River and the Santa Ana River merged to create a solid expanse of water from Signal Hill in Los Angeles County to Huntington Beach in Orange County, a distance of approximately eighteen miles.

As for Placerville, it was so placed that only Hangtown Creek caused any problem and that very little. Supplies had been cut off during the winter but they were now receiving them again, even if from different routes and towns.

With all of this in mind, Mr. Landecker said, "They're saying that this terrible flooding is going to mount up to over $10 million in property damage." In point of fact, history would reveal that one-quarter of the taxable real estate in the state had been destroyed in the flood, creating a situation where the state came close to declaring bankruptcy.

John Hume said, "The Wool Growers Association says 100,000 sheep and 500,000 lambs were killed."

"Yes, I heard that," Robert chimed in. "Even the oyster beds in San Francisco Bay have been reported to be dying."

"Why's that?" Mr. Morrill asked.

"Because of so much fresh water entering the bay. It's full of sediment and it covers the oyster beds."

Mr. Landecker, evidently not a fan of oysters, countered. "We can live without oysters, but we can't exist without beef. With a quarter of the state's 800,000 cattle killed, there's going to be a food shortage."

"We've got to get wood to the mines to replace all the flumes, sluices and derricks that were carried away in the flood waters, too." Mr. Hume shook his head. "They've done a good job of rebuilding wagons quickly, as we can see from all those coming through town."

"The recovery can't happen too quickly to suit everyone," Mr. Morrill declared.

The other men simply stared at him, the obviousness of the statement beyond comment. The women had tactfully not entered into this part of the conversation, knowing that nothing was expected from them. Even Lucy, not without strong opinions on the topic, knew better than to offer them in such a social situation.

With that popular subject having been covered, the conversation lagged, and Lucy wondered how she could return everyone's focus to the letters. Louis Landecker started talking and saved her the effort.

Setting down his empty coffee cup, Louis said, "You know, two of my employees, Rehl and Williamson, got one of those letters just yesterday. They were so upset they could barely function. Of course, like everyone else, they wouldn't tell me what was in their letters, but they did share with each other and I overheard them talking." He had the grace to look down and away from everyone before refocusing on the subject. "One of them was evidently accused of filching money from a previous employer, which he staunchly denied, and I do believe him. The other man was accused of..." Here he hesitated and glanced at the ladies clustered together on the far side of the circle of chairs. To cushion the impact of what he was about to say after admitting the clerk's name, he lowered his voice as he said, "... of having had an affair with his own sister."

The men may have been aghast at such an idea, but the ladies who lived there in town and whose moral rectitude Mr. Landecker had been in fear of offending, simply laughed. They knew the clerk's wife.

Dolly turned to Lucy to explain. "His wife is a pretty woman who is also very much in love with her husband, and unfortunately for him also outspoken around her close lady friends. She has more than intimated that her husband is in public a very proper gentleman, but in private just the opposite. She recently joked that she's amazed she doesn't have a dozen children by now. So he obviously adores his wife, and has no need to turn to *any* other woman."

George Morrill looked at Dolly with admiration, which Mary Morrill didn't miss. "Very tactfully put, my dear," he told Dolly. "And here I've always considered him a dry stick of a young man. He never even glanced at some French drawings a freighter passed around. Now I know why."

In an effort to pour soothing oil on the embarrassing topic, Martha Hume said, "If all the accusations are so far off the mark, and that fact gets around, then no one should hesitate to say they received a letter. It'll just be assumed to be a nuisance prank."

Lucy glanced at Dolly before gently reminding Mrs. Hume, "Except that sometimes it must hit the mark or Mrs. Butterick wouldn't have made such a drastic choice."

"Oh yes, of course," Martha mumbled, her cheeks coloring.

After that it was as though no one knew how to add anything more. Realizing that the subject of the letters had been covered as much as everyone was willing to contribute, Lucy said, "Your coffee is wonderful. I'll have to be sure to take home the same beans you use."

"Mr. Landecker has them at his market. But I believe it's the way Mrs. Bates roasts them for us that makes the coffee so savory. I'm sure she'd be pleased to tell you how she does it."

Mr. Hume chimed in. "It's getting dark. Should we light the lanterns?"

Dolly stood up. "We really shouldn't keep Lucy out much later. Thank you for such a wonderful evening. The food, the drink, and especially the company was simply wonderful."

"But before we go," Lucy spoke up, "can we sneak into the nursery and look at the baby?"

"Oh, of course," Mrs. Hume exclaimed, all smiling eagerness.

After the women had left, Mr. Hume handed out cigars and the men lit up. There wasn't much conversation at first, just the contented puffing and appreciating of fine tobacco rolled into a convenient delivery system.

"I get these at the Post Office Exchange," Mr. Hume mentioned. "Mike Borowsky is a bit of an ass, but he's excellent at keeping his tobacco fresh. And he has a fine inventory of liquors. You're fortunate to be on the Plaza, too, George."

"I never found Borowsky to be objectionable," Mr. Landecker stepped in to defended his friend. "We both belong to the Masons, you know."

Mr. Hume looked at him closer. "Oh, yes, I do know." Then, about to change the subject, he was interrupted by George Morrill.

"He has a nice wife. I filled a prescription for her the other day and she couldn't have been more charming."

John tried not to sound accusatory when he asked, "Didn't you sell Mrs. Butterick the laudanum that she overdosed with?"

George glared at him. "She was an honorable and dignified lady. When she said she had lost the other bottle by dropping it in the wash water, I had no reason to doubt her."

John managed to look shocked. "Of course not. No one would have." He changed course immediately. "Do you think California's gold is going to help the Union through this war?"

Mr. Morrill looked at him with surprise. "Of course, it will. The Confederates would like to have it too, but that's a doubtful hope."

Robert spoke up then. "I think the Confederates would rather have access to our Southern California coast. They need an open harbor unaffected by the Union Blockade." He was referring to what was being called Scott's Great Snake, a path of coastline blockade that stretched south from the Carolinas, around Florida, across the gulf and north through Texas, then curled around Kansas into Missouri.

"That may well be true," Mr. Morrill pointed out, "but there's a strong secessionist faction in Southern California, unlike Northern California that's strongly Union. We're in the middle of those two, and so far there's not been any major confrontations. I hope that continues."

Mr. Landecker knocked the ashes from his cigar and looked perturbed. "Let's hope the Los Angeles Mounted Rifles and chapter of the Knights of the Golden Circle stay in Southern California."

All the men looked gloomy at the prospect of pro-slave ownership groups pressing into their midst, but chose not to enlarge on that topic. None of them were totally clear about the stand the others present might take on anything related to the war.

Only too eager to change the subject, Mr. Morrill chose to return to an earlier one. "I got some cigars from Sarah Burns over near Cedar Ravine. I was surprised how nice they were. Hard to admit a woman knows what she's doing when it comes to smokes, but she does."

Louis Landecker looked at him with an odd smile. "There's a woman just arrived in town who would claim that what you just said was offensive to women."

George was clearly startled. "Really? How so?"

"You're impugning her intelligence and ability," John Hume cut in, "and implying that she's not as capable as a man."

"This is the women's suffrage talk that started back east," Louis Landecker explained.

John Hume was nodding his head. "I believe women's suffrage is indeed what this Mrs. Helms is all about. She'll talk about her ideas to any man or woman who will listen to her. Bothersome female!"

George Morrill made a noise that sounded like "hurrumph", then said, "All a bunch of nonsense, of course. Women already have plenty of influence. In the home, where they belong."

John shrugged. "Some women in town own their own businesses and are pretty successful. Mrs. Irwin's millinery shop is always busy." He almost mentioned that most of the "houses of ill fame" were owned by women, but thought better of it.

"Of course, a millinery is owned by a woman," Robert spoke up. "Women need somewhere to purchase their fancy bonnets, and millinery is a very respectable trade for a woman. She employs two ladies who are also respectable, even though they work outside the home. But I don't know why women can't work at other places like the post office or the bank, or even the hardware store if they want. Women who need to work need respectable places in which to do it, beyond washing clothes and cleaning hotel rooms."

Robert colored slightly, looked down at his cigar, and stopped talking, afraid he had started the men thinking about what his wife used to do. But they considered themselves *men of the world*, and had long ago accepted Robert and even Dolly.

Mr. Morrill sighed. "Yes, but women don't run major businesses."

When Robert named three women who owned a brewery, a dairy, and a lumber yard, Mr. Merrill cut him off. "They may own those businesses, but they don't *run* them. They have a foreman to do that."

Knowing it would be wiser to say nothing more, Robert nevertheless persisted. "Yes, but it doesn't prove that they *couldn't* run their businesses if the need arose. California's Sole Trader Act back in 1852 authorized married women to transact business in their own names."

"But," John interjected, "only if they prove first that it won't financially harm their husbands. Society doesn't seem ready to give uncritical allowance to women to openly run large business concerns. But the suffrage movement isn't just about women working outside the home," John reminded them. "The movement is also about women continuing to own *whatever* property they bring to the marriage. And this woman staying at the Orleans Hotel was evidently one of the most outspoken attendees during the 1848 infamous meeting in New York."

"I thought it was about them getting the vote and serving on juries," George said.

John Hume, being an attorney, was more familiar with the whole subject. "It is about that for some, but I think the majority of women would just be happy to keep ownership of their own property after marriage."

Louis frowned thoughtfully. "I must admit that seems reasonable. They should at least have some say in what their husband does with it. Sarah is expecting, you know, and if it's a girl, I'd like to think that whatever I give her will still be hers after she marries."

George shrugged. "At least during the last few years they've been focusing on emancipation of the slaves. But I've heard it said that some of these suffrage women are harping about rights of all kinds." He took a hearty puff on his cigar and frowned. "Sitting on a jury, by God! Imagine! The next thing they'll want is to serve in Congress." He made a noise in his throat and puffed harder on his cigar as the other men laughed at the absurdity of his joke.

To get them off such a sensitive subject, John said, "Congratulations on soon becoming a father, Louis. Here, have another cigar for later." When George Morrill couldn't hide his envy, John laughed and handed him another also. Robert declined with a gracious smile and shake of his head.

The women were heard on the stairs, and Robert put his partially smoked cigar in a glass ashtray. When the other men kept theirs, Robert wondered if their wives were less vocal about their preferences than Dolly. But he turned his attention from the men as they talked among themselves, choosing instead to watch the women descend the stairs. Sarah Landecker moved down them quickly, ahead of the others as though in a hurry to get on with whatever came next. But the other three were more leisurely in their descent.

The skirts of the women's fancy dresses dragged on the treads behind them, while the silk and satin fabrics glistened in the light from the wall sconces. Martha Hume's diamond jewelry sparkled against the dark gray of her satin dress, but so did the gold nugget Lucy always wore on a chain around her neck. It was a memento of the gold rush given her by Jim years before, and she never removed it.

Dolly descended slowly, her back erect and her right hand moving lightly along the railing while her left hand lifted her skirt just enough to ensure that she didn't trip. Her head was cocked a little to the side as she listened to Martha Hume, her smile showing how much she was enjoying herself.

Lucy was just behind the two women, her hand also on the railing. The dark blue of her dress gleamed in the soft light and although a smile played about her lips, her eyes were focused on the men now talking in subdued voices behind Robert.

How pretty and charming they are, Robert thought, as though the three Graces have come to life. And even while he chuckled at himself for such a frivolous idea, he knew that this was a captivating picture that he would carry with him for the rest of his life.

After everyone had retrieved their wraps and gracious compliments had been exchanged, those with rigs out front hurried to them. Lucy stopped to look up at the night sky, so thick with stars. Dolly took her arm and hurried her forward, such a sight commonplace to her and lacking the romance of it that evidently Lucy found so captivating. The night air had turned cold, and Robert was waiting for them by the rig, eager to protect his women from getting a chill. Dolly and Lucy, however, were overheated by their layers of clothing and the stuffy warmth inside the house, and they were enjoying the refreshment of the cool air. Nevertheless, they allowed themselves to be helped into the black rig, after which Robert tossed a lap rug over their legs.

Before walking into the hotel, Lucy turned to wave to her friends, watching the rig until it turned left onto Sacramento Street. Climbing the stairs to her room, she deemed it the end of a pleasant evening that she had enjoyed more than anticipated. Having been in detective mode the whole evening, she was especially pleased. But she was tired, so she set aside those intriguing moments she had observed that she considered deserving of further thought.

CHAPTER 3

"They can only set free men free...
And there is no need for that:
Free men set themselves free.

James Oppenheim, The Slave

Saturday, May 31

Dolly was determined to attend town functions where women gathered, bringing Lucy with her. She knew it would generate sharp comment that *Mrs. Robbins* was suddenly more visible at public events, something Dolly usually avoided, but she thought Lucy needed to meet as many women as possible in order to gain insight into the possible letter writer. There wasn't much that went on in town about which most women didn't have at least part of the picture.

Mrs. Vespacia Helms had been in town for a month and was giving a luncheon in support of the women's suffrage movement that was the passion of her life. Consequently, most people were referring to her as "that suffrage woman". The difference between men and women, however, was that most women wanted to hear Mrs. Helms speak, and few men would admit to such a radical activity.

Mrs. Helms's claim to fame was that she had been at the famous but controversial convention held in July of 1848, in Seneca Falls, New York, known by many as the first major women's rights convention. It had been billed as "a convention to discuss the social, civil, and religious condition and rights of women." She had also been present two weeks later at another convention in Rochester, New York, which some claimed carried even more importance in the movement.

Because of such extensive involvement, Mrs. Helms was revered by those women who wished they could openly champion the cause, but were too fearful of public censure to do so. She was also somewhat feared by those who recognized a person ruled by a single passion, and who wanted followers in absolute agreement. However, most people in Placerville, both men and women, simply saw her as a curiosity.

There was, of course, a set of men who fervently wished her gone from their lives, and especially from their town. She was a threat unlike any they had ever dealt with before, one that reached into the sacred core of their lives known as *the home*. They couldn't draw her out into a physical fight, and they didn't know how to verbally counter her arguments. It was the closest many men had ever come to feeling powerless. Some felt that this just couldn't be tolerated, her ideas being a form of social license that could besmirch the innocence of their wives and daughters. Nevertheless, the best some men could come up with was to dictate to their wives and daughters that they were not to attend any function where Mrs. Helms would be speaking. In a few instances, they even got their way.

Dolly, having heard from Robert about men's views of Mrs. Helms as a woman with a bee in her bonnet, was eager to finally see this much discussed woman. She was even more interested to see Lucy's reaction to such an unusual woman, and therefore hurried Lucy along to the Orleans Hotel where the luncheon was being held in the large meeting room.

"Any husband or father," Dolly told Lucy, "who has posed an objection to the women in his family hearing what Mrs. Helms has to say, has at least won a partial victory. The most oft used phrase is, 'I won't allow that woman inside the walls of my house.'"

Lucy laughed at Dolly's deep-throated mimicry of a pompous man. "I suppose in that way they can, if necessary, claim that 'their women' attended the luncheon only out of curiosity, but not out of welcome." Dolly only smiled in response.

The two women stood in the doorway of the hotel meeting room, a sea of square tables draped in white linen cloths spreading out before them. They admired the room's highly polished, wood plank floors, crystal chandeliers that sparkled, and the glowing wall sconces. Place settings of china and crystal were set two to a side except for the side facing the raised platform at the far end of the room, each glass and plate a glittering pronouncement that this was a prestigious occasion.

Many of the tables were already fully occupied with women who had filled their plates from the abundance of food on the buffet tables set up at the side of the room. They were busy visiting as well as eating, creating a buzz of excited chatter underlain with nervous expectation.

Mrs. Helms stood just inside the room by the door so she could greet arriving participants and hurry them to their seats. She was regretting her idea to feed the participants, who were generously filling their plates with a gusto she wouldn't have seen from the more polished Eastern society she so dearly missed.

She watched the women uneasily while hoping that some of these Western women, often described as independent and self-sufficient pioneers, would have the financial means to refill her waning coffers. If she didn't receive donations soon, it would be difficult to pay her hotel bill that now showed the added expense of today's meeting. Of course, if she didn't get a sufficiently large number of donations, there was one person in town who she knew would give her money, especially if it was to assure that she was on the next stage out of town.

The women blocking the door in line ahead of Lucy walked away from Mrs. Helms, who then turned eagerly back to the door, ready to greet Lucy and then Dolly. In that moment, Dolly gave a little gasp at the same time that she bumped into Lucy from behind. When Dolly didn't apologize, Lucy glanced over her shoulder and saw that her friend had turned pale while looking past her into the large room. Mrs. Helms seemed not to have noticed anything untoward and was smiling as she held out her hand to be briefly touched. As Lucy shook the hand offered, she looked into eyes that boldly met hers without the least element of warmth.

Vespacia Helms was of average height, her torso slightly thickened by a love of good food and a rejection of strong corsets, which she classified as a product of men's control over women. Her silver hair was parted in the middle and swept back, collected into netting that hung down her neck, below a lace and silk flowered cap. Many of the women in the room also had their hair netted in such a fashion, while others preferred hair styles and bonnets less modern. For some, this was a preference, but for others they just could not afford to update to current fashion.

Observing the woman's purple dress, Lucy noted that it was fairly simple, the pagoda sleeves edged in white velvet braid, and a collar of white lace that gripped her neck. Gold pins and long necklace completed the three colors of the women's movement. Unpretentious in design her outfit might have been, but the dress was of fine silk fabric that could not have been cheaply purchased, and it fit her perfectly as only custom made clothing can. Lucy couldn't help wonder at the source of Mrs. Helms's money.

"Come in, ladies," Mrs. Helms invited, her voice unexpectedly deep. "I'm Vespacia Helms. I'll be speaking as soon as the ladies have filled their plates and are seated at a table."

"Nice to meet you, Mrs. Helms," Lucy told her.

Behind her, Dolly mumbled the same thing and then headed directly to the table filled with small sandwiches, salads of several varieties, and small pieces of cake. Waiting her turn at the buffet, Lucy watched Mrs. Helms greet the next woman at the door. A casual observer simply saw Mrs. Helms as a sharp-featured woman whose upright posture projected self-possession, anchored by a smile that never wavered no matter how many women she greeted. Lucy was pretty sure the woman had practiced this before a mirror.

There was a tenacious resolve about Mrs. Helms that Lucy had seen in only a few women in her life, and the thought occurred to her that she hoped she never had to cross her. As strong as she knew herself to be, Lucy wasn't sure that she could win a duel of wits and words with this imperturbable vanguard of *the cause*. The gleam in her eyes was not simply the excitement of the moment, but was that of a fanatic in the midst of potential acolytes.

Lucy and Dolly finished making their choices and then turned to the room, spotting Martha Hume and Sarah Landecker nibbling their food at a table with two empty seats. As they hesitated, Martha looked up and saw them, waving them over to her table with a bright smile of welcome. While Martha greeted Dolly with enthusiasm, Sarah Landecker did a poor job of hiding her displeasure. The other pair of women at the table rose and carried their plates to another table.

Lucy laughed and said, "I wonder what outspoken thing they overheard me say at some time."

Dolly simply looked down at her lap and swallowed hard, knowing their move had been because of her. Then appreciation of what Lucy had tried to take onto herself filled her heart, and she looked up with a bright smile while glancing around at what was for her a new venue. "What a lovely room. The addition of flowers on each table really makes it inviting."

"Yes," Martha Hume agreed, "and the food isn't half bad."

Lucy thought this a generous observation as she put down the dry ham sandwich that had been slathered too liberally with mustard. After one bite, she also avoided the sour coleslaw. She told herself that when she and Freda had fed the gold rush prospectors back in the early '50's, they never would have given them anything so vile. But she had to admit the cake was good.

Lucy felt a sudden wave of longing to talk to Freda, and wished she was with her right then. Freda had been mother, sister and friend for the last half of her life, and Freda's counsel had always been wise and comforting. This led to picturing her son's face and wondering if Roger was missing her, which led to a lurch somewhere near her heart. "Oh, this won't do," she chastised herself. "I have a reason for being here and I have to focus."

Lucy forced herself to observe Dolly, who now seemed recovered from whatever had caused her earlier distress upon entering the room. Still, she seemed a little more subdued and preoccupied than usual, several times unaware when Martha had spoken to her until her name was used. Lucy wondered if Dolly had seen someone in the room who upset her, but knew that she would have to be tactful when later asking about it.

Mrs. Landecker turned to Dolly. "Maybe you'd be more comfortable sitting at the table in back."

Lucy looked over at the referenced table and could see no difference between the three women sitting there and any of the other women in the room. Well, maybe their clothing was a little brighter, and they were wearing rouge and lip coloring. "Oh!" Lucy thought. "So that's who they are." She then wondered, "Was it these women of *the profession* that Dolly spotted upon entering, surprised to see them here?"

With cheeks aflame, and her throat tight with anger, Dolly told Mrs. Landecker, "I'll have you know I'm a lady."

"My dear, if you have to declare it, you probably aren't."

Dolly valiantly withstood the criticism. "It was your comment that questioned the fact. I would expect better from a fine lady such as yourself."

Mrs. Landecker shrugged her shoulders in a dismissive gesture and continued to eat her luncheon, seemingly unperturbed. She did, however, shift slightly so that her back was more to Dolly than previously. For a moment, they all focused on their food, Mrs. Landecker the only one not embarrassed by the exchange.

As close as Lucy was to her friend, she knew that Dolly could be sensitive to anything that might hint of criticism, aware as she was that her background was of dubious quality, even before her time in Nevada City. From the few comments Dolly had made about her early years, Lucy had deduced that Dolly and sister Melanie's childhood had not been a pleasant one.

Their father had deserted the family not long after they had arrived in California. Consequently, when their mother had demanded the girls marry at fifteen, they had no means by which to refuse. Unfortunately, their mother's choices for the girls had been abusive men. After Dolly's husband had died so suddenly, she had ended up in Nevada City, penniless and with no way to support herself.

This was as much as Lucy knew about Dolly's past, other than the fact that Dolly had not been in contact with her parents for years. The last communication had been after Dolly had arrived in Nevada City and had written her mother to ask for money so she wouldn't have to work in a brothel. The letter from her mother contained no money and only one line: "You made your bed, now you can lay your head on its pillow."

On the other hand, as Lucy had only recently learned, Melanie and her husband Vincent had settled close to their mother. This meant that Melanie's life had been dictated by both mother and husband, who had developed a close relationship. This had spawned strict rules of behavior for Melanie. Unfortunately, as Melanie once described it to Dolly, her husband had discovered that when she inevitably broke those rules, he enjoyed punishing her.

After Dolly had married Robert and moved to Placerville, she had several times invited Melanie to visit them, even sending her a ticket for the stage. In this way, Melanie could have a break from her dismal marriage. Dolly had told Lucy that Melanie always destroyed her letters immediately after reading them so she could tell Vincent that Dolly lived in San Francisco. She would indeed go there, but would then take a paddle-wheel boat up to Sacramento, and from there a stage east to Placerville.

Because Lucy felt bad for Dolly and her sister, who she had not yet met, it made her all the more aware of the difference in their backgrounds. Lucy's mother had died when she was twelve, but she had many warm memories of her loving nature, her sharp humor, and her loyalty to friends.

No matter what was happening in their chaotic lives, her mother had always made Lucy feel safe. She had also encouraged Lucy to read and ask questions, even if little of it had taken place in a school. After her mother's death, Lucy's teen years had been under the influence of Freda, and that was something else that filled her with gratitude.

When Mrs. Helms climbed the two steps to the platform and stood before the lectern where she had spread her notes, Lucy's attention returned to the present. She watched Mrs. Helms wince with pain as she stretched her back and then look down at those ladies at the table almost at her feet. With light laughter, she begged their empathy. "I have a bit of lumbago that acts up sometimes."

Mrs. Helms scanned the room that had finally quieted, expectation combined with nervousness hanging heavily in the atmosphere. "Thank you for joining me today," she began. "I know that some of you have had to contend with men in your lives who don't want you here. Whether you have stood up to them or deceived them in order to be here, I appreciate your attendance." The brashness of this remark hushed the last few inattentive ladies.

Mrs. Helms immediately launched into the subject of the 1848 Seneca Falls Convention. She explained that on the first day of the event only women had been present, and then described the first speech, given by Elizabeth Cady Stanton. Mrs. Stanton had exhorted the women to accept responsibility for their own lives in order to "understand the height, the depth, the length, and the breadth of your own degradation."

This caused a buzz of short remarks among the Placerville women, forcing Mrs. Helms to pause until everyone once again settled down. The general tone had been a little rebellious. Lucy guessed that these Western women, who had faced many challenges just to get to the West, much less Placerville, did not appreciate being classified as "degraded". She knew she certainly didn't.

Mrs. Helms continued quickly. "Lucretia Mott, considered the unofficial organizer of the convention, spoke next. She encouraged everyone to take up *the cause*." Whenever she used the words "the cause" her emphasis changed, and in one instance she put her hand over her heart as she said those words. Lucy hid a smile behind a quick grab for her napkin. No one was in doubt that Mrs. Helms was devoted to her topic, with a consecration that few women present had ever experienced.

She went on to describe how the Seneca Falls organizers had prepared a Declaration of Sentiments that had been read out to those assembled, after which it was discussed and a few changes made.

"They even discussed the possibility of seeking men to sign it, but after a motion made to that effect, it was tabled until the following day when men would be allowed to participate. On that second day, more changes were made to the Declaration, and Mrs. Stanton added verbiage about women's suffrage and their right to vote."

Mrs. Helms looked out at those in the room, reading accurately the shock on some faces at the idea of women voting. She looked pleased and even a little smug as she continued. "At the evening meeting, Mrs. Mott spoke about the progress of other reform movements and asked the men present to help women gain the equality they deserve. The next day the editor of the *National Reformer* in Auburn, New York, said that her speech was," and here Mrs. Helms looked at her notes before quoting, "'one of the most eloquent, logical, and philosophical discourses which we ever listened to.'"

She looked up at the room and produced an exaggerated shrug. "So I guess all men aren't selfish, unprincipled brutes."

It was a shocking statement, even if the underlying motivation for it was shared by some of those present. Consequently, if Mrs. Helms expected laughter or applause, she received mere polite attentiveness. But it was mainly because no one wanted to miss whatever provocative statements might yet be uttered by this audacious woman.

Mrs. Helms continued, but showed her irritation at her audience's lack of reaction to her estimation of men's character. "There was a large crowd there that second day. Mrs. Mott's husband, James, served as chairman of the meeting, since with men present among the women, it was considered inappropriate to have a woman serve as the chair." Her eyes swept around the room a moment to determine how her audience might be reacting to that. A little disappointed to see no sign of open rebellion, although there were many frowns showing, she challenged their placidity. "I hope there has been some progress in that department since 1848. Why shouldn't a woman chair a meeting with men present?" When she saw a few more women frowning, she took it as agreement and prepared to continue.

A young woman near the podium raised her hand and without waiting to be called upon, asked, "Did men sign the Declaration?"

Mrs. Helms smiled tolerantly.   "Before the signing took place, Assemblyman Ansel Bascom stood up to say that the New York State Assembly had recently passed the Married Woman's Property Act." The Placerville women responded with hearty applause, although most of them already knew about this, the act having passed fourteen years before. "He then spoke about the rights the Act secured for married women, which included ownership of property acquired after marriage. There were other comments, including some by the famous abolitionist Frederick Douglass. The Declaration of Sentiments was adopted unanimously. When it came to the signing of it, however, it wasn't deemed appropriate for men and women's signatures to be mixed together, so there were two sections laid out, one for women and one for men. Altogether one-hundred of the three-hundred people present signed, thirty-two of which were men."

Once more the room burst out in applause, but Mrs. Helms quelled it by raising her hands in a deprecating manner, as though it had been for her personally.

A young woman at the back of the room spoke up. "So only a third of those present, most of them women, signed. That doesn't seem right."

"We were happy to get that many. You must remember that this was fourteen years ago. I'm sure we'd get many more now."

Many of those present nodded in agreement and Mrs. Helms continued, feeling that she was finally reaching her audience. "You should know that there were many men there who absolutely refused to sign it, including Assemblyman Bascom and a number of lawyers who had come there to find out what we were about. They thought the Declaration too 'bold and ultra'." She made a grimace of disgust. "Some of them had even spoken openly against equal rights for women. They didn't speak out against it at the meeting, you understand. But after they retired to the hotel's bar room, they were very vocal."

Murmurs sounded throughout the audience.   "Now, ladies, you shouldn't be surprised at that, especially back then. The open and relaxed attitude that became common here during California's gold rush era did much to change acceptance of women's value, at least in the West.

"The next day at the meeting the eleven resolutions that had been posed during the last two days were discussed. The only one that caused some furor was Elizabeth Stanton's, the one that read, 'Resolved, that it is the duty of the women of this country to secure to themselves their sacred right to the elective franchise.'"

Someone was heard to say, "Our duty?"

Mrs. Helms found the woman nearby and looked her square in the eyes, her own ablaze with remonstration. "No less an august individual as Martin Luther once said that women should have children 'until they die of it' because that's 'what they are good for'. In other words, it's a woman's *duty* to bear children until they wear out and die. Do you prefer *that* use of the word 'duty'?"

There was a stunned silence for several seconds at being presented with such a strong challenge. Mrs. Helms looked down at her notes, took a deep breath, and continued. "It wasn't that the women present were against the concept of women voting, but they knew it might cause the other resolutions to be rejected along with that idea. It was important that as many resolutions as possible be given support. The right to vote was, after all, a political right. And most of the women present were more interested in the social, civil and religious rights of women."

Mrs. Helms paused for effect before continuing. "You might find it interesting that both Mr. and Mrs. Mott were against Mrs. Stanton's resolution. I heard Mrs. Mott say, 'Why Lizzie, you'll make us ridiculous.' Of course, Elizabeth defended the idea, saying that voting women would be able to affect future legislation and gain even further rights."

A spattering of applause filtered through the room as some of the women nodded with approval, one even daring to say, "Indeed!" These more liberal women were stared at with uncertainty and a degree of alarm by those less daring.

Mrs. Helms smiled knowingly, trying not to appear patronizing, but doing a poor job of it. "Frederick Douglass, a handsome and charismatic black gentleman with a wonderful speaking voice, then stood up and every eye was on him." She ignored the few gasps from those older women who found it shocking that a white woman would comment on a black man's appearance in such glowing terms. "He spoke eloquently in favor, saying that he could not accept the right to vote himself as a black man if woman kind could not also claim that right. He also thought that the world would be a better place if women were involved in the political arena." She looked down at her notes. "Let me quote him. 'In this denial of the right to participate in government, not merely the degradation of woman and the perpetuation of a great injustice happens, but the maiming and repudiation of one-half of the moral and intellectual power of the government of the world.'"

The same impatient young woman raised her hand and asked, "Did that have any impact on the vote?"

"Yes, it did." No one missed Mrs. Helms's look of self-satisfaction. "The resolution passed by a large majority."

One of the women at the back of the room stood up. "That's nice, but how was the convention received in the press afterwards?"

"It was mixed. The *National Reformer*, of course, thought it was the beginning of a new era in progress. It said that the influence of the meeting would continue until women are guaranteed all the rights now enjoyed by what it called 'the other half of creation'. The *Oneida Whig* did not approve at all. It called the convention the most 'shocking and unnatural incident ever recorded in the history of womanity.' It said, 'If our ladies will insist on voting and legislating, where, gentleman, will be our dinners and our elbows? Where our domestic firesides and the holes in our stockings?'"

The room erupted with hisses and outspoken declarations of disgust. One energized woman stood up and said, "In other words, he was admitting that men are helpless when it comes to taking care of themselves." The room filled with laughter, which allowed them all to relax a little and settle down.

Lucy could hold herself back not a moment longer and stood up. "To be fair to men in general, during the gold rush hundreds of men managed to survive on their own cooking. I suppose they even learned to darn a sock or two when not building sluices, diverting rivers with only shovels, and finding gold with the sweat of their brow and the bend of their backs. So the editor of that newspaper was not only under-estimating women's abilities, but also those of his own gender." She sat down to light applause, and not a few questioning looks.

Mrs. Helms decided it was time to take back control of the meeting before more examples of men's good qualities could be interjected. "I'm pleased that so many of you here today are enthused about these issues, and are even determined to be fair to men." She paused a moment for effect before adding, "But you still don't have the right to vote. And for some of you, what was yours before you married is still now controlled by your husbands."

The room fell into a silence that was profound. No one could argue that she was wrong. "The best that was said about the convention was by Horace Greeley, the editor of the *New York Tribune*, and who was in fact a visitor to this town only a few years ago. He said that when men are called upon to give some reason *against* women having equal participation with men in political discourse, they can only answer, 'None at all.' He then added, 'However unwise and mistaken the demand, it is but the assertion of a natural right, and such must be conceded.'"

The same young woman at the back of the room spoke out. "Well, that's a bit of a mixed bag of support, isn't it? He thought the demand mistaken, but still thinks it should be conceded to."

Another of the women at the back of the room pointed out, "Sounds like he was trying to please everyone and cross no one." There was a buzz of agreement.

The woman next to her let out a raucous laugh. "Just like a man. Wanting it both ways in everything."

Ignoring the sexual inuendo this might imply, considering the type of woman who had said it, Mrs. Helms quickly talked on for another five minutes. However, now she had deserted discussion of the famous convention, and was obviously off on her own tack. It quickly became clear that she was no fan of the male portion of the population, or the idea of marriage.

"Of course, even before the current war of secession got underway, most of us involved in the cause had set aside our drive for equal rights so that we could champion emancipation of the slaves. But hopefully the war will be over in a few months, and then we can go back to striving for what is due us. For although we have won the right to sue for divorce, and some states have property rights laws now, there is much more to be accomplished. A woman should think twice before entering the married state. She may have gained legal means by which she can leave it, but in the meantime she has much to lose."

One timid young lady, not yet married, hesitantly raised her hand as she asked, "What would that be?"

"For one thing, what women produce in the home that helps to support the family is never acknowledged as a real contribution. Even if she makes quite a lot of money from what she makes and sells — soaps, candles, garden produce, jam, clothing — she is seldom listed on the census as a manufacturer or farmer, even seldom as *wife*. She's just the name that comes after the head of the household, marked F for female, followed by a list of names in *his* household." Turning to the woman who had broached the question, she asked, "Does your husband ever comment on the fact that you contribute to the household's financial stability?"

"I'm not married," the young woman murmured, as though confessing to a shameful sin.

"Count yourself fortunate," Mrs. Helms drawled. Her eyes scoured the room. "How about those of you who are married? Has your husband ever thanked you or acknowledged your contributions in *any* way?" She gave the women no time to answer. "If, however, he brings in even a pittance from occasional employment he will be known as the family's *bread winner*, and will get all the credit for the family's prosperity."

One woman, married two years, said, "My husband doesn't act that way. He's proud of my sales of pies to the restaurants."

Mrs. Helms pounced on this with a swiftness that startled everyone. "If that's true, my dear madam, then you should count yourself very lucky indeed. I assume you were listed on the last census as a baker?"

"Um, no."

"Well, maybe he brags about your pies among his loutish friends as they swill their beer in the saloons at night." That got a wave of laughter from most of the women.

Mrs. Helms looked up and included all those present in the sweep of her gaze. "By the way, did you know that slaves are counted on the census as only three-quarters of a person? Do you wonder at the fact then, that women who are dedicated to the concept of equality for themselves, are also fighting to end slavery? Men still hold us down; white men, I might add, the only ones in power and most of whom fear losing that power. Men still do not respect us, not our intellect or our abilities. We must do all we can to gain influence in the legislature so we can throw off the chains of repression by husbands, fathers and brothers. We start with those rules and customs of the town in which we live, then the State laws, and eventually the Federal ones. If we cannot influence our town, village or city, how can we expect to go higher?"

One of the women who had spoken earlier from the back of the room again stood up, obviously not afraid to question some of Mrs. Helms's claims. "What about the Sole Trader Act here in California that allows women to own their own business? Isn't that a sign of progress?" She sat down harder than planned and had to reach up to steady her hat.

Mrs. Helms smiled. "Oh, yes. But progress allowed by men."

The young woman popped up again. "But it allows for $500 of community property or the husband's separate property to be invested in her business. Then that becomes her separate property as part of her business and isn't subject to his debts."

"Yes, which is a good thing in case he becomes a degenerate or loses his money gambling," Mrs. Helms smirked.

"But that means the Sole Trader Act is good, doesn't it?" The young woman sat down again, this time with more grace.

"Of course, it's good. But none of it takes place without the woman going through a difficult process. A man can put a board across the stump of a tree to hold a bottle and three glasses anywhere he wants, and he's immediately recognized as 'in business for himself'. A man can own two broken down mules and call himself a packer and no one questions that he has the right of ownership of 'his business'.

"For a woman to take advantage of the Act, she has to find a newspaper to publish her intention for four weeks, and then she must appear in court to prove to a judge that her intent is not to defraud her husband's creditors. Hopefully, the judge doesn't have moral or religious prejudices against a woman working outside the home and he approves her plea."

After absorbing the gasps and murmured reaction to that comparison, Mrs. Helms continued in a slightly louder voice. "She then must swear that she is going into business with her own money to support herself, and if she has children, them as well."

An older woman at a table next to the speaker's platform said, "But that implies an absent husband, and at least in California he doesn't have to be gone. Here, she doesn't have to prove that without the business she and her children will starve."

"I must say I'm impressed that some of you are so well informed about the Sole Trader Act." If she had been a cat, she would have licked her shoulder in satisfaction at this point, but only because she knew what she was going to say next. "Yes, California has always been more progressive with its rights, as long as men allow for those rights. But let's not forget that this married woman with all these rights and privileges we're talking about can't apply to the courts without her husband's permission if he *isn't* absent from the family. I'm not talking legally. I'm talking about men's influence over their wives. How many wives that you know will cross their husbands in something like this just to have her own business, knowing how inharmonious will be that household if she does? And if he goes to court and objects, that's the end of her plans for a business."

No one offered any argument, and everyone's attention was riveted on Mrs. Helms. "And think about this. She might have a business of her own when single, but the minute she marries she is under the auspices of someone society says is her superior called 'husband'. At that point her marital status becomes a burden to her, an act of reduction of her person-hood. The last thing a woman does completely of her own volition is when she utters the words 'I do' during the marriage ceremony."

The young woman who had asked the original question about the Sole Trader Act stood up again. "You seem to feel that we should think of men as the enemy. Isn't the inequality of our status the real enemy? Can't we ask for more rights without hating men?"

"I'm not advocating that you should hate men. But it is after all men who vote 'no' when the subject of more rights for women is brought up in any legislature, whether State or Federal."

"But some states have voted 'yes' about allowing more property rights."

"Good for them." Mrs. Helms barely resisted curling her lip in disdain. "But until every state of the union, and given our current war the size of that union is in doubt, we are not done." The young woman started to say something more, but Mrs. Helms cut her off. "When you have fought this battle as long as I have, my dear, let's see how broadminded you are toward men in power."

The reference to the war was a sobering reminder. Until recently, most people had taken for granted that the war would be a short-lived event that would soon be resolved to everyone's satisfaction. However, even the most optimistic of people were beginning to change their minds about that as the second year of the war began and neither side was clearly winning.

Mrs. Helms took a moment to fold up her notes before continuing. "I now have an announcement to make. I have moved here to Placerville, since it is the county seat of El Dorado County. Here I will put down roots and continue my campaign for the rights of women." She raised her right hand, palm outward, as though swearing before a judge. "No man will stop us now!"

There was a stunned silence, most present still trying to absorb the impact of her previous statement about her having decided to live there. Many of the women present had placated their husband or father by assuring them that Mrs. Helms would soon be moving on, and therefore out of their lives. A number of men had made it clear that the only reason they were maintaining any tolerance of her at all was because they thought she would soon be some other town's problem.

Mrs. Helms charged on, oblivious to the consternation her announcement had caused. "Do you realize that back in 1636 that Roger Williams, the man who founded Providence, Rhode Island, was a man with what were then and still are radical ideas? He was cast out of the Massachusetts Bay Colony because he was critical of the restrictive Puritan influence over civic life. So he established what he called Providence Plantations on land he had been given by the local Indian tribe because he had been a champion of theirs. This is the colony that became Rhode Island. It was the first secular state in the New World and its people could worship anything they wanted, or not at all if that was what suited them. There was no persecution either way. Every plot of land was equal in size and women were allowed to own some of that land. Women were even allowed to have a say about what went on in the town. Of course, things have changed since then, even there."

A hum of what might have been discontentment spread through the room. Mrs. Helms seemed gratified at the sound and continued. "I plan to follow that example and make Placerville a town where all is equal for man or woman. If the responsibility involved in voting in a national election intimidates you, some counties now allow women to vote in city council or school elections. That's where we will start."

To lighten the shock that she could see in the room, she smiled broadly and said, "Unfortunately, I will have to work with a man to find a permanent residence." She couldn't hide her chagrin when no one laughed at what she saw as sharp irony. She cleared her throat. "So as soon as I've settled in, we will have a rally where we can march down Main Street with placards displaying our goals. Of course, we'll make sure the newspapers here and afar report this in detail. Doesn't it gall you that even if we are given the right to vote, or to do anything else that is currently forbidden us, that it will be men who make that decision?" Her voice raised almost to a shout, she repeated a favorite slogan of the cause. "Take us off the pedestal and put us in the voting booth!"

Lucy waited for the rallying cry from those around her, but it did not come. It seemed as though no one knew quite how to react. The married women thought of their husbands and the single ladies thought of the men they wanted as husbands. A few even thought of what was necessary for them to open or keep their small business, which approval of course came from men. On the other hand, no woman wanted to offend their luncheon guest, so there was polite but subdued applause.

Pushing on, Mrs. Helms declared, "In our schools, the boys are taught to think about their future work and so the importance of learning math and knowledge of history as they read wonderful books that expand their horizons. The girls are taught how to cook and do laundry, since they're expected to marry and raise a family. Consequently, their education is cursory unless they put forth much effort on their own. Boys are expected to graduate, but girls are not. And if girls aspire to a higher education, there are few universities in the country that will accept them. Those families with abundant means must send their girls to England, where there is greater opportunity for a university education, even if denied a real degree. Of course, right now that country is still in deep mourning for Prince Albert, and they're concerned for Queen Victoria as she deals with her grief."

Mrs. Helms hesitated a moment to show that she was capable of sympathy, but then weakened that when she said, "Maybe now she'll become the leader she was always meant to be." Stunned silence followed, but Mrs. Helms seemed not to notice. "It has been said that 'the men of the 18th century preferred his women fragile and the modern 19th century man prefers his women ignorant; but of whatever generation, they expect their women to be good.'" She offered what she thought was an ingratiating smile. "Of course, what that means is open to interpretation. But in whatever sense it is meant, it is always open to the restrictive dictates of a man who has power over some woman who he considers as belonging to him, even possibly feeling he owns her. But with all of us working together, we can change all of this."

Realizing the difficult situation of the suddenly restive ladies around her, who all but herself lived there in town, Lucy decided this last statement was a good place for this harangue to end. She stood up and declared, "We owe you much, Mrs. Helms. Not only for today with the information and motivation you have bestowed upon us, but also for all that you have done in the past to advocate for greater rights and privileges for women."

Martha Hume realized before any of the others that Lucy was providing an opportunity to bring the meeting to an end. She stood up and began applauding, with Dolly only a beat behind her. Sarah Landecker quickly joined them, and then the other women in the room stood up with what looked like enthusiasm but was mostly relief.

For some of them, the ideas expressed had been, if not shocking, then at least uncomfortable to consider. However, there were women present who found themselves stimulated when thinking about the freedoms that women might someday enjoy, even if thinking of them as 'a right' was as yet beyond their comprehension. Most of them also found it disconcerting when they thought of the reality of their current situation, both in society and in their homes, and the personality of the men who currently ruled their daily choices. No matter their situation, every woman who had heard Mrs. Helms speak was now somewhat disquieted as they questioned their life choices, and what might be available for their daughters.

As the women left their tables and began milling around, Mrs. Helms merged into their midst. However, before she could approach very far into the room, Martha Hume murmured to Lucy and Dolly, "Sarah has already left. Let's do the same. There's a side door to this room."

Soon they were on the sidewalk watching a long line of freight wagons, spring wagons and riders on horseback navigating the traffic on Main Street. They were each sharply aware in that moment that all of this before them was under the control of a man, and most were moving east to the main route over the Sierra that would take them to the other half of California, and new adventures. These men were focused beyond Placerville, even far beyond the Sierra, their goal the opportunity to succeed at whatever they might attempt.

The women watched them, more aware than ever before that these men had the absolute freedom to choose where they were going. If they decided at some point to turn right instead of left, or even to turn around, they could do so without anyone's permission or judgment. They could wear what they wanted, eat and drink whatever and wherever they might choose, and consort with any man or woman who appealed to them. It was a form of self-determination every man on that road took for granted, and every woman standing to the side considered an impossible likelihood for themselves. At least for the time being.

Uncomfortable with this thought, Dolly spoke up. "I ate very little of what was served, and I'm hungry. Would either of you like to get something to eat?"

Martha breathed out, "Oh, yes, please."

Struck with an idea, Lucy said, "The City Bakery isn't far from the Cary House where I'm staying. Why don't we purchase some goodies at the bakery and take them to my room? It has a small table in it and we can order up some beverages."

This was met with enthusiasm and soon the women had an indoor picnic spread out before them on the table, as well as the long dresser and a corner of Lucy's bed. A grinning waiter from the dining room brought them a pitcher of fresh water and two large pots of hot tea. The young man couldn't wait to tell his fellow waiters what the interesting Mrs. Murphy was doing in her room.

The women devoured hot rolls filled with ham and cheese, and savored small, folded cherry pies. After cleansing their palates with grapes Lucy already had in her room, they were ready to nibble lacy Florentine cookies with their tea.

The unconventional aspect of the occasion lent a light and frivolous atmosphere to their little party, and therefore the conversation was such that it prompted much laughter. But there was also the sharing of little secrets and anecdotes thought to be of no great moment. Lucy, however, filed them away in case they might have some future importance.

An example of this was when Dolly told them, "My sister should be arriving tomorrow. She still lives in Los Angeles." As long as Lucy had known Dolly, this was something about which she seldom spoke.

"Melanie's marriage hasn't been very successful." Dolly's eyes watered and she quickly took a sip of her tea.

Martha couldn't resist asking, "Weren't you married before your current marriage to Robert? If I'm not being too bold."

Dolly swallowed hard, although it was not with food. "Yes, I was, back in the early '50's. My mother had married me off the minute I turned fifteen. The next winter my husband was chopping wood one day and hit a hard knot. The axe bounced back and hit him in the forehead. I was told he died instantly. I was not yet 17, but circumstances brought me to Nevada City and I quickly found myself destitute. Being not well educated, I lost several jobs because I couldn't do them well. My mother had married off my sister only months after ridding herself of me, and she refused my return home. She wanted to get on with her life unencumbered, and eventually she remarried." Unspoken was that all that was left to her was the choice she had been forced to make. Lucy knew that Dolly had been more fortunate than some girls, as the house mother where she had worked had not mistreated *her girls*.

Martha didn't need Dolly to put any of this into words. Instead, she placed a hand gently on Dolly's arm. "We all do what we have to in order to survive, my friend. Those of us who were here during the gold rush know that more than most. That's when my husband and his brother came here from Indiana, and their trials along the way were harsh ones."

Martha's acknowledgement of the challenges that were a part of the era just past brought nods of agreement from both Lucy and Dolly. But it was hearing herself referred to as a friend that cleared away much of the shame Dolly sometimes still felt, no matter how justified she had been in choosing "the life". With a burst of relief, she leaned forward and gave Martha a spontaneous but brief hug. Martha laughed, a little embarrassed but obviously pleased as she picked up the plate of cookies and offered it to her friends. They all took one and Lucy poured them more tea. As she did so, she almost laughed aloud at how a little self-revelation and cookies could bond together three women from such different backgrounds.

Lucy waited to see if Dolly would add any further information to her resume. Like the fact that her first husband's accident while chopping wood had occurred the first day that Dolly had been able to get out of bed after having miscarried her baby because her husband had beaten her so severely. Or the fact that Dolly had left town the day after his funeral, before too many questions could be asked. But Dolly said nothing about any of this, friendships allowing for trust only after they mature.

Lucy steered the subject away from husbands and death. "Did you grow up close to the beach, Dolly?"

"Close enough that we could ride a burro there in half an hour. We lived in a small Mexican community of very nice people. It was a quiet and small Los Angeles town of hardworking people with businesses and gardens, groves of fruit trees and what seemed like miles of grape vines."

"Did you have a happy childhood, then?" Martha asked, hoping that at least this might have been a good time in Dolly's life.

"No," Dolly stated boldly. "Father deserted us not long after we arrived in Los Angeles, and died during the rush. I was thirteen and my sister was twelve. Mother worked three jobs to keep us in our home and fed. I worked sweeping out shops before they opened, and my sister worked at a fish cleaning station where fishing boats brought their catches up from the ocean. But Melanie seemed not to care that our life was hard. She was always the sweet, kind one. There was a family next door to us even poorer than we were, and Melanie would save the fish heads so the mother could make soup for her family. I was the naughty one trying to see what I could get away with."

Martha had not led a particularly sheltered life before marrying Mr. Hume at eighteen, but she was still appalled at the thought of such young girls having had such a difficult life. She didn't know what to say to express her feelings without accidentally saying something insensitive, so she remained silent.

Dolly continued, "When Melanie was fifteen, there being only eleven months between us, Mother married her off to Vincent St. John, a wealthy businessman she's still married to. After my husband died, Melanie wanted me to move in with them, but Vincent wouldn't allow it. He was never a very kind man."

Martha and Lucy sensed this last to be an understatement of vast proportions. They were all suddenly filled with over-whelming gratitude and appreciation of their husbands. Acknowledging that they didn't always agree with them, or their husbands with them, they knew they were always treated with respect, and had nothing to fear from them physically.

After they had each taken a turn visiting the facilities down the hall, Martha surprised her friends by pulling out from her purse a bag of hard candy that she had purchased at the bakery. They helped themselves as Dolly asked, "Did you hear that Peter and Caroline Beck are divorcing?"

Martha sighed. "Yes." She told Lucy, "Caroline does washing over on Cottage Street near Coloma. I'm not surprised at the news, considering how much they're known to argue. Still, I always think it's a shame when a couple can't stay together."

"Yes," Dolly agreed. "But they're not the only ones to have recently filed for divorce. The Bantas come to mind."

Martha was visibly shaken. "Oh, I didn't know about Ann and Henry Banta." She shook her head and fell silent.

Lucy quickly searched for a less tragic subject. "I heard someone say that you and Mr. Hume visited Sacramento recently on your way to the coast. How was it there?"

"Recovering from the floods more quickly than I'd expected," Martha answered her. After taking a sip of tea, she added, "There are still areas that are somewhat swampy, but on the whole things are getting cleaned up and rebuilt."

Dolly eyed the cookies, then forced herself to look away. "I heard Mr. Hume mention during your dinner party that he wants to visit his family."

"Oh, yes," Martha sighed. "He's wanted to go back to Indiana to see them for some time. It's just a matter of finding the right time in his busy schedule. It's a long, arduous journey and I worry about that."

Good grief, Lucy thought, this is not getting us to the point. She decided it was time to risk being forthright. "Martha, did you know Mrs. Butterick?"

Both of the other women put down their cups and looked at her with surprise. Anyone in Placerville who had spent much time with Lucy on past visits was aware that she was a somewhat free-speaking individual, so Martha told herself that she shouldn't be surprised at so probing a question, even such an unpleasant one.

Having almost forgotten why Lucy was really in town, Dolly rose to the occasion. "I've wondered the same thing. Mrs. Butterick seemed to be involved in so many charitable causes, but I couldn't really warm up to her."

Martha nodded. "I know what you mean. I've known few women to volunteer to help on a committee as much as she would." She sighed and shook her head. "If we needed someone to bake for a fundraiser, she was the first one to step forward. If we were a few dollars short of our goal, she supplied it. Her church is certainly feeling her loss."

"She always seemed a little closed off," Dolly mused. "But I thought that was just to me, because she disapproved of me."

"It sounds to me," Lucy surmised, "as though she was trying to make amends for something she felt guilty about."

Martha thought a moment before answering. "You might be right. But it must have been a long time ago, because she'd been here since just before the '56 fire. Still, the anonymous letter writer must have said something that made her think her secret was known."

It was a sad idea, and although Lucy too was affected, she pushed on. "Thankfully, no one else has been so despondent over whatever was said in their letters as to have felt the need to do what she did."

"For now," Dolly said.

Lucy picked up the thread of the thought. "Yes, but I wonder if there isn't someone out there who's more angry than despondent. So angry, perhaps, that if they find out the identity of the writer, they'll cause them physical injury. Many men are certainly angry enough to do that."

"If it's a man who figures it out, maybe," Martha said. "But if it's a woman who discovers the truth, I would assume they'd turn the writer in to the law."

"It would depend on how they know the person, wouldn't it?" Dolly suggested. "I mean, if it was a friend or relative, maybe they'd just talk to them about stopping."

Martha gave a deep sigh. "Maybe that would be the best resolution, after all. No arrest, no reason to make public comments, and no one fearing that the writer would speak out at a trial about those things they learned about various people in town."

"Which," Lucy mused, "brings up the question of how the letter writer gains their knowledge about everyone."

Dolly looked askance at the plate of cookies, shrugged and then reached for one. "She probably has several ways of gaining knowledge about others." Aware of the quantity of letters sent, she added, "She must know a lot of people."

"Or socializes with a lot of people," Martha added, thinking of how many social groups she frequented, and how many people she and John regularly entertained in their home. "Gossip is such a mainstay. I wonder if the sender is an *elderly* lady."

"Why do you say that?" Dolly asked.

"The elderly are the best at gossip. They've developed over time the knack of conveying or gaining information without giving offense."

Dolly laughed. "Or giving away what they're doing."

"Yes," Marth nodded. "Good gossip is such an art."

Abruptly changing the subject, Lucy asked, "How long has Mrs. Helms been in town?"

Dolly shook her head. "I've been hearing about her for the last month, but I hadn't seen her until today."

Martha considered a moment before answering. "I think for at least a month. I remember because the letters began to arrive about the same time she did, but over the last week I don't think anyone has received a letter."

"I received another one just yesterday," Dolly exclaimed, "so they have started up again."

The other women looked at her, momentarily stuck for what to say until Martha spoke up. "I admire your honesty, Dolly. I'll match it. I received one yesterday, too. It wasn't all that offensive, just asking what was John 'really' doing when he was working late at his office."

"I suppose that's the ridiculous nature of most of them," Lucy speculated. "But some letters must be much worse, or Mrs. Butterick wouldn't have felt the need to end her life before her secret got spread around. But about Mrs. Helms, I wondered how long she had been here because several of the ladies today seemed to already know her."

"That's right," Martha agreed. "I think she spent her time here up to now simply getting to know as many of the women in town as she could. Many of my friends have been talking about her opinions for weeks." She chuckled. "And also what their husbands think of her. Men's resentment of her ideas has gone from jokes and scoffing, to fear and even threats against her."

"Who were the young women asking so many questions today?" Lucy asked.

Dolly spoke up. "The one closest to the podium was Maria Price. She does washing, as does the other one, Anne Radigne. Maria works on the north side of Main near Sacramento, and they arrived at the meeting together." Lucy noticed that Dolly gave no reference to the demimonde at the back of the room who had asked questions.

"No, dear," Martha interjected, "Anne works in a saloon."

"Really? I must have her mixed up with someone else. What does Anne do in the saloon?"

Martha drew herself up as she exclaimed, "I wouldn't know that, would I?"

Dolly stammered, knowing she had made a social gaffe. "Of course not. I should have known that."

It was an interesting exchange that reminded Lucy that no matter how broad-minded Mrs. Hume might appear to be, she was still the wife of a prominent and important person. Martha therefore had to be careful at all times what she said, and how she presented herself to others.

Dolly quickly continued. "The only women I know who do washing, but who weren't there today, are Caroline Beck on Cottage Street, Nancy Edward on Cary Alley, and Maria Piarein over on Cedar Ravine."

"I know some of them, too," Martha said. "Nice women. In fact, two of them do our washing." She switched back to the original topic. "Two of my friends received a letter a couple of days ago. They also told me they thought their husbands had gotten one, although they said they didn't know what was written in them."

"Why didn't the men show their wives their letters?" Lucy asked. "Because what was in them was true, or because they simply thought the wording so foul that it would offend their wives' tender ears?"

The other two women laughed at Lucy's sarcasm, although that didn't mean they thought there was no truth in it. Many men had been raised in a culture that taught that it was a man's responsibility to protect women from anything crude or vulgar, which they gently termed *unseemly*. It wasn't any sillier than the Victorian dictate of calling a leg, a *limb*, whether it belonged to a person -- or a piano. Acceptable words spoken in polite society might have been used to avoid censoriously raised eyebrows, but the code was understood by everyone.

Martha frowned. "It tends to make one think that when a couple of weeks go by without a letter being received, that it may be because the writer is out of town."

Dolly looked at her friends with a new idea dawning. "Or she might simply be too busy to spread out the tools of her trade, so to speak."

Martha added, "Or maybe there are too many people present in her home to allow for the creation of the letters."

"Yes," Lucy agreed. "Maybe she's hindered by a husband who returns home after being gone, like a freighter or packer or stage driver."

Martha stood up. "Well, this has been most enjoyable, as well as giving us much to think about. But I need to start my walk to the Orleans Hotel where I left my rig if I'm to be home when John gets there."

"Would you like me to have a hotel steward escort you?" Lucy offered.

"Oh, thank you, my dear. But it's only a block away, and it's a fine day. I'll be glad of the exercise."

Dolly too stood up after looking down at the small watch in the form of a brooch that was pinned to the shoulder of her dress. "I had no idea it was getting so late. Lucy dear, do you mind if I leave all of this for you to clean up?"

"No, not at all. And I think I'll just stay in and read, so I won't see you for supper."

Dolly tried not to show her relief, thinking that she could now make a simple meal for Robert, considering that she wouldn't be hungry when he was. Besides, there was something else she wanted to do that evening, and without anyone's knowledge.

When the women were gone, Lucy gathered the remnants of the food not eaten and wrapped it in her cloth napkin, putting it all in a drawer of the dresser. Everything else she stacked on a tray that she placed on the floor outside the door to her room. It would soon be taken away, quietly and without fuss. Lucy so enjoyed life in a modern hotel.

CHAPTER 4

"Rumor is a pipe, blown by surmises, jealousies, conjectures."
Shakespeare, Henry IV

Saturday, May 31 – Wednesday, June 3

Lucy made sure she had her key in her purse before leaving the hotel through a back entrance that many people didn't know existed, and which was used mainly by those who lived in the hotel full time. The day's suffrage meeting and the makeshift picnic had been thought-provoking, but she longed for some time by herself. She wanted to walk along Main Street while thinking about all the information she had gathered since arriving in town, while at the same time figuring out what her next move should be. Investigating the malfeasance of people was not something she had ever anticipated doing, and she wasn't sure how to proceed.

Even this late in the day, heavily-laden freight wagons were still on the road heading out of town, having missed their chance to get ahead of those freighters who had started earlier. But if they could get at least as far as one of the stations where they could stop overnight, hopefully where there was still room in the corrals, then in the morning they would be ahead of those who had stopped in Placerville for the night. With so much traffic on the road through Johnson's Pass and Hope Valley, it paid to keep on the move if you wanted your freight to sell out quickly upon reaching its destination. That, at least, would not become a problem in Virginia City until a number of years in the future.

Turning away from a window display that had caught her attention, Lucy became aware that everyone around her on the sidewalk had come to a sudden stop. Following their gaze out to the street, she saw that between two freight wagons filled with hay was a group of five women mounted on riding mules. They each had a valise tied on one side of their saddle, and a hemp bag for food on the other side. More startling was the fact that they were not riding side-saddle, but rather astride, something a lady who cared about her reputation would not choose to do.

It was difficult to determine if these were *soiled doves* or not, such women having been seen riding through town like this before. The women now before them were at least wearing riding attire of split skirts, tall boots, and heavy jackets. Most important of all, their bonnets were understated and without adornment. It was possible that this group consisted of *good women* after all, and were just well-prepared for a long, arduous ride. Upon closer observation, however, it could be seen that they were wearing a considerable amount of make-up and the top button of their shirts were not fastened. When one of them threw a kiss to a group of men by the side of the road, and then laughed when the men offered cat calls in response, that made up the mind of the by-standers. The women on the sidewalks hurried on, although few of the men left as quickly.

Watching them pass by, because of her unconventional background, Lucy knew that these women would probably sell their mules when they arrived in Virginia City so they would have the funds to buy their way into a good parlor house, if they were considered of sufficient quality by the house mother. If not that, then they would attempt to join the protection of a bawdy house of decent repute. Only if these preferred options could not be obtained, would they use their money to purchase or build a crib *on the line* at the outskirts of town.

Occupying one of these tiny one-room cabins was the lowest rung of the ladder in their profession, although some women preferred it because they didn't have to pay a portion of what they earned to a keeper. Soon worn out by too many customers, too much liquor to dull reality, and too little hope of better, it was in these huts that many suicides took place. And although pregnancy was something most of them knew how to avoid, disease was not, no matter the so-called quality of their customer.

Lucy said a silent prayer of thanks for how her and Dolly's lives had turned out, then turned back to the front of the Fredrick Barss Jewelry Store. Drawn in by the sparkling displays within, she entered the store determined to only browse and not purchase. It was a small space, the walls lined with shelving crowded with bottles of scent and pomades, and down the center of the room a row of glass cases filled with all types of jewelry for women, as well as pocket watches and other jewelry for men. On the wall behind the counter hung five beautifully carved, wooden clocks, their brass pendulums swaying in rhythm together. Framed prints hanging by chains were anchored to the walls near the ceiling, leaning out at the top so those walking beneath could better appreciate them. At that moment, however, it was the wooden chair in front of one of the glass cases that interested Lucy, and she sat upon it to rest a moment.

Mr. Barss, his long, neatly combed beard covering his chest, walked over to her and asked if he could assist her. He was a man of substance, more military in his bearing than one might expect of someone who dealt in delicate pieces of jewelry, but his eyes were full of good humor.

"I'm interested in the little stick pin in this case. I think my husband would like it."

"Ah, your husband must be a man of distinction." He pulled it from the back of the case and laid it on a black velvet pad in front of her. "It's a small gold nugget found in our own Hangtown Creek some years ago."

Lucy reached to her neck and pulled free from her collar the gold nugget she always wore on a chain around her neck. "It's shaped much like the one my husband gave me. That's why it caught my eye."

"So it is." When he named the price, Lucy bit her lower lip and hesitated. It would mean not ordering another dress, but she knew that if she didn't buy it, she would at some point remember the moment as a regretted, missed opportunity. "I'll take it."

After half an hour of strolling casually along the sidewalks, Lucy took a seat on a wooden bench outside the open door of the Pebelie Barber Shop, beneath a wooden sign painted in the traditional form of a barber pole. The barbers in Placerville did no blood-letting, so the sign was not a true representation of the red stripe representing blood, the blue stripe of the vein that was tapped, and the white stripe representing bandages. Of course, if truly necessary, Mr. Pebelie might pull a tooth if the town's visiting dentist was out hunting, or sleeping off the effects of the night before.

Lucy immediately realized that she could hear the conversation between the four men inside while they were unaware of her presence. One customer had his face covered in a thin layer of creamy lather while getting a shave by a portly barber who was wielding the long blade of a razor with practiced skill. Every once in awhile he wiped the razor on that day's towel, and then went back to work. The other customer was having his hair trimmed by a young but efficient barber who tactfully took his time with a head of hair that soon would no longer have all that many strands left to be cut.

While men of the time might shave themselves at home or carefully clip a bit off their beard, for a haircut most men went to a barber. It was well worth 5 cents, even if they didn't add 3 cents for a shave. At home a man might pat a little soothing balm to his freshly shaved cheeks, but at the barber he could be pampered with hot towels, exotic lotions and dusted with scented powders; and all with no question of his masculinity.

He could also indulge himself in the latest gossip without being seen as doing so, especially if he had been made to wait on one of the benches along the wall at the back of the room. Provided there for his entertainment were the usual newspapers and magazines, but in this shop, they waited beneath wall posters not appropriate for the home. There was even a deck of cards with which to while away the time, the backs decorated with three red, vertically placed stars.

Lucy recognized the voice of Leo Bernathowitz, the older of the barbers, because he boarded at the Cary House. But it was the younger man they called Hal who was cutting the hair of Mr. Tony Leon, the husband of Jane Leon, a woman with whom Lucy had formed a friendship on her two previous visits.

The young barber asked, "How was your trip this time, Mr. Leon?"

"The mules fared well, I got there and back without undue excitement, and I got paid." He laughed. "So, for me, it was a good trip."

Mr. Bernathowitz leaned down closer to his customer, a freighter having made trips through town the past two summers. "Mr. Leon is a packer. He lives here."

His customer didn't dare reply with the razor still dragging across his face. However, as soon as the last remnant of lather was washed off, he turned to the wiry man in the next chair. "How do you do? I'm Jeff."

"Nice to meet you." Mr. Leon politely didn't ask for a last name from the rough looking freighter, but he wondered why it hadn't been offered. "I'm Tony Leon. We live just north of town on Coloma. Been gone a week and just got back. Thought it'd be a good idea to trim up before I take the wife out for dinner tonight."

Jeff told him, "From what I've heard this time through town, you missed the arrival of one of those suffrage women. She's been talking up her radical ideas all over the place."

"Oh, yeah?"

Hal spoke up. "Some woman by the name of Helms."

Mr. Leon became very still. "She's been talking suffrage, has she?"

"Yeah, all over town," the young barber answered. "Why?"

"Oh, just curious. My wife has read some of those kinds of pamphlets and I wonder if she's talked to her. She knows I disapprove." A frown settled across his brow as he pulled a gold pocket watch from a small vest pocket, and glanced at it. There was something etched on the back of the case, but his hand obscured it. Returning the watch to his vest, he said, "She didn't mention anything about it, but then again I wasn't home long before coming into town."

"Your wife might have talked with her," Jeff informed him. "According to what I've picked up in the saloons from unhappy men, lots of ladies have. In fact, your wife might have been at a meeting held at the Orleans Hotel at lunchtime today."

"Well, I'll talk to her about it later." His tone made it clear to the men, as well as Lucy, that it would probably be a lively conversation.

The men launched into a heated discussion about the idea of women having legal rights to property, or heaven forbid, the right to vote. The barbers seemed less concerned than the freighter and the packer, but they all agreed that these were radical ideas being promulgated, about which none of them were comfortable. They did, however, grudgingly agree that it was "probably only fair" that women keep what they owned before marriage. The barbers and the freighter agreed that any spending of money while married "should of course be governed by the husband". Tony remained quiet on the subject, and the others tactfully refrained from questioning him.

Soon the conversation ran to pure gossip about who was getting divorced and why, which man was sleeping with what woman on the side, and the bank clerk who was "let go". Lucy realized that maybe she should leave when they began talking about the status of the new *house* on east Main and heard them use the term "humpery". But since they mentioned several townsmen's names, she stayed where she was. She was beginning to realize the abundance of personal information available in casual conversations, and that it could easily find its way into a threatening letter by some unprincipled individual.

Only when the discussion turned to the impersonal topic of the increased cost of goods and the clean-up of the winter's flooding in Sacramento, did

Lucy quietly leave her place on the bench. She walked to a nearby café for a pot of tea, needing time to make notes in a small notebook carried in her purse. She wore down her pencil considerably before she finished.

Lucy was now fully cognizant that there were many sources of gossip in Placerville, as there was in every town. Just because men and women could be scrupulously polite, socially adept, and even capable of grace and kindness, it didn't mean they couldn't at times be catty or mean-spirited.

Lucy had to admit that people were much the same everywhere. They sometimes argued, coveted, feared, and schemed, and most probably had things in their past they didn't want publicly exposed. She forced herself to add, "Even here in my favorite, lovely town."

Although Lucy's honesty tended to make her sometimes too forthright with others, she treated herself no differently. Therefore, she confronted the fact that she had over the last few years formed a somewhat utopian picture of Placerville. It had become for her a place of refuge, and therefore she had gotten into the habit of thinking of it as having unusually high standards, perpetually congenial people, and year-round beauty. "Well," she chuckled to herself, "at least I can hang onto that last claim."

But no town was a utopia, even if the county had been named after the fabled city of gold called *El Dorado*. She told herself that it was time she faced that fact and let go of what was only a chimerical fantasy. If she was going to be of any real help in resolving the disturbing situation of anonymous, hurtful letters, she was going to have to be willing to deal with the harshest of realities. What people chose to display was on the surface, with what lay beneath often a more complex and truthful reality. She thought of the mining that was the history of the area and then of the task to which she had set herself. To reach the motherlode of what people might prefer to hide, Lucy knew she would have to dig deeper than might be comfortable for those being interviewed by her. It certainly wasn't going to be comfortable to be the one doing it.

Placerville might have been so special to Lucy because she had been there in 1848 right after coming into the custody of Freda, back when the town had been Old Dry Diggings. Back then it had been nothing more than a muddy track between log cabins and canvas tents. To Lucy, the town's progress was a symbol of what hope married to perseverance can produce.

While all this was playing out, the fact of the war was not ignored by those in Placerville. Being so far from the fighting, even if not the politics of it, the horror of the war was not a daily reality. Nevertheless, since the California discovery of gold back in 1848, hundreds of people had moved there from eastern and southern states, which meant that many of them had relatives currently fighting on one side or the other. Many citizens were therefore pre-disposed toward either the Union or the Confederacy, which occasionally caused a shouting match or even a fist fight if the discussion was carried too far. This was especially true in the southern half of California, where men were heavily aligned with the Confederacy. The northern half of the state had more Federalist leanings. Placerville was situated between these, and because of its increasing commerce, the townspeople tried hard to remain neutral, at least publicly.

News of the war's progress had come to them first in the few newspapers brought by the Pony Express at the beginning of the war. With that service recently ended, the growing presence of telegraph service across the country brought news more quickly. Cross-country stages passed by the slower moving wagon trains and brought not only newspapers but also letters from relatives close to the fighting. Although the trip around The Horn or across the Isthmus of Panama took months, it also brought people escaping the war and who were interviewed by newspapers once they came to rest in the West. In whatever way it arrived, news of the war was always welcome.

Of course, we now know many details of the broad picture of that war's progress, but in 1862 what people in the West heard was not all that encouraging if you were hoping *the upheaval,* as some politely called it, would be short-lived. The first few months of this second year of the war saw the Confederates routed at the southern border of Kentucky and defeated at Elk Horn in Arkansas. Fort Henry on the Tennessee River and Fort Donelson on the Cumberland were taken by General Grant of the Union Army. Consequently, with the loss of these forts, it necessitated that the Confederacy abandon Kentucky and Nashville.

Roanoke Island, on the coast of North Carolina, was taken, and Norfolk was thus threatened from the rear. A small victory, unproductive of much success at Valverde in New Mexico, was the only Confederate success. The frontier of the Confederacy had thus been pushed back in what was considered the West to Arkansas and Tennessee, and the coast of North Carolina passed into Federal occupation. This meant that at this point in the war the South had been waging a defensive war, its movements determined by the movements of the Northern armies.

In March, the sunken frigate *Merrimac* had been raised by the Confederates, plated with railroad iron, and armed with a beak or ram. After being renamed the *Virginia,* it attacked the Federal fleet, sank the *Cumberland* and captured the *Congress.* Right after that it encountered the iron-coated and turreted *Monitor* of the Union. After a battle that would become famous, it was an undecided win as the *Monitor* retired into shoal water and the *Virginia* withdrew to Norfolk to repair damages. Their fates were not good ones. A couple of months later the *Virginia* was blown up by her commander, and later in the year the *Monitor* would be lost in a storm.

Avoiding excruciating historical detail, the news during this second year was alternately encouraging to both sides, but especially the Confederacy as it increased its battle victories. This uncertain and wavering progress on both sides would continue until the eventual escalation of victories for the Union, and the war's conclusion in 1865.

But in the summer of 1862, there was much uncertainty about the next news to reach the California population. And always there was the realization that by the time they had received that news, more battles would have taken place that might have changed the status once again. Nevertheless, each communication was latched onto as *current,* and celebrated or mourned accordingly.

Lucy arrived at Dolly and Robert's house late on the morning of Monday the 2nd of June well rested and eager to begin her investigations. They had all agreed that Sunday would be a day of rest for them all, and had not ventured out after returning to their respective abodes after church services.

As soon as Lucy entered the Robbins home, Dolly eagerly rushed forward while leading a pretty young woman by the hand. She was dressed in a burgundy two-piece traveling suit that would have served her well even in fashion-conscious Eastern cities. With the top half separate from the skirt, it allowed for a versatility welcome when traveling, as long as one had packed both a white and a black waist. Lucy realized that Dolly's sister had not been lacking a decent clothing allowance, even if her marriage was unsatisfactory.

"Lucy, I'd like you to meet my sister, Melanie St. John. She got here yesterday, all the way from Los Angeles."

Lucy immediately saw the resemblance. Although Melanie was thinner than Dolly, both were blonde and voluptuous. Both women had dark blue eyes and a smile that gave them a flirtatious air, but that at the same time didn't cheapen them. Melanie's complexion was like porcelain, although Lucy could tell the girl used a light dusting of blush. Her hair, parted in the middle and swept back, as was the current fashion, was exceptionally sleek and glossy. Melanie was looking at Lucy with wide-eyed animation, her eyes actually sparkling.

According to Dolly, her sister had never had to deal with the wider world as she and Lucy had, having gone straight from her childhood home to her husband's home. Maybe, Lucy thought, that's why she seems to be clinging to much of her youthful, wide-eyed wonderment. Nevertheless, Lucy thought she sensed an underlying tension and wariness in Melanie that didn't match the sweetness of her smile.

"Oh, Mrs. Murphy, I'm so happy to meet you," Melanie gushed. "I've heard so many wonderful things about you from Dolly."

"Please call me Lucy." She extended her hand. "It's a great pleasure to meet you, too. I ..uh .. I'm glad you're here when I am." She had started to claim that in all the years she had known Dolly, until recently she had not known that Dolly had a sister. However, she realized just in time that Melanie might not appreciate hearing that. "I'm sorry if I seemed to stare, but you have one of the most beautiful complexions I've ever seen."

"Oh, thank you," Melanie beamed. "I do try to wash it regularly. I don't believe in the popular fear of soap and water."

Dolly transferred her gaze away to the front window and rose up suddenly to leave the room. "I'd better check the roast in the oven." But Lucy caught the sudden drop of Melanie's eyes as she avoided looking up at Dolly, and wondered what history between these women she might have unknowingly brought up.

Robert came home for his mid-day meal, and they all sat around the kitchen table, eating and chatting. Lucy found Melanie a delightful young woman, but she had to readjust her thinking, because although Melanie was only eleven months younger than Dolly, she acted even younger. Her voice was often louder than society dictated for a refined woman when in conversation, and she gestured more than a lady should. In fact, she acted much as one would if they had been without the benefit of practice in social situations.

Most women of Melanie's age had either matured into social poise, or had at least learned to rein in any natural, youthful exuberance. But then Lucy remembered that Melanie had lost the influence of her mother, as well as Dolly, when only in her mid-teens. This brought to her mind having once read that regarding the proprieties of a Victorian lady, that 'wise mothers trained their daughters, sensible girls trained themselves, and the more fortunate husbands trained their brides'.

After Dolly informed Melanie about some of the more mundane happenings in town, such as theater events and new arrivals in the shops, Melanie abruptly awoke the elephant in the room. "So, Dolly, have you gotten another of those letters?"

Robert cut in with a mock frown. "Hey, don't you care if I've gotten one?"

The three women looked at him with surprise before Melanie asked, "Have you?"

"Yes, I have." He actually looked proud. "It was on the forge this morning."

"Well?" Dolly demanded.

"Well what? Oh, you mean what was in it? It accused me of...um... using the hay for more than the horses."

Melanie looked blank, as though waiting for more information. Lucy and Dolly, however, burst out laughing, having gotten the implication. Dolly turned to Melanie. "The writer was implying that Robert has had a 'roll in the hay' with some woman. You know, had relations there."

Melanie was aghast at the idea. "But he'd never do that!"

Robert smiled and sat back in his chair, obviously pleased that he was held in such high regard by his sister-in-law. It was, indeed, something he would never do. He couldn't imagine desiring any woman as totally as he did his wife.

"No, of course he wouldn't," Dolly responded. "And that's the context of most of the letters. They claim or accuse things that no one, knowing the recipient, would believe of them. But those who don't know them might believe it. And every once in awhile, the writer seems to come across with amazing accuracy about something the recipient is loath to have others know."

"Oh, I see." Melanie was suddenly quiet, her gaze wandering beyond the window next to the kitchen table, and after a moment it was as though she had forgotten where she was. She was so long at this that Robert almost looked out the window to see what was so interesting in their backyard. But it was obvious that she was simply deep in thought.

Everyone silently continued to eat, but after several minutes without conversation, Dolly began to feel her role as hostess. "I told Melanie about the luncheon with Mrs. Helms. She was very interested."

Melanie brought her attention back to the moment. "Oh, yes. I heard talk about Mrs. Helms when I was in San Francisco with my husband last fall. We were there at a grower's convention." She turned to Lucy to explain. "Vincent owned fruit orchards and vineyards, but they were mostly wiped out in the recent floods." Returning to the topic of Mrs. Helms, Melanie told them, "People said she was quite a forceful speaker, and I'm sorry that once again I missed meeting her. I know that several women of our acquaintance who did hear her, felt that their eyes had been opened to new ideas."

Lucy wondered if Melanie often jumped from one subject to another like this, or was she pre-occupied with something beyond what they were discussing. Melanie kept glancing at Dolly as though expecting her to say something, but Dolly refused to meet her sister's eyes.

Robert spoke up. "I'd like to hear this Mrs. Helms. All I ever get is other men's opinions."

"You mean," Dolly asked, showing her surprise, "they've heard her speak?"

"Well, no." Then, glancing at Lucy with a crooked smile, he added, "But that doesn't mean they don't have opinions based on what they've heard about her."

"From other men," Lucy pointed out, "who also haven't heard her speak. They're going on pretty thin information, aren't they?"

Robert shrugged. "Of course, they also get their wife's point of view and quotes of what Mrs. Helms has said. But you know how inaccurate repeating something you've heard can be."

Dolly felt the need to stand up for her fellow townswomen. "I'm sure women at least convey the basic ideas they hear directly from Mrs. Helms."

"Probably," he agreed. "But many men are against the broad concept of women having any more rights than they already have."

"Which isn't that many," Lucy mumbled.

Robert ignored her. "On the other hand, those who are okay with the concept, are hesitant to say so."

Lucy spoke up. "I saw on the billboard in the hotel lobby that Mrs. Helms is going to be speaking Wednesday evening at the theater. And men are invited."

"Okay then, let's all go." Robert was eager to finally see this woman that he'd heard so much about, both complimentary and condemnatory. There had been several conversations he had over-heard in the saloons and his livery that he would never recount to these women. He felt shame for his friends every time he remembered what some of them had said, so crudely disrespectful of women in general had they been.

Robert had once asked a couple of such men, while together in a saloon, if when they had been crossing the country with their wives if the women had not driven the wagon, cooked meals in the dirt, milked the cow, and washed their clothes on rocks? Of course, the men had to admit to this. Robert had then asked if their wives had done all of this while also caring for the children. The men who had not understood the point he was making had asked Robert why he was speaking in such a challenging manner. When he had explained that he was just showing his admiration for women's efforts under difficult conditions, he had been informed by one man that he expected no less from *his woman.*

No wonder, Robert concluded as he remembered that discussion, that some women had a bad attitude toward men, specially if their lives had not contained a generous sampling of men who had treated them with respect and kindness.

Dolly had explained to him that possibly men objected to women having more rights out of fear. He had wondered what there was to fear, and Dolly had referenced Mrs. Helms. "She says it's the fear of losing power, and therefore control over everything in their lives, including *their* women." Robert now began thinking about the definition of power, and how it was being wielded in the war, and possibly misused.

Dolly turned to her husband, seeing the deep frown creasing his forehead. Whatever he was thinking about, she thought it deserved to be interrupted, so she laid a hand on his arm. "Is it okay with you if I get a new dress for the occasion? Sarah and Agnes Murphy over by Cedar Ravine have a number of partially constructed dresses that only need a bit of fitting."

"Of course," Robert smiled. Then, feeling a need to compensate for the thoughtless men about whom he had just been thinking, he told her, "And get a new bonnet to go with it, if you wish."

Dolly beamed as she turned to Lucy. "We'll meet you in the Cary House lobby at ten o'clock tomorrow morning and we'll go shopping." She didn't even try to hide her enthusiasm, which was as much about spending the day with other women as it was about buying a new dress.

"If you don't mind," Melanie spoke up, "I'd rather not go shopping. Is it okay with you if I just stay home?"

"Of course," Dolly told her, unable to hide her surprise.

Lucy didn't say anything, but was certainly curious as to why a young woman would pass up the opportunity to visit the shops. Maybe she just couldn't afford to buy anything, although the dress she wore had certainly not been inexpensive. And the high-button shoes that covered her trim ankles were new and of fine leather.

The next morning, with her brother-in-law at work and her sister absent, Melanie soon found her chosen isolation tedious in the extreme. Her temporary lethargy of the previous day had passed off, but she still wasn't in the mood to spend the morning at a dressmaker's or visiting the shops.

Unlike Dolly, who was used to artfully applying powder and rouge so as to still look natural, Melanie followed the standard of the day and wore nothing more than a light dusting of rice powder over her nose. She was fortunate in that her lashes were dark, and her brows evenly spaced and well-formed.

Melanie had admitted once to Dolly that she knew she was pretty, no matter how much her iron-fisted and self-righteous husband had criticized the shape of her ears, nose and mouth. She was tired of strapping down her voluptuous curves beneath corsets while wearing drab clothing styled for mature matrons. It gave the impression to other women that she had no fashion sense, or more often the impression that Vincent was a controlling husband. She had found some satisfaction in the fact that he was recognized as such by the women in their narrow social circle.

But on this day, Melanie was free of her husband. She was even wearing her corset loosely tied, and was enjoying being able to take a deep breath. She laughed as she did just that. It was a simple celebration of freedom, a victory won because Vincent was unaware of her current location.

Melanie had left him a note to find upon his return from a short trip to San Diego. It said she was sorry, but that she had gone to stay with a friend in San Francisco who was ill, but that she would return in a few weeks. She framed her apology in the most profusely groveling manner she could produce on paper, in order to stave off any urge he might have to come after her. Still, she knew he would be very angry.

Just in case he might decide to follow her and drag her back home, or ask questions at the stage depot there in Los Angeles, she had indeed taken the stage to San Francisco. But after only one night there at a low-class hotel, she had taken a stage to Placerville under an assumed name, as well as dressed far differently from her normal habit.

Thinking about her cleverness, Melanie laughed as she admired herself in the dressing table mirror. After stuffing a folded handkerchief in a pocket of her jacket and a small purse full of coins in the other, she set out for town. These coins were partly what she had squirreled away over the years, but also part of what she had stolen from the secret compartment in Vincent's desk. They were hers now, and she cherished them as earnings hard-won.

This not being Melanie's first visit to Placerville, she thought she would visit her friend Sue Ellen. Only a few years older than herself, Sue Ellen had a small lady's beauty business. Melanie had met Sue Ellen several years before on a rare visit to see Dolly, and they had kept up a correspondence ever since. Although Sue Ellen visited most of her women clients in their homes, she had also set up a small salon on the ground floor of an office building with an entrance off the alley in back. It was the nicest portion of any alley in town, since she swept it every day and had a half-barrel planted with geraniums next to the door.

Inside, there were comfortable chairs facing each other over a small table in the middle of the room where Sue Ellen could work on clients lit by a large globed lamp, since the front window was kept covered by curtains. A walnut-framed mirror was hung on the wall over a small table next to the door, allowing clients to admire the results of their visit while leaving their money on the table.

On their way to the far corner of the room, ladies could view paintings and sketches on the walls showing the most exotic hairstyles throughout history. Once at the back, a folding screen hid a table with a large water pitcher and wash basin set behind the back of a stationary reclining chair. These had been available since 1850, and Sue Ellen had been fortunate to get one shipped to her from San Francisco.

Sue Ellen's customers were those women who wanted to look their fashionable best, but didn't want it known that they couldn't fashion their own hair, pluck their own brows, or who might need facial hair removed. Consequently, Sue Ellen honored their privacy and served only one woman at a time. Considering how long an appointment took to complete, this meant no more than one customer in the morning and another in the afternoon.

Because of this penchant for anonymity, no door stood open in welcome, and no signage denoted the shop's location. There was just a small, plain door next to the back stairs leading up to businesses above the shops facing Main Street. On one side of the door out in the alley was a large water barrel that was filled each morning by two young boys, next to a post and ring where a horse could be tied. There was nothing feminine about the area other than the small barrel of geraniums, but many shops on Main Street had flower boxes out front.

Customers trusted that Sue Ellen would never comment on how they looked with wet hair, or before she artfully plucked and waxed what they wanted removed. Best of all, these women loved the time spent visiting while enduring all that she offered, whether their hair was wrapped around long cloth strips to create cork-screw curls, or combed straight over a towel covering their backs. It was then that their nails were trimmed and buffed with just a hint of carmine. Oh, not enough that they might be thought tawdry, but just enough for them to appear as the natural beauties they never had been, but so much wanted others to think they were.

If they wanted more attention paid to their physical beauty, Sue Ellen supplied it. While the woman's hair dried after having been washed with Sue Ellen's secret solution of borax, soft water and oil of lavender, she rubbed their hands with pure glycerin. For those whose hands needed more than an occasional treatment, she recommended white cotton gloves worn at night over a layer of her personally formulated salve; both of which she sold in her salon.

Once into the beautification habit, women would also purchase her face wash made from rain water that she touted as preventing redness of the skin. Of course, she gave no indication that the three ingredients of powdered borax, pure glycerin and camphor water could be easily and cheaply obtained at the general store. What Sue Ellen charged for it could in no way be considered moderately priced, but it did satisfy women's desire to maintain a youth that was inexorably slipping away.

To be fair, she also counseled against the use of rouges from France that were expensive and often contained dangerous substances such as mercury, although called *vermilion*. Instead, she sold her customers, at a reasonable price, rose-powder that was a simple white powder that she mixed with carmine and ochre to match their skin tone.

To assist in the illusion of stylish perfection offered in the salon, there was a large selection of human hair pieces in various colors from which to choose. These would be adhered to the head so that the woman's natural hair could be used to give the impression of luxuriant, natural abundance. Attached by hidden clips and jeweled combs, these hair pieces found their way in and out of fashion for many years. They were also her most expensive investment, since the hair before she styled it sold for $5 to $10 an ounce. She added a modest profit, but sold them only occasionally. Considering that miners and laborers made less than $4 for a twelve-hour day, one hair piece could cost a good portion of a month's wages.

The most delicate specialty of her trade, both literally and figuratively, was the removal of facial hair. She used a resin tempered with wax, with a strong anodyne added to block the pain of removal. But she was expert at heating the concoction to just the right temperature so it was firm enough to adhere to the hair but not scorch the skin.

Sue Ellen's trim figure was always impeccably dressed in a simple black dress that was covered in a scrupulously clean, white apron. She also kept her dark hair slicked back into a knot at the base of her neck so as to never be in competition with a customer. Because she kept her appearance as plain as possible for her customers, when she stepped out with her husband

Gabe in the evenings, she arranged her hair and applied makeup so skillfully that she was completely transformed and seldom recognized.

She spoke to her customers in soothing, soft tones as one might if approaching a nervous animal, and she made sure to lavish them with whatever truthful compliments she could. After several hours of such pampering, her customers were so relaxed that they were barely aware of what they said as they unburdened themselves of their fears and frustrations.

On this day, Mrs. Sterling was wishing that she was not at the end of her appointment, as she was dreading going home to see how poorly the daily girl had cleaned the stove. She looked into the large mirror on the wall by the door and smiled with satisfaction, adjusting her bonnet carefully forward of the fresh curls cascading down the back of her head, only some of which was her own hair. Sue Ellen turned her back to seemingly fuss with something on the sideboard so that the lady could discretely leave a small stack of coins on the table under the mirror.

"Good-bye, Mrs. Sterling. I'll see you again in two weeks." As soon as the door closed, Sue Ellen swept the coins into a small metal box that she quickly returned beneath a loose floor board in the far corner of the room. She replaced the rug over the board, waiting to count the money until later before taking most of it to the bank.

Suddenly hearing her stomach growl, Sue Ellen was glad that she had made room in her schedule for a mid-day meal. She was just thinking about taking this break when the front door opened and she prepared to object to the unscheduled arrival. Her displeasure turned to delight when she realized it was not a customer.

"Melanie!" She hurried forward and clasped her friend's outstretched hands. "I didn't know you were coming to town."

"There wasn't enough time to write and tell you. Besides, I wasn't sure I could follow through with this trip."

"How long are you staying?"

"I'm not sure. Vincent and I have separated."

"Oh, my dear. I'm so sorry." Even with all her sophistication, Sue Ellen was still shocked at such news. She knew well how harshly society treated *a divorced woman*, a title usually spoken in a whisper.

"I'm not sorry at all." And indeed, Melanie looked more relaxed and at peace than Sue Ellen had ever seen her. "I've never felt freer or happier."

Sue Ellen laughed. "That's the spirit!"

"However, that information is not for the public yet."

"I understand. I was just leaving to get something to eat. Come with me and be my guest."

"That sounds wonderful."

They entered the National Restaurant on the south side of Main between Coloma and the Plaza. The waiter asked where they would prefer to sit, their choice being where they could be conspicuously seen by others or where they would be hidden from those entering or passing the front windows. Sue Ellen, in accord with her penchant for being unnoticed, quickly pointed to a table in a quiet back corner. Soon they were enjoying their ham steak, sliced tomatoes, and cornbread, while catching up with one another's lives.

Eventually, Sue Ellen could restrain her curiosity no longer. "Now tell me, how does Vincent feel about your separation? Is he trying to get you to come back to him?"

"I'm sure he's angry. You see, I left him a note saying I was going somewhere else, when in fact I came here. And I took the money he kept in the house for emergencies. Now I'll write to him and tell him that I won't be returning to him and want a divorce. But I'll have a stage driver mail it from San Francisco where Vincent thinks I am."

"Oh, Melanie, why would you do that? It will hurt your standing in society. You'll be a *divorced woman!*"

"I know." A spasm of uncertainty passed over her face, but then she squared her shoulders and looked Sue Ellen in the eyes. "Vincent angry is Vincent dangerous. This way he'll feel in control, and can play the martyr if needs be. And he won't be so quick to focus his wrath on finding me."

"How will you support yourself?"

"I can stay with Dolly while I figure that out." She looked across the room to the edge of the window visible from their table. Her eyes misted over as she explained what was in her heart. "I'd like to have a little shop where I can sell household decorations, crafts created by local artists and those in big cities like San Francisco, and maybe even plants suitable for indoor growing. Maybe sell books about art and travel, and the natural world. I'd have chairs placed so people could enjoy the books right there among the beauty of the shop." She looked at her friend and blushed. "I know it doesn't sound like anything already here, but that's the point." She looked down at her empty plate and murmured, "I just want loveliness in my life for a change, and to be appreciated."

Sue Ellen didn't want to dampen such enthusiasm, or squelch anyone's dream, but she felt that a drop of reality was needed. "That will take a considerable sum to set up."

"I have a plan for that." When Melanie didn't explain further, Sue Ellen tactfully said nothing, knowing that the best way to draw someone out was to appear disinterested. But she didn't miss Melanie's tiny smirk of satisfaction as she said, "Let's just say that I know something that a certain someone wouldn't want known."

Sue Ellen frowned. "You were careful to keep their gender out of your statement, I see. Well, just be careful. That can be a dangerous game."

Aghast at what Melanie thought Sue Ellen was suggesting, she put a hand to her throat. "I'm not planning to blackmail anyone! If it's easy for them to give what I ask, and I ask only once, there should be no problem. It'd be a loan."

Sue Ellen hesitated a moment before saying, "You never used to be so... calculating." She then placed a hand on Melanie's forearm. "Has your husband hurt you so badly?"

Melanie swallowed with an effort. "Humiliation leaves deeper scars than simple pain." Melanie added more cream to her coffee, unwilling to meet her friend's eyes or to impart more detail.

Sue Ellen sat back and shook her head. "I hear that much too often from women."

"Really?" Melanie looked at her in amazement.

"You don't think you're the only one, do you?" When Melanie only shrugged, Sue Ellen told her, "Well, you're not. Don't get me wrong. I also hear women talk about the fine things their men do for them and how proud they are of them. But it seems that most women need someone to complain to about the unpleasant or frustrating little things in their lives, and I'm the one to hear it. Most of their complaints are incredibly petty, but some of their confessions I'm embarrassed to hear."

"For instance?" Melanie leaned forward, eager to learn of someone else's shame to compare it to what she had to bear.

Sue lowered her voice. "Like affairs they've had, or pregnancies that weren't completed, or unfulfilled lustful desires, or how they fantasize about other men when with their husbands. One woman thought she was confessing something terrible when she said she wanted to have sex during daytime hours."

"With someone other than her husband, you mean?"

"No. With her own husband."

Melanie laughed, but not with much enthusiasm, having herself never done that. To cover her unease, she commented, "You do serve as a type of confessor."

"I suppose so." Sue Ellen took a sip of her coffee before saying, "Gabe thinks it's funny."

"You don't tell your husband what these women tell you, do you?"

"Oh, no! I'd never do that. Well, I tell him the stories sometimes, but not who told me."

It wasn't until later that day that Melanie remembered that Gabe worked across the road from the alley entrance leading to Sue Ellen's salon. If he watched, he could easily see which woman walked down the alley toward his wife's shop, there never being more than two in a day. But Melanie knew Gabe, and didn't think he could possibly be the letter writer, any more than Sue Ellen could.

They finished their luncheon and went their separate ways after promising to meet again soon. Melanie wandered through the news agent's shop, where clusters of customers had stopped to visit. Able to easily overhear parts of these conversations as she moved through the shop, she realized there were more ways for private information to be uncovered than she had ever thought about before. "Wouldn't it be nice," she smiled to herself, "if I could find out who's sending the letters before Lucy does?"

But she found it difficult to hold back what she had heard from Sue Ellen, or what she had overheard while purchasing the latest *Godey's Lady's Magazine* where she knew there would be drawings of the latest fashion, short stories, and poems. Although there would be articles of such current interest, women appreciated that it was the publisher's decision to not include anything about the war.

That afternoon, while helping Dolly and Lucy prepare supper, Melanie told them what she had discovered. At the end of her recital, she slewed her eyes over to Lucy and smiled. Dolly had seen that self-satisfied, mocking look before, and wondered if Melanie might not be determined to find the sender of the letters before Lucy could do it.

Why Melanie had set herself this challenge, Dolly couldn't imagine. Instead of tasking herself with finding out the answer, however, she pushed the question aside. She had always given in to whatever Melanie wanted, unwilling to do anything to cause dissention between them. They had had enough of that with their parents.

Lucy, on the other hand, had no problem figuring it out. For some reason, Melanie was jealous of the relationship between Dolly and herself. Lucy could understand this basic human emotion, knowing how closely the sisters must have been while growing up, so she felt a little sorry for Melanie. Therefore, she was more than ready to compliment her on her bit of detection. Melanie's response was to look at first pleased, and then sulkily resentful.

"Oh, dear," Lucy thought, "she must have interpreted my praise as condescension. And I didn't mean it that way at all." However, knowing that at this point anything more she might say on that subject would be taken wrong, Lucy kept silent.

Dolly wasn't unaware of what was taking place between the two women she loved so dearly, but once again she decided it was simply best to change the subject. She pondered out loud, "I wonder how many people who are told something in confidence actually keep it to themselves, telling absolutely no one else."

Melanie quickly looked away and Lucy fought the urge to laugh as she said, "Probably not many."

As for herself, Lucy knew how damaging a secret revealed could be. She had events in her own past that she didn't want known, and even a few events that if revealed could adversely affect her future. But there was only one event that could land her in prison. Her fingers started to the scar on her cheek, but she dropped her hand to her lap before the women could spot the movement. Other than Jim, only Dolly and Robert knew this particular secret, and they could never tell without endangering themselves.

After Lucy left, and while Melanie was out to the market for Dolly, Robert returned home. He looked out the back window of the house at Dolly as she poured hot water from an iron kettle into a large metal tub on a wooden stand. She lifted in the washboard and sloshed it with water before dumping in a number of her more delicate items that she refused to have laundered by anyone else.

Robert decided to take advantage of being alone with his wife as she worked at the gravel-lined laundry area he had prepared for her after they had purchased the house. There was a clothesline on one side of it and a work table on the other, with two tin tubs on stands in between. He walked to the back door and watched her for a moment before turning away, having changed his mind. But she had seen him out of the corner of her eye. At first Dolly thought she would let him reveal whatever it was he wanted to say in his own time, but after several repetitions of this uncertain movement, she turned and faced the door. "Robert, do you want to tell me something?"

He walked slowly to her, for several minutes watching her rinse the delicate items. "Is it true that the Helms woman is going to organize marches down Main Street like the women in the East have done? With signs declaring their goals and criticism of men?"

"She said something about it at the meeting. She might even talk about it again when we attend tomorrow night's meeting." She then added cautiously. "Why?"

He hesitated only a moment before asking, "You're not going to do that...are you?"

She wiped her hands on a towel and moved to the wicker loveseat in the shade of a large nearby tree. "I'm glad you changed that to a question." She smiled to show that she was at least partially joking, but she received no smile in return. "I hadn't thought about doing any such thing," she reassured him. "It isn't something that appeals to me."

Robert sat next to her with his arm around her shoulders. "The rumor of it sure hasn't gone over well with most of the men."

"Am I supposed to be surprised at that?" She couldn't keep the sarcasm out of her voice.

"Do you think it's something Lucy would do?" He knew if Lucy decided it was a good idea, Dolly would certainly be right alongside her.

"I don't know." Dolly thought a moment, then shook her head. "I just don't know."

"I don't think it's something Jim would approve of," he volunteered, knowing he sounded like a petulant child and hating himself for it.

Dolly looked at her husband for a long moment before responding. "Whatever he might feel about it, I don't think he'd tell her. He'd leave it completely up to her, and support whatever decision she made. Unless she asked for his advice, of course."

Dolly found great satisfaction in the fact that his color deepened. He murmured something about getting back to work and left for town, while Dolly returned to her laundry. As she hung on the clothesline her fine cotton drawers, chamises, and lace cuffs, she tried to think how the suffrage issues might affect men raised with traditional attitudes.

How did the "proposed freedoms" threaten them, both from the point of view of their everyday life, as well as their accepted assumption that it was their right to be the only decision-maker in a household? Maybe, she thought, it was the use of the word *freedoms* that rankled. After all, to suggest that women needed freeing put them in the *slave* category. Of course, she wasn't so naïve as to think it was the same type of slavery that was being fought over in the war, but that didn't mean that at some level men were not troubled by what that phrase indicated about their relationship with their wives and daughters. Dolly sighed and changed her focus to what she should plant in her neglected vegetable garden. It was pleasant contemplation, and the other was not.

Robert soon discovered that he was not the only man concerned about the planned march. As he worked in his livery stitching together pieces of leather to make a new apron to wear when working at the forge, several men gathered to stand around the large opening to the cool, shadowed interior. Tereise Guidici, owner of a boarding house on Reservoir Street not far from the Robbins home, had come there to feed his horse some apples going bad. A tall, thin man with a short brown beard matching the hair sticking out around his old straw hat, he was friendly and outgoing, with a deep voice tinged with an Italian accent.

Ollie Sprague, the stage agent who boarded at the Orleans Hotel, had just returned his horse after spending the night at a friend's house just south of the town of Coloma. Except for his almost pure white hair and lack of any beard, he was a close match to Tereise in height and build. These two men could have left the livery as soon as they finished with their errands, but that would have meant going home or to work. It was more enjoyable to hang around this popular stronghold of male sovereignty. At least here, they knew women would not be congregating. And that suited the mood they were in just fine.

Ben Turk, a man with a thick, well-groomed beard of which he was inordinately proud, leaned against one of the open double doors. He spent a part of each day lounging there, talking to any man who couldn't avoid him, although those same men sometimes sought him out when they were in a mood to argue their opinions on various subjects. Robert thought of Ben as he did a spider on the edge of its web waiting for movement so he could pounce on its source.

Ben was married to a woman also not afraid to voice her views, and Robert often wondered whose idea it was that Ben spend so much time away from home when he wasn't working at his job as a day laborer. On this fine June morning, Ben had until then found no one interested in *chewing the fat* with him, his favorite expression. But now that Ollie and Tereise were there, Ben was a happy man, as there was something definite on his mind.

"Are your wives planning to march with the Helms woman?" he asked the others.

Ollie looked at him with a total lack of comprehension. "What the hell are you talking about?"

Tereise cut off Ben's answer. "Good God, man, haven't you heard about that? The suffrage woman who's in town wants all the women to march down Main Street with a sign demanding the right to vote. Not only that, she wants freedom for the darkies everywhere in the country, even in the South."

Ollie looked at him as though he had been speaking in his native, foreign language. Then he burst out with, "I'll be damned! The wife didn't say anything about such a march. Probably because she knows I wouldn't let her do it."

"That's what I told my wife," Ben said. "Do you know what she had the nerve to quote at me? Some poet Mrs. Helms told her about, name of John Milton. He evidently said, 'He for God only, she for God in him'." He removed his hat and scratched with ferocious determination at his scalp. Slamming the hat back on his head, he asked, "What the hell is that supposed to mean?"

Tereise said, "I think it means that this Milton fella was claiming men should look up to God as their superior, but that a woman should look no further than her husband for the one she should obey." He smiled broadly. "Gotta like that *obey* part."

Robert couldn't hold back. "He meant to imply that a husband is superior to his wife in all things, and she should gratefully accept that."

The other men looked at him for a long moment before Ollie turned back to Ben and asked, "Was your wife criticizing this Milton's statement or agreeing with it?"

"I'm not sure, if you want to know the truth." Ben shook his head. "After she told me this guy lived almost 200 years ago and that attitudes should have changed by now, I thought it best not to go into it with her. I just changed the subject. Frankly, I'm not comfortable claiming that a woman shouldn't pray to God when she wants to."

Ollie searched his pockets for his plug tobacco, bit off a piece and chewed thoughtfully. "I think it's a damn fine statement."

A fourth man walked up from the stall where he had been grooming his horse. He was greeted by them all before Ben said, "Morning, Brad. Did you hear what we were talking about?"

"Yes, I did." *Brad* Bradshaw was younger than the other men by several years, and had been educated in the East. He owned a book and stationery store on Main Street, and was considered the local intellectual. "I don't care if my wife wants to do something like march or talk to Mrs. Helms."

The other men responded together, part words and part sputters of protest. Robert's interest sharpened. Ben finally got out, "Why not?"

"I'm a realist," Brad told them. "She gets to feel whatever it is she needs to feel from having marched alongside other women. But when she's back home, she'll still make my dinner, wash my clothes and take care of the house and kids."

"For now," Ollie grunted.

Brad shrugged, but Ben frowned, ready to take exception to the suggestion. Then he realized he wasn't sure what Ollie meant. "What do you mean?"

"I've heard about women back East who left their families and went off to spend all their time marching and protesting against men."

"No!" This was news to Ben, and he looked over at Tereise, who was also showing his shock at such a thing. But Brad simply nodded his head like the wise sage he wanted everyone to think he was.

Robert tried to pour a little calming oil on the men's troubled waters. "They're not protesting against men. They're protesting against the *control* men have over them."

Ollie, wanting to hold center stage as long as possible, glared at Robert. "Oh, yeah? Well, these marching women will just get our women all het up and dissatisfied with their lot in life."

Robert forced a smile through his clenched jaw. "Maybe we should make sure their lot in life is a good one. Then they won't have anything to protest against."

Tereise ignored this, unwilling to even consider that something might need improvement in his wife's life. "All I can say is that we need to get rid of this suffrage woman!"

All eyes turned to him, mostly surprised but also alarmed as they realized the anger underlying their normally placid friend's words.

"How do you propose we do that?" Ollie asked, a little afraid of the answer and already forming some reason he needed to be elsewhere.

Tereise shook his head. "I don't know right off, but we should think about some way of doing it."

Robert frowned when the four men accepted Ben's suggestion that they talk it over at the Oasis Saloon. He was uncomfortable with the direction of the men's conversation, but he told himself that they were good men and just needed to blow off steam.

Unfortunately, this kind of talk was not isolated to livery stables and saloons. Even in the nicest houses in town and the most prosperous businesses, one could hear the same confused resentment and declarations of resistance. Accepting that there wasn't anything he could do about changing other people's attitudes, Robert set about feeding the horses and mules their evening hay. He could then go home to his own wife, who he was pretty sure didn't feel the need to protest for a better life. "Yeah," he thought, "*pretty* sure."

CHAPTER 5

"Thou shalt not kill; but needst not strive
officiously to keep alive." A. H. Clough

Wednesday, June 4 & Thursday, June 5

Late the next morning, Lucy rushed to the door of her room in answer to rapid and persistent knocking. It was Dolly, and she was white and trembling. Lucy led her to the edge of the bed and pushed her down onto it. "What's the matter?"

"She's dead."

"Who?"

"Mrs. Helms. Dead in her room at the Orleans Hotel. Blood dripping from her temple. Eyes staring and glassy." She gave an involuntary shudder and gripped her stomach with a shaking hand while breathing heavily.

Lucy sat next to her and put an arm around her shoulders. "How do you know all this?"

Dolly looked into Lucy's eyes as she swallowed with difficulty. "I found her. I went there to ask her to have breakfast with us, knowing the rest of her day would probably be full. When I knocked on the door, it swung open."

"Oh, my dear! You must have narrowly missed the killer."

Dolly leaned away from her, clearly horrified. "Why do you say that? He might have been gone for hours."

"No," Lucy said gently. "You said the blood was dripping down her face. That means it had just happened. Blood coagulates pretty quickly."

"Oh," Dolly whispered.

Before Dolly could think too much about what she had seen, or how close she had come to also being a victim of the killer, Lucy made her drink the last of the coffee in her morning's pot. "This should help you rebound from what I'm sure has been a terrible shock."

Dolly nodded and obediently swallowed the coffee. Her hands wrapped around the cup's warmth, she said, "I don't understand why someone would want to kill her."

"Don't you?"

"Oh, Lucy, none of the men here would kill a woman just because they didn't like her politics."

"My sweet friend, of course a man might. Not most men, of course, but it could be someone whose anger and hatred of women has been festering for years. He may have learned how to hide his strong emotions so that those who know him would be totally unaware of what he's really feeling."

"I suppose you're right. Men talk about what they think, but almost never about what they feel."

"Mrs. Helms's aggressive behavior may have in some way triggered some man's suppressed rage. Some of her statements about men might certainly do that."

"Goodness, Lucy, you have such a vivid imagination!" Lucy shrugged and said nothing, letting Dolly think about it. After a moment Dolly gasped and turned to Lucy with her eyes wide. "That could be any man we know." Dolly was so startled at this realization that it removed the ugly visions of Mrs. Helms's dead body from her mind.

Lucy nodded, already having tried to visualize the character of a person so unhappy that they felt it necessary to write anonymous, fear-producing letters. Would someone like that also be capable of murder? "You were going to ask Mrs. Helms to join us for an early breakfast? What time were you there?"

"It was close to six-thirty."

"That's pretty early to call on someone."

"I know, but she had mentioned that she was a very early riser, usually before dawn. The desk clerk said Mrs. Helms hadn't left the hotel, so when she didn't answer my light tap, I knocked harder. That's when the door swung open and I called her name. Then I saw her on the floor by the bed."

"Do me a favor. Before anything else fills your mind, describe the room to me."

Dolly looked at Lucy with eyes large and startled. "Why?"

"You brought me here to discover who's back of the letters. This might be connected to that."

"Oh, okay." She closed her eyes and recalled the scene. "She was partially dressed. She didn't have on a jacket over her waist, and nothing on her head. The base of the lamp was on the floor next to her, with her head toward the bottom of the bed. Kerosene had spilled on the rug and splashed onto the bedspread. I could smell it, although only faintly. The room was a mess."

"Like someone had ransacked it on purpose in anger? Or like they had been looking for something?"

"Neither." Dolly frowned. "I'm not sure, but I felt that something wasn't right with the room. The bed hadn't been made up yet, for one thing. A few newspapers were folded in half and stacked on the dresser, with a pair of long scissors on top of them. Next to them was a pot of paste with the wooden lid next to that."

"Were there scraps of newspaper in the trash?"

Dolly's eyes flew open. "Goodness, Lucy, I don't know. I'm surprised I remember that much. What with Mrs. Helms lying on the floor with blood on one side of her head." She looked out the window and mumbled almost to herself, "I still can't believe it was her."

Lucy started to ask who else it would be, considering that it was Mrs. Helms's room, but there was a knock at the door and a jangling of keys. She got up to pull it open and found that it was the chambermaid, Mary Mahon. Lucy had talked with her several times and she appeared to have adjusted to her work at the hotel. Nevertheless, one of the chambermaids had commented that Mary still resented having been dismissed from the Hume household.

"I'm sorry, madam," Mary said. "I thought you'd gone out."

"It's alright, Mary. We're just leaving." Lucy turned to Dolly. "Come with me. We'll get something to eat in the dining room."

They were soon seated with coffee, the only thing Dolly wanted. Lucy decided she too would forego food and picked up their earlier conversation. "Someone struck her with the heavy lamp?"

Dolly thought a moment. "I would assume so, since it was on the floor next to her. The lamp's chimney had fallen off and had rolled partially under the bed, but the base was thick glass and looked very heavy. And the burner and its wick had come loose and was also lying next to her."

"Which was why the kerosene had splashed out. At least that means that whoever hit her, didn't necessarily go there to kill her. If they had, I would assume they'd have brought a weapon with them. What did you do next?"

"I backed out of the room and screamed." She looked at Lucy, suddenly embarrassed. "I don't know why. Then I rushed down the stairs to the front desk, calling out for someone to help. The clerk came back up with me and he assured himself that she was dead. He told me to come down to the office and wait there with him while he sent someone for the police."

"Who showed up?"

"Deputy Sheriff Chapman and City Police Officer John Reynolds. John and Robert are friends. He lives on Pacific Street not far from us. You met him the last time you were here. His presence made a difference to Deputy Chapman, I think, because he treated me very kindly. The clerk swore that I hadn't been gone long enough to have killed someone, and certainly not long enough to have had an argument that might have led to such a thing."

"Thank goodness for that." Lucy relaxed a little, even though she began tapping her fingers on the table. She wanted more than anything to see Mrs. Helms's room before it was cleaned by the hotel.

When she said this to Dolly, her response was what Lucy expected. "Oh, Lucy, what a thing for you to say!"

"Why? Because a lady should have sensibilities too delicate to see a room where a murder has taken place?"

"No. Because a lady shouldn't *want* to see such a scene."

"We both know that's absurd. Women care for the sick and dying, lay out the dead for funerals, assist in births, and have walked most of the 2,000 miles across the country next to their wagon. But we're too delicate..."

Dolly took Lucy's hand, stopping her mid-sentence. "If Mrs. Helms could hear you now, she'd want no one else to find her killer. Do what you must, and damn the opinion of others."

"Have you told all of this to Robert?"

"No. I came here directly after leaving the police. I left the house this morning before Melanie was up, and right after Robert had left early for work."

Before doing anything toward an investigation, Lucy went with Dolly to her house, waiting with her in the parlor until Robert arrived home for lunch. She had intended to leave Dolly in Melanie's care, but she was in bed nursing a sick headache, and Dolly didn't want to disturb her. When

Robert did arrive home, before they could tell him what had happened, he burst through the door talking rapidly and loudly.

"Did you hear about someone breaking into Tony Leon's house last night? The funny thing is that Mrs. Leon says she can't find anything missing. Tony says there might have been a stack of coins on his desk, but he can't remember for sure. So maybe it was just a petty thief who looked through the French doors behind his desk and saw an easy grab for money." Robert then became more aware of his wife and realized how pale she was, reclining on the sofa sipping a cup of tea. "Dolly? Honey? Are you okay?"

In answer, Dolly started crying, put the cup on the table and held out her arms to him. Robert rushed to her side and held her while she wept onto his shoulder. Flummoxed by this display, he looked up at Lucy for explanation.

When she finished describing what Dolly had told her, Robert commented upon the obvious. "This happening on the same night as a break-in, not to mention a knife fight in one of the saloons, these reports are going to make people fear the town is becoming unsafe. Other than a brawl in a saloon now and then, we have very little violent crime here nowadays. The courts see far more mining and property disputes. But then again, there's so many strangers passing through now."

Leaving Robert to care for his wife, Lucy returned to the Cary House, where she responded to a growl from her stomach and walked into the dining room. Just as she took her seat, Officer John Reynolds walked in and Lucy quickly invited him to join her. More frequently referred to as "J. J.", he was a tall, broad-shouldered young man in his twenties. He had a strong, clean-shaven jaw and dark, intelligent eyes that missed little of what was going on around him. Although ladies thought him kind and helpful, men saw the toughness underlying that. He wore a dark suit and string tie over a clean white shirt, his badge pinned to a vest beneath the coat so it could be hidden or easily flashed to those who didn't know him.

"It's nice to see you back in Placerville, Mrs. Murphy. Can I assist you in some way?"

"Officer Reynolds, I must admit that I'm interested in what has happened to Mrs. Helms."

"Oh?" He looked at her with an intensity that was characteristic of him. He saw before him an attractive woman a little taller than most, with a pale scar on her cheek that made him even more curious about her than he might otherwise have been. He also saw a woman that exuded a quiet confidence borne of a tested self-reliance, and worn as comfortably as she did her wedding band. Remembering that his friend Robert Robbins had called her "one formidable and clever lady", he decided it might be to his benefit to pay attention to what she had to say. "Why are you interested, Mrs. Murphy?"

"Dolly is a very dear friend, and I want to make sure no one suspects her of Mrs. Helms's death."

"Oh, no one suspects her," he reassured, relaxing now that he knew where she stood.

"Not now. But if the guilty person isn't found, they might."

"I suppose so," he admitted. "But with the stack of newspapers in the room along with paste and scissors, it looks to my superiors that Mrs. Helms was the letter writer that's caused so much tension around town."

"That doesn't make sense." Lucy frowned. "How would she know so much about the people here?"

"She'd have to know someone living here that could pass on the information to her. Or maybe several people."

"She'd have to pay for such information, and I got the impression that money was a problem for her. Besides, why would a determined woman fronting for such an important cause want to do such a thing? If she was discovered, it would divert focus from everything she had been proclaiming to be important to all women. What would she gain from sending such hurtful letters that would compensate for that?"

His shrug expressed his lack of certainty. "Maybe the person giving her information on people was also giving her money. Maybe she was a bit crazy. Plenty of people thought so."

Lucy leaned forward. "Can you get me into her room?"

The suddenness of the question not only took him by surprise, but he couldn't hide the fact that he was a little appalled at the suggestion. "Why would a lady like you want to see where such a crime happened?"

"I assure you that I've seen my share of horrific things. It's just that the way Dolly described it sounded odd. I want to see it for myself."

"I'm not sure the blood has been cleaned up."

"That really won't bother me." Lucy's smile reminded him of his favorite childhood schoolteacher, Miss Warner, when she had found a bullfrog in her desk drawer. She had simply smiled, lifted it out and then lectured the class on its habits before setting it free. Officer Reynolds looked at Lucy a bit dubiously, but he slowly nodded his head.

Lucy walked down the street to the Orleans Hotel, having received permission from Officer Reynolds to use his name as a reference. The clerk working on this sunny morning was an older man who Lucy had never seen before. He introduced himself as Mr. Bradley, his mutton-chop side whiskers framing his face like fuzzy parentheses. That, and the interjectory manner in which he spoke, gave the impression that everything he said was an after-thought.

"I'm not sure, for several reasons, that I should let you into the room, considering everything," he told Lucy. "After all, and I'm sure you'll agree with me, you're not a member of the police, or at least you have no official capacity. You might be affronted by the condition of the room. It hasn't been, uh, cleaned up yet."

"You're correct, Mr. Bradley, that I have no official capacity. But I'm looking into the matter on behalf of close friends of Mrs. Helms. She made many friends during her short time here. If you would like, you can check with Mrs. Hume or Officer J. J. Reynolds."

"Why?"

"What I mean is that you can check with them regarding my being someone who has a right to look into the situation."

"Oh, yes, of course. Mrs. Hume, you say." That was evidently the magic name, even above that of a police officer. He turned to the wall behind him and took down a key next to an empty pigeon-hole used for guest messages and mail. "I'm glad to be of any help I can, my dear madam," he told her, suddenly ingratiating and obliging, "considering, of course, that everyone in the hotel is so disturbed by what has happened."

Lucy took the key with a sweet smile and a mumbled, "Thank you." But after a few steps she stopped and turned back. "Why hasn't the room been cleaned by now?"

He pulled a wry face. "The maids refuse to clean it, because of the blood on the floor, which by now has dried, and I must say I can't blame them." Having shown his human side, he added, "I should probably do it myself, since I'm the Assistant Manager."

"I'm sure they would appreciate that." But experience told her that he would leave it for some young chambermaid who was easily intimidated and would be unable to refuse him.

The room had a sour, musty smell that immediately told Lucy she would spend as little time there as possible. The short wall to the left of the door had an unlit wall sconce, beneath which was a small table covered in a lace doily highlighting a small crystal dish. A wicker trash receptacle sat empty beneath the table. The wall perpendicular to that backed a long, dark dresser. She looked at the commonly used white pitcher that was half-full of water next to a matching bowl that gave soapy evidence of Mrs. Helms having used it for her morning ablutions. A small towel was neatly folded next to it.

Surprisingly, the newspapers, scissors and paste pot that Dolly had mentioned were still there. The police evidently did not think them important, or had decided to leave them in place for some reason.

The room's back wall was the outside of the hotel, and in front of the window was an over-stuffed chair in the left corner next to a small table with a two-globe lamp on it. Next to that was a pine wardrobe closet that matched those in the other rooms. From the righthand wall, the bed protruded into the room next to an enclosed nightstand nearest the door. An oval, tightly woven, rag rug in shades of blue covered the open space between the door and the bed.

There had been a clear glass kerosene lamp on the night stand, but that was gone now since it had been the murder weapon. If it was the same as in the other rooms, the base of it had been made of thick, heavy glass with a single, loosely anchored chimney. Lucy visualized the thick stem connecting the foot of the lamp to the kerosene well, making a convenient hand grip. The wick assembly must have been put on loose after refilling or the kerosene wouldn't have splashed out when she was struck. Lucy could still vaguely smell it.

The pool of blood near the foot of the bed was partially on the floorboards as well as the edge of the large rug. From this, Lucy pictured Mrs. Helms falling onto her right side away from her assailant, after having been hit on the left side of her head. The killer must have been standing next to the night stand where the lamp had been. That begged the question of why Mrs. Helms would have stood so close to someone if she had feared them at all. Had she said something that had enraged her visitor, and before she could move out of their way?

Lucy walked to the dresser and looked through the few newspapers there: *Mountain Democrat*, *Placerville Daily News*, and the *Placerville Republican*. Next to them was a small crock of flour paste somewhat hardened, the wooden lid lying next to it. A pair of long-shafted steel scissors lay on top of the newspapers like a paper weight. Lucy picked them up to admire the ornate handles or "bows", then carried them with her as she wandered around the room. After fumbling with the heavy instrument in her gloved hands, she gripped them by the long blades and pondered the possibility of Mrs. Helms being the author of the anonymous letters.

She still thought it doubtful that Mrs. Helms would want to upset so many people in the town by sending such letters to them. Admittedly, most of the letters had been petty or so outrageous that they were of little consequence. But they had still been upsetting, and had shown some degree of familiarity with the recipients. Had it been some kind of ploy so Mrs. Helms could swoop in and take advantage of women while they were feeling uncertain and vulnerable? Did she have some perverse idea that this would help her convince women that she was their champion? Ah, but men had also received letters. Of course, that could have been just a smoke screen so no one would think the greater quantity of women recipients were the real target. Lucy's head began to ache. It all seemed to defy reason.

She turned back to the bed. The blanket and the dark blue spread had been hastily drawn up to the pillows, but still showed clearly that only one person had slept there, and that the occupant had stirred little while sleeping on the near edge. Mrs. Helms's night clothes were hung neatly in the wardrobe, and Lucy remembered that both Officer Reynolds and Dolly had said Mrs. Helms had been dressed for going out.

There was no breakfast tray in her room, further evidence that it had been very early when Mrs. Helms had received her killer. Lucy was puzzled about that, since Mrs. Helms would not have received just anyone so early. It had been pushing propriety for Dolly to have called at the time she did, but at least the sun was up. Maybe Mrs. Helms had initially planned to meet someone at a restaurant for breakfast, but was kept from leaving by the unexpected arrival of her visitor. After all, if they had been expected, wouldn't she have hidden the newspapers and paste?

The fact that the glass lamp had been used as the weapon seemed to show that the person who had come to her room had not come there with the intention of killing her. But if not, Lucy queried as she looked down at the scissors in her hands, why didn't they stab her with these? The long blades were strong and sharp, and very pointed. It was that last detail that probably made them so useful when cutting out small parts of a newspaper's printing.

At this point Lucy remembered her discussion with Dolly about the blood still being wet. There was something about that fact that tickled at the back of her mind, but she couldn't place it. And there was something about the room itself that bothered her. But try as she might, she couldn't figure out if it was the product of her imagination or something actual.

Having gotten all that she could from the room, Lucy locked the door behind her. She ignored the fact that the door to the room across the hall was open a crack, with a watery eyeball trained on her. When she returned the key to Mr. Bradley, he was obviously restraining himself from asking questions.

As she stood on the wooden walkway trying to decide what she should do next, Lucy watched the traffic slowly passing down the street. The rigs and riders on the road, the large wagons heading east carrying mining equipment and cases of poultry, all caused dust to rise up. She could barely see across the road after a small herd of cattle was chased down the street by herders on horseback. What the cattle left behind was ground into the dirt by the wagons that followed.

Nearby, a man on foot with only a pack on his back negotiated a ride on a wagon in exchange for helping with the team of ten horses. Watching this, Lucy smiled with fond remembrance of when she had done much the same thing seven years earlier. It seemed much longer since those desperate days. Although thinking about them was not pleasant, some of what had happened had made such a deep impression on her that it was not always easy to push away the memories.

A young boy of about ten ran up and stood in front of Lucy, grabbing her attention as she sensed his urgency. He was wearing worn but clean overalls over a red shirt, and the length of his brown hair was neatly combed off his face. This was no street urchin, she decided, but someone's well-maintained child.

"May I help you, young man?"

"You the lady asking questions about letters?" Large brown eyes studied her with hopeful expectation.

"Yes."

"You interested in the killin' of that suffering woman, too?"

"Suffrage. And yes, I am. Why?"

"My older brother, he's a friend of J. J.'s. He says I should tell you somethin'." He looked at her as though waiting permission to proceed.

Swallowing her eagerness for the information, she calculated that the details of what was coming might be more easily obtained if she dealt with the boy in a relaxed setting. She had discovered that this method often worked well with her son, Roger. "Why don't we sit down on the bench outside the bakery? At the same time, I'd appreciate your sharing a pastry with me."

His well-scrubbed face brightened at that. "Oh, yes, ma'am. I think that would be a very good idea."

After Lucy watched the youngster devour a large fried donut, she decided it was time to come to the point. "Now, what's your name?"

"Billy Dooris. My mom sells fruit on the south side of Main in Upper Placerville."

"What is it that your brother thinks I would like to hear?"

"Yesterday afternoon a man asked me to deliver a note to the lady what got killed."

"Did you?"

"Clerk wouldn't let me bring the envelope to her room. He said she was out, so I gave it to him. He put it in one of the little square holes in the wall behind the counter, the one numbered 201. I figure that must've been her room number."

"Did you know the man who gave you the envelope, Billy?"

"No. Well, I've seen him around sometimes. I think he's a miner outside of town 'cause he's only here some of the time. Mostly on Sundays to do his shopping and such like. You know, like the prospectors always do. Anyway, he said some woman wearing a head scarf gave him two bits if he'd give the note to some kid he trusted. My instructions were to deliver it to the Orleans Hotel. Then he gave me the nickel that she'd given him for the kid. The words *Helms* and *Orleans Hotel* was printed in ink on the envelope. And before you ask, it was sealed and I didn't open it."

"I would never have asked you that. I can see you're a man of integrity." Billy grinned and she asked, "Do you know if the man who gave you the note is still in town?"

Billy shook his head, then licked his sticky fingers before wiping his hands on his pant legs. "I'd better get home. Supper will be ready soon." With that, he dashed down the street toward Upper Placerville, that small community where the town extended east just past Cedar Ravine. The Ravine had been one of the first areas of prospected wealth, and there were still active mines further along its twisting length.

Lucy was left deep in thought, but extremely satisfied. "So this morning's visit had been an appointment made through a note delivered yesterday," she mused. "But not directly delivered by the visitor, who was obviously someone trying to hide their connection to Mrs. Helms. Was the woman who approached the man with a note also someone employed to move the note along?"

One of Lucy's previous assumptions now changed. Mrs. Helms and her visitor had probably not been planning on going out together. The visitor simply wanted to talk to Mrs. Helms alone at a time of day when it was less likely they would be seen, indicating that the visitor didn't want to be associated with Mrs. Helms. Lucy suddenly realized one thing that had been bothering her about the description of Mrs. Helms's body. If she had been intending to immediately go into town with someone, she would have been wearing a jacket and bonnet. A self-respecting woman of her age and status might substitute a shawl for a jacket, but they would never go out in public without some kind of head covering.

She once again wondered why Mrs. Helms had not hidden the letter-making items. Did the visitor already know she was the one sending them? Thinking about the visitor's arrival that morning, Lucy reasoned that they must have waited until the clerk was away from the front desk and then darted up the stairs. There must also have been an exit strategy, but any thought about that could only be pure conjecture. Although, the killer had indeed gotten away unseen.

Lucy took her time returning to the Cary House. As she passed the Bye & Stewart Store, she was reminded of the tree that had once stood there, now merely a stump in the store's basement. It was from that tree that several men had been hanged in 1854, back when the large oak tree had shaded the back of the Jackass Inn, long gone from the town. The other town hanging, having taken place before that in 1850 of *Irish Dick*, had been from a tree that had at that time stood where the Cary House was now located.

The death penalty more recently carried out, of two Indians for the murder of an Irishman named Guy, had been lawful. Of course, there were those still there in town who would argue that the earlier hangings had also been *lawful*. It just depended on your definition of the word. Consequently, there were those who still embraced the name *Hangtown*, and those champions of progress who resolutely avoided that name.

Lucy went back to her room at the Cary House and spent the rest of the afternoon making notes. She paid a runner to take a message to Dolly saying she was staying in, not caring to explain more than that. Feeling a little despondent, Lucy realized that she was missing Jim. She was used to talking things over with him, and longed for his wise counsel. Concluding that she was mainly just tired, she had a light meal delivered to her room and retired to her bed earlier than usual.

Lucy was fortunate in the location of her room in the three-story brick hotel. On the second floor and well back from the street, the noise of the freight wagons, which traveled through town at night as well as during the day, was somewhat muted. Unless, of course, the blustering drivers got angry about something and started shouting. Or if a full-throated drunk lurching home in the middle of the night began singing. Consequently, when she awoke with a start during the night, she sat up in the bed and listened for whatever sound must have awakened her so abruptly. She had not closed her drapes and the light of a full moon night glowed into the room. After a moment, she heard the raised voices of two men from down the hall and realized the sound that had awakened her had been these men arriving home.

Feeling thirsty, she climbed out of bed and poured a glass of water from the pitcher on the dresser. Still half asleep, she placed the empty glass back on the dresser. Or at least that was her plan. In the darkness, she missed the edge of the dresser and the glass fell onto the rug. Bending over to pick it up, she groped around for it and finally felt her fingertips come in contact with it. As she straightened up, a slight twinge caught in her lower back. Laughing to herself, she thought, "Whoa, I'm much too young to have lumbago."

It was simply a momentary twinge that passed off quickly after stretching, and she got back in bed. However, a moment later she sat up again, now wide awake and her heart pounding. Mrs. Helms had claimed to have back pain if she wasn't careful. There was no way she could have worked bent over the low dresser or bed in her room while making those anonymous messages.

Picturing the layout of the room, Lucy realized the large easy chair on the other side of the bed probably would have been too heavy to move closer to the bed. Even if Mrs. Helms could have moved it, she would still have had to lean forward while working on the letters spread out on the bed. No one with back problems would do that.

In that case, where had Mrs. Helms constructed the anonymous letters? Or had she made them at all? But if not, what was the paraphernalia needed to make the letters doing in her room? Lucy had from the beginning found the idea of Mrs. Helms as the letter writer incongruous with the woman's stated goals. Was it only this juxtaposition of ideas that had bothered her about the room?

As soon as it was daylight and the dining room was open for breakfast, Lucy hurried downstairs to eat and organize her thoughts. Officer Reynolds had gotten there just ahead of her, and had already finished off most of a small silver rack of toast.

He stood up to pull out a chair for her. "I was about to send a maid up to see if you were up and dressed yet."

"Oh? Why?"

"Sheriff Hunter thinks there was a letter writer who stopped sending out the letters after Mrs. Butterick killed herself. But he also thinks Mrs. Helms took over and started them up again."

"Why would she do that?"

Picking up a piece of toast, J.J. spread it with jam heaped in a crystal dish. "He thinks she thought it a good cover for the few letters she was sending out to blackmail people. And that one of *those* few killed her.

I'm not sure I agree with that. The thing is, if he's wrong but still wedded to that idea, I'm not sure how much effort will be put toward finding the killer. Maybe when Jim Hume, John's brother, takes over, he'll think differently."

"As Street Commissioner I hear James Hume plans to have the Main Street gutters cleaned out, as well as the road graveled. I must say, I'm impressed with his ambition."

"Yeah, he's a good guy. Back in the early, somewhat lawless years, he was a lawyer here and also served as a constable, one of the few law officers trying to keep order. He was later our first mayor, so he's learned a lot over the years about crime and human nature, and I trust his instincts." Having finished that piece of toast, he reached for another. "He's right that there was a space of time between Mrs. Butterick's death and when the letters started up again, which was around the time Mrs. Helms came to town." He frowned as he picked up his toast and took a large, almost ferocious bite.

"It will be interesting if any more letters are received now that she's dead." Lucy smiled as the observant waiter brought her coffee, along with more toast for the table without being asked. When he had walked away, she told Officer Reynolds, "I take it you're not content to accept your superior's conclusion."

John looked around, making sure no one could hear his reply. "It just doesn't make sense to me. She was so caught up in her ideas. The sheriff never met her, but I talked to the Helms woman a couple of times because my wife is so fired up over this women's rights stuff. I mean, how can I really know my wife if I don't understand the issue from a woman's perspective, or at least as much as I can?"

Lucy sat back in her chair and looked at him with amazement. "You're a very forward-thinking young man. I only hope there are more like you in the town."

Officer Reynolds washed down a mouthful of toast with a large swallow of coffee before commenting. "Oh, there are. You might not think so if you listen to the older guys in the saloons, but some of us do agree with certain aspects of change. Like the property part. Why should a husband be able to just take a woman's property? Or keep the children if she leaves because he's violent with her?"

Seeing his color deepen as he said that last, Lucy asked, "Why does that upset you?"

He hesitated a moment before again lowering his voice and leaning forward. "Last year I was sent to retrieve two young girls who had left with their mother when she escaped her brute of a husband. Everyone knew he was cruel to her and the girls. If he got those girls to raise, there was no telling the abuse they'd take when he got drunk. No, ma'am, I wasn't happy about that assignment."

"Did you find them?"

Again, he hesitated. Lowering his voice to almost a whisper, he looked Lucy in the eyes. "No, I didn't! They got clean away."

Lucy smiled, picked up her coffee cup and looked at him over the rim of it. "Good." What the young officer couldn't realize about Lucy was that she recognized in this compassionate young man someone who was conscientious and brave, but also willing to bend the rules. That could come in handy at some point.

She changed the subject by asking, "Did you question the chambermaids who regularly cleaned Mrs. Helms's room?"

"No." He frowned, afraid he had slipped up somewhere. "Did something you see in the room cause you to wonder?"

"I was just thinking that it would be interesting to know if they had ever seen newspaper scrap in her waste basket prior to the night she died."

He thought about that, following the train of thought this triggered. "You mean that maybe the stuff on the dresser wasn't hers?"

"Yes. Did you see any scraps?"

"That's it!" He leaned forward eagerly. "There wasn't any of that in the trash, but there was a small shred of newspaper on top of her. I saved it to show to the sheriff, but he didn't seem to think it important. But I still have it. Why would a piece of paper be on her back unless it was dropped there *after* she was hit and lying on the floor? Maybe it had been clinging to the stack of papers and dropped off when..." He sat back and frowned. "Well, I don't know."

"Why would the visitor have moved some of the stack after the murder if, as we're assuming, it was a spur of the moment act?" Lucy watched him closely to see his response to her question.

"If it was unpremeditated," he said slowly, "just an angry lashing out, and she wasn't the letter writer..." Again the officer couldn't follow through with his reasoning. "But the newspapers and stuff *were* there. Why else would they be there if she wasn't working with them?"

"I'm going to let you think about that," Lucy told him with a smile. "I have an idea taking shape, but I want to see if you too come to the same conclusion, to check my thinking."

He looked a bit chagrinned, but Lucy could tell he also appreciated the challenge and was already trying to work it out. Since J. J. had to get to work, he departed from Lucy, leaving her to finish her breakfast while looking over a list she had made earlier, and which Sheriff Hunter might have found interesting.

She studied the two columns of names, put together with Dolly's help, that covered the people known to have received a letter. One column was of those who had received a letter *before* Mrs. Helms had arrived in town, and the other was of those who had received a letter *after* her arrival. According to Dolly, they all knew one another at least to some degree. Lucy read through both lists, some of them known to her. Could one of them be the writer, having sent a letter to their own home in order to obscure their guilt? Some of the letters had been delivered during the night directly to homes or places of business, so that had to be taken into consideration.

"If only," Lucy told herself, "I could have seen the envelopes of those letters received through the mail." Dolly had said one of her letters had been mailed there in town, but that another had a Coloma post mark on it. Yet another had been mailed from Georgetown. Given how often Placerville citizens traveled to these nearby towns, this wasn't all that helpful. But it did indicate that the sender was someone who could leave town without anyone marking the occasion as unusual.

One woman on the list had acute arthritis in her hands so she couldn't have cut out all those tiny words and phrases from a newspaper, at least without great pain. Two of the men who had received a letter couldn't get around without a cane, and another was almost blind. She crossed all these people off the list. She then sat and stared at it again, but nothing stood out to her.

She returned to wondering if anyone had asked the chambermaids about newspaper scraps in the trash. Or had they heard something not mentioned to the police? Had the young women said nothing, not wanting to get involved? Or had it not seemed unusual to them? Had they ever observed the stack of newspapers in her room when they went in to clean? She folded the list, stuck it in her pocket and hurried from the hotel.

Lucy had to wait until the chambermaids at the Orleans Hotel were allowed a break from their duties, but eventually she joined several of them in the little room set aside just for their use. They all wore the same uniform of black dress beneath a white pinafore apron and white stuff cap. Long sleeves, high necklines, and bell-shaped skirts hid anything of individuality or femininity, which allowed them to fade into the background and be easily ignored. To most people, they were servants, practically non-persons. Consequently, people often said things around them that they would never dream of saying in front of most people.

Lucy had introduced herself as a friend of Dolly Robbins, but it was Robert's name that brought out giggles from one of the younger maids. She was immediately shushed by the others. However, when Lucy laughed, they became less wary, especially when she explained that she had been asked by Dolly to help find the anonymous letter writer.

The girls heated water in an iron kettle on a small sheet-iron cook stove made at the town's foundry and vented through a black stovepipe directed out the side of the building. As they made themselves tea, Lucy opened the bakery bag of cookies that she had brought with her and stacked them on a large platter. As these proceedings took place, they made small talk about the latest troupe of entertainers appearing at the theater in town and news of the latest fashions.

Although the fashions in the East, influenced by those from Europe, was characterized by skirts so full they had to be supported by crinolines and hoops, such style was not practical in Western towns. Simpler in design and less full-skirted they might have been, but with the discovery of the first chemical dyes back in 1856, they could at least now reflect bright colors. This was an exciting event for these young women. The first new colors had been mauve and bright purple, but now they could obtain fabric with bright pink dyes called magenta and solferino.

Lace, however, was popular and might be applied anywhere, as well as embroidery in silver or gold if the dress was to be used for an evening event. Day dresses with pagoda sleeves worn over undersleeves called *engageantes*, were popular in the East and even with some women recently arrived from there. But the necklines could be counted on to be up around the neck, possibly enhanced by lace or tatted collars, especially if it contributed to a demure look.

The girls with Lucy knew all about modern fashion because it was illustrated as black and white drawings in magazines that dictated to women what they should be wearing. The models were drawn as willowy creatures with haughty expressions of superiority, and the chambermaids looked upon them as near goddesses. But these Placerville chambermaids were paid a basic wage and could only dream of owning something so luxurious and sophisticated. Their best dresses were of calico or light wool, and they considered themselves fortunate if they could afford to add a bit of lace to any part of them. Those who knew how, crocheted collars and scarves, and were grateful for that.

By the time Lucy and the chambermaids were seated together around the table in the middle of the break room, it was as though they had been friends for a long time. Grateful for their welcoming attitude, Lucy decided they deserved nothing less than her honesty.

"I won't try to present my reason for being here as anything other than what it is. As I said, I was asked to find the writer of the anonymous letters. But now one of your guests has been killed." Lucy explained her interest in the death of Mrs. Helms, since she was sure that by now they knew Dolly had found the body. "I'm hoping that you're all observant and don't mind speaking up."

The four women nodded their heads, but each one with a degree of caution. "We were the day crew that week," the one known as Nancy told her. "At night there are two maids on duty just in case a guest needs something. We rotate the schedule, since that's pretty easy duty."

"That makes sense." Lucy nibbled at a cookie and sipped her tea. "Have you all cleaned the room of Mrs. Helms at one time or another during her stay?"

They all nodded, but only one spoke up, even if hesitantly. "I think I probably did it most often. I certainly did the room the day before she was killed, and I was scheduled to do it that day, too."

"What's your name?"

"Marsha, ma'am," she answered barely above a whisper. "I've worked here for almost a year now."

"Then let me ask you. At any time did you see newspaper in the trash when you took it out to be dumped?"

"Yes. Once or twice."

"Whole newspapers, or scraps of them?"

Marsha frowned before saying, "I don't know what you mean."

"Were the newspapers tossed in the basket like anyone else might do after having read them? Or were the pages cut up?"

"It was just like everyone else. In fact, they were in such good shape that I took them out and brought them in here so we could all read them when we had the chance."

"What about the rest of you when you cleaned her room?"

They variously shrugged, looked blank, or shook their head. Seeing that she had gotten as far as possible in this regard, she asked, "Did any of you ever see visitors coming to her room?"

Marsha, usually so shy that the others called her Mousey Marsha, spoke up again. "I saw a man once come to her room. But it was a couple of weeks ago. He works as a packer here in town."

"Do you know his name?"

"Mr. Leon, I think. I remember because I thought it odd that his last name was like what a first name should be."

Lucy smiled, trying not to show too much interest. "Yes, I see what you mean. Do you know how long he stayed?"

"For a little while, because I was waiting to get into her room. It was my last on the floor, and I was getting impatient to get in and clean it. So I guess he was there with her for about half an hour or so."

"Did you hear any part of their conversation?"

"No." But she didn't sound sure about it. "Well, I mean, not distinct words. But Mrs. Helms, her that was always so polite and considerate, was angry about something. At one point she sounded especially upset and, um, exasperated I think the word is. Just fed up, like. Then the door opened and as he left, I heard her say, 'It can't be too long before I see you again.'"

Nancy frowned. "That's an odd way of saying you don't want to see someone again."

Clare, the only one to have remained quiet up to that point, said, "Or does it mean she hoped to see him again as soon as possible?" She was ignored by everyone except Lucy, who thought it a perceptive point of view.

Lucy asked them, "Was there anyone else you remember seeing with her?"

Nancy nodded so vigorously that her little maid's hat came loose from its pins on one side. "I saw a woman come see her once. Lots of long hair in old-fashioned ringlets down the back. Blonde she was. Nice figure. Hat with a short veil."

"Had you ever seen her before?"

Nancy shrugged. "I only saw her briefly from the side just as she was entering the room. Just before she left, though, I heard one of them say loudly, 'That's not fair.'"

"When was this?"

"Early evening of the day she held that big meeting here at the hotel. In fact, Mrs. Helms was barely returned to her room from having been out for her supper."

Clare spoke up again. "Now I come to think about it, I saw a woman I could describe the same way. She went into Mrs. Helms's room mid-morning the day following that big meeting here at the hotel. Average height, and as the men might say, *stacked*." The other girls giggled as they poured themselves more tea. "And I did hear Mrs. Helms raise her voice during that visit several times, but I couldn't make out the words."

Lucy could tell from their furtive glances at the door that the girls were done with their break and were eager to get back to work. Clare mumbled something about their supervisor, so Lucy rose to leave, not wanting to get them into trouble.

Marsha, however, had enjoyed the change in their routine and didn't want it to end. "I often saw Mrs. Helms leaving alone in the mornings and not coming back until well into the afternoon. Is that helpful?"

"It could be." Lucy shrugged and shook her head. "At this point, I'm not sure what's helpful."

Nancy asked, "Are you working with the police to find her killer?"

"In a way. Do you think it would be possible for me to see her room again? I've been in there already once with Mr. Bradley's permission."

Marsha told her, "I'll take you up. Mr. Bradley said that I should clean it, but I haven't gotten around to it yet. Frankly, I'll be happy to have you with me the first time I go in."

When Marsha had used her skeleton key to open the door, Lucy pushed forward so that she was in front as they entered. She knew exactly what she wanted to see, and turned to the young maid. "I suggest you bring a bucket of very hot water mixed with borax, two scrub brushes and a stack of old towels." Marsha said nothing as she hurried away.

Lucy quickly scanned the room, noting that the soiled rug should be rolled up for removal. She found it surprising that the newspapers were still on the dresser, but when she walked to them, she saw that the scissors were gone. Looking around, she couldn't find them anywhere else in the room. The paste pot was still there, however.

So enmeshed in her thoughts was she, that when Marsha spoke her name, she jumped. It took them half an hour, and several trips to change out the water, but they got the unpleasant task completed. The two women also rolled up the rug and tied it with twine. As Lucy bid farewell to Marsha, she knew that she had made at least one friend at the hotel, and maybe an ally.

Lucy also knew something else. She knew what had bothered her about Dolly telling her that the blood had been wet on Mrs. Helms when she had found her, but that the smell of the kerosene was faint. Was it possible that Mrs. Helms had not died immediately following the blow from the lamp? Had there been a space of time between the attack with the lamp, when the kerosene had been spilled, and when Dolly had found her? Enough time that the kerosene had partially evaporated? And during which time a second person could have entered and struck her a blow so hard that it broke the skin, causing death at that time? These questions would continue to plague her for some time.

On her way out, Lucy stopped at the counter to express her gratitude for being allowed to talk to the chambermaids. As she started to walk away, she looked to the wall behind the counter and noticed that hanging from the nail beneath room 201 was only one key. Most of the others had two keys hanging below the pigeon-hole assigned to a room. When she questioned the clerk, he explained that the second key to Mrs. Helms's room had recently been lost.

Lucy walked out of the hotel, thinking to herself, "Lost, or stolen?"

CHAPTER 6

"I slept and dreamed that life was Beauty;
I awoke, and found that life was Duty."
Ellen S. Hooper

Saturday, June 7 - Monday, June 9

At the end of Lucy's first week in Placerville, she found herself sitting with Melanie in the parlor of the Robbins home, herself on the sofa and Melanie in one of the two chairs across from her. It wasn't what she had planned when she had set out to see Dolly, but sometimes plans go awry and we must simply do our best in the circumstances. And that was what Lucy was trying to do.

The Saturday morning sun flooded the east-facing kitchen and extended its light into the parlor, where fresh mountain air was coming in through open windows. With Robert at work, Lucy and Melanie were drinking coffee from Dolly's fine china cups while waiting for that busy woman to return home from a quick trip to the Chinese market just down the street on Sacramento. She wanted a share of the fresh vegetables just received, knowing they would sell out early.

Melanie was commenting on the poor turn-out at Mrs. Helms's funeral at the Union Cemetery on Bee Street just north of town. Fumbling for something to say, Lucy informed Melanie, "I was told that the money she had with her was divided between the hotel and Mr. Roy, who served as undertaker."

"Oh?" Melanie returned, just as desperate to find something bland to say. "He runs the furniture store that reupholstered these chairs for Dolly." After a moment, Melanie added, "I did think more people would have turned out if for no other reason than out of curiosity."

"The fact that only women were there made quite a statement of its own. She would have appreciated that, I think."

"Yes, possibly so."

"I'm sorry. I should have asked how you're feeling. I understand you had a sick headache recently."

"Yes. I get them sometimes. Such a nuisance."

"They must be."

And this ended their short burst of constrained conversation, and Lucy was fast approaching a state of embarrassed awkwardness. She had exhausted all the small talk she could think of that Melanie might find interesting, or at least about which she might be willing to offer a comment.

This did not mean that there were not a multitude of questions that Lucy would have liked to ask. She had always been curious about Dolly's childhood, and here was a singular source of that information. But Lucy was stopped from any such inquiries by an overwhelming sense of unfriendliness coming from the pretty young woman across from her. It felt like a physical wall between them, expressed partly by furtive glances cast in her direction and partly from some subtle radiation of attitude. In whatever way she knew it, there was no doubt in Lucy's mind that Melanie was holding onto a deep well of resentment.

After a long silence between them, and with a firmness that signaled something of purpose to follow, Melanie put down her cup and leaned forward toward Lucy. "Who *are* you?"

Lucy blinked, her mind scrambling to understand the meaning back of the question. "Who am I? You know who I am."

"I mean, why did my sister ask you of all people to come here to discover who wrote the letters? It seems that she just assumed you would be able to figure it out and that no one else would."

"Well..."

"And you accepted her request, so you must think that you can do exactly that." So far her tone had been merely one of curiosity, but it suddenly sharpened. "What makes you so special that she turned to you and not the police?"

Feeling on the defensive, Lucy fought to establish an aura of simple reasonableness. "I'm not sure it's because she thought the law *couldn't* figure it out. Rather that Dolly thought they weren't taking it seriously enough. Of course, now with the murder of Mrs. Helms they are, although they're not convinced the anonymous letters to townspeople and the murder are connected."

"Forget about the murder. Why did Dolly think you could be of help in finding out who's sending the letters?"

"I guess she respects my ability to solve problems. I'm not without knowledge of the town and its citizens. Most of those whom I've met I like very much."

Melanie looked directly at Lucy and studied her for a long moment. "No. It's more than that, I think."

Lucy felt an irrational urgency to defend Dolly's decision to seek her help, as well as her own decision to accept. At the same time, she was irritated that Melanie was acting as though there was something underhanded going on. "I've been included in the social circles of a number of people here on occasion, so I have access that the police don't have."

Melanie ignored where this might have led. "Dolly doesn't talk about her time in Nevada City." This sudden change of direction took Lucy by surprise, especially as it was one that she too avoided. She realized this was the real purpose of the questioning when Melanie said, "It was almost seven years ago that Dolly married Robert and left there. And I know that she met you there. But other than the obvious reason you had to leave," and here she glanced at the scar on Lucy's cheek, "she has never gone into any detail about why you were in a brothel in the first place."

Clenching her jaw, Lucy snapped, "I was a cook. And only a cook." She wasn't going to volunteer any further information about her past or what had taken place in Nevada City when she had worked there. However, when Melanie continued to simply stare at her, Lucy felt compelled to add, "It was a long time ago and it has nothing to do with what's going on here. Let's just leave it in the past."

But Melanie was not good at dropping a subject upon which she was fixated, especially if it had anything to do with her sister's past. Being so close in age, the girls had when children formed an alliance in their defiance of the strictures placed upon them by their mother. This had started when their father had left so suddenly after they were in their Los Angeles home, which necessitated that they take care of one another while their mother worked.

Just recently Dolly, trying to make peace with her past, had expressed to Lucy the fact that she was just beginning to realize how the stress of such a circumstance could turn a parent into a strict disciplinarian. Melanie, however, was not quite so willing to accept this, possibly because she was still bound in a marriage both demeaning and frightening.

Melanie, sensing with satisfaction that she was making Dolly's usually self-assured friend uncomfortable, pushed on. "Was it so awful for you there in the parlor house where you met Dolly?"

Lucy smiled, determined not to let Melanie get under her skin. Exaggerating the false sweetness of her tone, she said, "I'll tell you what, my dear. You tell me first what you endure in what I assume is an unpleasant marriage, and then maybe I'll tell you what was going on in my life back then."

"My private life is none of your business!" Melanie snapped at her.

"Exactly." Lucy picked up her coffee cup and took a sip as she looked over its rim at the young woman before her.

For a second Melanie stared back at Lucy with something beyond distaste and just this side of loathing. When Lucy continued to meet her eyes, Melanie forced herself to lightly laugh away the moment. But it was clear that each woman resented the other's intrusion into what they considered private territory. Lucy knew that she and Melanie would never be close friends, but she still wanted at least cordiality between them for Dolly's sake.

When Dolly opened the front door shortly afterwards and stepped inside, she immediately sensed the tension between the two women silently sipping coffee while trying to pretend the other wasn't there. She started to ask about it, but instead began talking about her morning and what she had purchased for supper that night.

As she set her woven shopping bag on the kitchen table, she called to them. "I overheard some men talking. Evidently there's a shortage of wagons with so many wrecked in the floods. Freight has been stacked in the hills around town until freighters can return from the east side for it. Wagons are being built, of course, but I imagine they'll be expensive."

Melanie sat back. "The freighters can afford them, considering what they charge and how busy they are. Too bad they don't spend some of their money on bathing more often."

Dolly came into the parlor and sat in the chair next to her sister. "Well, dear, if you sat behind the back end of a team of mules or horses for hours on end, I doubt even your lavish use of perfume would help."

"Are you saying I use too much scent?"

"Sometimes." Dolly smiled at her and patted her shoulder. "But it's a lovely choice and shows your good taste in such things."

Melanie looked only slightly mollified, but she said nothing. Sensing a cross current of meaning between the sisters, Lucy rose from the sofa. "I think I'll spend the rest of the day in private pursuits." She didn't linger to dispense formal farewells, or to be accompanied to the door. She simply walked from the house, trying not to look like one escaping.

As soon as the door had closed behind Lucy, Dolly turned to her sister. "Did something happen between you two?"

"I think I may have been less than tactful. Nothing serious, I assure you." Melanie gave her sister a bright smile and retired to her room.

Dolly hated confrontations in general, and with her sister in particular. So, although she was pretty sure there was more to what had happened between Lucy and Melanie, she chose to accept Melanie's claim and focused on preparing that day's meals. It would take up much of her day, what with everything fresh and made from scratch, but it was worth it to see the satisfaction on her husband's face as he rose from the table. Besides, tinned goods were sometimes unstable, although the previous year she had purchased a tin of Underwood Deviled Ham and they had enjoyed it. The thought flitted through her mind that tinned food would probably grow in popularity during the war, and she was correct.

Meanwhile, Robert left his Main Street livery, leaving his assistant, Paul, in charge. He didn't do this often, because although Paul was honest and reliable, he was also exceedingly slow. In spite of that, Robert knew he could trust Paul to safely look after the animals, and finding someone to replace him would not be as easy as some might assume.

Once in town, Robert visited several saloons, not staying long in any of them. Those who knew him well would have found this sojourn between saloons surprising, since Robert was known to drink very little even when the drinks were free from someone in a celebratory mood. While those around him would toss back all they could ingest, Robert would stick with his two beers.

On this day, his unusual ramble between drinking establishments ended at one of his favorites. The other saloons had been crowded and noisy, but he had still been able to start a few conversations that gained him access to the current buzz of gossip among men. With the death of their favorite shared enemy, Robert had been curious how Mrs. Helms's sharpest critics were reacting to the murder of "that interfering suffrage woman".

Robert leaned on the white, painted bar of his favorite saloon and watched the bartender, Harvey Goldbloom, known to everyone as *Goldie*. He was an older man of 55 who was far beyond being surprised by life. He also had a definite opinion on any subject raised in his presence, and was not shy about sharing those opinions. When adamant, however, he had an unfortunate habit of emphasis in his speech that was somewhat jarring, and made Robert glad that women were not allowed in saloons. Robert liked Goldie's place because it was smaller than most, on a side street away from traffic, and the noise of gambling was confined to a back room.

Some said that when Goldie was angry, his long, gray beard actually bristled. They might have said the same about his hair, except that he didn't have much of it left. The small amount of cheek that showed above his beard was that of withered apples laid over with the stubble of a man who had lost his razor and wasn't interested in looking for it. But it was his eyes that held fast people's attention. Black as coal and usually red-rimmed, his eyes glared with contempt at a world he considered in worse shape than himself.

Robert leaned on the bar with a foot resting on the brass rail as he accepted a mug of beer. "Sure is a pretty day out there. Almost makes it a crime to be indoors."

"Goddamn right!" Goldie exclaimed.

"I'd like to go fishin'," Robert continued, "but I have too much work."

After a discussion on the best places for that activity to take place locally, amid interruptions from thirsty patrons, Goldie began wiping dry those glasses that had been soaking in a bucket of tepid water. He made no attempt to draw anyone into conversation and Robert was wondering how to start one in the direction he wanted.

A tall, thin man in a rumpled suit moved up to the bar and stood next to Robert. He was clean-shaven, with finely drawn features and long brown hair combed back and held in place by his hat. The stranger ordered a beer and while waiting for it, looked around the room with a critical eye, as though assessing the general friendliness of the assembly. Picking up the mug of beer when Goldie placed it before him, the man looked at it with deep appreciation before drinking it half-way down in a few gulps. He'd just gotten off the stage and was thirsty, hungry and tired, a condition not unusual for one traveling by stagecoach. He asked Goldie if he could buy two of the pickled eggs from a large jar on the bar, and when served, quickly washed them down with a swallow of beer.

Robert turned to him and asked, "Did I hear the soft, lyrical drawl of someone from the South?"

The man turned slowly toward Robert, only too aware that he was not always welcomed by those who were staunch Unionists. But when he saw Robert's smile and a hand extended for shaking, he smiled in return, shook Robert's hand, and asked, "Are you a sympathizer of the southern causes?"

"Not really," Robert answered honestly. "I'd prefer the Union to remain intact, so no, I'm not a Sesesh. But I feel a degree of compassion for a Southern society feeling itself torn apart. At the same time, I don't hold with slavery of any people."

The man nodded. "I agree. But you see, for a long time there have been folks who have tried to convince themselves and others that the blacks are not people like us. Just property to be used or traded for profit." Before Robert could object, which the man could see he was about to do, he added, "I know that's absurd, but it's what basically good people have convinced themselves of in order to keep the Southern economy and society the way they want it."

Goldie, having been born in Oklahoma and lived the last thirteen years in California, asked, "Is it true the slaves are regularly beaten and the women raped by their owners?"

The stranger hesitated a moment before speaking, and then as though the words were being torn from him, said, "Yes, sometimes. In fact, more often than is comfortable to think about. But there are also those plantations where that doesn't happen. Where the food is decent and the housing adequate, and such discipline is rare." Still, his face as he looked into his mug was grave. "But even on the best of the plantations, it doesn't mean a child won't be sold away from its parents, never to be seen again. As the Southern economy worsens, it'll happen more often, since it's a form of readily available income for the owners."

Robert fought the lump in his throat. "Is that why you're here and not there?"

"Partly. I'm a southerner, but not one who wants states to secede, nor do I approve of slavery." He took a long draw on his beer. "I wasn't far from Fort Sumter in Charleston last year in April. I watched from afar with throngs of other people when the Confederate ships began shelling the Federal garrison out on the island. At first it was like watching a noisy play, with people observing the action from across the waterway on their roofs and balconies."

"How long did that go on? I'm still not clear on that."

"It started not long before dawn on Friday, April 12, and didn't stop until mid-afternoon the next day."

Goldie shook his head. "That's a lot of shelling."

"Yeah, about 4,000 shells they say. It didn't stop until the fort was in flames. While it lasted, they closed down the telegraph so reporters couldn't alert their papers, and all trains were kept from coming in or going out of the city. Reporters who were Southern sympathizers, like those they now call Copperheads, even if representing Northern newspapers, were harassed and threatened, and sometimes arrested. They were then put on out-going trains as soon as the shelling stopped. And not always in good condition, with some even needing hospitalization. When it got around that this was happening, some reporters escaped the area by wearing disguises, even dressing as a woman if they could get away with it."

"Wait a minute," Goldie exclaimed.

While Goldie rooted around in the back room, the stranger told Robert, "It was strange, watching the shelling from so far away, looking out over the water to the small island fort. It quickly became a public spectacle, with hundreds of people sitting on their balconies and roofs, making sport of what was happening and betting on the result. Even stranger, though, was when the shelling stopped and the smoke was slowly cleared by the breeze."

"Oh, yeah?"

"Yeah. The American flag was still there, flying over the fort with all its glory still in evidence."

"I'm surprised it wasn't shot down."

"Oh, it was. It was hit by a Confederate shell, but a soldier risked his life to rush out and retrieve the flag, and then mount it on a shorter pole. The stripes showed a few holes, but the diamond pattern of 33 stars was intact. After the surrender of the fort, a Major Anderson lowered the flag and brought it to New York City for a patriotic rally in April, where it was flown from the equestrian statue of George Washington in Union Square.

I was there along with 100,000 other people, the largest public gathering we've ever known. Now it's being taken to different cities to raise money for the Union effort."

Gus, having returned in time to hear this last comment, said, "It's almost enough to make a person want to go to church." He shook his head and laid a newspaper on the bar. "I've kept a number of papers brought here from the East. This one is from April of last year." He held up a copy of the *New York Herald* with the headline 'The War Has Begun', with a wood-cut drawing of the new Confederate flag. "The editor predicts that the war could last as long as twenty years and says 'oceans of blood' will be spilled, and that 'millions of treasure wasted, with no other imaginable end than to leave the country exhausted, impoverished and wretched, and worst of all, despoiled of the freedom purchased at such cost by our forefathers.'" Goldie looked up at the other two men with distress written clearly on his face. "Do you think he could be right?"

The stranger said, "Sadly, I don't think it will take twenty years to achieve what he describes."

Robert swallowed hard. "A longer or shorter timeframe?"

"Oh, much sooner, I think. Men are dying by the hundreds, on both sides. The fighting will have to stop when the country runs out of men of fighting age."

The three men bowed their heads and were silent for a whole minute. Whether in contemplation of this horrible, sad truth, or in tribute to all the brave men who would die in the struggle, was for each of them to know in their heart.

Goldie's prodigious sigh brought them back to the moment. "This idea that the South needs to secede to be separate seems damned odd to me. Everyone knows that the North and the South are already distinctly different. That's a form of separate."

"True," the stranger said, "both socially and politically. They've hated each other as long as I've been alive. The laws, manners, and traditions of each are very different."

"Yeah," said Goldie, "but both areas think of themselves as populated by the most courageous, the most welcoming, the most creative, and so on."

The stranger laughed. "I think every group throughout history that has been in conflict with another has claimed that." Grinning, he added,

"But, of course, we know that here in the West all of those things apply more than anywhere else."

Ignoring the humorous challenge in the man's last comment, Robert asked, "Did you live in Charleston, South Carolina? Is that why you were there when the bombing of Fort Sumter began?"

"No. I was there on a short assignment for my South Carolina newspaper." He drained his glass. "I got my story, and I also found I could dress convincingly as a woman while boarding a train." He winked at the men, and having consumed only the one drink, he shoved the trade bit given him in change back toward Goldie and walked out. Goldie picked up the brass bit coin with the name of his bar stamped on it and shrugged. Tossing it into a basket with many others, he plucked a dripping glass from the wash bucket, and slowly began wiping the glass with a fairly clean cloth while deep in thought.

From his post across from this activity, Robert struggled to find a way to direct the conversation toward recent town events. He knew Goldie was a man who heard a lot of talk among his customers.

Robert drained his glass, which was one of the smallest used in any saloon in town, and shoved it toward Goldie. "I think I can handle another of these."

"Goddamned right!" Goldie handed him another as he said, "You seem kinda down today."

"Oh, I guess I'm a little concerned about the death of Mrs. Helms."

"Didn't your wife find her body?"

"Yeah. It really upset her."

"Goddamned right it did! That's nothin' for a woman to see."

"I guess some people are saying the letters will stop now."

"Some say they found the makings of them in her room." Goldie looked at Robert for confirmation.

Robert didn't give him a direct answer. "Do you think someone who was afraid of what she knew about them killed her?"

"Could be." But Goldie didn't look convinced.

"Or it could be," Robert tried again, "that it was someone who didn't like her views about giving women more legal rights. He might have thought she was going to be a threat to his relationships with the women in his life."

"Naw!" the bartender scoffed. "I've heard many a man talk against the suffrage ideas, and some even get pretty heated about it. But they're not that afraid of it. From what the police say about the killing, it looked like an attack from someone in a sudden rage."

"You're probably right. Maybe Mrs. Helms tried a bit of blackmail on someone and it went badly for her."

Goldie nodded his head slowly, followed by a mumbled, "Could be you're right about that."

Having milked the discussion for all he thought he could get out of it, which conversation Robert had to admit hadn't been all that fruitful, he decided to return to the livery. As he walked, he inhaled deeply, enjoying the smell of something sweet hanging in the air that was wafting to him from a nearby garden. "June," he thought, "is a wonderful month for nice days."

A beautiful day it indeed was, and Lucy knocked on the door of the Jones residence after an enjoyable walk down Main to Coloma Street. Zelda Jones answered it, and couldn't hide her surprise, her dark skin turning even darker and her eyes opening wide in surprise. Zelda was of Mexican-American descent, tall and lovely, and she carried herself with an elegance of movement that Lucy envied. Her husband had come from Mexico during the Mexican War back in the 1840's, and after it had ended, he had stayed to join the gold rush that had immediately followed the conclusion of the war. Lucy remembered Joseph's wonderful, deep laugh, but also the dourness of his frown when displeased. Being Saturday, Lucy could hear Joseph Junior playing marbles in the back of the house with two other boys.

Lucy quickly responded to Zelda's hesitant, somewhat cool greeting with an apologetic explanation. "I thought I would stop by and say hello, Zelda. I've been in town several days now and I didn't want you to think that I'm ignoring you. I've always enjoyed our visits."

"So have I, Lucy. Please come in."

As they settled in the small parlor, Zelda glanced nervously toward the kitchen. Lucy could just see part of Joseph Jones's leg where he sat at the kitchen table. When he didn't immediately join them, Lucy sensed something not quite right.

"The weather is so fine," she told Zelda, "that I thought I would get out of the hotel and call on a few old friends."

"Yes, it is fine. Oh, would you like a cup of coffee?" She glanced toward the kitchen. Her long black hair was held back by a white ribbon, and although it fell forward with her jerky movement, it didn't hide the uneasiness in her eyes.

When Zelda made no move to rise, Lucy got the point. "Oh, no thank you. I can't stay. And I know you must have things to do, it still being morning. I just wanted you to know that I hadn't forgotten you."

"How kind. I did hear that you were in town, but I knew you must have a lot of people to call on, being that you don't usually stay for more than a week. You've made so many friends here over the last few years."

Realizing that Zelda was for some reason anxious about her husband hearing more than a formal conversation between ladies, Lucy made a few casual comments about a hat she had seen in the Wolf Brothers store and then declared that she needed to meet someone. She hesitated at the door and whispered that she was going to stop for lunch at the Hope & Neptune Restaurant on the Plaza.

An hour later Lucy was seated at a table in that restaurant, sipping a cup of coffee, and hoping Zelda would soon arrive. Her attention was diverted to three women at the next table who were talking about Mrs. Helms. A waspish lady dressed in dark purple from head to toe, including a hat wrapped in swirls of toile, had just said, "That Mrs. Helms was an obnoxious woman. No wonder someone killed her."

The woman next to her, wearing a small bonnet blooming with silk flowers, pointed out, "If that was a reason to kill someone, we'd have a fuller cemetery. Women don't get killed just because they're obnoxious."

"To hear my husband talk, they should be." This third woman, younger than the other two, had large, fancy combs holding back her hair instead of a hat.

The first woman gave her a sharp look aimed down a long nose, a common pose that was known to cease many a rebuttal to her opinions. "I suppose it depends on whether or not Mrs. Helms's words or actions had something to do with her death." She leaned forward and whispered almost louder than her spoken words, "Did she have dangerous knowledge about someone, I wonder?"

"Well," the second woman said, savoring the word as though it were a tasty appetizer to what was to come next, "if the person sending the nasty letters can find out things about people, I would suppose Mrs. Helms could have, too. She certainly talked to a lot of women after she came here." Then, with an aura of innocence, she added, "And we know how some women gossip." They all joined together in a judgmental nod of their heads.

Lucy almost burst out with a snort of disbelief, but she was stopped from such an inappropriate display when a tall, stately woman in her late thirties walked into the restaurant. She was accompanied by her teenaged daughter, both with luxuriously long black hair and dark eyes that didn't hesitate to meet those of anyone who acknowledged them. Their dresses were simple but well made, and as they passed other tables people nodded to them and smiled. They were immediately seated on the far side of the room by the window, and two waiters hurried toward them, one giving way to the other with reluctance. This incident grabbed the attention of the three women.

Not knowing the trio of women's names, Lucy appointed them each a designation as she thought of *Macbeth* and the bubbling cauldron tended by the three witches.

Third woman said, "She's a rather attractive girl. Better than her mother. The girl has character showing in her face."

First woman spoke up. "Yes, but it's too bad her eyes are so close together."

Second woman sat up straighter and said, "Well, be glad she didn't inherit her mother's nose. I wasn't going to point it out, but...well..."

First woman smirked. "You don't have to say anything about it. It speaks for itself."

Laughter that could have been interpreted as cackling followed, and Lucy found it exceedingly uncomfortable to hear. She had the urge to defend the woman and her daughter, who she knew as both kindly disposed people, but she didn't want to make a scene and draw attention to herself. Feeling shame for her gender, and a little for herself for her hesitancy, Lucy was glad when Zelda finally arrived at straight up noon.

Zelda Jones came through the door of the restaurant with her homemade, cloth shopping bag over her arm and her eyes darting around the room even after they had located Lucy. She had the rattled look of a woman who had watched her favorite bonnet blown under the muddy wheels of a passing wagon. But her bonnet was firmly in place, partly covering her hair now wrenched into a severe twist, and shadowing her face with a short veil. But nothing could hide her dark beauty, and several men irritated their female companions by watching her as she hesitated just inside the door.

Deciding there was no one present who might report her to her husband, Zelda made her way to Lucy's table. After the waiter took their order for soup and a roll, Zelda told Lucy, "I know you probably wanted to talk about the anonymous letters and I just couldn't have you bring them up around Joseph."

"Why not?"

"The whole subject upsets him, and he has forbidden me to discuss them. He says they're dangerous."

"Has he gotten one?"

"I think so. He did mumble something about it not being unusual for a plain man to have a beautiful wife who was faithful to him. But he doesn't know that I've also gotten one. If his letter upset him so much, he might think that whatever was in one of my two letters was true."

"Was it?"

"Not at all." Zelda sat back with a slight shrug. "The first one accused me of beating our dog. But we don't have a dog." She didn't comment on what was in the second letter, and Lucy didn't ask.

"Then show it to him so he knows how silly they can be."

"I can't. I tossed it into the fire. Even though it was nonsense, it was still frightening to receive it. It's upsetting to know you're the target of some woman with such hate in her heart for others."

"Do you know many other women who have received one?"

"Oh, yes." Zelda leaned forward and lowered her voice, her dark brown eyes boring into Lucy. "It's gotten around that you're interested in solving our little problem. That's why I was afraid to talk to you at home. But many feel that with Mrs. Helms dead, the letters will stop."

"I don't think Mrs. Helms was the sender."

Zelda looked down at her bowl, reached for her roll and began tearing it into small pieces without eating any of them. "That's interesting. I've thought the same thing. It just doesn't feel right. I was at the talk she gave, and she was so...intense."

"Exactly. Her goal was to enlighten and strengthen women, and convince men that there was nothing to fear about women having more rights. Making everyone afraid and suspicious is the opposite of that."

"How do you plan to find the one sending them? I'd like to help, but Joseph would be angry if he found out."

"All I need from you is a list of the women you know who have received a letter, and how they might be tied together."

"You mean, like clubs, churches or interests?"

"Yes. Anything that might give them something in common. I'm trying to see why certain women have been targeted and others not. I think the few men who got them was a blind, and that women are the real target."

Zelda agreed to do what she could, then hurriedly finished her lunch and left. The waiter, referred to as *Young* Tom in deference to his father referred to as *Old* Tom, brought Lucy the bill for the meal, as she had instructed him to do in advance of Zelda's arrival.

Placing a silver salver with the bill on it on the table, he scowled over his shoulder at the table just deserted by the three catty women who had been so difficult to please. In a low voice, he told her, "I heard you and Mrs. Jones talking about the letters. Come see me at three o'clock at the Orleans Hotel. Room 5, at the back end of the corridor." He walked away before she could say anything, and she decided to return to her hotel room.

Questioning the wisdom of going alone to a strange man's room, even one so well-known, just before three o'clock Lucy walked the short block west of the Orleans Hotel. She knocked lightly on Tom's door and he greeted her politely, smiling with welcome. "Good afternoon, Mrs. Murphy. Won't you come in?"

He stood back and Lucy entered somewhat cautiously, one hand ready to dive into her purse for her companionable derringer if it was needed. She then noticed that Tom had set up a small table with a coffee pot over a kerosene warmer. Next to it was a glass bowl full of crushed brown sugar and a pitcher of thick cream.

Tom pulled out a chair for his guest, and after noting with approval that he had left the door open, Lucy seated herself. She removed her gloves and laid them across her lap as Tom sat down and took in hand an unusually large mug that more closely resembled a beer stein. After pouring coffee into it half way up, he poured in a generous amount of cream, raising the level of the now pale liquid by an inch. With the addition of two large scoops of brown sugar, the rim was nearly reached. He handed the sweet, beige concoction to Lucy, who accepted it with a polite but wavering smile. The first sip made her eyes bulge. Her effort not to gag was valiant and she even managed to look pleased. Freda would have been proud to know that her years of training Lucy in how to be a proper lady had paid off.

While Lucy recovered her ability to speak, Tom declared, "These letters have me angry!" He ran a hand through his blond hair, and she noted that his clean-shaven, youthful features were unusually tense. "I've heard some of the things the letters have accused people of, and even if only some of them are true, well, I mean, how on earth does the writer know these things? Are conversations being overheard and reported to someone? If so, I didn't want us to be overheard, so I invited you here."

"What didn't you want others to overhear you telling me?"

"I think you should go talk to Mrs. Hall. She lives permanently here in the Orleans Hotel." He sat back and folded his arms across his chest as he announced, "Right across the hall from where Mrs. Helms was killed."

Lucy smiled, remembering the eye staring at her through the crack in that very door. "You think she might have heard or seen something important?"

He leaned forward. "A friend of mine works here as a steward, Bill Hooper, and he says she's a right busy-body." He then added hastily, "But very nice."

"Thank you for the information. I'll follow up on it. But how did you know I'd be interested?"

He blushed. "Truth to tell, a number of people have cottoned on to how you're asking a lot of questions about the letters and Mrs. Helms. Some think you're just nosey, and others think you've been asked by someone to look into the letter problem."

"What do you think?"

"I don't care as long as the letters stop. My mother got one." He once more ran his fingers through his unruly mop of hair. "It was the day before Mrs. Helms was killed. I heard Mom crying after she'd wadded it up and thrown it into the stove fire. And it's hurting businesses in town, especially the trades where the clerks are usually talkative with their customers. And now those few people who used to leave me a gratuity have stopped doing it. Maybe they're wondering if I eavesdrop on people's conversations." He stood up and began to pace. "I just hate all this."

"I see. You're an admirable young man." Lucy stood up and moved toward the door while pulling on her gloves. "Thank you for the coffee, and the information. If you hear anything you think might be important, you can leave me a note at the Cary House."

"I'll do that. Good luck to you, ma'am."

Being only mid-afternoon, Lucy decided to call on Virginia Edsel. While waiting for her knock to be answered at the small house on Spring Street, she pictured Virginia in her mind. Here was a woman who had never in her life thought that there was anyone who would not delight in hearing her opinions.

Although Lucy didn't know it, Virginia's childhood companions had assumed she must know more than they did and had therefore listened to her while waiting for that something to be revealed. It had made them wonder if they were too stupid to have recognized the point Virginia was making. In her teen years, those she sought out remembered their training in good manners drummed into them at home and school, and so nodded with half smiles until they could retreat from her. As an adult, most people still fell into one or the other of these reactions.

There were, however, a few people in town who found her outgoing confidence endearing and enjoyed spending time with her. These people had connections to those with the previously described attitudes, and in order to show Mrs. Edsel that they could be as open and confiding as she was, they often found themselves conveying what they had heard about their friends. Because of their motivation, it never crossed their minds to classify what they passed on as gossip.

To Mrs. Edsel's credit, she thought nothing of such things as whether or not a woman wore the latest fashion, or if she worked outside the home. To her, all women were sisters under the skin. She also served a homemade wine of epic potency. Waiting for her knock to be answered, and wondering if she would be offered some of Virginia Edsel's famous wine, Lucy heard a hoarse chuckle. Looking up, she found a raven on the branch of a nearby tree watching her with what appeared to be disdain. He uttered again that guttural, chuckling comment so common to his kind, then looked past her and began mumbling.

Lucy had met Virginia Edsel, a dozen years her senior, the previous fall when she and Jim had been in town for their last visit just before the rains began. Virginia Edsel was one of those women who had always looked older than she was, and the prim attitude she regularly adopted didn't help that. But because Jim liked Mr. Edsel, Lucy had been determined to make a friend of Virginia. With this in mind, the previous autumn Lucy had rented horses for herself, Dolly, and Virginia, and they had headed out onto the three miles of trails south to Diamond Springs to enjoy the fall foliage. Virginia had packed a picnic lunch for them and it had been a pleasant, companionable day that Lucy now remembered fondly.

Virginia finally answered her door and was happy to see Lucy, chatting constantly while pouring them tiny glasses of her wine. "After all, it is afternoon," Virginia justified, "and whatever you had for lunch will settle better with a little of this in you."

One sip made Lucy almost long for Young Tom's coffee. After the second sip, however, she began to think it not so strong. After the third sip she was brought to a point of pleasant relaxation that almost made her forget her reason for being there. She resolutely put the glass aside after asking for water that she hoped would dilute the effects of the wine.

"Virginia, you may have heard about the anonymous letters that are going around."

Virginia hesitated only a moment, but it was a significant pause considering what she said next. "I've heard something about them. But not having gotten one myself, I haven't paid much attention."

"So, you don't know of anyone who might have received one? Someone in your social circle, for instance?"

"No, not at all." Her lips pursed and she sat up even straighter than her corset necessitated. "The people I know wouldn't discuss something so crass. And frankly, Lucy, I'm surprised that you're involving yourself in finding the perpetrator."

"What makes you think I am? I mean, considering that you haven't paid any attention to what's going on."

"I'm not deaf." She smoothed her skirts and sniffed. "I do hear some of what people are saying, especially with you asking around so much."

Lucy had seldom seen anyone so uncomfortable. Virginia was practically squirming, and was obviously relying on years of practice in controlling her emotions to hold them back now.

"I'm sorry if you disapprove of what I'm trying to do," Lucy told her as calmly as she could, considering her disappointment in Virginia's attitude. "I thought we had formed a close enough acquaintance that you'd be honest with me. I'm trying to see if there are common connections between those who have received the letters. It's a big town and only a relative few have received them. Any commonality among recipients could help point to who is sending them. But if you simply don't want to discuss the subject, I'll respect your wishes, of course."

"I told you I don't know anything about them." Virginia stood up and Lucy followed her lead. "Now then, if you'll excuse me, I have to change and go to an appointment."

Lucy thanked her for the wine and made her way to the front door. "I'm staying at the Cary House if you ever want to talk." The resolute woman before her remained stiff and quiet, plainly not caring where Lucy was staying. Lucy walked out, hearing the door firmly closed behind her. "Well," she sighed, "I guess that's a friendship I've ground into the dust." The raven, still in the tree as though awaiting her return, looked down on her and chuckled.

Finding that the wine's influence was still somewhat with her, Lucy walked carefully down the road to Main Street. She took a deep breath of fresh air and was grateful that it helped clear her head. She continued on, puzzling over Virginia's reaction. On the other hand, maybe it wasn't all that unexpected if she had received a letter that contained an embarrassing truth.

Once in town and walking down the sidewalk, Lucy spotted a large bonnet coming toward her amid a crush of people. She didn't need to see the face beneath it. Mrs. Bowers, one of the few women Lucy would have preferred to avoid, was known for choosing the largest hat available as a means of advertising her millinery business. Although she was addressed as *Mrs.*, she was not married, but was given the traditional title as a show of respect for her age and ownership of a business.

In her attempt to back away from the grinning woman rapidly approaching, Lucy was immediately pressed up against the outside wall of a store. She felt like a condemned bug pinned to a board by a collector.

"Lucy dear," Mrs. Bowers gushed, "I heard you were in town. I thought you would have looked me up by now." Her large bust, inadequately reduced by the stays of her corset, nearly brushed against Lucy while the tall woman loomed over her. Lowering her voice, Mrs. Bowers said, "I hear you're asking a lot of questions about the anonymous letters. I could tell you a thing or two about those."

Lucy was no longer in a hurry to get away. "Really? You think you know who the sender is?"

"Oh, no." Mrs. Bowers drew herself up and took a small step back. "Well, I have my ideas, of course."

Lucy could tell Mrs. Bowers was caught between wanting to be truthful while yet wanting the attention that knowledge would bestow upon her. "I hear things, of course, when ladies come in to try on my bonnets." She bit the corner of her mouth to stifle what Lucy was surprised to realize was a giggle. "Sometimes I get more gossip than sales." Suddenly aware of what this might indicate, she hurriedly added, "Oh, but I'd never repeat anything of what I hear. Or do anything with it."

"Oh, of course not." Lucy hoped she hadn't sounded insincere. "Not for a moment would anyone think that you could be the writer."

Mrs. Bowers backed off from Lucy and looked at her with a raised brow. Ignoring the fact that it was not Lucy who had broached the subject of the conversation, she said, "You *are* good at getting information from people! Well, good luck to you."

And Mrs. Bowers unpinned Lucy from the wall as quickly as she had attached her to it, the collector having suddenly realized that this bug was not one she wanted to keep.

On her way back to the hotel late that afternoon, Lucy stopped by Dolly's house, relieved that Melanie was absent.

"I'm only stopping long enough to say good night before heading back to the hotel. I'm longing to take off my shoes and change into a dressing gown." She gave Dolly a brief hug and moved toward the door where she stopped and turned back. "Dolly, you never told Melanie about how I got this scar, did you?"

"Of course not! I've never told anyone."

"I was sure you hadn't."

"Why did you ask then?" Dolly was a little flushed and Lucy knew she was perturbed that such a challenge to her integrity would be asked of her, especially by Lucy.

Lucy decided it would be best if she was totally frank. "Melanie tried to suggest that you had."

Dolly was obviously shocked. "Why would she do that? It's none of her business."

"I pretty much told her the same thing, and she wasn't at all pleased with me."

Dolly moved to the middle of the room, her hands clutching and releasing at her waste. "I never would have thought she could be that rude." She turned back to her friend. "I'm so sorry, Lucy."

"You needn't apologize." She smiled brightly to show there were no hard feelings. "I'd appreciate it if you wouldn't bring it up with her, though. It might embarrass her and create an awkwardness between the three of us."

"You're probably right. Lately I've noticed that she can sometimes be less than tactful, but I'm sure she's not aware of it. I think her marriage is very much on her mind. I won't be surprised if she asks to stay here and separate from him for at least a little while."

"That could certainly be the explanation." Lucy hoped she sounded as though she believed it. "The poor girl is probably overwrought and trying to hide it."

Although Dolly had decided to accept this explanation, Lucy had not. As she walked back to Main Street, she remembered the sense of antagonism she had felt from Melanie. The only explanation she could think of that might apply was that Melanie was jealous of the closeness between herself and Dolly. Melanie's sweetness as a child may have long since evaporated under the weight of all that had befallen her since then. Women tended to use words like "harsh treatment" or "difficult relationship", which people usually accepted at face value. But the details might be so horrific that they would never be spoken, even to a close friend or sister. Few women of Lucy's era thought it proper to "bare their souls". It just wasn't done.

The following day was Sunday, and Lucy was still not ready to cease her calls upon those she knew in the town. But she waited until Monday afternoon, skipping Sunday to avoid offending anyone with a social call on the Sabbath. Some of those whom she wanted to ply with questions she had met only once, and that at a large gathering. But at least there had been an introduction, which was imperative.

Most of those who were willing to speak with her that Monday were women, but some were men who owned stores, as well as two who were miners. But few of them had any knowledge to impart, and those she thought might have received a letter were not readily forthcoming. Keeping the day from being a total loss, she finally came across William Norris, a stage driver who roomed at the Cary House.

She invited him to sit with her in the lobby, where he was happy to open up about what he had heard regarding the letters. He didn't feel he needed to clean up some of the more salacious details for her, as he knew Jim and figured that the wife of a professional gambler shouldn't be as easily offended as most women. He considered, therefore, that he was cleaning up his language well enough. Regardless, the desk clerk came over to them once and asked that Mr. Norris lower his voice.

From Mr. Norris, Lucy learned that many people knew which man was regularly visiting the houses of ill repute, and that although some of these men would not mind if that got around, others would. And all of their wives would mind very much if it was openly discussed. Then there were the rumors of employee theft, women who secretly drank or used snuff, the minister who had left a previous post under dubious circumstances, and other audacious items related to Lucy with relish. All of what he told her found its way into her notebook, but without names attending the details. Those she committed to memory, as Lucy refused to have anything in writing that, if found by someone else, could make life more difficult for anyone.

One of the most interesting of the people with whom Lucy talked that day was Charlie Johns. Many described him as an "idiot", others as simply "slow". He was indeed a reserved young man in his late teens, but she had several times before gotten into conversation with him and found him uncannily observant. He simply "didn't much like people", as he put it, especially men. Women were more tolerant of him, and although they were sometimes patronizing or bossy when he helped them with their gardens, they at least didn't tease or insult him.

As Charlie and Lucy sat outside the news agent's shop sharing a bag of freshly roasted peanuts, Charlie glanced angrily at a man walking past who pointedly avoided looking at Charlie. The man wore a pressed suit and a white shirt, and looked to be a prosperous gentleman of business.

Lucy leaned sideways towards Charlie. "Why don't you like him?"

"He's a doctor. He told my ma once that she should have me sent away."

"You mean put in an institution?" Lucy was shocked at such a thought.

He nodded and slowly crushed a peanut, shell and all, in one hand. He let the pieces fall onto the wooden sidewalk beneath the bench, carefully placed a boot over them, and resolutely pushed down. He smiled with satisfaction at the sound of the crunch. If this was his way of releasing his anger, Lucy thought it effective, as Charley looked up at her and grinned.

"I assume," she told him, "that your ma took exception to such a suggestion."

He laughed with satisfaction. "She told him off good and proper. She tried to explain to him that I learned as well as any boy, but just differently and the teachers didn't have the patience to deal with me." He shrugged. "I don't guess they had the time either. But most of them were kind to me even when I frustrated them."

"But not all?"

"There was one schoolmaster who thought he could whip the stupid out of me with a switch when I got a bad grade or gave him an answer that he called insolent. He thought I'd learn the day's lesson better that way, I guess."

"Oh, how awful!"

"Ma came to the school, took up the switch from the edge of his desk where he always kept it, and took the switch to him." He chuckled at the memory. "She only hit him on the shoulder before breaking the switch into pieces, but he reported her to the city police. They just told her to take me out of school and teach me at home. She did, too."

"I think I like your mother very much. And you sound better educated than many of the boys I've met."

He grinned again. "My reading isn't as fast as I'd like it to be. But when Ma reads out to me books, I remember what's in them, and I can pass any of the tests given at school. But back then they wanted me to write down the answers. That's where I'm not much good."

"How are you with sums?"

He perked up. "Good! I don't get numbers mixed up like I do words."

"So I gather whoever is sending out these anonymous letters hasn't sent you one?"

He laughed at that. "No. What could they say? Maybe it's because most people already think I'm different. At least they don't pay much attention to me."

"And that's good?"

"I think so. I think I even saw the person who's doing it."

Lucy stared into the distance and purposely said nothing. Eventually, Charlie added a little more. "I saw someone carrying a letter. Well, an envelope. They put it on the anvil at the Robbins Livery."

Lucy was glad Charlie couldn't hear her heart thudding in her chest. "A man or a woman?"

"Not sure. They had on a long black coat and a big floppy hat."

"Tall?"

"Not very."

"Fat or thin?"

"Hard to tell. It was a big coat. But I can tell you things about some of those letters that I've overheard."

He proceeded through a litany of vile suggestions, absurd assumptions, nonsensical jumps to conclusion, and hurtful accusations. He put no names to any of it, and Lucy was glad.

Charlie suddenly stood up when he saw a man approaching that he evidently didn't like, since he said nothing to Lucy before stalking off. The man seemed vaguely familiar to Lucy, but she continued to shell peanuts in her lap. The first she was aware of the man's near presence was when she saw his dusty boots only a foot from her own, and pointed at her. She looked up from the peanut she had been shelling and admired his pressed suit and fancy vest.

He said nothing, but removed his hat and banged it against his leg, raising a small cloud of dust. Nevertheless, upon resettling the hat atop his head it was just as filthy as before. It occurred to her that he might have something to do with one of the local mines, possibly the Coon Hollow Mine a mile south of town that was being hydraulicked, the hillsides washed away to find the gold within. But she couldn't remember having been introduced to him.

A tall man, stiff and upright, and seemingly at attention as he looked down at those with whom he conversed, he was a man who didn't invite casual conversation. Someone had once told him that he looked like an old soldier. Since then, he had carried himself in such a way that many believed it true, especially when they heard his experiences in the war with Mexico. Truth be told, he had never gotten closer to a battle than those he had read about in books.

Lucy felt she should stand up, but he was so close that this proved impossible, so she asked, "May I have the pleasure of knowing your name?"

"No." His voice was muffled by the abundance of thick beard covering the lower half of his face. Between that and the brim of his hat, all she could see were green eyes that glittered malice and determination. "I don't know what you think you're doing asking so many questions about who got the anonymous letters and what's in them. But you need to stop."

"I assure you that I don't care what is claimed in them about any specific person. It's enough that they're disturbing the peace of this town. But if I can find out who's sending them, that will stop them. Don't you want that too?"

"Do you mean that?"

"Which part?"

"That you don't want to know what's in them?"

"Of course. What little I have heard about is laughable and preposterous. If some of it hits the mark, it seems to be pure chance and few people would probably believe it."

He seemed to consider this, remaining silent while Lucy waited uncertainly. Finally, he spoke. "Just be careful. You could be treading on very sensitive toes."

Lucy nodded her head, and taking this as agreement, he turned and walked away toward the Plaza. She looked around to see if there was someone nearby who might know the man's identity, but saw no one on the sidewalk she could ask. She quickly walked into the news agent's store, the old wooden boards creaking beneath her feet as she made her way to the counter.

"Excuse me," she asked the clerk, so young he looked as though he should be in school instead of working.

"Yes, ma'am?" He licked his chapped lips and ran a hand over his mouth and chin, a new habit as he waited eagerly for his beard to begin growing. But he had a nice smile and Lucy thought it a shame that someday it would be covered over with facial hair.

Focusing on the task at hand, she asked, "Did you see the man in the suit that I was just talking to outside?"

"Yes, ma'am."

"Can you tell me his name?"

"No. But I know he works somewhere in the court buildings."

"Oh." That surprised her, and she wondered if the man had gotten his information about what she was doing from Mr. Hume. Or maybe it was someone associated with the police. Maybe Officer Reynolds had shared some of their conversation. As curious as she was about the source of the man's information, she was more concerned about whether she had been warned or threatened.

Lucy walked down Main Street past the courthouse to stand at the beginning of Bedford Avenue, remembering the delightful dinner party at the Hume residence. She looked up the steep, winding road that led past the homes and eventually entered an area of active mines, which was a reminder that this was the origin of the towns throughout the area.

Realizing that she was ready for a few minutes of rest, she walked to the small park behind the courthouse and followed the rock-lined path to a bench. The trees recently planted by the town ladies who maintained the small, green oasis were still young, but were showing healthy growth. Two round flowerbeds were full of colorful plants, their fragrance subtle but their bright colors uplifting. Lucy soon found herself feeling refreshed and ready to continue her wanderings.

She walked back through town toward the Plaza, where she prepared to cross the road and return to the hotel. But she was startled from her pleasant anticipation of refreshment when she saw Melanie walking up Center Street away from her. Responding to her curiosity, Lucy followed at a distance and saw Melanie turn up Coloma Street, where she hesitated at the front corner of the small house belonging to Tony and Jane Leon.

Lucy quickly pressed into the side of a neighboring house, and only when Melanie's back was turned did she carefully draw closer. It was then that she realized Melanie was standing outside the glass-paned French doors to Mr. Leon's study. So absorbed in whatever she was looking at to the right of the desk just inside the door, Melanie was unaware of anything around her.

After several minutes, Melanie stepped back onto the road and headed toward town, just missing Lucy hiding behind a tall fence. The look Lucy saw on Melanie's face was hard to interpret. It was a mask formed by lips more smirk than smile, and eyes that were partly closed, so that the whole was of a calculating nature. Melanie's hands were also clenched at her sides, as though holding in an intensity of emotion.

Lucy was confused, and a number of questions raced through her mind. Of course, in the lead was why Melanie would do such a discourteous thing as spy into someone's home? Melanie had never mentioned knowing Jane and Tony. Had she started to visit Jane and then saw that she had company, and therefore decided to return at some other time? But she had not gone to the front door. Nevertheless, she might have heard someone inside through the French doors and therefore had not gone further. Lucy assured herself that this must be the answer.

Half an hour later, Lucy had made her way to the Orleans Hotel so deep in thought that she had passed three people without being aware of their greetings. She was soon outside the door of the "nosey neighbor", she of the observant eyeball that had watched Lucy leave Mrs. Helms's room. When Lucy had asked about the woman from Mr. Packard, the clerk at the front desk, he had warned her that Mrs. Hall was "a bit batty half the time".

Lucy's response was to inquire how Mrs. Hall acted the other half. The clerk laughed at her mild jest, but sobered quickly. Aware that he might have been less than tactful about a guest, he quickly said that Mrs. Hall was pretty normal in the main. Lucy didn't care one way or the other, as long as the woman had seen or heard something useful that could help in an inquiry that was proving to be more difficult than she had anticipated.

CHAPTER 7

*"That which is everybody's business
is nobody's business."* Izaak Walton

Monday, June 9 – Wednesday, June 11

Mrs. Hall opened her door, the first on the right at the top of the stairs, and took a brief head-to-toe scan of Lucy. She then announced, "I didn't send for you!"

Lucy smiled warmly. "No. I'm a friend of a friend of yours, Bill Hooper, who works here."

"Oh, you know dear Billy!" Lucy didn't try to clarify this error. She simply smiled as Mrs. Hall stepped back. "Come in, my dear."

Before the door could close, waiter William Hyman from the dining room arrived with a tray of tea things. Seeing the plate of scones and jam, Mrs. Hall's hands flew to her cheeks as she started to explain that she hadn't ordered it. She didn't want to tell them that she couldn't afford such lavishness, being able to barely afford living in the hotel. Lucy, however, had an inkling of this from the scuffed toes of the woman's worn shoes showing beneath the hem of her plain calico skirt.

Lucy assured her, "This is just a little treat from me for your being willing to take time out of your day to visit with me."

After placing everything on the table, William carried the tray away and closed the door behind him softly. He smiled with pleasure, eager to tease Bill Hooper, also known as *'Dear Billy'*, about his favorite old dear having such a nice treat. Even if it was from the somewhat bold Mrs. Murphy.

Mrs. Hall glanced at the arrangement of tea things now spread out on her table and gave Lucy a sideways, coquettish smile. "What if I had turned you away?"

Lucy made an elaborate gesture, throwing up her hands in surrender and saying with exaggerated resolve, "Then I guess I would have had it all to myself back in the dining room."

Mrs. Hall giggled like a schoolgirl. "I appreciate a person who understands contingencies." She sat at the small table in front of the room's only window, motioned to the other chair for Lucy to sit, and poured out their tea. It gave Lucy time to glance around the room.

It seemed large, having in it only a small, narrow bed in one corner at the end of which was a small trunk. With a pine wardrobe and long dresser taking up the back wall, it allowed room for the small table and two chairs, along with a comfortable easy chair and ottoman. These sat next to a small table holding a kerosene lamp and a crystal water carafe on a crocheted doily, along with several small books stacked on the edge of the table.

Books, in fact, filled three wall shelves. They were also stacked in corners, next to the bed on the night stand, and various places on the floor. Lucy noted that the subjects were wide-ranging, from classics to travel monologues.

She transferred her focus to Mrs. Hall. She had a small, sharp nose, a triangular smile, a dainty chin and gray hair pulled back into a small knob at her neck. Everything about her was sharp, including a watchful and suspicious eye.

Mrs. Hall stirred her tea. "You noticed all my books. I suppose they're my escape to other places around the world. In the silence of long days, one can't escape from oneself, so I escape into a book. I suppose if I could listen to music when away from a music recital, I would escape into music as well." She looked up and smiled with pleasure at such an extraordinary idea.

"I imagine you have many friends here."

"Oh, I do," she nodded eagerly, her face lighting up with pleasure at the acknowledgement. "And they're very kind, but they have their own busy lives. Although I'm asked to dine often with them, there are still many days when I'm my own best company."

Lucy liked how much better it was to think of one's self as "my own best company" instead of that dreaded word *alone*. But Mrs. Hall was continuing. "I receive letters from my nieces and nephews in the South," she announced proudly. "It's by their generosity that I live here. Well, that and some stocks I have in some mines." Then, referring to an earlier comment, she added, "They're certainly having to think about contingencies. Things are changing quickly for them. But hopefully this trouble will soon be settled and we'll be back to one great big, happy family of states."

"I wouldn't expect to hear something like that from a Southerner. You don't want the southern states to secede from the Union?"

"Not all those in the South feel that way, and I suspect that not everyone in the North wants slavery to end. Some men in the north no doubt have investments in the South that profit them."

With a new respect for the lady's acumen, but aware that Mrs. Hall had not answered her question, Lucy asked, "And you think those businessmen would be okay with the status quo in the South even at the expense of continuing to enslave people under brutal conditions?"

Mrs. Hall gave Lucy a pitying glance. "Oh, my dear, of all the dubious talents of human beings, self-justification is one of the most common. And one of the most treacherous. Not only for others, but because it demeans the value of one's own character." She reached for the jam pot and plopped a large spoonful onto her scone. Before taking a bite of it, however, she added thoughtfully, "People talk about how travel expands one's horizons, which means of course a different awareness of the world around them. Maybe they should spend more time being honest with themselves about themselves. That would expand an even better horizon." She gave Lucy a meaningful look. "By that I mean a greater understanding of themselves. It would make a big difference in their choices, don't you think?"

"Um, yes, it would." Lucy looked at Mrs. Hall with wonder. Her clear blue eyes sparkled, and it was obvious that she had her wits about her. Lucy wondered why the clerk had thought otherwise.

Mrs. Hall suddenly cut to another subject. "You don't live here in Placerville, do you?"

"No. I live in Jamestown. I'm here visiting friends. But this isn't my first visit. I was fortunate to arrive in time to hear Mrs. Helms speak here in the hotel."

Shaking her head, the elderly lady reached for her cup. "That whole thing is so disturbing. Such poor, unhappy ladies are to be pitied. It must make for a difficult life to carry so much anger inside."

"Does it make you uneasy being so near to what happened?"

"Not really." And, indeed, she didn't seem perturbed in the least. "This was obviously aimed at her alone. Of course, like everyone else, I do wonder what she must have done to bring something like this upon herself. I mean, people don't go about bashing women over the head without provocation."

"A lot of men hated her goals."

"So did a lot of women." Mrs. Hall dabbed delicately at her lips with a white linen napkin. "I got tired of hearing her running diatribe myself whenever I visited with her, which wasn't often. But I don't think that would have set someone off enough to strike her down."

"Did you hear anything that early morning?"

"Which time?"

"The morning Mrs. Helms was killed," Lucy explained patiently.

"I know, dear, but there was more than one coming and going that morning."

"Well, yes. When the killer arrived and when Dolly Robbins came at six-thirty and found the body."

"Oh, no, dear. I mean before Mrs. Robbins found the body."

"Really?"

"Oh, yes. I heard someone knock on her door around five-thirty that morning. Then, about half an hour later and after some loud, angry shouting, I heard the door close and footsteps hurry down our creaky stairs. Then maybe half an hour later I heard someone come up the stairs and go into her room without knocking. That puzzled me. But they came back out so quickly that I didn't have time to get to my door to peek out."

"Did you look out the first time?"

"I didn't think to. People come and go here all the time, even that early. If I looked out every time, I'd be at the door more than in my chair." She leaned forward as she colored slightly. "I sleep in my chair much of the time." Sitting up straight, she told Lucy, "I thought it might have been hotel staff bringing her an early breakfast tray. She ate breakfast in her room every morning."

"And then Dolly arrived and found the body."

"I heard her, of course. Well, I heard her scream, as well as the clerk come up with her, and all the hub-bub that followed."

"Did you see or hear anything else?"

"No." But she hesitated and Lucy caught it, so she continued to look at Mrs. Hall expectantly. It paid off when Mrs. Hall added, "I have the lingering feeling that whoever it was on the stairs, they were light rather than heavy."

"Which time?"

"Now about that, I'm not so sure." She frowned in her effort to recall. "It's becoming mixed up in my mind the further we are from the event. It was just a slight thought I had that she wasn't being visited by a large man." She stared off in the distance for a moment. "But that any man would enter her room so early surprised me. Of course, a few weeks ago one did, but it was in the afternoon." She looked out the window and frowned. "She just didn't seem the type."

Lucy avoided asking her what type that would be. Mrs. Hall seemed to be fading in energy and focus. Knowing she could always return on some other day, Lucy thanked her new friend for taking the time to visit with her and left Mrs. Hall with the last of the scones and tea.

It was late in the day before Mrs. Hall realized that she didn't know why she had received a visit from the nice lady who had brought her the lovely tea.

Lucy lingered in bed the next morning, paper and pencil next to her, wondering if she had really learned anything of substance thus far. She had certainly talked to a lot of people, but what had it netted her that the law didn't also know? Maybe the answer was that now she had a conviction, even if based on very little, that Mrs. Helms had not been the letter writer. Of course, that didn't mean she wasn't blackmailing someone.

It had netted Lucy one thing the evening before as she returned from supper at a nearby restaurant. A man had stepped toward her from an alley, but not so far that he escaped from the shadows. With his hat pulled forward and down, she had no idea who he was, or even if she had ever met him. On the other hand, he did seem vaguely familiar, and she assumed his gravelly voice had been disguised as he told her, "Back off, lady. Someone just might slam the door in your face one of these times you come a knockin'. Maybe *on* your face. It'd be a shame to see that pretty face of yours all messed up."

Lucy had stepped back out of his reach, but at this point had recklessly told him, "I gather you don't want the anonymous letter writer unmasked. Or is this about the murder of Mrs. Helms?"

There had been no answer except the crunch of boots on gravel as the man had retreated back down the alley. But the tread had been light, and she had recalled what Mrs. Hall had said about the footsteps on the stairs. Thinking back on this exchange in the alley, Lucy wondered if she had been threatened by the killer. Even though now in the safety of her room, a chill crawled down her spine.

A knock on the door made her jump and her pulse race, until she remembered that she had ordered coffee and rolls for this time of morning. She was soon sitting at the table in her room with her paper and pencil, reaching for a sweet roll and thinking how she should enjoy this time of living in a hotel before once again being mired down in domestic duties. She was of course eager to once again be surrounded by home and family, but part of her wondered if it meant that her life would never again hold adventures that would test her self-sufficiency and courage. If she could have looked forward into the next couple of decades, she would have chosen domestic routine and been glad of it.

Focusing again on the challenge at hand, she had to admit that the most confounding detail lately garnered was what Mrs. Hall had said. Who had come to Mrs. Helms's room almost half an hour after she had heard the earlier first arrival? This time, however, Mrs. Hall said the visitor had not knocked. Was it because they knew there was no one alive in the room who could answer the door? That would mean they also knew the door was unlocked. Had it been the killer, having left something behind that needed to be retrieved? If so, it had to have been very important to justify possible exposure by returning.

Lucy then tried to form a theory based on two different people visiting Mrs. Helms that morning; one person who had knocked and been admitted, and another person who had a short time later entered without knocking. The latter scenario presumed the individual would have known the door would be unlocked, possibly because Mrs. Helms was expecting them. That idea bothered Lucy because they would have to be on exceedingly close terms to bypass the politeness of even a cursory knock on the door before entering. And Mrs. Helms wasn't supposed to know anyone in Placerville that well. And then too, there was the fact that right after that Dolly had arrived to find Mrs. Helms not long dead. But the person who entered without knocking hadn't been in the room but a very few minutes, hardly long enough to have interacted with her before deciding to kill her.

No, it felt to Lucy as though the first visit had been when the murder had taken place after some time spent in conversation. And the second visit was the same person coming back for some reason. Still, there was something wrong with that reasoning. But what it was escaped her at the moment as another question arose in her mind.

Why had Tony Leon been seen going into Mrs. Helms's room two weeks prior to the murder, as noted by the chambermaid? And although Mrs. hall hadn't known his name, she too had been aware of this visit. What was his connection to Mrs. Helms? Maybe that was an avenue of investigation down which she should be traveling. But there was no reason she could think of that would allow her to approach him, considering that she had never been introduced to him. Maybe she could find some excuse to spend time with *Jane* Leon, whom she did know. Would Jane know that her husband had visited Mrs. Helms, much less why? And if not, should she tell Jane?

A short time later Lucy walked out onto the sidewalk in front of the Cary House, then hesitated as she realized it was too early to call on anyone. A sulky sun was trying to break through a layer of clouds casting a depressed vitality upon the day's beginning. But even as she watched, the sun's weak glow was completely veiled by a misty cloud, dropping the morning into an unexpected crepuscular gloom. In the shops, kerosene lamps were lit, gas wall sconces turned up, and women out shopping considered returning home.

On a day like this, women didn't want to be late putting the mid-day meal on the table, usually referred to as *dinner*. It would take at least two hours to complete preparations for it, unless the stove was already hot, and even then, wood would have to be added to the fire box. Hopefully, it was cut and stacked next to the stove. So much work just to cook a meal. It would count in the thousands, if it could be known how often cooks had fantasized about the ability to light a stove by just a flick of the wrist. For many working men in town, this mid-day meal was their largest of the day, with *supper* in the evening less substantial. All conscientious wives thought about the preparation of the day's meals first thing in the morning. Lucy felt *almost* guilty that she wasn't doing the same thing.

Early summer it might have been, but as Lucy walked down the sidewalk, she was reminded that in the mountains that doesn't guarantee warmth, especially early in the morning. The smell from cooking stoves was today enhanced by fireplaces sending up smoke from pine and cedar fires just catching. The aroma of frying bacon wafted from a nearby café, and Lucy felt a wave of something akin to nostalgia that startled her as she recognized its source.

She didn't want to be merely a visitor here. She wanted this town to be *her* town, where she felt more at home than any place she had ever lived. She thought back to when she and Freda had been here at its beginning, when there had been mere crude cabins, stores and gambling halls in tents, and a muddy track connecting it all. From that to what it was now had spanned over a dozen productive years and several destructive fires, so that the townspeople were understandably proud of their town.

It had also been here in '49 that she had met Jim, a young gambler with a good reputation, while she had been only a girl of thirteen and indentured to Freda and her husband. But she had not been too young to summon her courage, and had therefore saved his life. Now, looking back, they each felt that the other had been the savior. A number of years had passed, with many challenges met, but eventually they had been able to marry. Yes, Lucy thought, Placerville is very special to me.

With all of this in mind, it made Lucy even more determined to discover the source of the letters, and if possible, also whoever had murdered Mrs. Helms. But she now realized that it had become more than the challenge of solving the source of the letters. Not only had the letter writer tainted her sense of the town as her personal refuge, but the writer had stolen from many good people their sense of trust and faith in one another. So much had this been the case for Mrs. Butterick that she had taken her own life rather than lose her standing among the community. The injustice of no one being held accountable brought to mind the phrase "a viper in Paradise", and heightened Lucy's determination to oust the person from *her* paradise.

She turned to her right and made her way to the Round Tent Store. Rebuilt after the fire of '56, it was no longer round or in a tent, even while retaining its original name. Its brick façade, rounded on one corner, extended into the road so that the sidewalk now swept around the front of the building in order to continue down the street. This created a narrowing of the road that sometimes caused a bottleneck in the flow of traffic, but it was also a favorite place to cross because it meant less time on what was often a muddy street.

Walking across the store's freshly swept, wood plank floor, Lucy scanned the neatly folded men's clothing laid out on rough lumber tables that had been whitewashed and covered in sheeting. She knew there would be nothing for ladies here, but she thought she might find something for Roger, as it did stock clothing for boys.

The rest of the store all the way to the back contained tables and shelves laden with men's shirts, pants and boots, and racks of men's suits. Rolling ladders along the walls gave access to the upper reaches of the shelving, while barrels and boxes intruded at the edges of the wide central aisle.

But the most interesting thing in the store for Lucy was Jane Leon, off to the side of the room. She was running a hand over the rough surface of a bolt of durable upholstery fabric, her brow furrowed as she looked up at alternative bolts on a near shelf.

Without stopping to think through what she was going to say when she reached her, Lucy made her way directly to her target. "Mrs. Leon! How delightful to see you."

"Hello, Mrs. Murphy." Jane Leon took great pains to match her face to the perkiness of her words. Nevertheless, Lucy could tell that it took a definite effort as Jane politely added, "This store is surely a nice alternative to being outdoors today."

"Yes, my thought exactly," Lucy smiled. "Are you purchasing fabric for some specific project?"

"Yes." She gave no details, asking instead, "And you, Mrs. Murphy?"

"Oh, please call me Lucy. Our acquaintance has been of long enough duration that it pleases me to think of you as a friend now."

"You're quite right. I feel the same." Jane suddenly relaxed and her smile was genuine.

"I came in to see what items might be available for my son." Lucy looked again at the fabric in Jane Leon's hands.

Seeing this, Jane said, "My husband's desk chair in his study needs recovering." Jane then chuckled and shook her head. "That's what we call a corner of the parlor where he sits at his desk. We even have it screened off to give him some semblance of privacy. Fortunately, the French doors behind him give good light during the day."

"How nice for him."

"He jokes that I have the whole rest of the house and control of the money. So he says that when he's home from his pack trips, he should have some little place that's just his." She smiled as she added, "My part of the parlor has the fireplace, so he can have his drafty old corner."

"Is that the room that was broken into?"

Jane frowned and nodded her head. "That was so odd."

"In what way?"

"Nothing was taken," she declared, her tone still one of amazement. "The catch on the French doors had been forced and mud from the garden had been tracked in on the floor. But that was all that seemed amiss."

"Do you think the burglar was interrupted?"

"Possibly. Tony was very upset over it. More than I thought the incident warranted. I teased him that it was supposed to be the woman who over-reacts to such things."

Lucy laughed appropriately. "How did he take that?"

"Oh, fine. I don't think he was less upset, but he hid it better."

Jane had a clerk take the bolt of fabric to the counter for cutting, and the two women walked through an area full of miscellaneous items. There were supplies for leather repair, racks of knives of all kinds, and other small tools a man might desire.

"I need to buy a new pair of scissors," Mrs. Leon sighed. "I lost mine somewhere in the house."

Lucy picked up a long velvet pouch and pulled out a pair of scissors with beautifully sculpted, ornate handles. "These are nice."

Jane shook her head. "No, they're for normal people. I'm left-handed, and my scissors were made for left-handed users." When Lucy frowned down at the ones in her hand, Mrs. Leon took them from her. "You can tell the difference at a glance, because with these the shearing edge is visible. If I use them with my left hand the cutting edge of the scissors is behind the top blade, and it's more difficult to see what I'm cutting."

Lucy switched the scissors to her left hand to see what was being described. "So with left-handed scissors, all of that is reversed and you can indeed see what you're cutting."

"That's right. Now I just need to see if they sell any here. They're not that common, and that's why I feel like such a dunce for having mislaid mine."

Scrambling in her mind for a way to bring up either the anonymous letters or the murder of Mrs. Helms, Lucy decided to just dive in. "I guess you heard that my friend Dolly Robbins was the one who discovered the body of Mrs. Helms."

"Yes." She turned to face Lucy. "Was it very upsetting for her?"

"She was shocked at first, of course." It flitted through Lucy's mind that Dolly's shock had very quickly turned to curiosity. But then, she could say the same thing about herself.

"What a thing for a young woman to have seen!" Jane declared, expressing the proper comment expected of a lady. But she couldn't hide a tinge of prurient interest when she asked, "Was there much blood?"

"No, I don't think so." Lucy decided to come right out and ask what she really wanted to know. "Did you and Mr. Leon know Mrs. Helms?"

"Oh, no." Jane moved further down the aisle, stopping at a table of men's gloves. "Tony did tell me of the gossip about her that he'd picked up in the saloons. That was just before he left on his last trip. So I knew what men were saying. But I wanted to see and hear her for myself. That's why I went to the same talk you attended."

"Oh, I didn't see you." Feeling herself at a disadvantage, she quickly added, "I would have come over to say hello if I had. There were so many women there."

"The flyer she had circulated said 'any and all women invited'. That was a mistake. Even a few of the soiled doves decided to attend."

"Yes, I saw them at the back of the room. A couple of them even asked questions."

Jane shook her head with indignation undisguised. "Imagine such women casting votes if the suffragists get their way!"

"Some might assert that they're still citizens, and therefore have the right to participate in voting for those who run the state or country in which they live."

Jane looked at her with a scandalized expression that Lucy knew could put an end to any further conversation, so she quickly added, "I mean, that's probably what Mrs. Helms and her supporters would say."

"Oh, well, I suppose so. If one thought the subject a proper one to debate."

"Would you like to vote?"

Jane hesitated only a moment. "Yes! Yes, I would." She smiled at Lucy. "I have no doubt you would."

Lucy laughed, taking it as a compliment, whether it was meant that way or not. "Why do you say that?"

"Oh, Lucy, if you could, you'd single-handedly choose the State's next governor. And possibly do a good job of it, too."

Lucy laughed again. "Thank you. I think."

Jane smiled fondly at her friend. "Have you run into much opposition about your trying to find the letter writer?"

No longer surprised that it was popularly known that she was doing this, she said, "Some. I've even received a few threats."

Jane showed her alarm. "Oh, do be careful, Lucy. You never know with some people." She looked directly into Lucy's eyes. "Men and women."

"Mrs. Helms did give an interesting talk, I thought," Lucy commented, unwilling to speculate about possible danger to herself. "But she obviously had a jaundiced view of men."

"The minute you stood up to thank her on behalf of everyone, and thank you for doing that, I got up and left. Tony was due to come home any day and I had baking to do. He'd had several short packing trips over the spring and I was hoping he would be staying home for awhile."

"Where does he go on his trips?"

"Up into the mountains to mining camps where wagons can't get into because of the remoteness of the mines. He brings them supplies until there's too much snow for him to get through. But by then most of the prospectors have come down into town here or Coloma or Auburn. Maybe all the way to Stockton or Sacramento."

"Let's hope Sacramento and the other towns damaged by the flood will be in shape by next winter to receive them."

Jane laughed. "Oh, I'm sure they will be. They need to get businesses up and running as soon as possible. Commerce is a powerful motivator to progress."

Other than inviting Jane to share in some refreshment, which the nature of their meeting and the time of day made awkward, Lucy didn't know how to prolong their visit. Consequently, she excused herself and left the store, unaware that Jane Leon watched her go while wondering why Lucy hadn't purchased anything. Or for that matter appeared to have been all that interested in doing so.

Lucy walked east, past saloons, shops, the theater, and Hinds Blacksmith and Wagon Repair. Her destination was the single story, stone building housing Pearson's Soda Factory, where she purchased a bottle of their soda water. She put it in her shopping bag, looking forward to later pouring it over ice and lemon slices. When she stopped for lunch, she was tempted to drink it then, but forced herself to wait until that evening.

Feeling at loose ends, she wandered into the book store that was housed in a large, but nevertheless claustrophobia-inducing space. After running her eyes over the walls lined with floor to ceiling shelves packed with books, she turned to the tables taking up floor space at the front of the large room. They held stacks of newspapers and pamphlets, some weeks old. Old lithographs framed in dark wood filled the few open spaces on the walls and the ends of shelving units that crossed through the room. Several oil paintings hung on the wall behind the counter next to the front door, offering the brightest colors in the shop.

On this gloomy day, gas wall sconces had been lit and kerosene lamps placed on the tables at the front and back of the room. Customers often had to bring a book near one of the lamps and turn up the wick for greater light if the embossing on a book cover was to be clearly visible.

As used to the presence of kerosene lamps as she was, Lucy still shuddered at the thought of how quickly the room would go up if one of the lamps was knocked over. There were, as in all businesses, buckets of sand on either side of the front door and at several points in the room, most of which had been used to put out cigarettes and cigars. There was also a large, heavy bell next to the door to ring at the first sign of trouble, but she doubted the fire brigade could be fast enough to stop the flames from consuming the whole building. Fire was the most feared event in any town, even one rebuilt with brick buildings after suffering large fires as Placerville had in 1856. After reminding herself that there was a back door to the store, her anxiety abated.

Mrs. Martha Carrasco, the very proper, elderly owner of the bookstore was puttering behind the counter when Lucy entered. Petite and gray, Martha balanced a delicate pair of wire-rimmed glasses on her rabbit-like nose and smiled with contented satisfaction as she began her day.

Martha pulled her shawl up around her shoulders as she watched her only customer meander along the shelves. She wondered if the coolness of the day warranted lighting the small stove. It was next to the counter and she had arranged several chairs near it for those who liked to read next to its warmth. Not only did this offer the customers an inviting change of pace to their day, but it gave Mrs. Carrasco an opportunity to stay current with the latest "news" via overheard conversations.

Someone had suggested that she might bring in more customers if she had coffee available for them, but who had ever heard of such a thing in a book store? It was shameful! It might suggest that she thought people were incapable of providing for themselves. Or worse yet, that she was pandering for business out of desperation. She *was* desperate to make more money, but she was determined that no one would ever suspect it.

Having earlier picked up her mail on the way to the shop, Mrs. Carrasco took her place on the tall stool behind the counter, made sure her skirt was draped to completely cover her ankles, and picked up the letter opener with its pewter handle and thin, sharp blade. She slit all the envelopes, neatly stacked them, and methodically opened each one while briefly assessing their content — bill, order, advertisement, correspondence — before moving on to the next one.

At the seventh envelope, she hesitated with it in her hands. It was addressed in printed letters such as a child would form, unlike the typical flowing script that looked as though a spider had crossed the paper after climbing out of an ink bottle. Proper penmanship was a thing of great importance, and one could often tell if it was the handwriting of someone in trade, a gentleman or lady of refinement, or someone with only a basic education. But printing such as this was beyond anything she had ever seen before in her mail.

The baker came in for his morning newspaper and Mrs. Carrasco put aside the unusual envelope. It wasn't long before it was buried beneath wrapping paper and books, and when she remembered it several days later, she realized it had probably been tossed out. She hoped it hadn't been important, and promptly forgot about it.

Lucy had moved further into the room. Inhaling deeply, she smiled at the singular aroma of mustiness from books sewn together and protected in old leather, those with only starched fabric covering cardboard covers, and boxed sets in thin wooden cases. A layer of dust clung to everything, impossible to eliminate in a town with dirt roads, even if feather-dusted every few days. But the dust didn't hide the glittering embossing on the spines of hundreds of books. The only other place in town that came close to being a large book depository, was a small stationery store on the

Plaza and upstairs at the Neptune Fire Department, where several hundred volumes could be accessed.

The books around Lucy seemed to cry out to her to be taken down, to be paid attention and appreciated, or at least be acknowledged as worth notice. Lucy almost laughed at herself for such a fanciful thought. But then it occurred to her that it was much the same as what people wanted for themselves. This set her to wondering if this thought had come to her because of something that had been said during a recent conversation. Had she missed an important clue?

She took down a small, thin volume at random and sat on a chair at the back of the store next to a large round table. Pulling the lamp closer, she turned the screw that lifted the wick higher, but deep in thought she barely glanced at the book in her hands. Paper protective covers known as dust jackets were not yet applied to books. Instead, book covers consisted of textured hard boards deeply embossed with fancy gold or silver lettering spelling out the title of the book, and occasionally accompanied by designs or simple scenes.

When Lucy finally did look down at the book, she saw that the dark blue, pebbly cover was embossed in gold with the title "*Five Hundred Mistakes Corrected*". Inside, the title page continued the title "*...of Daily Occurrence in Speaking, Pronouncing, and Writing the English Language, CORRECTED*". It had been published in New York in 1856, the same year as Placerville's major fire. She then noticed that across the top of the title page it said, *"Never Too Late to Learn"*.

Being in a contemplative mood, Lucy took the fact that she had randomly chosen this particular book almost as a sign that her pursuit for the truth was appropriate. She was even more convinced that it was an omen when she read the small print beneath the title. *"It is highly important, that whatever we learn or know, we should know correctly; for unless our knowledge be correct, we lose half its value and usefulness."*

As she sat back and let her mind go where it wanted, ungoverned by prejudged dictates, it occurred to her that she was still bothered by the fact that Mr. Leon had visited Mrs. Helms. It must have been just before he had left on his last pack trip, which was about a week before Lucy had arrived in town. He hadn't been on a long trip, because she had overheard him in the barber shop just upon his return.

But Jane Leon had said that she and her husband hadn't known Mrs. Helms. Maybe that was true of Jane, but Tony Leon had known Mrs. Helms well enough to call upon her at her hotel room, and spend nearly half an hour with her. And with raised voices attending the visit.

Why, Lucy thought to herself, does my thought keep returning to Jane's silly left-handed scissors? And then she knew. It was because of the ones she had held in her hands while walking around in Mrs. Helms's room. They had been awkward in her hands because they had not been right-handed scissors, the bows shaped in a way she wasn't used to handling. Could they have been those belonging to Jane? If so, how had they gotten into the room of Mrs. Helms? And out again, since they had not been there when she went in with Marsha, the chambermaid.

Lucy stood up suddenly, the little book dropping to the floor. Scooping it up, she hurried to the front counter and paid for it, not taking the time to allow it to be wrapped. She simply slid it into her shopping bag and hurried back to the Cary House.

Once in her room, she took out her notes and scanned them. She saw nothing there that would preclude the validity of the conclusion she was forming. If those had been the scissors belonging to Jane Leon, had they been brought to Mrs. Helms's room along with the paste and newspaper? Had they been brought there by the killer or someone else for reasons of their own? Would that account for the shred of newspaper found on *top* of the body? If brought there before the murder, it could indicate premeditation of what followed. But in that case, why not stab Mrs. Helms with the scissors? No, the newspapers, paste and scissors must have been brought there *after* the killing.

Lucy was almost dizzy with what this, if true, might mean. Of course, it didn't necessarily mean that Mr. Leon had killed Mrs. Helms, but it might fit in with him or Jane being the anonymous letter writer. But why would either of them do such a thing to the town? And then there was the break-in at their house sometime during the same night as the murder, which meant they too had been victimized. Or had they? Could Tony or Jane have simply made it look that way?

Lucy sat back in her chair, looked out the window, and felt as gloomy as the weather. She was feeling that sudden, plummeting sensation that follows the discovery of an exciting theory when it is realized that one has no idea what to do with it. How could she prove that Jane or Tony was the perpetrator, if she came to the conclusion that they were? Did one of them bring those cut up newspapers into Mrs. Helms's room to divert suspicion onto her? Was it simply to suggest that one of the recipients of the letters, sent by Mrs. Helms, had killed her in a rage?

Lucy decided to clear her mind with some other activity. Reclining on the bed with her back against the headboard, she opened the little blue book she had purchased that day. Before long, however, she had dozed off while contemplating supper that evening at Dolly's house. Unfortunately, she slept right through until almost midnight.

That same night Jane Leon watched her husband sleeping soundly next to her, his regular breathing interrupted occasionally by his signature snort. He hadn't been sleeping well lately, showing an exhaustion unusual for him, so Jane was glad that he had finally fallen into a deep sleep.

Now it was Jane's turn to deal with sleeplessness. Her conversation with Lucy buzzed through her mind like an angry wasp, but she staunchly refused to bat it away. Earlier, she felt that Lucy had harbored a special reason for engaging her in conversation. But after having reviewed several times what had been said between them, she wasn't sure if this was true. It had seemed so typical of any such meeting between women, but somehow Tony had been inserted into the conversation more than she would have thought necessary.

Tony *had* become unusually tense and anxious lately, and she couldn't understand why. She had several times started to ask him, but he never seemed to be in the right state of mind for anything approaching a confrontation. And he was home so seldom. It was easy to justify avoiding the subject.

However, now she wondered if anything untoward had happened on this last trip of his to make him so unusually distant and pre-occupied. He had even snapped at her several times, something he had never done before, although she often sensed that he was on the verge of saying something sharp. But he had always pulled back. It bothered her a great deal that she couldn't pin-point the source of his recent fretfulness. Most of the time she found it easy to lead him in the direction she wanted. But that was when she was sure of his mood. This change seemed to have started immediately after the break-in. "But nothing was taken," she repeated once again to herself.

It then occurred to her that maybe what the intruder had wanted was still there. But what on earth could that be? Sliding out of bed, she didn't bother pulling on a robe over her long, bleached-cotton nightdress, but instead quickly and silently closed the door of their bedroom behind her.

Sitting in the chair behind Tony's desk, Jane nerved herself to do something she had often thought of doing, but each time could not summon the courage. Now, however, she felt different about it, and she went through the drawers of his desk without further hesitation. Bills, fliers for businesses, advertisements of goods and services, and notes made to remind himself what to take on his trips were all jumbled together in the large drawer to the right of the knee hole where he kept envelopes for correspondence.

The shallow middle drawer contained pencils and note pads, beneath which she found his scissors. This reminded her of the pair she was missing. She had always kept them on the table next to her chair near her sewing basket, out in the open readily at hand. This only added to her puzzlement as to where they could be.

Tugging on the large, left-hand drawer, she found it locked. Knowing that Tony carried no key ring, she remembered once seeing him reach to the back of the middle drawer. After groping along the back of it, she found the small key that fit the drawer. She pulled it open slowly, as though expecting something to leap out at her. But all she saw was a box of white drawing paper. Lifting out the box of paper, beneath was revealed a pile of shredded newspaper.

Looking more closely, Jane realized that most of the newsprint was composed of headlines and sub-headings neatly cut from newspapers like the one neatly folded in the drawer. His old collar box was also in the drawer, now full of cut out individual words. As much as she fought it, as she poked through these and saw the nature of the words in the box, she could not avoid an obvious conclusion. She also fought a rising wave of fear-induced nausea.

A sound startled her, but she quickly realized it was just a bush scraping the side of the house in the rising wind. Nevertheless, she put everything back the way she had found it and quickly locked the drawer, returning the key to exactly where she had found it.

In an effort to still the heavy beating of her heart, she sat back and closed her eyes. When she opened them, she was facing the tall shelf of

books on the wall to the right of the desk. Tony was a great reader, proud
of how many books he owned. However, the top shelf held those books
she had never seen him take down. This was a location beyond her reach
when she was dressed because of the confines of her corset. Now free of
that wretched undergarment, she stretched up and brought down one of
the books. Opening it to the title page, she read there a scrawled note:
Happy Birthday. M.A. 50.

Jane put it back and took down another. This one was inscribed *Happy
Anniversary*, and the Roman numeral for five. Several of the others simply
had a book plate on the inside of the cover: *Property of L. Anthony.*

Making sure the books were exactly as she had found them, she moved
from behind the screened desk to her chair by the unlit fireplace. She
stared at the cold ashes and bit her lip. Who was L. Anthony and why
were these books on her husband's shelves? Were these from an old flame
of his? She knew he had been "busy" before they were married, a thought
that didn't sit comfortably but one she had accepted years ago.

A more comfortable thought was that many times people had given
him goods in lieu of money when paying for the supplies he brought them.
She smiled as she remembered the chicken he had brought home for her
to cook, the fishing rod he still used, and a small painting of a stream now
on the opposite wall. He had even brought her a small bundle of papers
that had turned out to be a short story written by some fellow named
Clemens, whose handwriting had been difficult to read. Consequently,
after struggling through one reading of the story, they had used it to start
that evening's fire. With a shrug, Jane relegated the books to the category
of payment in trade for services.

She could not so easily forget the locked drawer. This was a problem she
could not solve simply by ignoring it, but she also didn't want to confront
it right then. She made her way back to the warmth of their bed, and soon
her shock and fear was swallowed up by the blessed blackness of sleep.

When Jane awoke the next morning, the other half of the bed was
empty. She found this surprising since Tony always slept late when he was
recently home from a trip. As she slipped into her bathrobe, she walked to
her dressing table and found a note from Tony lying there. It said he had
an early appointment and would be back for a late breakfast.

However, by ten o'clock he had not returned and Jane was becoming
irritated at his thoughtlessness. The biscuits were cold, the bacon only fit

for a sandwich, and the eggs fed to the neighbor's dog. However, being somewhat quixotic in her moods, all of this irritation vanished when she heard footsteps on the gravel path leading to the front door. Hearing the door knocker bang gently, she wondered why Tony would not just come on in and hurried to open it for him.

"Lucy! And Officer Reynolds." So many questions and fears raced through Jane's mind that she couldn't say anything more. Had they discovered that it was Tony who had written the letters? Oh, God, what would become of them now?

"Jane, may we come in?"

"Oh, yes. Of course, Lucy." She moved aside and led the way into the parlor.

Lucy took Jane's arm and guided her to the sofa where she sat next to her. Taking Jane's hand in her own, Lucy said, "We have some very bad news. You must prepare yourself. Mr. Leon was found this morning, dead."

"What? That can't be." Jane shook her head, then explained. "He left here early this morning for an appointment."

Officer Reynolds spoke then. "Do you know who it was with?"

"His note didn't say." She turned back to Lucy. "Where is he? He can't be dead." Nevertheless, her face was white and her chin was quivering.

"He was found at the Robbins Livery. He was in the stall of a horse."

Jane stared in horror, first at Lucy and then at the officer. While allowing Mrs. Leon to absorb the shock of what she had just been told, Officer Reynolds stood looking down at the two women, but his attention was focused on Mrs. Leon. After several minutes while Jane fought to control her emotions, he told the new widow, "The horse had not killed him. He was already dead when he was put into the stall."

Jane took a moment to think about what he was saying, then asked, "How do you know?"

"We just do. Take my word for it." He couldn't tell this woman that the horse had not after all trod on the lifeless body of her husband as the killer had probably assumed when he placed the body there. If that could have been believed, it might have been thought that was the cause of his death, and the death therefore ruled as an accident. But the crushed skull had been caused by something other than a horse's hoof.

Lucy went into the kitchen and found the pot of hot coffee on the stove. She poured out a cup and added a good helping of sugar to it before bringing it to Jane. "Here, drink this."

But Jane just stared at it. Lucy forced her to take the cup, and after an effort to swallow some of it, Jane looked up at Lucy. "I need to show you something."

Lucy and Officer Reynolds followed her to Tony's desk and watched her retrieve the key to the locked drawer. She handed the key to Lucy and moved away from the desk to sit in her chair by the fireplace. "You'll want to see what's inside the left-hand drawer."

As Lucy sat down, she was just able to see Jane beyond the screen in front of the desk. Opening the drawer, she looked down into it and said, "I don't understand. What's so odd about a box of paper?"

"Look under that."

After removing the box of paper, she said, "There's nothing beneath it."

Jane went even whiter than before, then bound forward to look into the empty drawer. "But...but..."

"What did you expect to be in it?" Lucy asked gently.

Jane looked at her friend. "I don't want to say."

"Tony was the letter writer, wasn't he?"

"I..." Her face flushed red and her throat went dry. Jane groped her way back to her chair as she said, "Yes. I just discovered it last night. There were cut out headlines along with words and phrases, all organized in that drawer. When I woke up this morning, I was going to confront him, but he had left the house."

"I'm so sorry," Lucy told her.

Jane turned to Officer Reynolds. "Do you have to tell your superiors? I mean, now that he's dead, the letters will stop."

"I'm sorry." And in fact, he looked a very unhappy man. "I have to put it in my report. What they do with the information is up to them."

"Yes, I see that." She shut her eyes. "Oh, God, I'll be so despised."

"But like you said," Lucy told her, "he's dead, and it wasn't you that wrote the letters. You'll be characterized as having been betrayed by your husband. You'll be pitied, not despised."

Jane met Lucy's eyes. "I'm not sure but what that's worse."

As Lucy and Officer Reynolds walked back into town, he told her, "Thank you for coming with me. I figured she would take the news better from a woman. But I had no idea you'd figured out that Tony was the letter writer."

"I wasn't sure and was trying to find a way to confront him about it. Evidently someone else figured it out first."

"And violently." He shook his head as he remembered seeing the bloodied body of someone he had known, and how his stomach had lurched.

Lucy frowned at him. "But why kill him?"

"Why? Because they were furious." It seemed obvious to him.

"But why? Did Tony threaten to make public something he had discovered about them? Someone who would write anonymous letters might not balk at a little blackmail. On the other hand, the newspaper pieces in the drawer that Jane found might not have been of Tony's creation. He might have taken them from someone and was holding onto them."

"You mean he attempted blackmail of the letter writer? I wouldn't have thought him that stupid, and that would have been a very stupid thing to do." Following this thought to its logical conclusion, Officer Reynolds told Lucy, "Still, he must have removed the letter writing stuff from the drawer of his desk, and brought it with him to the meeting at the livery. Having the cut-up newspaper pieces with him would have served as proof that Tony was the anonymous letter writer. Or, as you surmised, he might have stolen the stuff from the person who was. Either way, his knowledge must have been harmful to whoever he was meeting with. His victim must have been terrified of exposure of some kind. So much so that he struck out when he had the opportunity."

"And evidently the killer did have the opportunity," Lucy reasoned. "What part of his head was struck?"

"The back toward the top."

"Then he had turned his back to the person with him." They looked at each other, not missing the significance of what this meant. "What was he hit with?"

"Whatever it was, it was heavy and the doctor says round."

"For it to partially crush in a man's head, I would imagine that it would take a lot of strength."

"Fury or desperation can ramp up a person's strength."

"True."

After a few moments walking in contemplative silence, Officer Reynolds said, "Funny that Dolly found Mrs. Helms's body, and Robert found Mr. Leon's body."

Lucy stopped and faced him squarely. "Are you hinting that they had anything to do with these murders?"

He turned red, but continued. "I can't see that they'd have a reason to do it. I mean, Mrs. Robbins wanted you and her to have a meal with Mrs. Helms like so many women did, which was why she went to see her, right? And Tony's body was probably in Robert's stable because that's where Tony kept his mules and his horse. Still, it's an odd coincidence."

"Yes, it is," Lucy admitted reluctantly. "I do find it interesting that the meeting had to have been set yesterday, and yet Jane knew nothing about it, meaning that Tony kept the meeting a secret from her."

"Or so she says," Officer Reynolds pointed out. Before Lucy could comment, he hurried on. "One thing I noticed at the scene of the crime. The killer had dragged Tony into that stall, but only just inside. I could see the drag marks. They'd been scuffed at with a shoe, but I could still see what they were."

"Could you tell what kind of a shoe did the scuffing?"

"No. Too much straw on the ground."

That evening it was a somber gathering around the Robbins kitchen table as the women waited for Robert to arrive home for supper.

"It's so hard to believe," Dolly said again for the fourth time.

"Oh, for heaven's sake, Dolly," Melanie snapped at her sister. "Can't you say something else?"

Dolly stared at her in surprise. "Well, I'm sorry. But I feel sorry for Jane."

"How much had you ever talked to him?" Melanie asked sharply.

"I never did. I saw him a few times in passing at Robert's livery and on the street, but I never had occasion to talk to him. I never even looked him in the eyes." She couldn't hide her embarrassment. "I seldom do with men. I don't want to be accused of... well, you know."

"Flirting?"

"Something like that."

"Well," Melanie said, "I did talk to him." That got her the focus of the other two women, and she couldn't hide her gloat of satisfaction. "I saw him at the post office the other day as we lined up at the window. He asked me if I was your sister and I said I was. He mentioned how much he liked Robert and the way he cared for his animals. Then the line moved and it was his turn at the window."

"That was it?" Lucy asked.

"Yes. He was gone by the time I was finished mailing my letter."

"What was your impression of him?"

"He was just another man, although..." Melanie hesitated. "Oh, I don't know. Maybe what has happened colors my judgment, but I felt uncomfortable. There was a speculative look in his eyes. You know how men assess an attractive woman."

"Could be," Dolly told her. "Everyone says he has a roving eye. Um, *had* a roving eye."

"Yes," Lucy put in, "but I wonder if he ever actually cheated on Jane."

Melanie gasped out, "Damn his soul to hell!"

Surprised at the degree of venom in her words, Lucy was about to tell them that Tony had written the letters, but she hesitated a moment too long. Robert opened the front door, and Dolly rushed out to him. "Are you okay?"

"Yes. The police had a number of questions, especially after they found that it was my anvil hammer that was the weapon used."

"How do they know that?"

"It had his blood and hair on it." Dolly swallowed hard, trying not to picture it. At the same time, she was grateful that Robert had not treated her like some "frail flower of womanhood", a phrase often attributed to women in popular literature.

"The horse really didn't stomp on him?" Melanie asked from the kitchen door.

"Even if it had, it couldn't kill a dead body."

Melanie shuddered and returned to the table with Lucy as Dolly told him, "Supper is ready."

"I think I'd like a drink first. You gals go ahead without me."

Robert moved to the sideboard's silver tray holding a number of bottles and reached for his favorite whiskey. Dolly went into the kitchen and brought the pot of chicken and dumplings to the table, serving it up for the three of them.

As they ate, and Robert sat on the front porch with his drink, Lucy stared into her bowl. Why would anyone bother to move the body? Why did it matter if it was thought to be the result of a bashing with the heavy iron hammer, or a stomping by a horse, if the murder weapon was to be left behind and not even wiped clean? Maybe it showed that the killer, unused to such violence, was too upset to think clearly. Or maybe that he had heard someone coming and hid the body in case he was found there before escaping. Would he have been willing to kill anyone who found him there, or would he have tried to convince them that the horse had killed Tony?

Decades later, the police might have tried to lift fingerprints from the hammer, but such a possibility was not yet developed. Footprints had been considered, but nothing of note had been seen in the straw-padded dirt of the livery other than a few splashes of blood and the drag marks. Without the science of forensics, only an item found at the scene of the crime would have attracted attention. Even photos were unavailable, but sometimes a police sketch artist might make a drawing of the scene for the records.

On her way home, Lucy shook her head and took a deep breath. No wonder Jane had told them that Tony had seemed anxious lately. He had discovered that some of the cut newspapers on top of his desk, along with the paste pot and Jane's scissors, had been stolen the same night that Mrs. Helms had been killed. Then later, when they were mentioned as being in Mrs. Helms's room, he couldn't help but have realized that it meant someone knew his secret, which opened him up to exposure or even blackmail. So why was Tony dead, and not whoever knew his secret, because Lucy didn't doubt that Tony would have been capable of killing someone to protect his secret. And, in fact, may already have done that to Mrs. Helms.

Had Tony killed her and then brought the letter making items there to make the police believe she was the sender of the letters? Had he then remembered that the scissors were unusual enough that someone might connect them to Jane, and so he came back for them?

As Lucy pondered the situation, she concluded that whoever had made a second visit to bring the letter writer's paraphernalia to Mrs. Helms's room had known she was dead already, either because they had killed her, or knew who had. But if it wasn't Tony who killed her, why would the person who had killed her want to divert suspicion away from Tony and onto Mrs. Helms as the letter writer? One name came to mind immediately, along with two troubling questions. Did Jane really have no prior knowledge of Tony being the letter writer? And had their marriage really been a happy one?

CHAPTER 8

"I'm not denyin' the women are foolish:
God Almighty made 'em to match the men."
George Eliot

Thursday, June 12 and Friday, June 13

Robert had gone to town earlier than was his normal habit, eating little of his breakfast. So when Lucy arrived at Dolly's house, she pitched in to help prepare the mid-day meal, knowing Robert would be hungry sooner than usual.

Lucy asked, "Why did he go to work so early?"

"I don't know." Dolly started to say that she had been afraid to ask, but held that back. "He often does this when there's some horse he's preoccupied about."

The two women worked comfortably together with little conversation until Lucy asked, "Where's Melanie?"

"She went into town to visit with a friend."

"I'm sorry I haven't been able to solve the mystery of who killed Mrs. Helms." She hesitated, wondering why she had not yet informed Dolly of her conversation with Jane Leon and their conclusion that it was Tony Leon who had written the letters. Every time she had started to tell her, she had pulled back. Having learned to always listen to her hunches, Lucy also didn't tell her now. And once again, she felt a prick at her conscience.

After several moments where Lucy chopped vegetables and Dolly stirred the stew on the stove, Dolly spoke up. "Lucy, I need to tell you something." Lucy stopped chopping the green peppers and gave Dolly her full attention. When Dolly spoke again, it was almost in a whisper. "That last letter I received hinted that my first husband had not died by accident."

Before Dolly could say more, Lucy turned back to the chopping board while saying, "It was declared an accident and that's all that matters if anyone looks up the coroner's record."

"But..."

Lucy looked over her shoulder, directly into Dolly's eyes. "It's done and over! Now, do you want all of these peppers in the cornbread batter?"

Dolly slowly nodded, but they both knew it wasn't about the peppers. Nevertheless, Lucy dumped them all into the batter before placing the pan into the oven.

A few minutes later Dolly addressed Lucy's earlier comment. "Maybe you haven't found out who sent the letters, but I get the impression that no more have been received by anyone. Evidently, whoever was sending them has decided it's unwise to continue, and that's possibly because of all the questions you've been asking." She turned to Lucy with a cagey smile. "But they might start up again once you leave, so maybe you and Jim should move here."

Lucy looked at her for a long moment. "I guess we could."

"Oh, I was just kidding!" Dolly laughed.

"But why not?" Lucy shrugged. "The only reason we settled in Jamestown was because it was where I came to rest after... well, after I left Nevada City." It was an understatement, considering that leaving when she did had been a matter of survival. "After I inherited the house in Jamestown from the woman I was caring for, it made sense to stay there. I do like the town very much, but there really isn't anything keeping us from selling up and moving here."

"Oh, Lucy, how I would love that!" Dolly gave the stew a couple of stirs before turning back to Lucy. "Wait a minute. Why aren't you more surprised by the idea?"

Lucy's eyes crinkled with humor. "Let's sit and have a cup of coffee while the cornbread bakes." Both women appreciated being able to sit down for a break, so Dolly removed the stew pot from the stove and poured them each a hearty mug of coffee, foregoing the more usual cup and saucer formality. After they were settled at the kitchen table, Lucy said, "I received a letter yesterday from Jim saying that a new family has come to Jamestown. The man has something to do with railroads. They asked Jim if he might be wanting to sell the house, offering him far above the market value. The man said our house and its out-buildings suited as nothing else in town would. Jim told him it was my decision because the house was left to me."

"Did you write him back yet?"

"I telegraphed him." She actually flushed as she looked at her friend, knowing how important her reply was to her. "I said it was okay with me, but the final decision was up to him."

Dolly giggled. "That was very tactful of you."

Lucy smiled in return. "No doubt Mrs. Helms would have been disappointed in my deferring to a man when I didn't have to. And Jim may even have laughed when he read the telegram. But that doesn't mean that somewhere in his masculine soul he doesn't appreciate that I did defer to him."

"Do you think he'll accept the offer?" Dolly felt herself holding her breath. She loved these visits from Lucy, but they were spread too far apart and were followed by several days of realizing her loneliness, which was odd given that she had a husband and many local friends, not to mention busy days of chores. But she and Lucy had a shared past about which few had knowledge, and when with Lucy she could relax and just be herself. And Lucy had always been her champion. As much as she had been accepted in town, Dolly knew there would always be those women who would never accept her because of her past.

The memory of one of Lucy's visits flashed to mind. They had been at a party, and Dolly had made mention that she admired the fact that so many women in Placerville had their own businesses, and that a few of the married women even worked outside the home.

One old cat had loudly remarked, "Yes, you know all about being a *working girl*."

Dolly had turned red and looked toward the exit, but stopped when she heard Lucy snap back, "Because it's so much more honorable to marry an older man, not for love but for his money."

The woman had walked away, red-faced and in a huff. No one at that party ever openly criticized Dolly again, even when Lucy was not in town. Now, with moments like this in mind, Dolly waited for Lucy's answer.

"Yes, I think he'll accept the offer. He'll send me a telegram when everything has been finalized. I've written him to say that once everything is set to go, Freda and Roger should come ahead by stage and Jim can drive our rig along with the freighter bringing our things. It'll take a bit longer than if he rode ahead on his horse, but we'll have a rig of our own here."

Dolly couldn't hold back her laughter. "Lucy, you should be planning campaigns in the war!"

Lucy smiled as she said, "I am a bit of a planner, aren't I? But so is Jim, and I'm just being practical."

In a spontaneous gesture of pure joy Dolly rushed at Lucy and embraced her. It was at this moment that Melanie walked into the kitchen, having entered the house without their having heard her. Correctly reading the glint in Melanie's eye and the curl of her lip, Lucy knew she was about to say something snarky. To head her off, Lucy turned to face her. "Dolly is excited about some news she just received."

"Oh, yes!" Dolly exclaimed. "Lucy and Jim are moving here."

After a short pause, Melanie said, "Really? When?"

Lucy answered as Dolly returned to the stove to put the dinner back on the fire. "We'll move here as soon as Jim completes the sale of our house in Jamestown."

Melanie started to say something, but Dolly swung around at that moment. "I just remembered! I have a friend with a fairly large house over on Cedar Ravine that would be perfect for you. They're wanting to sell, but haven't been successful."

"Is there something wrong with the house?" Lucy asked.

"Not at all. But it's too large for some people. It looks small across the front, but it goes back quite away from the road, and there's a second floor." Hearing the front door open, Dolly removed the pot from the stove and put it on a large tile in the middle of the kitchen table. "Here's Robert." She rushed at him as he entered the kitchen while visibly sniffing the good smells welcoming him home. Dolly grabbed his arm and asked, "Sweetheart, can you let Lucy and me have a rig this afternoon?"

"Of course." He grinned as he added, "But can we eat first?"

Dolly patted his arm and returned to the kitchen, catching him up with the over-all plan while she cut into the pan of hot cornbread and placed large pieces on a plate. While Lucy carried the plate to the table, she watched Melanie. She had taken on a stillness that might have looked like poise, but was belied throughout the meal by the tenseness of her shoulders and a jaw so tight she could barely chew her food.

She ate little and remained quiet as the conversation around her continued. It was clear to Lucy, although obviously not to Dolly or Robert, that Melanie was not at all pleased with the idea of Lucy moving to town. Not surprised, but still a little hurt by it, Lucy was grateful that she and Dolly were leaving Melanie at home while they took the rig into town for shopping as well as to Cedar Ravine.

The house was indeed a large one, and not far off Main Street. The ground floor had a reasonably large parlor, a dining room, and a kitchen large enough for a small table in front of a window facing the side yard. A steel range enrobed in just enough burnished nickel plating to make it enviable but not ostentatious sat next to the back door that was not far from the wood shed. Up a narrow flight of stairs were four bedrooms, the largest with two wardrobe closets. There was also a box room for storage, and a ladder-accessible attic.

A bath house had recently been built onto the rear of the house complete with a small stove to heat water next to three large tubs for washing clothes or people. One of the tubs had a new clothes wringer attached to its side by large butterfly screws, and Dolly paid particular attention to it, not hiding her envy. The property also had a small barn large enough for their rig, as well as four horses if they ever had that many.

The owners, who had remained in the parlor while Lucy and Dolly walked through the house, were thrilled at the offer Lucy made them. When they accepted her handshake to settle the deal, Lucy was impressed. Nevertheless, the husband insisted on meeting with Jim when he got to town so they could be assured of his approval, and the men could then sign the transfer of deed. Lucy fought an ironic laugh as she thought again of Mrs. Helms.

On the way back into town, the two women stopped at the telegraph office so Lucy could notify Jim. As they left, Dolly commented that she hoped Jim wouldn't be too surprised at Lucy's audacity to make such an arrangement without him. But Lucy said nothing, aware of Jim's complete trust in her judgment. Upper most in her mind was the thought that they would have a house soon after her family arrived in Placerville. Lucy looked up at the gathering of summer thunderclouds and knew a sense of peace that was profound.

Later that day a telegram was received back from Jim with only one word. "Satisfactory!"

With everything in her personal life fitting together so well, Lucy was even more disappointed that she had not discovered who had killed Mrs. Helms. And now there was the additional puzzle of Tony Leon's death. Although she knew the solution of the letters, even though she still had not admitted this to Dolly, there was still the question of who had tried to make it seem as though Mrs. Helms had been the writer of those letters.

Until something pointed in another direction, Lucy was assuming it must have been Mrs. Helms's killer who brought the letter making supplies into the hotel room. She just wasn't sure why they would have done such a thing. Of course, by deflecting attention about the letters *onto* Mrs. Helms, it at the same time deflected attention *away from* the actual sender. And, at the same time, attached the motive of her killing to the letters. But, Lucy wondered, was there more to it than that?

She had given less thought to the murder of Tony Leon because she had thought it an active police investigation. However, according to Officer Reynolds, the police had run into a dead end with both murders, and didn't know what more to do. But unlike the police, who had concluded that Mrs. Helms was the writer of the letters, Lucy knew otherwise. Officer Reynolds did too, and had explained this to his superiors. Even so, they were still inclined to think Mrs. Helms had been trying to blackmail someone. The police had also decided that Tony had been killed as part of an effort to rob him, because his pockets had been searched and were empty, and his pocket watch had been taken.

J. J. had, of course, explained again to his superiors all that Jane had said to him in front of Lucy. But they had pointed out that even if Tony had been the letter writer, which they continued to doubt because it was usually "a woman thing", that fact probably had nothing to do with his death, which looked like a simple robbery gone bad. Sensing that his opinions were not being welcomed, J.J. ceased trying to convince them otherwise.

After the women had completed their shopping and returned the rig to Robert's livery, they walked down Sacramento Street and through the Chinese District to Pacific Street. They felt perfectly safe here, although in some towns no white woman would have considered it wise to linger in such a neighborhood, as the perception of the time by most women was that such districts consisted of heathens, opium dens and "other vices". But in Placerville, to most people the Chinese were considered to be just people providing for their families like everyone else, even if their habits were peculiar and their religion not understood. Of course, there were always those who carried prejudices and talked against them, so the Chinese residents kept primarily to their own part of town.

At the corner of Sacramento and Benham Streets, Dolly stopped to purchase dried fruit at a small, stone-fronted market. Upon leaving, she stopped to introduce Lucy to a Chinese man lounging on a bench out front.

"Lucy, I would like you to meet Tuck Hing. He's been a merchant here since last year. He's a 'Tai' or community leader, and he acts as an arbitrator if there are disputes among his people. You can always trust the quality of his products."

He was a small man, like most of his race, but this did not keep his bearing from being imposing. His eyes were kind, but piercing in their depth of perception, with his mustache and small, pointed beard neatly trimmed. He was dressed in white cotton pants, a dark tunic with a simple round collar, and a pill-box hat sitting above the long braid down his back. But it was his hands that caught Lucy's attention. Long, gracefully tapered fingers held what at first looked like a stick, but upon closer observation turned out to be a strange looking pipe.

Lucy told him, "It's a pleasure to meet you."

"You come get vegetables next week. Corn very good this year."

"Thank you. I will."

Mr. Hing puffed on his pipe and looked toward town, the two women dismissed from his attention. They took the hint and continued on their way.

They passed what the whites called a Joss House, but was more accurately called a *Mue*. It sat atop a steep flight of thirteen steps leading up to what looked like a type of colorful temple. Lucy admired the architectural details of tiles, peaked shingled roof, and beaded accents over doors and windows. During the gold rush, the Chinese had been harassed and taxed out of business, and in many towns still were. Lucy was glad that in Placerville they were accepted as a colorful part of society, at least as long as they "toed the mark", as some men expressed their acceptance of the Chinese presence.

After walking up the steepness of Pacific Street, they were pleased to find Melanie greeting them with a tea tray that included sandwiches and freshly baked cookies. Melanie offered to serve, and poured out for Lucy first. She did so with a smile of contrition that Lucy graciously accepted without comment.

After Dolly enthusiastically described to Melanie the interior of the Cedar Ravine house, Lucy spoke up on a different topic. "Something I've been told by several people keeps gnawing at me and I would like to bring it up."

Dolly's eyes widened, surprised more by the serious and tentative tone of Lucy's delivery than by her words. Melanie's already upright posture stiffened and she turned her full attention onto Lucy. Dolly offered assurance. "You know you can say anything to us."

Lucy took a deep breath. "It may well be a coincidence, but a woman was seen going into Mrs. Helms's room that could very well describe either of you."

"The morning she was killed, but before I found her?" Dolly gasped out.

"No. Within the few days before she died." She left it at that and didn't ask outright if it had been one of them. Both women turned alternately pale and then red.

Melanie stood up. "I don't know about Dolly, but I take great exception to what you're suggesting."

"I haven't suggested anything." Lucy stirred her tea, not looking at either woman.

Melanie turned to her sister. "See the kind of person you've invited into our life? Is this the action of a friend?" She didn't wait for an answer, but picked up her purse from where she had set it on the sideboard and stomped out the front door.

Dolly was aghast. "I'm so sorry, Lucy. I don't see why she needs to react so strongly. There are other women in town who look somewhat like us. It simply needs to be said that it couldn't have been one of us."

"That's right."

"But if you'll excuse me, I think I'll go after her. She needs calming."

"I've things to do in town anyway. I'll see you tomorrow." With that, Lucy quickly left the house. However, when she looked back after passing down the street, she saw that Dolly had not left the house to follow Melanie, who was just disappearing up Reservoir Street toward Main. Lucy wondered why her friend had decided against going after her sister.

Not long after seven o'clock the next morning a light rap on the door to her room brought Lucy to it, thankful that she was an early riser and already dressed. "Dolly! What brings you here so early? Is something wrong?"

"I need to talk to you." She was pale, but there was also a determined set to her mouth.

"Why don't we go down to breakfast and talk in the dining room?"

"No!" She brought herself up sharply. "I mean, this is too private a subject to be discussed where anyone else might possibly hear us. I have a confession to make."

Lucy struggled not to place too much importance on those last words, but considering how nervous Dolly was, it was difficult not to do so. "Come in and sit down."

Once settled at the small table, Dolly rushed into speech. "There's something about this whole business with Mrs. Helms that you should know. I went to see her the same evening as her talk at the Orleans Hotel. I had a light dinner prepared for Robert when he came home that night and as soon as he was at the table, I told him I had to check on a sick friend in town. But I really went to call on Mrs. Helms." Her voice seemed to hang up in her throat as she gasped, "I've never lied to him before." Lucy poured her a glass of water from her nightstand carafe and Dolly swallowed it eagerly.

"Why did you go to her room?" Lucy asked gently, feeling as though if she spoke sharply, Dolly would flutter away like a startled sparrow.

Dolly put the glass on the table and looked down at her lap. She removed a lace-edged handkerchief from beneath the edge of her sleeve and began twisting it into a knot. "I went to her room because I recognized her."

"Was that why I heard you gasp behind me as we entered the meeting room?"

"Oh, you heard that, did you?"

"Yes. But why didn't you say you knew her? Or greet her as an acquaintance?" Lucy frowned, thinking that the same could have been asked of Mrs. Helms.

"Because I didn't want anyone to know she was my mother."

After forcing herself to absorb what she had just heard, Lucy struggled to find an appropriate response. She settled for another question. "Why didn't you want that fact known?"

"I was shocked to see her, and was forced to realize that the Mrs. Helms I'd been hearing about was my mother. Then too, I knew she wasn't going to be popular here and I didn't want to be associated with her views. It's been difficult enough for me to find acceptance. Besides, I hadn't heard from her for years. Years ago, I tried to convince myself that mail from back east is easily lost, but eventually I faced the fact that she wanted no communication between us. And frankly, that was fine with me."

"I thought she was still in Southern California."

Dolly looked down, unable to meet Lucy's gaze. "I never said she was, but I did let you think that. Actually, she left Los Angeles as soon as Melanie and I were both married. I did tell you that we'd grown up in Illinois. It was there, when I was eight, that she left us with our father and went to New York where she got caught up in the suffrage movement. That's when she was at the convention in Albany. When she came back to us in Illinois, something we weren't sure she was even going to do, Father brought us across the country to California. He said it was to join the gold rush, but I think it was mostly to get Mother further away from Eastern influences."

"That makes sense, I guess."

"Then Father got swallowed up in the gold fever of the rush, and we never heard of him again. Then I got married and the following year so did Melanie. Mother went back to New York. That's why, after my husband died, I asked to live with Melanie rather than Mother, although I wrote to ask her. After Melanie's husband wouldn't let me live with them, the one letter I got from Mother was her glib remark that I had made my bed and had to lie in it. And I did. In a Nevada City brothel, where some time later I met you." The bitterness was sharp in her voice.

"But you went to your mother's room that evening after the meeting. Why?"

"She had shown no recognition of me when she greeted me at the talk that day. I needed to know if she really hadn't recognized me or if she was just good at play acting. Since I had thought all this time that she hadn't known how to get ahold of me, I felt it was up to me to approach her."

"How were you received?"

Dolly hesitated. "As though I was just a mere acquaintance, and not a very welcome one at that."

"Oh, Dolly, how awful for you."

"I wasn't surprised that there was no effusive welcome, but I at least think she might have pretended to be more pleased to see me. Her main concern was that it might be thought that the reason she had come here to speak, and to live, was because of family ties. She felt that would weaken her message. She didn't want to be seen in a domestic role."

"You mean as a mother?"

"She said she had worked hard to be defined as an important advocate of a cause of great consequence for all women everywhere. I assured her that I too wanted to avoid being associated with her."

"Ouch!"

"Oh, but she didn't take offence at all. In fact, she relaxed after that and we had a short but pleasant chat about the town. She even told me about some of her adventures traveling through the Isthmus of Panama to get back to California."

"Wait a minute! Your last name before you married Robert wasn't Helms. You only told me once, and I don't remember what it was, but it wasn't that."

"I used my married last name the few times I had to use a last name, like at the bank. It was Farraday."

"Oh, that's right."

"Mother told me that after she was able to divorce father on the grounds of desertion, and assuming he was dead, she married a Mr. Helms who died a year afterwards."

"How was it left between you and your mother?"

"We agreed to have no further private meetings, and would only see one another if we were in a public setting with other people. She asked me if Melanie was in town, and I told her she was to arrive the next day. She made me promise that I wouldn't tell Melanie that she was here, as she hoped to avoid her as long as possible." Dolly looked at Lucy with shame evident in her expression. "Other than telling her I thought her unfair, I let her comment pass. I should have challenged her more, but we were finally on a decent footing and I didn't want the moment to become acrimonious.

I told her that Melanie would be staying only a short time, needing to return to her husband, so they would probably not run into one another as long as Mother didn't start her marches down Main Street. She agreed to hold off until after Melanie left town."

"Well, that clears up some of the confusion. I appreciate your telling me."

"I'm only sorry I didn't tell you sooner. I still haven't told Melanie. But I didn't see how it could make any difference to what happened to Mother."

"It probably doesn't. It simply clarifies what witnesses have told me."

As Dolly rose to leave, Lucy stopped her. "You didn't also go to her room very early on the morning she died?"

Dolly was obviously surprised at the question. "As you know, I did return to ask her to breakfast. I thought it would have been within the realm of our agreement if there was someone like you with us. But that was the only time that day that I went there, and then I found her dead."

"I just wanted to clarify that."

Dolly left the hotel still fretting over that last question from Lucy, wondering what had been back of it. She thought she had told Lucy everything she felt Lucy needed to know about the woman now known as Mrs. Helms, but maybe Lucy had sensed that Dolly was still holding something back.

Only a few minutes after Dolly left, there was a knock on the door. Thinking Dolly had returned to add something to her story, Lucy quickly pulled it open. It was the hotel clerk just coming onto the day shift. "I just noticed that someone left a note for you in your box. It must have been yesterday evening. I thought I should bring it up to you in case it's important."

"Oh, thank you." She reached into her purse and handed him a coin.

"Thank you, ma'am!" He touched the brim of his cap and hurried away after handing her a sealed envelope. The note read: *Please forgive this intrusion, but I think I have something to tell you that you should know. I will call upon you at your hotel at 10 in the morning. If you're not there, I will not bother you again. – Mrs. Holliday*

Lucy hurried after the clerk and caught him just as he was descending the stairs. "Do you know a Mrs. Holliday?"

"Not to say *know*, but I know of her. She's an older lady of good repute. She keeps to herself mostly. A widow lady."

"When she arrives later this morning, please tell her to come up to my room."

"Yes, ma'am."

Lucy opened the door to Mrs. Holliday upon hearing her knock at exactly 10 AM. Her first impression was of a somewhat old-fashioned and fussily dressed stereotype of an elderly widow. She smelled of lavender, and her skin was translucently white against the black of her dress. Her pale face almost blended into the bezel of white hair around her face, and upon her head perched a simple black hat with a short veil. She had latched on to the proper image of a recently bereaved widow, and was not going to let go of it, even though her husband had died twenty years earlier.

Accepting a chair, the lady perched on its front edge and nervously glanced around the room. She hesitated as Lucy, having ordered a pot of coffee, poured out for them both. As soon as Mrs. Holliday had taken a sip, she returned the cup to its saucer and looked Lucy straight in the eyes.

When she spoke, her voice was strong, with an emphasis of certainty underlying her words. "I had best come to the point." Without acknowledgement of why she thought Lucy might want her information, she said, "I was out walking very early the morning that Mr. Leon was discovered in the livery stable. As I passed the livery, I heard voices raised in anger. I know it was naughty of me, but I looked in through the side window and saw Mr. Leon talking to someone toward the front of the livery. I thought I had heard him talking to a woman who was speaking in frantic tones, but when I looked in, I could see Mr. Leon talking to a man in a long black coat. The man was gesturing wildly in an excited way."

Hiding her own excitement, and remembering an earlier description of someone in a long, black coat, Lucy forced herself to ask almost nonchalantly, "Did you recognize who it was?"

"No. His back was to me and the voice that I couldn't clearly hear wasn't familiar. Besides, he had the coat collar pulled up and it hid his face as well as muffled his words. He had an old cloth hat pulled low, too. It was an odd tableau, because Mr. Leon was holding a shallow basket in his arms and seemed very agitated, the tone of his voice pleading. The basket was filled with what looked like a couple of newspapers, a small wooden box like men's collars come in, and some pieces of newspaper. I wondered what articles he might have cut out from a paper that would so disturb the man with him. He was thrusting it all forward, like an offering from a supplicant. I heard Mr. Leon say he was going to take something, I couldn't hear what, to the sheriff and tell him everything."

"Did you hear the response?"

"Something about it being better for him not to do that because it would only create confusion, well, about something or someone. At that point I heard footsteps nearby and I darted around the corner of the livery and hurried home."

"Have you told the police about this?"

"Oh, no!" Mrs. Holliday blushed a deep crimson. "I couldn't bare anyone else knowing that I eavesdropped. I trust that you'll keep private our conversation."

Lucy didn't actually promise, but she also didn't think the police would do anything with it even if they knew about it. There was nothing to prove it had anything to do with Tony's death.

After Mrs. Holliday left, Lucy wondered if Tony had confronted someone with the fact that he was the letter writer and they had been so angry that they had struck out at him with the hammer from the anvil. Or was she wrong, and Tony was confronting someone who was the writer? Had he after all confiscated from someone the paper segments Jane had seen in his desk?

No, that didn't account for the paste and Jane's scissors in Mrs. Helms's room. Lucy still thought that Tony was the writer of the letters. Why would anyone not want him to confess this to the police? "Well," she told herself, "everyone would know that Mrs. Helms was *not* the letter writer. And it would be known that the newspapers, paste and scissors had been put in her room to disguise the real reason for her murder. That would have forced the police to delve into new areas of inquiry." Victim or perpetrator of the letters, Lucy definitely wanted to know who the person in the livery with Mr. Leon had been.

Later, when Dolly heard about Lucy's meeting with Mrs. Holliday, she exclaimed, "Oh, I know her. We go to the same church and I serve on the refreshment committee with her. Such a nice lady." She laughed shortly. "But she is a bit on the nosey side, so her actions don't surprise me." The obvious truth hit her then. "Does this mean that Mr. Leon was the letter writer?"

"I think so." Lucy didn't tell her that this was something she had already concluded.

"And all this time we were so sure they were sent by a woman. How unhappy the poor man must have been to do such a thing. And poor Jane, too. I only know her casually, but I've always thought her a decent woman." After a moment's hesitation, Dolly asked, "Why did you ask me if I'd been in Mother's room the morning of the murder? Had someone said something about a woman seen there that morning?"

"Not seen. But the person coming to her room was heard, and the witness said the tread seemed light. She also thinks she heard a woman's voice raised in anger. And one of the chambermaids had seen you when you came there the evening of the speech."

"Oh, I see." Dolly frowned and looked away from Lucy.

Lucy put a hand on Dolly's arm. "Just because I asked you that, it doesn't mean that I thought you would have been there to kill her. It could have been just as innocent a meeting as your first one with her."

Dolly nodded and looked relieved. Lucy left her friend busily working in the kitchen, obviously satisfied with this explanation. Lucy only wished that she could feel as reassured.

Lucy decided to call on Jane Leon to see if she could be of any assistance to her grieving friend. And, of course, to also see if there was any further information to be gleaned in that direction. She was still convinced that Jane was holding something back.

On the way, she stopped at the Davis & Roy Periodical Depot for a newspaper. She found herself standing in a short line behind Mrs. Fairweather, one of the local school teachers about to retire. Her hair, dark and luxurious when she had started teaching, was now streaked with silver and partially hidden by a conservative bonnet. Tiny wire-framed glasses perched precariously on her nose, and whenever she reached up to adjust them, she was prone to long sighs apropos of nothing in particular.

"Good morning, Mrs. Fairweather. You're looking fine in that Paisley shawl."

"Oh, hello, Mrs. Murphy. Thank you. It was a gift from parents whose four children all graduated due to my tutelage. I so enjoyed our talk when you were last here. In fact, I'm on my way to treat myself to pie and coffee. Would you care to join me?"

"I'd be delighted."

Once seated, and after catching up on local events, Mrs. Fairweather acknowledged that she was aware of Lucy's activities in the town. After a bite of pie had been swallowed, the teacher asked a question that sounded more like chastisement. "Do you think that such as you're doing is appropriate for a respectable woman?"

Lucy felt herself smiling. "Yes, I do. I'm sure the police are making inquiries, but I also know how people hesitate to be frank with them. With me, they'll repeat gossip as well as observations."

"'The motive-hunting of motiveless malignity – how awful it is!'" She smiled and added proudly, "Samuel Taylor Coleridge said that."

"Yes, of course, some motives are indeed hidden," Lucy agreed, "but most are innocent and need not be hidden. I'm simply attempting to allay the fears caused by the anonymous letters, not to mention two recent deaths."

"I'm sure you're doing it with good intentions." She leaned forward and lowered her voice. "If you insist on this course of action, I would look for fear or hate as the motive. I say this because of the weapons used in both killings. Such impromptu violence must have arisen suddenly from a deep well of hate or fear."

"You keep saying *or*, but sometimes there are both hate *and* fear present. The question is, which came first? And, of course, the reason for it is no doubt particular to the killer. If we list the possible reasons for rage against Mrs. Helms, like the kind of threat she posed, we can deduce at least a short list of possible attackers. And we can do the same for Mr. Leon. A name on both lists will be someone I want to talk with."

The school teacher leaned back and looked intently at Lucy, the corners of her mouth twitching. Ignoring the poor syntax of Lucy's last sentence, she said, "Maybe you're wise enough to do this after all." She picked up her coffee cup, but before drinking looked steadily at Lucy. "Be careful, though. The closer you come to successfully discovering the culprit, the closer you will be to danger. The people you're after don't hesitate to kill. Just because Mrs. Helms and Mr. Leon were killed by someone striking out with something heavy, it doesn't mean whoever killed them doesn't carry a gun or knife."

Having departed from Mrs. Fairweather, Lucy soon after found herself sitting in Jane Leon's parlor. Not that she wanted refreshments, but she had not been offered anything as was usual. Nevertheless, Jane seemed relaxed as she sat on a low chair knitting and chatting. In fact, she appeared quite content.

After discussing several mundane topics and reassuring Lucy that she was well, Jane told her, "I'm not floundering as much as some women might who have so suddenly lost their husband. I miss him, of course, but I've always had control of our money, so I know what I'm doing there. I never asked his permission to spend it either. After all, he was sometimes gone for weeks at a time. I got used to making repairs to things or ordering it done if I couldn't do it myself. When he was home, I gave him a modest allowance so he could drink a reasonable amount with his friends, or spend it any way he saw fit."

"Did the two of you agree on what constituted a reasonable amount?"

"Oh, he often asked for more money," she chuckled. "And most of the time I gave it to him, especially if it was later in the month and he had good reason to have run out."

Lucy swallowed hard. "He gave good reasons each time he asked, did he? Reasons you approved of?"

"Oh, yes. He was very proud of me, you know. You could see the pride on his face when I'd tell him about some odd job around the house that I'd taken care of while he was away." She smiled fondly. "I used to tease him that I really didn't need him at all. But I was always quick to add that I kept him around because I was fond of him."

Lucy looked at her with disbelief, stunned that a woman could be so ignorant of how a man would feel hearing such a thing. "You know, Jane, it's often said that men need to be needed. Few of them understand the ties we women feel to those we love, but don't also need."

Jane shrugged. "Oh, he was fine with it. Besides, I don't think he ever accepted the idea that I, a mere woman, didn't need him."

"My dear Jane," Lucy began, her throat tightening, "have you not asked yourself why he felt the need to write the anonymous letters?"

Jane looked up and stared at Lucy for a long moment, her knitting hanging from her hands. "I assume it was because he just wanted to cause trouble. He'd always had a mischievous streak. He loved practical jokes."

"Just little pranks?"

"Some of them were more than that, even a few causing men a degree of injury. Still, he loved seeing their embarrassment, and would laugh about it for days. He enjoyed it so much that I knew he would never stop, so I didn't ask him to." Seeing the startled look on Lucy's face, she quickly added, "But he never played tricks on women or children."

Lucy looked at her friend without trying to hide her incredulity. "No, he just wrote women anonymous letters that disrupted their lives and caused them anguish."

Jane looked down at her knitting, which continued apace. "Yes, he did do that."

"But *why* did he do those things? There had to be some underlying reason for wanting to cause upset to so many people, especially women."

"You're talking about what is referred to as a psychological reason, aren't you?"

Lucy remained patient. "A person plays hurtful pranks and sends out anonymous letters because they feel powerless or have a need to get even, and they express their resentment by making others unhappy." When Jane remained aggravatingly sanguine, Lucy lost a little of her patience. "I mean, wouldn't you think so?"

Jane sighed with an answering impatience of her own. "What you're not saying is that he wanted others to be as unhappy as he was. But I never thought of him as unhappy." After a moment's hesitation, she asked, "But if he was, I suppose I should understand why, shouldn't I? I just don't see any reason for him to be unhappy. He had a reasonably good life. Maybe not as good as some, but far better than some, too."

Realizing that she had waded into a very personal part of Jane Leon's life, Lucy was feeling acutely uncomfortable. "Well, it's not for me to say, really. And maybe it doesn't matter so much now."

Jane looked at Lucy and blinked. "You mean because he's dead. You're right in one sense. There's nothing I can do about it now even if I was in some way responsible for his unhappiness. But hear this, Lucy. He *was* with me the night Mrs. Helms was killed, and I mean that. If I knew he'd done something like that, I wouldn't cover for him."

"I believe you."

They sat in somewhat tense silence for several minutes. Lucy looked out the front window at a squirrel running up a tree and wondered if she should stay or go. She had seldom felt so awkward and hesitant, and was wondering how to gracefully take her leave. Thankfully, Jane put down her knitting and gave vent to her thoughts.

"I suppose if I ever hope to remarry, it would be a good idea if I knew whether or not I should change in some way. I wouldn't want to engender unhappiness in my new husband."

"Are you thinking of remarrying?"

"One never knows, does one? Let's face it, after playing the grieving widow for a decent length of time, remarrying would restore me to a more permanent respectability."

Lucy left soon after that, thinking about how controlling, even cold-bloodedly calculating, Jane Leon could be. Of course, that didn't mean that what she had said wasn't true. Life was certainly easier for a married woman in a world that gave women few legal rights, and that sat in judgment of everything she did. Nevertheless, Lucy felt she was getting a glimmer of what had motivated Tony Leon.

Tony may well have felt that having a thoroughly capable wife was all well and good if it meant not having to worry about her while absent from town. But no man wanted to think they were unnecessary to the point of being dispensable. Add to that the fact of having to ask for spending money from his wife, and it would be logical to assume that Tony's pride had suffered. If his sense of powerlessness had been acute, attended by resentment held in for years, Lucy wondered if he might have sent those letters to give himself a feeling of being in control of something, even at the expense of other people's peace of mind. Was this why most of the letters had been sent to women?

"Poor Jane," Lucy thought, and then added, "And poor Tony."

Lucy sat on a bench under the awning overhanging the entrance to a stone building on Main Street known as The Placerville Melodeo, but more often simply referred to as "the theater". She idly watched people passing by, admiring the dresses of several ladies, and even at one point patting the head of a dog being led by one of them. It was too early for the Friday evening's parade of young, single women who sauntered down Main Street in order to be noticed by men sitting on the sidewalks to observe them. It was a tradition held over from the gold rush years, when the number of women compared to men had been much less. The women pretended they were simply "taking the air", and the men pretended they were resting after a hard day of labor.

Lucy thought back over the people she knew in Placerville and wondered who there might be that had an attentive ear for what was happening in town. Her memory somewhat reluctantly recalled one person, a man who probably knew a good deal and might be willing to talk if properly handled.

The one time she had met him, she had come close to being thoroughly intimidated by him. Well, as close as she ever was around any man. If men wanted to get him to open up, there was usually no problem, especially if they stuck to topics considered safe, like hunting, fishing, or oddly, the war. For a woman, it could very well be an insurmountable task to get him to even acknowledge her presence.

Nevertheless, Lucy set out, unsure of the exact location of *Old Gus*. She wondered if there was anyone in town who knew his last name. She did remember that his cabin was down an alley between two buildings, and that there was a small, directional street sign fashioned to look like a feminine hand with a ruffled cuff that pointed down the alleyway. She then remembered that the feminine sign was next to the Confidence Engine House, a very unfeminine location. It had been known as the Mountaineer Engine Company until they had purchased a pumper with the difficult to remove, engraved name on the side of *Confidence*.

Because Lucy was in a pondering mood, it occurred to her to wonder why this feminine signage that pointed the way forward had become so popular. Why was this directional indicator a feminine hand instead of a man's hand possibly gloved or with a cuff showing below a coat sleeve? Was it a matter of trust, the supposition being that it would be safe to believe a woman telling you to proceed?

After all, Lucy thought to herself, society was always telling women they were the mainstay that gave substance to the sacred place of *The Home*, where every "normal woman" could be found. This was a common argument offered as to why women should not be given more rights that allowed for their independence. The idea being that society, and therefore the whole country, would fall apart without women remaining at home cooking, cleaning, mending socks, and having children.

Unfortunately, this reasoning gave every *unmarried* woman over twenty the ignoble title of *spinster* with which to burden their self-esteem. The thought then occurred to Lucy that maybe the world needed unmarried women if they were dedicated to such fields as education, invention, music, and literature –– something they were far less likely to involve themselves in if married and raising children. Looking out at the throngs of people on the road and the sidewalks, Lucy came to a stop. What, she wondered, will happen when the earth has absorbed all the human beings it can house and feed? She quickly laughed at herself, thinking that would surely take many hundreds of years, if ever.

Having found the location of the alley, Lucy refocused her attention and headed toward a small cabin at the far end, passing the side entrances of the San Francisco Laundry to her left and the fire department on her right. Crates and barrels sat outside the alley doors, waiting to be brought inside while among them scuttled unseen, rustling critters. She assumed they were mice, rats and lizards hoping to escape the three feral cats she saw hunting for them. Such things bothered her not at all, and she kept walking, resolute in her determination.

Lucy hoped Gus was at home, although he was among the grossest men she had ever met. She smiled at this, considering that when she had crossed the country as part of a wagon train in the 1850's, she had walked next to men who had seldom bathed, changed clothes or shaved for weeks at a time.

In the case of Gus, people said it wasn't so much that he reeked of undefined bodily odors, which he did, but that his manners when eating redefined the word *disgusting*. Steeling her resolve, Lucy knocked gently on the cabin door, as she had the impression that the door might not stand up under a more aggressive application. Besides, being that the cabin was only about nine feet across, she assumed that if Gus was home that he couldn't be far away. However, when the voice within called out "Come on in" and she opened the door, it was to find the interior more spacious than she had assumed. It was what some refer to as a *shot-gun house*, meaning very narrow but deep, one room leading into the next.

Gus was a small man with a proud paunch beneath a faded red shirt, beady eyes above a scraggly beard, and a crop of hair to match. It was his hands, more properly belonging to a much larger man, that immediately grabbed her attention. Unfortunately, Lucy had caught Gus at a time when he was eating, and those hands were full of something dripping grease.

He sat at a small table of raw wood covered in a faded red and white checked cloth in need of a good washing, and stared up at his unexpected visitor over a plate of roasted fowl, possibly a chicken, but Lucy wouldn't have sworn to that. All the time they were talking, Lucy had to fight the urge to stare impolitely at his mouth as his tongue moved food from one cheek to the other in search of available back teeth with which to chew. From the amount of shifting, it seemed there might be very few.

"I know you," he declared by way of greeting. "You're that nosey woman friend of Robert's missus."

"Yes," Lucy smiled with an effort. "I'm Mrs. Murphy. We met the last time I was in Placerville. You were helping Robert at his livery."

"Oh, yeah. Well, have a sit and tell me why I'm of interest to you." He took another bite of roasted fowl and chewed slowly, giving Lucy her turn to talk.

Lucy pulled out the rickety wooden chair opposite him and tried to gather her thoughts as she gingerly perched on its edge. His manners, and his faded home and clothing aside, Gus had the reputation for keen awareness and astute observation. He was not a formally educated man, but had lived through a lot of challenges in his 60 years, and occasionally revealed wisdom gained from surviving varied and colorful experiences. He was also a voracious reader, as was evidenced by the stacks of books along the walls.

Lucy had taken too long to begin, and he told her, "When I finish here, I'm going into town, so you best cough out why you're here."

"Sorry. You're right. I know you to be a very observant man, and someone who people seem to confide in."

"They don't confide so much as feel free to say what's on their minds. They consider me someone who doesn't gossip." He looked at her with meaning.

Meeting his honesty head-on, Lucy told him, "Well, then, let's say I'm interested in information you've gathered from paying close attention to others."

Gus scowled at her for a moment before his head bobbed up and down to the accompaniment of deep chuckles. "Okay. In regard to what?"

"I'm trying to find out who killed Mrs. Helms and Tony Leon."

She waited to hear him laugh at her for thinking she could do any such thing, but he surprised her by asking, "You think it's the same person? I kind of thought the law had settled on some unhappy person having gotten an anonymous letter from the suffrage woman and killed her for it. And Tony, well, he was a very nosey person, always prying into people's lives. They say he was robbed." He looked steadily at Lucy before saying, "He sometimes took a long time to pay his gambling debts."

"Did he cheat on Jane?"

"Not that I know of, but he was as randy as a goat and not nearly as smart. Why?"

"A witness saw him arguing with someone who might have been a woman. It took place in the livery the morning he was killed."

"'Might have been a woman'?" he repeated with surprise. "Didn't the witness know a man from a woman?"

"The person was seen from the back, and although it could have been a man, it could also have been a woman wearing a man's coat."

"No kidding?" He took a minute to think about a woman wearing men's clothes. "Well, I'll be damned. That'd sure be bold, and also agin the law." He took another moment to think as he drank the last of the coffee in his tin mug. "Don't know why anyone would kill him, though." He took a leap forward in his reasoning and added, "It's even harder to believe Tony would've had a reason to kill the suffrage woman. His missus kept a pretty tight rein on him."

"Would you be surprised if it turned out he sent the letters?"

His eyes squinted at her. "Huh. Not so much." He took from his back pocket a white handkerchief so large it might have been a small table cloth, wiped his hands, and then blew his nose on it. "Yeah, he might have done something like that. It would have tickled him to think of people's reactions. But I also think it would have upset him to think that one of his pranks caused someone to take their own life, like that woman who did. But didn't the sheriff say they found the makings of the letters in the room of the suffrage woman?"

"They could have been put there by the person who killed her to make it look like she wrote the letters, and was therefore killed because of that."

He sat back in his chair and folded his arms across the old red shirt encasing his chest. "You've worked it out that way, have you? But that makes it look like Tony was the one who killed her, if he was the one who did the letters. Of course, anyone could gather up some newspapers and put them there."

"But the newspapers were accompanied by the paste and scissors from Tony's study."

"But why would Tony want to kill her?"

"Actually, I don't think he did. I think someone who knew he was the letter writer stole the newspapers and things from his house and put them in the room of Mrs. Helms. His house was broken into around the time she was killed. As to who might have done all this, I don't know. That's what I'm hoping to get a clue about from talking to various people."

He stuck a finger into the back recesses of his mouth to dislodge a morsel of his meal before speaking. "Well, all I can say to that is to say you'd best be careful. Someone's out there killing people for some reason we don't know, and you don't want to get in their way."

Lucy stood up. "Yes, that's occurred to me, too." She smiled at him. "Thank you for talking to me. It's helped me organize my thoughts."

"Just why *did* you want to talk to me? Most women avoid even walking past me."

"Back in the mid '50's I crossed the country on a wagon train. Part of the time I walked next to a man who wore dirty and even ragged clothing, and smelled horribly. During one of our very interesting conversations, he told me that body odor had been a problem for him no matter how much he bathed, even when he had been a professor at a prestigious university in the East. He taught me a lot about literature, the law, and important events in history." She couldn't hold back a smile as she added, "Some of it, I even remember."

"Ah, but what you really learned was not to judge by appearances."

"Yes. And I'd once heard you talking to some men on the sidewalk about the war, and it showed a depth of reasoned discourse in which I longed to participate. But, of course, being a woman, the option wasn't open to me."

Hearing the resentment in her voice, Gus laughed and scratched the back of his neck. "So you were a supporter of the Helms female?"

"Of the basic principles of freedoms and rights for women and blacks, yes. Of her method of presentation, no." She smiled at him. "Again, thank you for sharing your views with me."

"Any time. I don't often talk with a female who thinks like a man." When he saw the flush to Lucy's cheeks and her jaw tighten, he added, "I mean that as a compliment."

"Yes, I know you do." Lucy surprised him by giving him a friendly smile and saying, "We'll keep it for discussion at some other time."

He watched her leave, muttering under his breath, "Huh!" But he remained where he was until the venturesome lady, who had dared visit him in his lair, had walked away from the cabin. He then got up, scratched a few places, and sauntered to the front window. Deep in thought, he looked out through the shadowy gloom of the alley to watch Lucy walk toward the bright sunlight of the street. He then expelled another "Huh!"

CHAPTER 9

"Three things women most excel at
are weeping, weaving and lies."
Chaucer

Saturday, June 14 – Monday, June 16

Being a nice day with no wind, Lucy found Jane Leon on the back porch of her house sitting at her spinning wheel. The long skirts of her old calico dress, worn only when at this task, lifted rhythmically as her foot moved up and down on the treadle. She had accumulated a nice amount of spun thread and was peddling steadily to keep the large wooden wheel turning, the fluff of the white wool having settled over her and the surrounding ground. So automatic was this activity to Jane that it allowed her to give freedom to wandering thoughts, and so deep into them was she that when she became aware of Lucy standing nearby, her fingers faltered only a moment in feeding the flock to the spindle.

"Oh, Jane, I'm so sorry," Lucy pleaded. "Startling you was what I was trying to avoid by not speaking up. I entered only because your front door was standing open."

"Nothing done that can't be fixed. I had the door open to get some cooler air inside." Her tight smile belied the casualness of her remark.

Lucy looked down at the large wooden wheel. "This is something I've tried to do, but I don't seem to have the knack for it. Freda used to use an old wheel I inherited with the house, but it broke."

"I find it relaxing as well as practical."

Lucy didn't miss the clipped delivery of Jane's words and knew she wasn't really welcome. Nevertheless, she persevered, hoping Jane's mood would lighten. "But you don't wear homespun fabrics."

"I can well afford to buy my fabrics, but there are still those women of little means who weave their own, so I give it to them."

"How kind! What did Tony think of you doing that?"

Jane's right hand fumbled in its task and the thread slipped from her left thumb and finger, winding itself up sharply on the spindle. She gasped, pursed her lips, and turned to Lucy with irritation showing clearly before turning back and unwinding the thread and making the join in the wool. She restarted the wheel with a light touch of the hand and settled down with a determined calm.

"If you must know," Jane responded, her lips pursed at the memory, "he thought I should charge them something. It was an on-going point of contention between us. I refused to ask for money for something I intended as a gift."

"I've always thought of you as a thoughtful person and now I'm even more convinced."

"How about you? I know, because I serve on many committees, that you give to several charities here."

Lucy blushed, feeling unreasonably shy at having been caught out. "Yes. As we do in Jamestown. But we don't want recognition for it."

"Neither do I." Although curious as to why Lucy was taking her time stating her business, Jane was too well-trained in social rules to ask outright. Instead, she adhered to proper etiquette and said, "I could benefit from a cup of tea. Will you join me?"

"Yes, thank you."

After they had settled on the sofa with a tea tray before them that included cookies with currents, Lucy knew it was time to broach the subject of her visit. "I felt bad about our conversation yesterday and wanted to apologize if I over-stepped any boundaries. I know this is a stressful time for you, and I hope I didn't add to it."

"Don't worry about it, Lucy. I know your heart was back of what you said."

"I do have another reason for stopping by."

"Is it to tell me that you're moving to Placerville?"

Lucy laughed. "You already know about that?"

Jane smirked with satisfaction. "I wanted to show you that I'm not outside the range of news that spreads so quickly through the town."

"I look forward to having you visit when we're settled." She took a sip of tea. "I was also wondering something. When your house was broken into, you said nothing was taken. Have you since changed your mind about that?"

"Well, nothing of value."

"You told the police, and me, that there was nothing."

"Oh, well," she hesitated. Then, with a deep sigh, she said, "The cupboard in a corner of the parlor beneath the book case was empty. You know the one. It's just inside the French doors, to the right of Tony's desk. Tony said there had been nothing in it except some naughty French cards some man had given him."

"Really?" Lucy struggled to hold back the temptation to laugh, picturing Jane's offended reacted to such a thing being in her husband's possession.

"Sometime ago, before he could close the door of the cupboard, I came upon him unexpectedly. He closed the doors to it, and even locked it, but he knew I had seen the envelopes in it. That's when he told me about the cards they contained." Jane blushed to admit that she understood that these cards were engraved with black and white wood cuts of half-dressed women, the more expensive ones being hand-tinted. However, any knowledge that some of the art had been of completely naked women, she would *not* admit to knowing.

"And that was all that was taken?"

"I think that my scissors might have been stolen then, too. Tony got them in trade from some miners on a trip where he took them supplies and then found they had run out of money to pay him. And had found no gold."

"Now, after thinking about it, do you still think that cupboard only held the cards?"

"No," Jane snapped, her jaw tight. "I think it held some of the letters he had not yet mailed to those in the town. I mean, why would such cards have been in envelopes with names printed on them? And before you ask, I didn't see the names clearly enough to see who it was." She shook her head. "I've thought a lot about what you said during your last visit. Maybe the way I treated him made some difference to him. But there was something else."

When Jane gulped her tea and hesitated, Lucy encouraged her. "Yes?"

"Tony was married to a woman in San Francisco before we met. I won't tell you how I found that out, but it wasn't from him. I've even wondered if he was legally divorced from her. Such a thing wasn't that uncommon during the rush."

"Oh, Jane." The enormity of this news was beyond words she could express, so she simply asked, "How long have you known this?"

"Not long," she answered evasively. "Several times he made very nasty comments about soiled doves, and I think maybe he had tried to save one of them by marrying her, and it didn't work out. Don't you think that such a marriage may have been part of why he resented other people's happiness?"

"Quite possibly."

Jane looked at Lucy with challenge showing clearly in her face and tone. "But you think that the way I treated him at least added to his past negative experiences with women, and was what tipped him into a form of revenge through writing the letters. Don't you?"

"I've no way of knowing that, Jane." Lucy had no desire to add to Jane's distress. "But I do know that all of that must have been difficult for you to consider, and I admire you greatly for your willingness to do so. I know from experience that it takes a singular type of courage to look honestly at one's own actions."

"Thank you for that," Jane murmured.

"In fact, I want you to know that I'm hoping that once the killer of Mrs. Helms is discovered, that it won't be necessary to reveal who wrote the letters. They will have stopped, and that's all everyone wants."

"Is it?" Jane's voice was hard.

"You mean that without a definitive answer as to who it was, people will be living with the fear that the letters could start up again?"

"Yes. I'd hate that." She looked at Lucy with tentative hope. "It would be another thing if they thought it was Mrs. Helms who sent them."

In a quandary about how to respond, Lucy stood up and walked slowly to the door. "I won't lie about that, or mislead anyone into thinking that's true. But if it's not asked of me, I also won't volunteer what I know about Tony. On the other hand, if his activities are somehow connected to his death or that of Mrs. Helms, no one will be able to keep it quiet."

"You're referring, of course, to the fact that he might have killed her. He didn't. I'll swear he was with me that night, because he was."

After a moment's hesitation, Lucy asked, "Was he still with you after you fell asleep? You didn't hear him leave the house the morning he was killed, when you woke up and found his note."

Jane stood up and began gathering together the tea things. With her back to her guest, she said, "Good-bye, Lucy."

Without further words, Lucy left the house and began her walk back to the hotel. Had she irreparably damaged her friendship with Jane? Maybe they shared too many dangerous secrets that would act as a divide between them. If true, she felt badly for Jane, and even a little sorry for herself.

It was taking too long to gather enough evidence to confirm the idea she was forming, and Lucy was beginning to doubt that such evidence existed. In her mind she could see the sequence of cataclysmic occurrences that might have taken place, with the whole of them leading to the death of two people. The letters, and Tony's reason for having sent them, she had settled in her mind. But the murders were another story.

Lucy knew almost instinctively that Tony sending the letters somehow tied in with his getting killed. After all, Mrs. Holliday had seen newspaper items in Tony's arms while talking to someone in the livery. When stealing the papers from his desk the night of Mrs. Helms's murder, had the interloper into Tony's home also taken the unsent envelopes in the cupboard? If Tony had carelessly left the newspapers out on his desk, he might also have left the cupboard open. If so, it was no wonder he was so upset after the break-in of his house. Or had Tony already sent the letters in the cupboard to their addressees before the break-in?

Lucy wondered about the actions of Mrs. Helms and Tony during the years or even the months leading up to their deaths. She suddenly realized that it was the nature of their character, who they were as people, that had contributed to what had befallen them. Their fundamental character was back of the choices they had made in their lives, how they had treated other people, and even how they had thought of themselves. She wished she knew why Tony Leon had been in the room of Mrs. Helms a couple of weeks before her death, and why their voices had been perceived as arguing. Was this the moment of clash that precipitated both of them dying violently? Had Tony killed Mrs. Helms for some reason as yet unknown, and then someone had killed him for some reason unrelated to Mrs. Helms? Or had the same person killed them both, even though there seemed to be no connection between the two victims?

With no immediate purpose in mind, Lucy arrived at Dolly's house and found her in the small garden she was nurturing back of the house.

Dolly looked up from the weeds she was hoeing, the long white apron covering her dress streaked with mud. "Have you come to rescue me? This began as an enjoyable challenge and has become a chore that's about to overwhelm me."

"Dolly, you're just not used to working the soil," Lucy laughed. "It's outside your realm of reference."

"Ah, there you're wrong." She wiped the back of her hand across her forehead and leaned on the hoe. "Growing up, it was my chore to work in our garden in Los Angeles."

"Come sit in the shade with me and give yourself a rest."

"Good idea. I spent an hour this morning squeezing lemons and making a pie, and I had enough left over for lemonade. I'll get us some."

Dolly soon joined Lucy already seated in a white wicker chair with a high rolled-edge back, while Dolly reclined on the matching love seat. Settled beneath the shade of a large tree, they tasted their cold lemonade and for several minutes simply enjoyed the quiet pleasure of one another's company. There was no need for immediate words, the near presence of the other being enough. But Lucy knew her friend well, and realized that Dolly wasn't one to remain silent for long. Lucy decided to choose the topic of their conversation.

"Do you remember what it was like living in Los Angeles at the beginning of the 1850's?"

"It would be difficult not to remember." Dolly took a swallow of her drink before continuing. "It was a very violent time. The whole area was known for the vast quantity of cattle and horses raised on ranchos. And in 1851, also known for the rustling of those animals."

Lucy nodded. "It still has that reputation. But so much of the large herds of cattle and horses drowned in the floods. And the orchards and grape vines you once mentioned were lost as well."

Dolly sighed, trying not to show her sadness at the thought of such loss. "You have to realize that in the early 1850's, when only a state for a couple of years, it was still wide open country. Other than around a garden to keep out deer, or around corrals to keep in a few animals, there were no fences between properties. The old trail between the missions was little more than a track, but it got people between Los Angeles and San Francisco. Hundreds of unfenced acres of one rancho flowed to meet those of the next. Thousands of horses, and even more cattle and sheep, thrived on the endless pastures.

"The town when we first arrived there was just a scattering of buildings, and clusters of homes banded into little neighborhoods, but it was beginning to grow larger. Not far from us was a large warehouse, with more being built, and we lived in what was called a *square*. These were mostly adobe buildings on four sides of an open space used for communal purposes, but more and more wooden buildings were going up."

"What were the buildings used for?"

"Oh, businesses of various types, like in any burgeoning town. Offices and markets, of course. But also gambling dens, saloons, dance houses, and small hotels and boarding houses. There were only a few rough, rutted roads leading to the pueblo, and they cut through vast tracks of cattle range."

"Is that where the rustling took place?"

"Yes. The Governor back then declared that the losses in cattle and horses was one of the state's major economic problems. There were bands of rustlers sometimes fifty or more in number, and they did this stealing over several years. If caught, they were hanged from the nearest tree or dragged behind a horse until dead. But they knew it was high risk for high reward."

Lucy was surprised at how casually Dolly said this. But evidently she wasn't totally inured to the violent memory, as she hesitated a moment before continuing, taking a long sip of her cold drink.

"In one month alone in '54 there were a dozen violent deaths in Los Angeles. All the men in town carried a pistol, rifle, or shotgun, along with a bowie knife. In '56 bandits killed two City Marshalls and in '57 they killed Sheriff Barton and three of his posse. That brought in U.S. troops who joined with citizen groups, and even a large number of local Indians. They caught up with the bandits in the Santa Ana Mountains, killing some and arresting others. Some, of course, got away and disappeared. About ten hangings followed."

"You saw all of this?"

"I had married and moved away during much of it, but Melanie continued to live there even after her marriage. Vincent had invested in some of the ranchos. Between the violence in her marriage and in the society around her, I'm surprised it hasn't turned her into a nervous wreck. But she's the same sweet girl I grew up with."

Lucy's mind raced down a dozen avenues in an effort to find a tactful way to disagree, but she hit a dead end at every one of them. She decided to just smile and change the subject to the previous winter's floods, and the excessive damage it had caused throughout the state. Men always found this a safe topic, and now so did Lucy.

What no one knew in the summer of 1862 was that a year later they would be talking about being in the midst of a historic drought, one that would last well into 1864. Over 100,000 cattle and horses would die on the ranchos for lack of water, along with thousands of sheep. Crops would fry and blow away, and the state's economy would flounder worse than it had during the rustling and the floods. The result would be the elimination of most of the native California landowners, and would initiate the subdivision of many of the great Spanish-Mexican land grants.

The days of mile upon mile of unfenced rancho lands, of enormous herds of half-wild cattle and horses, along with numerous sprawling estates of wealthy and powerful men, would all come to an end. And a little of the romance of what had become part of the colorful legend of early California would fade into the dusty memory of history. It would take a full century of change and progress before the ranchos of early California, along with the history of the mission system, would be once again acknowledged. Then, many of these historic places would be renovated and restored -- and made accessible to the paying public.

On this warm summer day of 1862, Lucy knew only that the lemonade in her glass was refreshing and that she was enjoying Dolly's company. But Dolly was not ready to leave the past.

"It was during the 1850's that we heard news of the Indians from the Owens River Valley carrying off hundreds of horses and cattle from the ranchos of Los Angeles and Santa Barbara. Other tribes did the same in San Diego south of Los Angeles, and San Luis Obispo north of Los Angeles. One raid near Mission San Juan Capistrano netted almost 500 horses from old Governor Pio Pico's rancho."

"He was the last governor of Alta California, when it was under Mexican rule, right? Before it became the State of California?"

"That's right. He was also elected to the Los Angeles Common Council in 1853. All of that is why it was in the papers when his herd was rustled. The newspapers also said that the San Fernando Mission lost close to a thousand horses, and that over a period of five years Indian horse-thieves cost the rancheros of the southern counties at least $300,000.

"Of course, we know now that all of this wasn't due to the Indians, but to groups of Mexican bandits and white raiders, too." Dolly shook her head. "It was just such a violent decade for the southern half of the state."

"Time changes our perspective of the past," Lucy mused. "When I look back to the way I thought of the gold fields when I was a girl, they seemed like a bastion of civilization. I was too young to be aware that it was very far from that."

"But your experience traveling and working with Freda was a good one."

"In the main." Her thought veered away from the several times when things had been particularly rough. "I understand that the Indians around Los Angeles were treated poorly by the rancheros."

"Oh, that's such an understatement." Dolly paled as she remembered some of the things she had witnessed. "I'm not surprised that some of the tribes turned on the ranchos and stole from them."

"We've all heard of the poor treatment they received at some of the missions, but I wasn't aware of more than that."

Dolly took a sip of her drink before continuing. "Even now, ranchers complain bitterly about the Indian depredations they claim created a check to the prosperity of the southern California counties. But they don't bother to mention the degradation and injustices foisted upon the tribes in the area clear back to the 1840's. The tribes supplied most of the unskilled labor for ranchos, farms and vineyards.

"They worked like dogs, but were always accused of being lazy when doing anything other than herding sheep or working with horses. The Indian men were bought at auctions in the squares for a week's work, things like plowing or making bricks or felling trees. At the end of the week, when the job was done, they might be sold to another landowner to work in the vineyards. They'd also be picked up from the jail after a night of boisterous drinking, their fine paid, and therefore considered as owned by whoever paid their fine."

"What about the Indian women?"

"I know they were used for household help. But I also think I was probably sheltered from any harsher realities regarding them." Unwilling to contemplate that subject, Dolly switched topics. "While this was going on early in the 1850's, in one year there were thirty-one homicides in or near the pueblo. Not one of the perpetrators was caught. It's still more unsettled than many realize. But as it expands, people are demanding more law enforcement."

"And this is where your father brought you girls and your mother when he decided to come to the gold fields?" She knew she sounded judgmental and didn't care.

"That's where he parked us before going off to find his fortune. He came back once to see us, but only briefly." Dolly sighed deeply. "After that we never again saw Mr. Anthony, as Mother always referred to him. Melanie never referred to him at all, and I slowly gave up hope of ever seeing him again. But I missed his smile." She looked out into the distance. "He had such a wonderful smile and made us laugh with his funny stories." She bit her lower lip. "After a couple of years, we decided that he had probably died in the gold fields like so many men did, and we moved on with our lives, such as they were."

Lucy placed a hand on Dolly's arm. "No wonder you left that area as soon as you could after your husband died."

"That, and because of the questions that were being asked about my husband's death. But the hardest part of leaving was knowing that Melanie was stuck in the midst of it all with a husband not at all kind. Because of the way he kept her cloistered from other people in the town, she didn't even have a friend to support her."

"But her husband let her come to see you a few times after you moved here."

"Only because she used subterfuge to get away. One time when Robert went to San Francisco, I had him mail a letter to her from there so Vincent would think that's where we lived. I even had Robert write a line about the strictness of how Melanie was chaperoned during her visit."

Lucy stood up suddenly. "Let's go for a walk. I need a few things at the merchandise store." She had heard enough about grim realities, and she didn't want to return to the tales of *poor Melanie.*

As they came out of a shop, Dolly said, "Here comes Mrs. Blake. Do you know her?"

"I don't believe I've met her."

"I'm not surprised. She's usually home and in bed with some complaint or other." As the thin woman approached, Lucy saw that she looked drawn and pale. "Good day, Mrs. Blake," Dolly greeted the pale woman. "Are you enjoying this beautiful summer day?"

"Oh, hello, Mrs. Robbins."

"I'd like you to meet my friend Lucy Murphy."

"Nice to meet you." She turned back to Dolly. "John has a new job at the Pioneer Livery. However, right now he's off looking for color with some friends. He never gives up on the idea of finding that one large nugget that no one else has found." She pursed her lips and shook her head. "I've been feeling a bit under the weather recently, but nothing serious the doctor assures me. It's just so exhausting caring for a child learning to walk."

Dolly turned to Lucy. "Mary and John have the cutest child. Amanda is going to grow up to be a beautiful girl."

Mrs. Blake offered what she thought of as a smile, but which didn't convey much pleasure. "Yes, I fear you're right. It would be so much better for her if she could be plain. Easier to gain a good, solid husband. But Amanda is a lovely child, and already her manners are beyond her years." With another forced smile, Mary Murphy gave them a nod and walked on her way.

Dolly told Lucy in a lowered voice, "We escaped easily that time. The way she usually talks, you'd think she was the only woman to have given birth. I guess a long enough time has passed that she'll now be carrying on about her daughter's perfection."

Lucy stared at Dolly in surprise. "I've never heard you sound so waspish before."

Dolly was immediately contrite. "I did, didn't I? I'm sorry. I guess I'm a little frustrated that I haven't been able to give Robert a child." She turned to Lucy with a genuine smile. "And little Amanda is indeed a beautiful child. In fact, as pretty as your boy Roger is handsome." She sighed, the romantic streak in her nature coming to the fore. "Wouldn't it be wonderful if after you move here, the two children should meet and become friends?"

Lucy rolled her eyes. "Not if it means I have to spend time with the mother."

As they laughed and linked arms, the two friends walked on, soon the jest forgotten. Instead, the fate of the two children would be left to a later time in a mining town far across the mountain, a town that was as yet not established but that would someday pronounce its judgment upon both Amanda and Roger.

The next day was Sunday, and Lucy was treating herself to a leisurely breakfast when Officer Reynolds entered the dining room of the hotel. "Oh, Lucy, I'm so glad you're here."

"Good morning, John." Neither of them would have presumed to use first names around other people, but they were now feeling more friend than officer and citizen. "Has something happened?"

"Not exactly. But the coroner says Mrs. Helms was hit twice. It was two wounds right next to each other on her head."

Lucy sat back, nodding her head. "I wondered about that."

"Oh, yeah? I was surprised." He took a piece of toast from the silver rack and slathered it with strawberry jam from the generous mound heaped in a crystal dish in the center of the table.

"Look at it this way," she told him. "During an argument, Mrs. Helms is struck with the lamp, after which her assailant flees, thinking her dead. He then returns with the newspapers to put in the room, trying to make it look like she was the letter writer and therefore killed because of that. But he finds that she was only stunned. So he picks up the heavy bottom of the lamp and once again hits her with it, only much harder this time and breaking the skin. Then the killer runs away. Within minutes, Dolly arrives and finds her on the floor, dead and the blood still somewhat fresh."

Officer Reynolds stared into space as he pictured what she was saying, not even aware that the waiter had put a cup of coffee in front of him. "That must have been the way it happened."

"But," Lucy lamented, "it doesn't bring us much further along. We might know how it was done, and assuredly we know when and where. We can assume sudden rage, too, although we don't know the source of the disagreement. But we can't, from all of this, deduce the who. We can't even be sure of the gender of the killer since Mrs. Helms had recently had both male and female visitors."

Officer Reynolds gulped down his coffee and headed off to church with his wife. Shortly after finishing her meal, Lucy stepped out onto the sidewalk and hesitated while adjusting to the light. In that moment, a man walking past lurched into her, slamming her up against the brick of the hotel. Two other men came to her aid as she righted herself, and she assured them that she was fine. But her shoulder smarted, and she kept it to herself that she had heard the man utter the words, "Stop now, you nosey bitch!" Unsure whether she should report what had happened or not, she chose to say nothing about it.

The rest of the day was irritatingly unproductive, although she had to admit that it was reassuringly uneventful. She sat reading both the *Mountain Democrat* and the *Placerville Republican* for some time while seated in the small courtyard next to the hotel, then browsed the town's two book stores. She had a leisurely lunch while rewriting her notes so they were easier to read and reflected a more accurate timeline. After dinner alone in her room, she retired early to bed. However, before retiring, Lucy ordered coffee and rolls to her room for 7:00 AM.

Having received this order the next morning, and still in her robe, she took herself back to bed with her breakfast. Propped up on pillows, she read again the telegram from Jim that had been waiting for her at the front desk the evening before. He planned to be in town in two weeks, with Freda and Roger to arrive by stage soon after.

Lucy was torn between her eagerness to see Jim again, and her disappointment that it would be so long before she would once again be holding her son in her arms. But at least, she thought, my husband will be holding me.

She was still hoping that by the time her family arrived, she would have fulfilled her purpose for coming to Placerville. Yes, she now knew it had been Tony Leon who had sent the letters, and she even felt she knew something about why he had sent them. But was he killed because of this activity?

It would be a reasonable assumption, but he had gotten away with it unsuspected for so long. How had someone found him out? Was that someone willing to kill to keep a secret from being exposed? Or was it simply out of revenge? The only person who had died because of the letters was Mrs. Butterick, and she had no relatives, no spouse or fiancé, and not even that many close friends. But what damage might have been caused in some relationship because of the letters, about which she knew nothing?

If Tony wasn't killed out of revenge or fear of exposure, why else would someone want to kill him? Gus had mentioned that Tony didn't always pay his gambling debts. Or had he turned some of his discovered information into blackmail? That would mean he had turned from playing mean pranks in order to create fear and disruption, to making money off people's secrets.

Why would he suddenly want money? Almost in the same instant that she asked the question, Lucy knew the probable answer. He had decided to get away from Jane and a life that he felt stifled him. That led Lucy to another idea. Had Tony met another woman while on his travels out of town? If so, was Jane aware of this? And would she even care?

Lucy's dissatisfaction with all of these options expressed itself by her leaping out of bed to begin dressing. Only then did she see that sometime after her coffee had arrived, someone had slipped an envelope under her door. Opening it, she found a crudely printed note. "STOP NOW OR SUFFER THE CONSEQUENCES."

Several people had hinted that what she was doing could be dangerous, and feeling a twinge from her sore shoulder, she now knew they were right. She made sure the gun in her purse was loaded and then hurried to Dolly's house, hoping to catch Robert before he left for his livery. However, only Dolly and Melanie were home. Lucy immediately handed them the note before sitting on the sofa to await their reaction.

Dolly's response was what Lucy expected. "Oh, no! You must stop what you're doing immediately. It isn't worth endangering yourself. Leave it to the city police or the sheriff."

Melanie snorted with derision as she leaned back in her chair. "What do you expect, going around sticking your nose into people's business the way you've been doing?"

"Melanie!" Dolly looked at her sister with disbelief as she sat in the chair next to her. "I'm the one who started this."

"And wasn't that misplaced trust!" Melanie's cheeks blazed with color. "She's only made things worse. If someone comes after her when you're with her, you might get hurt, too."

Lucy stood up, slipped the folded note into the pocket of her dress and looked directly at Melanie. "I'm not going to stop. Not yet."

Dolly told Lucy, "It no longer really matters who wrote the letters. They've stopped being sent, and that's all that matters."

"Have you forgotten that there have been two murders?"

"But you don't know that they're connected to the letters," Dolly argued.

"I think they are." After a moment's hesitation, she sat back down on the sofa. "Because I know who sent the letters."

Dolly bit her lip in consternation, hoping Lucy wouldn't reveal to Melanie that Dolly also knew.

But Melanie simply stared at Lucy before growling, "No, you don't!"

Lucy turned the full intensity of her gaze upon Melanie. "Yes, I do. Why does that disturb you?"

"It doesn't disturb me." She calmly spread the skirts of her dress. "I just think you're bragging to bolster your position."

Dolly again looked at her sister, aghast at the way she was behaving. But before Dolly could say anything, Lucy cut her off. "I assure you that I know. And it wasn't Mrs. Helms. It was Tony Leon."

Dolly reached out to pat her sister's arm with reassurance. Careful not to let on to Melanie that she already knew that he was the sender, Dolly asked Lucy, "Did someone kill Mr. Leon because of the letter they got from him?"

"I don't know. But I don't think he put the newspapers in Mrs. Helms's room. I think whoever killed her did that."

"But," Dolly argued, "he could have done it. He might have put the letter-making stuff there to make everyone think *she* was the letter writer. You know, to protect himself if anyone ever suspected him of writing them."

"Oh, I think her killer wanted everyone to think Mrs. Helms was the writer. But the newspapers were stolen from Tony the same night or early morning that Mrs. Helms was killed. If he had been the one to put them in her room, he wouldn't have had to stage a break-in at his house. That only drew attention to him. And how would he have known he could get into her room without her knowledge, unless he also knew she was dead? No, whoever killed Mrs. Helms, broke into his house and stole the papers because they knew he was the letter writer."

"How would they have known where the papers were?" Melanie asked. "And the paste and scissors?"

They all avoided pointing out that Jane Leon easily fit this qualification. Lucy told them, "The person who put those things in Mrs. Helms's room either had been in the Leon house before at some time, or had spied on Tony." After a moment's hesitation, Lucy fixed her eyes on Melanie. "You know how easy that was to do, don't you?"

Melanie drew herself up, refusing to look at Dolly, who was now staring at her sister with her mouth agape. Melanie spoke softly to Lucy. "I don't know what you mean."

"Yes, you do." It was obvious that Lucy wasn't going to back down, and in her agitation, Melanie wadded a handful of her skirt in her hands. "I saw you looking through the French doors behind Tony's desk. If he had left the letter-making items on his desk, they could have been seen by you or anyone else standing outside."

"You spied on me?" Melanie tried for offended indignation, but immediately realized the futility of that. "Okay, yes, I did look into their house once." She wished she could avoid Dolly's shocked reaction. Unable to do this, she continued rapidly. "I had wanted to visit with Jane, but as I approached the house, I heard voices raised in anger. I knew it wasn't a good time to be visiting."

"Was Tony arguing with Jane?"

"No. It was Tony and some man, but I couldn't see either of them. They were beyond the screen in front of the desk that, as you know, sits just inside the French doors. But I was nosey enough that I wanted to see who it was." Her cheeks colored deeper at the confession. "But I didn't stay there long, as I'm sure you saw, because I was fearful of the savagery in the strange man's voice."

"Did you hear what the man was saying to Tony?"

"Not much. It was all muffled, but I could hear a few swear words. And then the strange man said 'I'm not going to let you do that.' That was all I heard before I hurried away."

Dolly turned to Lucy. "Are you now trying to find out who killed both Mr. Leon and Mrs. Helms?"

"Yes. I'm sure they're tied together somehow." She gave Dolly a look filled with compassion. "I'm sorry if that upsets you, considering who Mrs. Helms was to you."

Melanie stood up like a pistol had gone off behind her. She looked down on Dolly. "You knew she was our mother?"

Dolly stood up to face her. "Only from the time I saw her at the Orleans Hotel meeting. Do you mean to say this isn't a surprise to you?"

Melanie sat back down and nervously ran her hands over her skirts while breathing deeply. "Mother had written to Vincent last month telling him she was coming to Placerville to hold a meeting. She wrote him a couple of times a year, but never wrote to me. He threw it on the fire like he did all the others without letting me read it. But since he immediately left the room, I was able to catch it out before much of it caught fire. When I got here, I had the stage drop me off in front of the Orleans Hotel and they held my luggage while I went up to see her."

"Why didn't you tell me?" Dolly asked, the hurt in her voice apparent.

"Why didn't you tell me you'd recognized her at the meeting?" Melanie shot back.

"I didn't know how you'd react. I was still not sure how I felt about it." She purposely avoided saying that their mother had not wanted to see Melanie, and had made Dolly promise not to mention her presence in town.

"I was confused too, especially because she wasn't very welcoming. That's why I went back to see her while you two were out at the dressmakers and after I had visited with Sue Ellen. Our first meeting when I arrived in town had been very short. I just wanted her to know how awful my marriage had been. This was, after all, the marriage that she had arranged and insisted that I stay in." Melanie pressed her lips together to keep them from quivering. "She didn't seem to care. I left abruptly when she made me promise not to tell anyone of our relationship."

"Yes," Dolly nodded, "when I saw her the evening of the speech, she asked the same of me. I was glad to give her my promise."

"So was I." Melanie looked down at her hands now clenched in her lap, as though silently praying. But when she reached for a handkerchief in a pocket, Lucy realized that she was trying not to cry. Melanie took a deep breath before continuing. "But it was strange. The next day when I woke up, I felt free. She had released me from ever hoping there might be some resolution between us. I didn't have to be her daughter any more, or claim her as my mother. It was then I began to consider not returning to Vincent."

Lucy and Dolly looked at her in surprise. Both had assumed Melanie had made up her mind to that before even arriving in town.

Melanie continued. "Still, when I heard she was dead, it was a finality that forced me to realize that I had retained a little hope of getting some admission of responsibility for the horrid marriage she had forced me into. I know it sounds selfish, but it's the only thing that makes me sad about her passing."

Dolly rose from her chair and moved to her sister's side, bending down and wrapping her arms around her like she had when they were children. But Melanie did not hug her back. She reached up and grasped Dolly's wrists, disengaging the arms that had tried to wrap her in comfort.

Dolly returned to her chair and sat down, her face a mask of controlled emotion, most of which was hurt and confusion. After a sip of tea, however, she established the appearance of composure, saying, "I got Mother to admit to one thing. She said she was a very poor chooser of men. That was about my husband." She turned to Melanie and bit her lip. "She refused to admit the same about your Vincent."

"I'm not surprised," Melanie shrugged. "She told me she knew he was strict, but that I was just soft and spoiled. I tried to explain how badly he treated me, but she didn't want to listen."

Lucy sat and watched the two women with interest, at a loss for what to say. Melanie gave the impression of trying to control emotions Lucy at first wasn't sure were entirely sincere, although she certainly did seem distressed. Dolly sat back, still dazed by the rebuffing from her sister. She stared out the front window as though expecting someone to arrive with a good explanation. Lucy wondered if it was occurring to Dolly that the close tie that she had always felt with Melanie was no longer reciprocated. The harshness of their lives over the past decade had affected that bond more than either sister had realized, and possibly in ways they would never understand.

Dolly was indeed thinking this, but also that whereas she had finally made a good marriage with a stalwart and kind man, Melanie was not yet free of her disastrous, forced relationship. Having now become more fully aware of how different their lives were, she surmised that Melanie too had made this comparison, and might be resenting it.

Lucy was trying to imagine what it would be like to have one's mother express the desire not to see you ever again. How could a mother not want to even acknowledge her children's existence? Lucy coughed gently to clear a sudden lump in her throat and pulled herself together. Aloud, she asked, "Why would Tony Leon have visited Mrs. Helms a week or so before she was killed, and been heard arguing with her?"

That brought the sisters' eyes to her with intense interest, making it clear that neither of them had any knowledge of this. At the same time, Lucy found it strange that neither of them asked for further details. She found herself wanting to retreat from the idea that they were both misleading her. But instead of being put off by this, such an idea only made her more determined to go forward in her investigation. Consequently, she departed so abruptly that it left both Dolly and Melanie deep in thought as to why, although each of them arrived at a very different assumption. But their degree of consternation was close to the same.

CHAPTER 10

"Those friends thou hast, and their adoption tried,
Grapple them to thy soul with hoops of steel."
Shakespeare's Hamlet

Monday, June 16 - Tuesday, June 17

Lucy approached Robert's livery slowly, stopping to look at the aged, wooden building not far from Coloma Street that sloughed a little to the west. The long walk from Dolly's house had helped shake off the lingering uneasiness of what had been more confrontation than visit. Any lingering distress completely disappeared when she approached the open double doors of the livery and eagerly inhaled the pungent, heavy smells that greeted her. Mixed with the obvious equine odor was the rich scent of raw leather, the sharp bitterness of red-hot iron, and the nutty aroma of fresh straw. It was familiar, and somehow reassuring, and her spirits were uplifted.

Inside to the left, Robert worked the bellows to stoke the coals in the hot box where an iron implement was starting to glow. Adjusting the leather apron that covered his torso, he began work at his anvil. The loud, rhythmic clang of his hammer assaulted her ears while creating orange sparks that flew about like spring gnats on the hunt.

She realized for the first time the bulging strength of Robert's biceps, usually hidden beneath cloth, but now exposed below rolled up sleeves. "Thor's little brother," Lucy thought, trying not to laugh at the idea, and pretty sure she wasn't the first person to think it.

She stood in the doorway and glanced around, noting that although not as large as she would have expected, the stable's openness and well-organized interior made it appear spacious. That there was no dropped ceiling below the peak of the rough wood and cross-beam roof contributed to this impression. It was also a somewhat porous building, since she could see light between the boards of the side walls. Considering the frequent odors of hot iron, sweat and used straw, she thought the fresh air this afforded a fortunate circumstance.

To her right was a row of stalls with a window at the back of each one, their wooden shutters this day resting back against the walls. All but one of the stalls held a horse, a mule, or a burro. One of the horses had the companionship of a goat tethered just outside its door as a calming influence, the horse's head munching its food a near chomp away from its friend. Lucy noted that each animal was freshly curried, and recalled hearing many good comments about Robert's treatment of the animals in his care.

Behind Robert was a line of work benches below a wall from which hung rakes and shovels, an old bellows with the leather split, coils of rope, buckets, and tools of various types. Some needed repair, but others were ready to be pulled down for use. A shelf above the furthest work area was full of half-formed iron objects better suited to the kitchen, either made to order by Robert, or needing repair.

Pigs of iron were stacked in the corner. These were chunks of solid iron formed at a foundry, many of which were in New York. It was from these *pigs* that Robert would fashion his horseshoes, tools and kitchen utensils. It wasn't uncommon for them to be used as ballast on ships traveling around The Horn, but Robert had purchased his from the Placerville Iron Foundry. The foundry, at the west end of town on Hangtown Creek, was currently leased by Henry Morey, but he was hoping to someday be able to purchase it. In the meantime, he was shipping machinery to Virginia City that he had made in his shop.

Lucy took a step further into the interior and could see that across the back of the large barn was a row of wooden stands holding oiled leather saddles, the brass fixtures on them shining like jewels on brown satin. There was also a stack of thick, tightly woven blankets to fit beneath the saddles so the horses' hides would be kept free of sores from rubbing leather. Halters and bridles were hanging from pegs on the wall, some attached to bits and others not, while next to them were long, thin strips of leather that would become reins.

As Lucy's eyes adjusted to the shadowed interior, she realized there was a man standing at the back next to the row of saddles. He was deftly rolling a cigarette, pulling shreds of tobacco from a gauze pouch that he shoved back into his shirt pocket. His long, tobacco-stained fingers worked with alacrity to roll the shreds in the paper, the edge of which he licked across before putting the final product into his mouth. Pulling a match from his other shirt pocket, he scraped it across his boot and set the flame to the little cigarette as he inhaled deeply. He dropped the spent match into a bucket of water while Lucy waited for the smoke to be exhaled. When it was not, she wondered curiously where it had gone.

He was a man of forty who looked twice that, his brown leathery skin clean-shaven and his dark, hooded eyes squinting above the smoke curling up from the cigarette now dangling from his lips. He picked up a loose rope and began coiling it over his hand, the picture of nonchalance. Nevertheless, Lucy was certain that he had noticed her. In fact, she was pretty sure he noticed a lot more than some people might assume.

As the hatless man walked slowly toward her, she realized that although somewhat stoop-shouldered, he still registered as tall. The sinewy strength of his arms, bare below the rolled sleeves of his blue miner's shirt, gave evidence that Robert was not the only one who spent hours at the forge. When the wind whipped through the open doors of the livery, his hair blew up and out, and Lucy remembered Robert mentioning *Piney Paul*. He did indeed look like a pine tree bent over in a strong wind.

Paul had been around town since it had been *Old Dry Diggings* at the start of the rush. He was known for claiming that he would endure as long as the Sierra, because it was not only where he chose to live, but where he wanted to be buried. His old, crusted denim pants and worn boots looked to be already headed into antiquity.

Lucy anticipated his approach as he moved forward. Could this have been the person Mrs. Holliday had seen through the window, with his back turned to her and wearing a coat? The shadows of the interior, broken here and there by the light from structural cracks and windows, created a distorting picture of the interior. But why would Tony Leon have been discussing the anonymous letters with this man? Then again, why not?

Robert, seeing her hesitating at the entrance, ceased his work. "You want to see the spot?"

This stopped Paul in his tracks. He looked back and forth between Robert and this young woman in a simple but immaculate calico dress and shawl, her hair tucked up under a perky straw bonnet. He then glanced down at her leather, high-top shoes that showed a professional shine. He couldn't help but grin, thinking that no woman dressed so fine would want to sully herself by coming inside a livery stable.

"Do you mind, Robert?"

He barked out a short laugh. "Not at all." He stretched his back and swallowed a dipper of water from the bucket next to him. "Paul, will you show Mrs. Murphy where Tony was found?"

Paul hesitated, the idea not fitting in with his opinion of what a decent woman should be interested in seeing. Nevertheless, he motioned her forward while he remained where he was across from the forge.

"Here." Only one word, but it was full of grim meaning as he looked at the straw at the front of a stall with its door open, a small burro tied inside. "Can't see the blood now." When she didn't shudder or gasp, he frowned in disappointment.

Lucy looked down at the dirt floor in front of the stall, now covered with straw and scuffed over with boots and hooves that had tromped through the livery every day since the killing. What impressed her was the short distance between where Tony had fallen when killed, obvious because of the blood, and where Robert had found the body. Tony had been struck not far from the forge, then dragged into the nearest stall.

Lucy looked up at Paul, and then between the forge and the stall. "I'm trying to picture someone opening a stall and dragging a body into it with a horse inside that was possibly expected to trample the body to hide the fact that he was struck with a hammer." Paul grunted, but didn't say anything and Lucy continued. "Most horses wouldn't step on someone if they could possibly avoid them, afraid of entangling their feet. If there was a horse in the stall fractious enough that the killer expected it to go after someone on the ground, wouldn't a horse like that also attack the person doing the dragging of the body?"

She looked up from the floor of the stall to find Paul watching her with curiosity. "That's a good question, if there had been a horse in the stall."

Surprised, Lucy asked, "There wasn't?"

"Nope. Oh, there was when the body was found in the morning. But not when I closed up the night before."

"No one told me that." She tried not to sound querulous, but she couldn't hide her irritation.

Paul shrugged. "No one questioned it before. If they'd asked, I'd a told 'em."

Lucy looked at him and smiled. "So whoever killed Tony was able to enter the stall of a horse and lead it into this stall with the body. That means the horse saw the body on the floor and yet didn't kick up a fuss about entering. And stayed away from it all night."

"Yup. The killer picked one of the most well-behaved horses we were keeping at that time. It's gone now. The owner came and got him and rode on out of town."

"That was a major misjudgment on the part of the killer. Would that mean that they weren't used to being around horses?"

Paul only shrugged. "Could be they thought any horse in a stall with someone sprawled on the floor would at some point step on him."

Lucy shook her head. "Someone familiar with horses would know better."

Paul smiled at her, but said nothing. She thanked him before walking over to Robert. "Did you know that Tony Leon had visited with Mrs. Helms in her room before he left on his last trip?"

His surprise was genuine. "He knew her well enough to do that? I'll be damned. Does that mean they might have been killed by the same person?"

Lucy laughed. "If you want another job, I think you should apply to the police department. You came to that conclusion very quickly."

"Seems obvious, doesn't it?"

"If it has occurred to the investigating officers, they're being very close-mouthed about it."

Lucy turned and walked back into town while Robert continued on with his work, hammering on the tines of a hay fork slowly taking shape on his anvil.

Walking into town and trying to think of those people with whom she had not yet spoken, Lucy realized that there had been at least one woman who had been less than accepting of Mrs. Helms's ideas. That had been the young woman who had boldly questioned Mrs. Helms during her talk. There was probably no more to the questions asked than a woman challenging ideas that were a threat to her future, but Lucy was curious. She had not missed the notes of defiance and even scorn in the young woman's voice when she had asked her questions. And she had asked them from the table furthest from the podium, at the table sneered at by Mrs. Landecker.

When questioned, Dolly said she didn't know who the women were at that particular table, but she suggested to Lucy that Mary Nary, the laundress at the Cary House, might know, as she had a distant relative who worked in one of the *houses*. Lucy approached the smallest of the wooden laundry structures in back of the hotel, its windows on all sides open and its stone floor wet. Mary was in the process of washing women's lace collars and cuffs, along with underthings — chemises, corset covers, drawers and petticoats -- a lighter load than towels and bedding washed in the other outbuilding. Still, the woman was busy and Lucy hesitated to interrupt her, so she stood back under the overhang of the hotel's back porch to wait for a more approachable moment.

Mrs. Nary was working at a long wooden table just beyond the shed's open double doors and near three tin tubs. One of these was full of clothes in water kept hot from a heavy iron kettle on a sheet iron stove at the back of the room. The other two tubs contained rinse water, one hot and one cold. Lucy watched Mrs. Nary shave a cake of lye soap before dumping the shavings into the steaming hot water of the first tub, which she stirred with a short stick. She then mixed flour into a bowl of cold water until it was smooth before pouring it into a pot of simmering water sitting on one of the eyes of the stove. She now had starch to be used later when doing the pile of men's white shirts sitting off to the side.

Mary removed the ladies' items from the tub with what looked like a broom handle missing the broom, and transferred them to the first rinse tub of hot water. After a slosh through the second rinse tub with cool water, she wrung out the clothes by hand even though there was a mangle attached to the tub's rim. She carefully hung each item on a rope clothes line that ran down the side of the room across from the work table, and took a minute to stretch her back.

After dumping the soapy water onto the stones of the floor, she gave them a quick scrub with a string mop before rinsing the stones with the water from the cool-water tub, the water draining away through vents along the bottom edge of the walls. When all the tubs were empty, she turned them upside down and dried her arms with a towel from a peg over the work bench.

It was then that she looked up and spotted Lucy watching her from beyond the open door. "Can I help you with something, madam?"

"I didn't want to interrupt your efforts. I know what that's like when you don't want your hot water to cool and there's a lot to get done."

Mrs. Nary looked Lucy up and down. "You don't look like a lady that does her own laundry."

"I have a family, and believe me, I've often done it with or without help. But I've come to ask you a question." Mrs. Nary stepped outside and sank onto one end of a wooden bench next to the door. Lucy sat at the other end of it, shifting towards the woman now fanning herself with the hem of her apron. "Someone said you were at the talk Mrs. Helms gave at the Orleans Hotel."

"Yeah, I was there. I saw you there, too. It was a bit of a lark that some of us thought we'd go and see. All stuff and nonsense, if you ask me."

"I was told that you might know who the woman was at the back of the room asking so many questions."

"Oh, her," she shrugged. "That was Sweet Tooth Kate. She works in a house down Main Street toward Upper Placerville." She proceeded to give more detailed directions to the house, one of the fanciest in town. "The *mother* there won't mind if you talk to one of her girls."

"That's good."

Mrs. Nary stood up and removed her wet pinafore apron, hanging it on a peg next to the door to dry. Sitting back down with a small groan and a twist of her tired shoulders, she said, "You won't find any *black-eyed Susans* or *celestials* there. They're in other houses in town. No, Sweet Tooth Kate and her fellow creatures are too high-toned to consort with Mexican or Chinese girls. You'll know Kate when you see her 'cause she'll probably be sucking on a piece of rock candy."

"Thank you, Mrs. Nary. You've been very helpful."

Mary reached around to her back with both hands and rubbed the lower portion. "You're the one looking to find out who wrote them terrible letters, ain't you?"

"I've already done that. Now I'm hoping to find out who killed Mrs. Helms and Tony Leon."

"Oh, yeah?" She tucked a wisp of gray hair behind her right ear and twisted her lips into a grimace. "Well, let me tell you somethin'. You ever talk to Tony Leon?"

"No. I never met him."

"He had a funny sort of way of lookin' at you if you was a woman. Bold, it was. He'd come to the house to see my man and when we was alone, he'd comment on things. Nothin' special, but I always felt like he was waitin' for me to say somethin' back. I'd no idea what. Made my skin crawl." She rolled her eyes as she added, "My husband said I was bein' foolish, but I know what I felt."

"That's very interesting. Your husband was friends with him?"

"Not really. My Hal always said nice things about Tony's way with his pack mules, though. But I think it was because he didn't want to say anything bad about Tony his self, like how he looked at young gals. Trouble was, they didn't look back and I don't think that set well with Tony."

"A lady's man?"

"No, I wouldn't say that." She thought a moment before adding, "More like he was sad."

Lucy hid her surprise, but didn't ask for clarification, as she wanted to get on her way. Besides, she thought Mrs. Nary had told all she knew that wasn't mere surmising. She gave Mrs. Nary two nickels and thanked her again. The woman slipped the coins into a pocket without comment and began sweeping the area with an old straw broom that had been leaning against the wall.

Lucy was not a stranger to what would be found in a parlor house establishment, nor was she shy about entering one. But she knew if anyone saw her do such a thing, her reputation in town would be highly compromised. Therefore, seeing young Charley coming out of George Francis's clothing store on the Plaza, she stopped him and sent him to the house with a message for Sweet Tooth Kate. He was soon on the front porch relaying Lucy's request that Kate meet her at the Adriatic Restaurant on the south side of Main opposite Coloma, at a time named by Kate. In return, Kate was told she would receive a meal in compensation for her time. Charley made sure to emphasize that Mrs. Murphy was a lady, and also a very nice one who could be trusted.

Kate's curiosity and appetite were greater than her wariness, so she told the boy that she would meet Mrs. Murphy at the restaurant in an hour. Charlie hurried back to Lucy with the message.

Waiting at a table at the back of the restaurant, Lucy recognized Kate immediately upon her entrance and waved to her. She was pleased to see that the young demimonde was dressed conservatively and wore barely any makeup. Consequently, Kate brought no notice to herself even from men present who probably knew her quite well when "tarted up" at the house. And the townswomen present were unaware that the type of woman they referred to as "appropriate for the gutter" was in their midst.

Kate nodded in response to Lucy introducing herself. She sat straight and proud, and obviously on her guard, like a wild animal ready to spring up and run at the slightest provocation.

"I'm very grateful for your willingness to meet with me," Lucy told her. "I'm sure you'd rather be resting up for tonight." Kate blinked at what was a casually stated acknowledgement of what she did for a living, but that also showed no judgment. "I don't know about you, but I'm as hungry as a miner with a played-out claim. Let's order. Do you like beef steak?"

"Yeah, sure." Kate was surprised at being asked her preference, and that Lucy was willing to pay for the most expensive item on the menu in the middle of the afternoon. But she visibly relaxed, and even gave Lucy a tentative smile that lit up her face and showed how young she really was beneath the hard veneer she presented to the world.

After Lucy ordered the steaks, along with two side dishes, Kate showed her cautious nature by immediately asking the reason for the invitation. Lucy explained her interest in Mrs. Helms, but only to the point of admitting to curiosity and wanting to find her killer. Dolly and Melanie's connection to Mrs. Helms she would not have shared with anyone. In fact, she was still undecided whether or not she would ask the young woman any questions about Tony Leon.

Lucy pulled a small paper sack of clear rock candy from her purse and laid it in front of Kate. "I was wondering why you seemed to be challenging Mrs. Helms's ideas during the meeting at the Orleans Hotel."

Kate picked up the bag and hefted it in her hand similar to how Lucy had watched miners with a pouch of gold. Kate smiled and slipped the bag into a large side pocket of her skirt. But her dark eyes snapped angrily when she turned to the subject of Mrs. Helms. "I'd talked to the old bat a few days before that big meeting at the hotel."

"Oh." Lucy didn't know what else to say. It was clear Kate was no fan of the late Mrs. Helms.

Both women took time out to enjoy the steaks placed in front of them by the waiter, along with the creamed corn and sliced tomatoes and cucumber in sweetened vinegar. As the waiter walked away, he was almost overwhelmed with curiosity as to why a lady like Mrs. Murphy would be sitting at the same table as Sweet Tooth Kate. But he was well-trained, so he didn't linger, and consequently missed what followed from Kate.

"She came to the house to talk to Mrs. French, the owner. Mrs. French is strict, but she treats us well."

Lucy stiffened. "Is Mrs. French a woman of advanced years, tall and thin, and with a kind smile? Been in the business since she was young?"

"Why, yes." Kate showed her surprise, quickly followed by suspicion that she was being set up for something unpleasant. "How do you know her?"

"I think I met her about seven years ago when she visited a parlor house where I was the cook."

"You worked in a house?" Looking at the fashionably dressed woman across from her, wearing a wedding band and who was what Kate thought of as "quality", she found this most interesting. But she only said, "Of course, Mrs. French has a man who does her bidding and acts as bouncer for us girls."

"That's good. You want to be sure you stay on his good side." Having made this curious statement with a surprising degree of conviction, Lucy asked, "Did Mrs. Helms come to the house to convert or chastise?"

Kate laughed. "Plenty have done both. But she just wanted to talk to us about her usual topic of women's rights. And to be sure that we'd join her in the march through town she was planning. Still, she couldn't hide her condescension, and it irritated all of us."

"That wasn't very wise of her."

"She said that at least us girls had made a decision to live on our own, in our own way, and that we had 'charted our own course'." Kate made a hissing noise before exclaiming, "What bullshit!"

"Did you tell her how you felt?" Lucy was smiling openly, and Kate immediately warmed to this unusual woman asking her odd questions, and who wasn't easily offended.

"I certainly did." Kate stuck out her chin, her cheeks pink with remembered vexation. "I told her that she didn't know anything about what we have to put up with, and that I resented her pretending that she did. I told her that men are more in charge of our lives than a wife's, because at least a wife has a few laws that protect her." Adding with a heightened degree of defensiveness, she said, "And if not that, then at least a wife has society's rules of acceptance."

Lucy nodded. "Yes, your best protection comes only from how well and to whom your house mother gives her payoffs."

"That's right!" Kate leaned back in her chair and curled her lip. "All Mrs. Helms wanted was females to march in her idiotic parade. We didn't want her looking down her nose at us at the same time as asking us for a favor. We turned her away pretty sharp after we realized what she was really after."

"Did she go to all the other houses to do this?"

"I don't think so, 'cause I didn't hear anything about it from them girls. But then, we don't socialize much with the girls from other houses. They're just competition to us."

After Kate had left, Lucy remained at the table waiting for the waiter to bring the bill while finishing the last of the tea in the pot. She watched a man with a long, dark beard get up from a table across the room and slowly approach her table, a slight limp obvious as he made his way toward her. His eyes were red-rimmed, and his shoulders stooped. Lucy immediately labeled him as *old miner*.

He removed his felt hat, revealing a thatch of dark hair. "Excuse me, ma'am, but you look very much like a young girl I knew during the rush. Her name was Lucy and she was traveling with a woman who cooked for us miners." As he spoke, Lucy saw past the beard to realize that this man couldn't be out of his thirties.

"How nice to see someone from back then. Please join me." She put out her hand and he took it in his for a brief but almost reverent moment before pulling out a chair and sitting down. She told him, "I am indeed Lucy."

He slowly shook his head in wonder. "So you're the little lady who gave me food and coffee when I needed it most."

She laughed. "Not so little any more. I'm married and have a child almost six."

"Oh, my." He again shook his head. "You were such a boon to my spirits back then. The prospecting wasn't going too well, and all of us in my small group of friends were disheartened and talking about giving up.

"And did you?"

"No. After you were so kind to me, I felt such a surge of hope and good feeling, that I convinced them all to keep going until I'd recovered from my injury. Three days later we hit a good size strike. They own their own businesses now, and I just sold my saddle shop in Sonora."

The way he looked at her, Lucy thought, "I feel like a wounded bird cupped gently in his hands to be given warmth." But she only said, "The early days of the rush were very special. I never met so many men appreciative of good food and a bit of innocent conversation with a young girl."

"I didn't have this much facial fur back then," he chuckled. "I was the man with the wounded foot leaning against the outside wall of a cabin without water or grub. You were angry at my friends for not taking better care of me."

She looked into his smoky gray eyes and the picture as she had seen him almost a dozen years earlier came rushing back to her. She also remembered how concerned Freda had been about her wanting to bring food to some strange man uphill from where she and Freda had set up camp. Most of all, she remembered how grateful but also somewhat bitter the man had been.

"Henry, right?"

He almost glowed, his joy was so great. "I can't believe you remember my name."

"I guess it's because you gave me such a lecture when I mentioned 'the gold fields', a romantic term you scoffed at. You reminded me that gold was always down in deep, rocky ravines in cold streams and rivers, which was certainly true."

"Yeah. But now it's mostly hard rock mining."

After another fifteen minutes of general conversation and reminiscing, Henry left. At the door, he turned and looked back at Lucy. When she smiled and put up a hand to wave good-bye, he put his hat on and left quickly. Out on the sidewalk, he gave a quick blow on his handkerchief and headed for the stage about to leave town.

Lucy sat for several minutes thinking about those days so long ago, and how easily people pass through our lives without our ever knowing how our actions might have affected them. Back during the rush, she had been determined to chase after her dreams, just like thousands of gold rush miners who had also chased after theirs. But only a few men had found a strike that paid for the exorbitant costs of prospecting and everyday existence, much less enough to set them up for future success.

Lucy hurried to Dolly's house to tell her about her afternoon, only to find that her friend was in town shopping. It was Melanie who answered the door, and who invited her in.

"Would you like something cold to drink? Or a cup of tea?"

Lucy couldn't hide her surprise at Melanie's friendliness, or the fact that she was acting as lady of the house. "A glass of water would be nice."

"Of course. Make yourself comfortable while I get it."

Lucy was certainly not comfortable as she sat on the sofa. She was full of suspicion and had one eye on the front door, hoping Dolly or Robert might enter and keep the conversation on general subjects.

Melanie was back with her water in only a moment, saying, "I think I owe you an apology, Lucy." The look of contrition on her face was obvious, but Lucy was uncertain of its sincerity.

"Oh? What about?"

"I've not always treated you with cordiality."

"You mean that you've been rude."

A spasm of irritation flitted over Melanie's face, but was quickly sheltered and replaced with a smile. "Well, yes. And I'm sorry for that. It's just been such a difficult last few months for me. I came here expecting to find consolation and comfort from my sister, in the warmth and peace of her home, only to find that she was involved in trying to find the perpetrator of anonymous letters. With your help."

"In other words, she didn't immediately focus on you." Lucy wasn't in the mood to play to Melanie's act of reformed good will. She was sure it was being put on solely with some ulterior motive in mind.

Melanie forced a small moue of a smile. "You're not making this easy, Lucy."

"I'm not trying to. You've treated me with ill grace on a number of occasions. And you've also lied to me as well as to Dolly."

Melanie began to object, but instead looked down at her lap and retrieved a small lace handkerchief folded over the belt of her dress. She dabbed delicately at each eye. "Are you forgetting that I had a great shock in finding that my mother was here as the out-spoken Mrs. Helms?

Someone not acceptable to many people? I certainly didn't want to be seen as connected with her. I came to find refuge with my sister and found the dark cloud of our mother looming over my visit."

"I'm sure that was disconcerting for you. But I've been disconcerted by situations in my life, and yet I didn't find it necessary to be rude to new acquaintances." Seeing Melanie's jaw clench, she quickly added, "But I can feel compassion for how difficult it must have been for you. It certainly was for Dolly. But you said Mrs. Helms had written to your husband and you read the letter. So how much shock could there have been?"

"Yes, she did write him, but I wasn't sure she was telling him the truth about *when* she would be here, and I needed to get away from...home."

"Do you know how long ago she married Mr. Helms?"

"I only know that he died a number of years ago."

So, Lucy thought, she has had either more correspondence with her mother than she's indicating, or she had more of a conversation with her here in Placerville than she has let on. "What else are you keeping from Dolly and me?"

Melanie hesitated only a brief moment before saying, "Nothing."

Lucy let this pass unchallenged. "Did you know she was planning to live here?"

"You have no idea how upset I was when Dolly told me that she had announced that intention during her speech." Lucy noted again how Melanie always avoided using the term *mother*. "I think it made me even more anxious than I was already. And why I took it out on you, what with your being here also such a surprise. But that wasn't fair of me."

"So why are you trying to smooth over all of that now?"

Melanie took a moment to refold her handkerchief before laying it on the low table between them. "I guess I've come to the realization of how unfair I've been. My reaction was selfish and immature, especially for a married woman no longer in the first flush of youth."

Lucy relented, deciding to give Melanie the benefit of the doubt after all. "Well, let's forget the past. We can just proceed on the basis that we both love Dolly, and are happy to be in such a nice town."

Melanie bit her lower lip. "Yes, you're going to be living here with your husband and child. How nice for you, having your family around you. It should keep you very busy. Maybe so much so that you'll have little time to embroil yourself in the town's affairs."

Lucy fought back a sigh of disappointment, while also feeling disgruntled for having allowed herself to be taken in by someone she instinctively knew she shouldn't trust. "Is that your polite way of saying I should mind my own business in the future? I'm only trying to find the culprits involved in crimes."

Melanie couldn't hide the sudden, angry blush that spread over her face. "There you go again, minding other people's business. We have a police department in this town who look into crimes."

"Yes, but that doesn't mean a private citizen can't take an interest."

"It's not an appropriate thing for a woman to do. I don't care about your reputation, but since you're Dolly's friend, your actions may reflect badly on her."

In that moment Lucy knew without doubt that Melanie had no intention of leaving Placerville. "Dolly knows how to handle other people. And I'm sure you'll settle into the town just fine. You needn't worry that I have any interest in *your* affairs."

"You better not! You stay out of my life!" All effort toward amiable civility had evaporated from Melanie's demeanor, and she obviously no longer cared if it was apparent.

Unaware as to what she had said to trigger Melanie's sudden defensiveness, Lucy stood up and walked toward the front door. Anger welled up inside her, and she turned back to find that Melanie was standing with her fists clenched at her sides. Lucy smiled with feigned innocence as she aimed at Melanie's most vulnerable spot. "You didn't mention your dear husband. Missing him yet?"

The look of fury aimed at Lucy was replete with unladylike thoughts longing to be put into words. Instead of voicing them, however, Melanie turned and walked into her bedroom, slamming the door soundly behind her.

But while Melanie seethed with outrage, mumbling epithets and pacing within her room to release her frustration, Lucy felt guilty and regretful. She remonstrated with herself for giving way to feminine cattiness. Usually compassionate and quick to forgive, even with those who had harmed her, she couldn't understand why Melanie always seemed to get under her skin.

As Lucy walked back into town, she stopped a moment to watch a crew of Chinese men who were building a small, square building with rock quarried from somewhere nearby. So far, they had only completed the first floor, three doors across the front, with a second floor to be added in the future. Wondering at its use, she continued to Sacramento Street, and walked toward Main. Unbeknownst to Lucy, once completed, a rumor would circulate that the building was connected to Main by a tunnel so patrons of the stone bordello could enter without being seen.

As she walked, she was surprised to realize that right then she wanted nothing more than to feel Jim's arms around her, giving her comfort and support. It clashed with the picture she had of herself as independent and strongly self-reliant, which she had demonstrated countless times following a thoroughly unconventional childhood and adolescence. This domestic, feminine side of herself was more disconcerting to her than any other aspect of her character.

Nevertheless, at this moment she ached for the sight of Jim's lopsided, somewhat cocky smile. When he looked into her eyes and winked, flashing a message only she understood, her heart always beat a little harder. As she sighed and unlocked the door to her hotel room, she admitted to herself that Jim couldn't get to Placerville soon enough.

Jim Murphy was a gambler from the snappy clothes he wore clear through to his outlook on life. He entered a game not with a wooden expression determined to give nothing away, nor did he swagger like some professional gamblers who tried to throw the other players off their game with fear of his ability. When Jim sat down to play, his was not a face full of bland disregard, but rather that of animation and excitement.

He always made a point of shaking hands around the table, leaving the impression that they were all there to enjoy themselves in a companionable game among friends. He showed openly his eagerness and ardor for whatever game of chance was to be played, and he didn't care that it awoke in his fellow players their alertness.

When Jim held cards in his hands, he was most alive, and this joy never left him as he played and bet. Consequently, the other players couldn't tell if he was happy about his hand or was just happy about being where he was. It was unusual, and therefore unsettling, to see a professional gambler unafraid of showing such lively zest for the game, and who reacted to a losing hand with the same grace that he accepted the chips from a winning pot. And he won most of the times he played. Nevertheless, because of his low-key and friendly approach, he never garnered a reputation as did so many western characters.

Getting dressed the next morning while thinking about Jim's arrival, Lucy laughed at herself when she realized there were butterfly flutterings in her stomach. It always amazed her to hear other women talking about their husbands with disparagement or harsh criticisms. Beneath her love for Jim lay a deep respect for his character. The compassion she had often seen him display toward others, his patience with Roger, his willingness to stand up for those unjustly accused, his self-deprecating sense of humor, all were the basis of this respect. But above all that, he accepted his wife for who she was, and never chastised her for being outspoken or occasionally headstrong. Consequently, her respect for him was equal to that which he held for her.

Looking down as she fastened the buttons of her white, lacy waist, she realized that she had been neglecting her hands of late. They could definitely benefit from some attention, so she decided to stop by Sue Ellen's establishment to see if there was an opening on her schedule.

Lucy had met Sue Ellen on her last trip, and had liked the way she had washed and set her hair, all while being friendly as well as professional. After learning that Lucy was a friend of Dolly's, Sue Ellen had been even friendlier and they had found a number of things in common. Nothing draws two people together quicker than laughter, and they had laughed a lot.

Not surprised to find the door of the shop locked, Lucy knocked softly. After a moment, the door was opened and Sue Ellen cautiously peeked out.

"Lucy! I was expecting a customer who is very late." She stepped back and Lucy entered the cool, fragrant room.

"I took a chance by coming here, knowing you might be busy. But I need some attention to my hands."

"Oh, that's no problem. If my tardy customer decides to show up, she can wait until we're done. Serves her right." Sue Ellen smiled impishly and pulled out a chair for Lucy at the work table, whereupon she sat opposite her.

After turning up the wick on the lamp to create more light, she pulled open a drawer and removed jars, nail files and cloths. While Lucy's hands soaked in a foamy mixture of rose water, Sue Ellen laid out several implements on a soft towel. Removing one of Lucy's hands and drying it gently, she began work on the cuticles. Nothing was said between them for several minutes and Lucy felt herself relax into a state of near euphoria.

Then, without preamble, Sue Ellen said, "You've been very busy since you came to town." It was a statement that left no room for evasion on Lucy's part, and she was once again alert.

However, instead of commenting on this subject directly, Lucy surprised Sue Ellen by asking, "You're a good friend of Melanie St. John, aren't you?"

Sue Ellen sat back and laughed. "Dolly's sister? We're friends." Lucy didn't miss how non-committal this answer was, and wondered why.

"She doesn't like me," Lucy frankly stated. "In fact, from the moment we met, she decided to dislike me very much."

Lucy respected the fact that Sue Ellen didn't immediately reject this idea, but took a moment to consider it. "The sisters have always been very close. She may resent the rapport you and Dolly share. Especially if it's based on shared experiences about which she knows nothing."

"Oh, I'm sure of it." After a moment, Lucy added, "I also think her mind was made up not to return to her husband even before she came here."

"You may be right."

"You know I am, don't you?"

Sue Ellen only smiled and shrugged, hoping this would not betray Melanie's confidence, but also avoid lying to Lucy.

Lucy thought she would try a little shock tactic. "Then you know about the girls' relationship with Mrs. Helms."

Sue Ellen started to question what Lucy was referring to, but then changed her mind. "Oh, that."

Lucy was pretty sure Sue Ellen didn't know what she was talking about, but rather was trying to get the information by pretending she did. "Well," Lucy sighed, "it sure surprised me. Can you believe a mother not wanting to claim her children?"

It took a moment for Sue Ellen to get the drift of what Lucy was indicating, but when she did, she sat back and showed her surprise. "Their *mother*? But they already..."

When Sue Ellen stopped and bit her lip, Lucy prompted, "They already what?"

"Oh, nothing. I just meant they've had such difficult lives, and then to run into their mother here. It's just so unfair. They're such nice women."

"Yes. Unfair." Lucy was sure that wasn't what Sue Ellen had been about to say, but she also realized that pushing the point right then would be counter-productive.

"Do you by any chance know why Tony Leon would have been in Mrs. Helms's room a week or so before her death?"

"Was he?" Her voice cracked, and she got up to fetch them both a glass of water. "It's a warm morning, isn't it?"

"Yes." But Lucy wasn't ready to change the subject. "Tony was heard to be arguing with Mrs. Helms. Did you know they were acquainted?"

"I can't imagine. It's all so confusing."

Having finished with the cuticles, Sue Ellen quickly took a file to Lucy's nails while talking in excruciating detail about a new dress she had ordered. Lucy several times attempted to change the subject, but to do so would have been to interrupt the flow of Sue Ellen's almost breathless dissertation.

Sue Ellen then handed Lucy a small jar of glycerin salve. "Now, I'd better prepare for my next customer. You rub this in before you retire at night and your hands will soon look like that of a girl of ten."

She led the way to the door, smiling brightly, while Lucy protested that she needed to pay for the treatment. Sue Ellen waved her hand at the protest. "Oh, heavens, it was a pleasure. I had to be here anyway waiting for my lady to arrive."

"But I should pay you for the salve."

"Consider it a gift. Now, I hope to see you again soon. Good day, Lucy."

Feeling hustled out, because she had been, Lucy moved away down the alley toward the street. She maintained a posture of dignity, but she was mentally blinking at the abruptness with which her session had ended. What had she said that caused her to be treated like a bum ushered from a saloon?

Meanwhile, in Jamestown the intense eagerness Jim was experiencing as he looked forward to seeing Lucy again was not as surprising to him as it might have been to someone who didn't know him well. Men of his generation and background never discussed among themselves their finer and deeper feelings, so he was left to suppose that he was an oddity among males. For he loved his wife even more after six years of marriage than when he had proposed to her.

Thinking that he would soon be able to once again feel the warmth of her body next to his in the night brought on a longing that almost overwhelmed him. As an alternative, he tried focusing on her voice, but that made his heart ache with a loneliness that he'd seldom felt before. It made him push everyone around him to pack faster and leave behind the heaviest of the furniture, no matter how serviceable or handsome.

"We can always buy what we need once we see the house and what furnishings are there," he said again to Freda, who was getting tired of hearing this.

He may have been Lucy's husband, but as far as Freda was concerned, no one knew Lucy as well as she did. Only fourteen years Lucy's senior, Freda Carr had finished raising Lucy from the time she had been twelve until almost twenty, and under circumstances both challenging and rewarding. At times they had been more like sisters, while at others like mother and daughter, but seldom employer and employee. Lucy had been legally indentured to Freda until she had turned eighteen, but Freda hated what that implied and had long ago refused to admit to it. Parted for several years, after Roger's birth Freda had headed west from New York to become part of the family.

Freda knew what items Lucy would never consider leaving behind, and she therefore ordered onto the freighter's large wagon Lucy's rocking chair covered in petti point, the small pie safe that had belonged to the woman who had left the house to Lucy, and her own rocking chair that had been a gift from Lucy. She personally packed Lucy's china, placing each piece of it in the wooden barrels filled with straw, and with the silver flatware distributed on the bottom so no one would know it was there. And, of course, she demanded that Lucy's favorite books be included, along with a small crystal vase given her by Jim on their first anniversary.

Young Roger had to talk *Aunt Freda* into leaving behind the books his mother had read to him when he was a child, which he no longer considered himself. Freda told him he could explain to Lucy that it was his idea, but she did include his favorite book only recently outgrown, as it had been a gift from herself.

Paper-wrapped parcels of clothing were placed between everything to hold it in place and give it as soft a ride as possible. The freighter, knowing how shifting a ride it was going to be over rough dirt roads, down valleys and up steep hills, smiled and said nothing. Breakage was part of life to him. On the other hand, he had seldom seen such careful and well-organized packing as that done by the exacting Mrs. Carr.

When the new owner of the Jamestown house saw all that had been left for him, his joy took the form of a bank draft passed to Jim with a hearty handshake. The stage was not leaving town until two days after the freighter got under way, so Jim used that money to make Freda and Roger comfortable in the Jamestown Hotel in the heart of town. Built in 1858, it was known to have a fine dining room and comfortable, spacious rooms. Unfortunately, it would burn down the following year, to be rebuilt and that one lasting into the next millennium.

After departing from them, Jim tied his riding horse to the back of the black rig and proceeded to follow the freighter, a man he knew well. When he realized the freighter had hired on a young and experienced flunky, Jim reconsidered his need to tag along.

Almost to the north end of town, Jim heard a man call to him from the sidewalk. "Hey, Jim. Hold up there."

"Harry! What can I do for you?"

"I have a proposition for you."

"Oh, yes?" Harry always had a proposition for someone, and sometimes they were even good ones.

"I have an aunt in Sonora who's looking for a new rig just like yours. How about you sell it to me and then you'll have that extra money when you get to Placerville? You can also ride ahead and have a little time with Lucy without Freda and the kid around."

Jim laughed. "You've prepared the perfect argument, haven't you?"

Henry smiled, knowing Jim well. "I know how you must be missing your lady. And I owe my aunt a lot for all she's done for me."

The amount being easily settled between them, Jim mounted his horse and headed north. Even with this additional time gained, he tried to recall if there were a couple of shortcuts along the way. Nevertheless, he forced himself to slacken his pace, always mindful that his horse was a living thing with needs of its own.

The seventeenth of June in Placerville was a Tuesday that dawned clear and warm. One of the churches had planned for a rummage sale in order to raise money for repairs to the roof. The town ladies, and even a good number of men, were looking forward to it. So many people had donated items that the sale filled the surrounding area where usually people parked their rigs.

Lucy arrived shortly after it began and wandered between tables loaded with miscellaneous kitchen items, tools, remnants of cloth, coils of rope, fishing poles, boots, and books. Having found a reason to stop, she picked up book after book to read the title or flip through its pages. Many of them had inscriptions on the blank facing page, and she smiled as she read them. Birthdays, anniversaries, graduations, all were commemorated by relatives and admirers. Some were dated, but most of them were not.

Picking up a book with an inscription indicating that it had been an anniversary present with the Roman numeral for five, she felt an odd frisson of excitement. She couldn't understand why until she saw the title page and realized it was a Bronte novel that she had enjoyed a number of years earlier. She continued to look at books from that same stack and found several inscriptions signed with initials or, as in one instance, hearts and flowers drawn instead of words or initials.

Deciding there were several of the books interesting enough to purchase, one of which was Ralph Waldo Emerson's "The Conduct of Life", a collection of essays. She started to leave, but went back for another book, "The Woman in White" by Wilke Collins, having been told it was an exciting story about mysterious happenings. Maybe, she thought, when I'm done with these books, I'll take them to Mrs. Hall at the Orleans Hotel in case she hasn't read them.

She was soon back at the Cary House, sitting in the lobby near a west-facing side window, where the light was good for reading. She ordered a pot of tea, and soon a china pot with matching cup and saucer was brought to her on a small silver tray. There were even two sugar cookies on a small plate. Lucy sighed with pleasure, only too aware of how special and rare are such moments in one's life. She opened one of the books and began to read.

Not long after she had finished her tea and cookies, the desk clerk approached her. "Mrs. Murphy, there's a man here who would like to see you. He has considerately not entered the lobby." Lucy looked toward the door and saw Gus standing on the sidewalk watching a stage being unloaded of its Wells, Fargo and Company bags. In his most officious manner, the clerk primly suggested, "Maybe you would prefer to talk to the, um, gentleman while seated on the bench outside. It's down a little way from the door."

Lucy thought of several cutting remarks, as well as forcing the issue by inviting Gus to join her on the sofa. But upon consideration, she realized that would just make Gus uncomfortable. "Thank you. I'll do that."

Once outside, and having greeted Gus with a warm smile, she led the way to the bench. "Is something wrong?"

"Yes and no." He looked around to be sure no one could hear them. "I'm not an advocate for *all* that women want. I think society would change too much too fast. But I was drinking with some fellas last night, and one of 'em said no woman would ever have the courage or intelligence to make good political decisions. I immediately thought, 'I bet Mrs. Murphy would.' And then I thought that maybe there are other women like you who think like a man." When Lucy looked at him with a raised brow that bordered on a scowl, he quickly added, "Again, I mean that as a compliment!"

Lucy looked out at the street full of passing wagons, each one owned by a man and driven by a man, and laughed. "I know." She turned to him with a smile and asked, "Is that why you came here? To tell me you're taking a second look at women's suffrage?"

"God, no. I came by to tell you I overheard some guy threatening you."

"Where was this?"

"In a saloon. He was pretty loaded, but not so far gone that he didn't know what he was saying. He said if the suffrage woman could be done away with, so could you." He looked sideways at Lucy. "I told him that if anything happened to you, he'd be the first one I'd come after. And I'd make him sorry he'd been born."

Lucy smiled as she looked out at the street, but then sobered. It was difficult to accept that there were people who were adamantly opposed to the idea of someone other than the local law looking into crimes. The fact that it was a woman doing it probably made it seem to them especially unforgivable. "Thank you for telling me, Gus."

"I have a pistol you can have," he blurted out. "I can show you how to use it."

She looked at her new, somewhat strange friend, and placed a hand on the beaded purse that hung from her shoulder on a silver chain. "I carry a derringer with me always, and I know how to use it."

Gus shook his head, holding back a laugh. "I should have known."

With that as his parting statement, Gus rose and walked away. Lucy could only see the back of him, but those approaching him wondered why Old Gus was grinning.

CHAPTER 11

"Society is at the mercy of a murderer who is
remorseless, who takes no accomplices and who
keeps his head." Edmond Pearson

Thursday, June 19 – Sunday, June 22

Lucy awoke with a start, noting that it was just breaking dawn. Who on earth could be knocking on her door this early? Her heart raced with misgiving, and she began anticipating what calamity might have befallen someone. Was Dolly okay? Had Robert been injured?

Quickly slipping her arms into a wrapper, she hurried to the door. Then she stopped. Considering the number of alarming threats she had received, answering the door might not be the wisest thing for her to do. She pulled the little gun from her purse and slowly opened the door.

Her visitor didn't miss the weapon in her hand. "You always answer your door ready to shoot?"

"Jim!" She flung open the door and let her grinning husband into the room. He waited only until she had laid the gun on the dresser before pulling her into his arms, running his hands through her hair that cascaded down her back and smelled of lavender from the bedding. He clung to her as though he thought she might rise up and float away.

For her part, Lucy huddled in his arms, luxuriating in their protective warmth. For a few moments she turned over to him all the toughness, decisiveness, and resiliency that she had resolutely embraced over the last few weeks. He was her rescuer, arrived to give her comfort and reassurance, and she was tempted to relinquish her commitments and give way to being nothing more than a man's wife. But a lifetime of independence and an honest self-awareness rebelled at the idea. She pushed back from him and looked up into his face, relieved that it had been only a fleeting impulse. To cover any strange emotion she was showing, she smiled and said, "Welcome to Placerville."

"I thought about waiting until a decent hour, but I just couldn't. I've missed you so damn much."

He scooped her up in his arms and carried her to the velvet chair in the corner. With her sitting on his lap, he asked, "Now, tell me why you answered the door armed for trouble."

"It's a long story." She nuzzled his neck, kissed his cheek, and then slid off his lap. "Why don't you go down to the dining room and order us coffee and rolls. I'll pull myself together, and join you there."

He didn't look like a man wanting to share in that plan, having other priorities in mind, but he agreed. More than just wanting privacy to perform bodily ablutions, dress, and make herself up to look her best, Lucy also wanted time to gather her thoughts. His abrupt arrival had shoved her without preamble into the beginning of her role as wife, and soon also mother. She needed to find a way to also be the logical, clear-headed woman with an important mission still to be fulfilled. At the same time, her pulse began to race as she headed downstairs, eager to be with the man she loved. And thus the conflict begins, she thought to herself, not unaware of another sharp irony doled out by Life.

Half afraid she was going to find that Jim's arrival had been a dream that had lingered upon awakening, she entered the dining room with relief at seeing him at the breakfast table. Seated across from him, and having been revived with coffee, Lucy first asked about Roger and Freda. His reassurances of their well-being, a few minutes of bragging about his son's brilliance, and the retelling of a few anecdotes related to Freda's packing, all washed over Lucy like a warm, misty rain. This was her reality after all, and after accepting it as such, she listened to him in a contentment of spirit that was more delicious than the pork chops and eggs Jim had ordered for them.

She looked down at her plate and hesitated. As special and thoughtful as this order had been on Jim's part, she wasn't used to such a full meal so early in the morning. In fact, she was almost too excited to have much of an appetite for her usual toast and coffee. But the last thing she wanted to do was hurt his feelings, so she ate as much as she thought necessary to appear sufficiently appreciative.

"I received your last letter the day before I left Jamestown," Jim told her, cutting into a chop and obviously enjoying his breakfast. "I had planned to accompany the freighter bringing our things, but at the last minute he had a good helper with him, so I decided to sell the rig and ride on here.

Freda and Roger will come on by stage in a few days. This way, we have some time alone before they arrive and we begin the move into the house."

"I'm so happy to have you here." She laid her hand over his for a moment. Their eyes met, their thoughts went in the same direction, and they both colored with a shy self-consciousness unusual for them.

Jim squeezed her hand before letting it go. "I was told when asking for you at the front desk that the room next to you is empty. I asked for it for Freda and the boy, only to be told you had already made that arrangement." He flashed her a teasing smirk as he added, "Of course, I suppose Roger and I can take one room, and you and Freda can have the other."

"Absolutely not! There's no way I'm letting you out of my bed for so long ever again."

And in fact, that's where they spent the next hour after returning to the room. But eventually, dressed and ready to venture outside, they surprised Robert at his livery. Greetings and pleasantries having been exchanged, Jim asked to rent a rig. "We need to get to the court offices so I can sign and file the papers on the house. The owners left them for me before they left town. Then I want to see what I've purchased sight-unseen."

Jim grinned at Lucy, but found that she wasn't smiling back. In fact, she was looking over at the stalls and frowning. Jim and Robert both assumed she was thinking about Mr. Leon's murder, but in fact she was listening to the echo of Jim's words as he claimed that *he* had purchased the house. It was subtle, and certainly nothing to which she was going to call attention, but it was nevertheless a reminder of the world in which they lived. She idly wondered if such an attitude would have changed by the time a hundred years had passed. Her conclusion was that although the words might change, the underlying attitude would not.

Jim was not only pleased with the house, but actually eager to get settled into it. Lucy followed behind him as he wandered from room to room as he commented on the efficient flow of traffic through the house, the capacity of the water reservoir out back, the solid construction of the porches, and the splendid indoor gravity flow toilet. Finally assured of his approval, Lucy felt comfortable pointing out the appointments to the kitchen she wanted to add, the need for new curtains throughout, and the color of paint she had chosen for the parlor. Jim listened as though he cared, even nodding a few times.

The previous owners had left much of their furniture behind when they had moved out, and Jim decided that what little was needed could be easily obtained in town or freighted in from Sacramento or San Francisco. Lucy had hesitated to ask what had exactly been packed onto the freight wagon coming from Jamestown, and when informed that her rocking chair was on board, she yelped with joy. They had a good laugh and locked up the house until they could focus their attention on it.

Wrapped up in the excitement of Jim's arrival and plans for the house, Lucy spent little time thinking about the murders over the next couple of days. She finally decided to use Jim as a sounding board for all she had concluded. It acted as a refreshment and a clearing away of impressions that had clouded a clear perspective of what had taken place.

That night, finding her mind too stimulated to sleep, Lucy slid out of bed and sat at the little table in the corner of their hotel room. She looked out of the open window and listened to the sounds of the busy town brought to her on the night breeze. Noting how the town never completely shut down at night, being a supply town welcoming a constant flow of wagon teams, she once again marveled at how Mrs. Helms's killer had come and gone from the hotel unseen. Then she stopped and amended that thought. They may have gone *unnoticed*, but more than likely had been seen, at least outside the hotel. Obviously, their presence had just not been noteworthy.

She opened the window wider to let more cool air into the room. Shouts from those on the street reached her, along with the jangling chains of an ox team pulling a heavily loaded wagon. These sounds were familiar to her now, and she greeted them like old friends from whom she would soon be parted. Once they moved into the new house, there would be new sounds with which to get adjusted, as they would be nearer the hills and valleys southeast of town. There would also be new routines and new demands on her time. She felt a wave of urgency to sort out these murders as soon as possible. By now, it was obvious that the police had moved on from them, drawing conclusions that Lucy did not accept.

She pulled her notes closer, turned up the wick on the lamp, and began reviewing the questions she thought still needed answering.

Why did Tony hide from Jane the fact that he had been married to someone before her?

How did Jane find out about that, and why did she choose not to tell me the details?

Has Melanie found evidence of who might have committed either murder, and is trying to follow it up herself in order to make me look bad?

Why did Tony's killer pick Robert's livery as the place for their meeting?

Why did his killer drag his body into a stall?

Was Tony's watch the only thing taken off his body?

If Tony had newspapers with him, why did his killer take them away?

Was the person that Mrs. Hall heard the morning of Mrs. Helm's death, a man or a woman?

Was Mrs. Helms or Tony capable of blackmailing others?

An hour later, with her eyes growing heavy, Lucy stumbled to the bed and collapsed onto it, the night too warm for covers.

"Solve the whole thing?" Jim mumbled.

"Isn't there a game somewhere you can go lose?" she mumbled back.

Not missing her sarcasm, he chuckled with delight and fell back asleep.

The next morning Lucy left the room just before dawn while Jim continued to sleep soundly. Leaving a note on her pillow for him to meet her at the National Restaurant, she enjoyed the early morning walk down Main toward the Plaza. But having slept fitfully, she was too eager for coffee to linger in front of any store windows.

As soon as she was seated, she told the waiter, "Coffee, please." Hearing the eagerness in her voice and seeing the weariness in her eyes, he brought it immediately. He also brought her a sticky bun, since she had often ordered one in the past. "If you don't want this, Mrs. Murphy, I'll remove it."

Lucy grabbed at it as she smiled up at the young man. "No, I'll keep it. Thank you. You're very kind."

Of course, Lucy knew he probably also remembered that she always tipped for good service, something not yet expected by wait staff. But she didn't care. She quickly gulped down her first cup of coffee and welcomed a second, breaking off pieces of the sticky bun and savoring its sweet, buttery goodness.

Feeling better, her attention was drawn to the next table. Several men sat there, having continued their drinking through the night and just now sobering sufficiently to want food. They were loud, and either didn't care if others overheard their conversation, or were unaware how their voices carried.

"Did you hear that Hume wants to be City Marshall?" The man with the long beard punctuated this question with an unapologetic burp.

The smaller man next to him asked, "John or his brother James?"

"James, of course. Why would John want to give up being District Attorney?"

His friend answered this with a sulky glare and remained silent.

The third man of the trio, tall and thin, shook his head. "They'll have a lock on the law around here if that happens."

"Is that so bad?" the first man asked. "They're both good men."

The glaring man broke his silence with a laugh, his bitterness not buried as deep as he thought it was. "Then you'd better watch yourself. You may know James, but if he's the man of character we've heard about, he won't turn a blind eye to your shenanigans."

These men had known the Hume brothers since they had arrived at the beginning of the gold rush with several friends. John and James Hume had formed their own company and had crossed the country from the east in five wagons, too eager to reach the gold fields to join the protection of a larger and slower wagon train. These were brave, tough men, and those at the table in Placerville knew it was unwise to cross the Hume brothers. In fact, in 1883 it would be James Hume that would be in charge of the capture of the infamous stagecoach robber, Black Bart.

A loud belch brought that topic to an end. "A friend of mine who's gotten off the booze has written an article for the *Mountain Democrat* about his struggles with demon rum."

One of the other men pulled a wild turkey quill from his shirt pocket and prodded between his teeth. "Why would he want to embarrass himself like that?"

"Beats the hell out of me. It's going to be published on the front page of the June 28th edition."

They all shook their heads, although privately they thought the guy had real courage, at least more than they would have had. The belcher brought forth another, while regretting the last couple of drinks he'd downed that morning. The third man reached for a flask hidden in the inner pocket of his coat, looked at it somewhat dubiously, and slid it back out of sight. Lucy smiled behind her napkin and continued to enjoy the show.

She was so enthralled by the men's conversation that she almost forgot that Jim was soon to join her. She sighed with deep contentment. How nice it was to have her husband once again part of her life. After catching him up with the events of the past few weeks, he had asked only a few clarifying questions, but had offered no advice or opinion. Part of her was glad, but part of her wondered why he had not. Nevertheless, she knew that if she asked for his advice, he would give it freely. She just didn't want it yet.

On the other hand, some of what she was thinking about those killings she found very troubling and didn't want to share, even with Jim. Everyone involved was someone she knew personally, and some of them would have obviously benefited from the demise of Mrs. Helms or Tony Leon. For all she knew, maybe by the death of both. What haunted her was the feeling that there was something below the surface of what had happened that had as yet not become obvious. Her frustration came from wondering if she should already be aware of what it was.

Before Jim had arrived in town, Lucy had thought it an interesting challenge to find the person responsible for two murders. Now, however, she was feeling the pressure of getting the whole thing solved before the arrival of Freda and Roger. She knew herself well, and knew that upon their arrival she would become wrapped up in their needs as well as the business of the move. They would all be eager to get out of the hotel and into a real home. But there were repairs needed at the house, and of course the decorating of it. Freda would love doing that, even without Lucy's help. It never occurred to Lucy that there would be no conflict in her life if she just gave up trying to solve the mystery of the two murders.

Her thoughts moved to her son and beyond. Roger would need to be enrolled in the school; clothing purchased to fit a rapidly growing boy; shopping to fill the larder; and, of course, laundry and ironing to be done. She was determined to utilize Maria Piarein to do the washing, as she was nearby on Cedar Ravine. At the same time, the routine of baking and cleaning would begin. That meant she would need to find a daily girl to come in to do the basic work, but that shouldn't be too difficult. There were also delivery dates and amounts to be arranged with the butter and egg man. And she had better have the chimneys and stovepipes cleaned, not knowing when that had last been done. She had better find someone to chop the large pieces of firewood she saw out back into smaller pieces, too. And there was still an outhouse, so it might need to be limed. Wood ash could go in later.

Lucy sat back with a heavy sigh, less contented than earlier, and thinking to herself, "There I go, throwing all my thought onto the family and away from my first reason for being here, a task that still hasn't been completed. Damn!"

Jim arrived just then, looking rested, perfectly groomed in a suit, vest, and tie, and annoyingly chipper. Lucy wished she felt the same and resisted an urge to purse her lips to express her pique. After they had ordered their breakfast and Jim had enjoyed his coffee, he pointed to the newspaper he had laid on the table upon arriving. There was mention of the war in it, and it was this subject on his mind.

"I must admit I'm a bit conflicted about some of the aspects of this war." Surprised at this, Lucy kept silent and let him explain. "I mean, about my participation."

A stab of alarm hit her in the chest and came close to taking away her breath. "You're not a soldier who can go rushing off into battle!"

"Oh, I know that." He couldn't help smiling at the thought. "I'd be a risk not only to my own life and limb, but everyone around me. But there should be something I could do." Then, seeing her pale face and her naked alarm, he immediately sought to reassure her. "Don't worry. I'm not going to enlist. The war probably won't last that much longer anyway."

But Jim's feelings were not uncommon with men in the West. And as the war progressed over the next two years, such feeling only became stronger when everyone began to fear the war raging even into 1865. Some men in the West did go east and take up arms for the Union or the Confederacy, depending on their leanings. Those who stayed, formed relief organizations, sending money to the war effort to relieve suffering in hospitals, or to cover the cost of supplies for the soldiers. President Lincoln would rely on the wealth of the Comstock and other mines in the West to help the Union to its eventual success.

Changing the subject away from war, Lucy asked, "Do you think I'm pushy?"

Jim almost choked on his coffee. "Why on earth would you ask me that? Has someone accused you of being pushy?"

"Both men and women have expressed such an opinion, some in more polite words than that, but that was their meaning. They think I'm being too aggressive with my inquiries. Of course, if I was a man, no one would dare say such a thing."

"My dear, they wouldn't even *think* such a thing about a man."

"Exactly!"

"I'd say instead that you're assertive." He wanted to reassure her, but also knew better than to sound in any way patronizing. "You simply don't hesitate to voice your opinion, or go after what you want."

"Is that bad?"

"Do *you* think it's bad?"

"Are you avoiding my questions?"

Jim laughed, his voice deep and resonate, drawing attention from the men at the next table as they rose to leave. One of the men leaned over toward Lucy as he passed, having heard the beginning of her conversation with Jim. "Leave my wife alone, lady. And, yes, you *are* pushy!"

Jim started to rise up, but Lucy put a restraining hand on his forearm as she turned to the man and smiled her sweetest smile. "Thank you. Coming from you, I take that as a compliment."

The man drew back as though having been struck. He hadn't expected such a response, and wasn't sure if he should feel provoked or satisfied. He was left only to feel awkward and a bit silly.

Still smiling, Lucy told him, "I'm unaware of whose husband you are, so I can't promise to stay away from your wife, but I'm sorry if I've offended you or her."

"Uh, well, I meant nothing disrespectful, I'm sure." He turned and quickly joined his friends waiting by the door, who were ready for a quick exit after hearing their friend's rude comment to the lady.

Jim laughed again. "That's the best example I've ever seen of why women would do well in politics. But it also answers your question. Even if you are sometimes a little too assertive for some people's taste, you also know how to be gracious and charming when the occasion arises."

"Thank you." She sipped her coffee, feeling rather proud of herself, but still wondering whose husband that had been.

Jim continued with his thought. "I also think that if you're willing to stand up for fairness and justice, why should that be seen as *pushy* instead of simply on the side of right? Of course, to do that, you'll certainly appear to be boldly forthright."

"That's all well and good to say about a man," she told him with spirit. "But women are not supposed to be forthright. Mrs. Helms was, and look what happened to her."

"Do you really think that she was killed for being outspoken and free with views some think of as radical?"

Lucy stared down at her empty plate, looking a little sad. Whether it was on behalf of Mrs. Helms or the absence of the wonderful sticky bun, she wouldn't have dared say. "I think there was something much more personal in the attack upon Mrs. Helms. Of course, I could say the same about the killing of Tony Leon."

"Tony Leon," Jim repeated. "It's not often you meet someone with a last name that could have been the first name. I'm often referred to as *Murphy*, as people do when referring to men. Everyone who knows me, knows it's my last name. But a stranger might think they're calling me by my first name."

Lucy stared at him for a whole minute. "Oh, my God!"

"What? Is something wrong?"

"I think you may have just hit on a major clue to this whole thing."

Jim simply blinked at her, saying nothing. He could tell that Lucy's mind was racing, and didn't want to intervene. And indeed, Lucy was trying to fit together a number of moments that flooded into her memory. "Book inscriptions, Roman numerals, and 'Mother referred to him only as ...'." Lucy stood up like an explosion had taken place under her chair. "No! It can't be! Oh, Jane!"

Jim quickly paid for their meal and ushered Lucy from the restaurant, all eyes following them out and wondering what had overcome Mrs. Murphy.

On the sidewalk, Lucy said, "I have to go see Jane Leon. She may not be happy to see me, but I have to do it."

When she hesitated, Jim told her, "Just go. Don't worry about me, for heaven's sake."

She turned and walked rapidly toward Coloma Street, past the stable and feed yard, and up the road to the Leon home. Knocking on the door with more force than she had intended, she stood her ground when the door was opened and Jane confronted her with a scowl.

"I know I'm not welcome, but I must talk to you right now."

The urgency and determination in Lucy's voice reached Jane, and she reluctantly stepped aside. "Come into the parlor."

Once there, however, Jane did not sit down and neither did Lucy. "Jane, I'm not going to mince words in order to be polite." But instead of talking, she marched around the screen in the corner still blocking Tony's desk. The bookcase to the right of the French doors was empty of all the books that had once filled it.

Jane braced herself for the questions she sensed would follow as Lucy asked, "How did you find out that Tony had been married to someone before you?"

Thrown by the unexpected question, Jane stammered, "I don't have to tell you that."

"No, you don't. But it could clear up a lot about what happened to him and why he was killed."

Jane sank heavily onto the sofa as Lucy followed her further into the room. "I don't see how. But I guess there's no real harm in telling you. It was Sue Ellen, when she was working on my hair."

"How did she know such a thing?"

"She said someone had told her, and she thought I should know in case something came of it."

Frowning, Lucy sat on the edge of a chair across from Jane. "I think I know who that might have been. But it's not like Sue Ellen to share confidences with other women."

"I thought the same thing when she told me. She's known for her respect of women's privacy."

"That must mean she thought it important that you know about Tony's first marriage. I'm sure it wasn't to upset you, so why else would she have told you? How did you react?"

"At first I didn't believe it. I told her it was a mistake, and not true, that her informant was mistaken. She didn't push the point, but just shrugged and admitted that could be the case."

"Did she give you any details about the marriage?"

"No. She said she didn't know them, but I think she was holding back."

"When did she tell you this?"

"Only a couple of days before Tony's death. Of course, after I realized he was the letter writer, and then he was killed, I began to think it might be true. I mean, obviously there was a lot about him that I didn't know."

"Did Sue Ellen tell you that her informant suspicioned that there had been no divorce?"

Jane closed her eyes for a moment and swallowed hard. "Yes."

"Besides his claim of being single when he met you, is it possible he might also have changed his name?"

"Why on earth would he do that?"

Lucy shrugged and asked, "Did you fear others finding out that you might not have been legally married all this time?"

"No!"

"Some could think that you killed Tony to keep such a fact from becoming known."

"If that was my state of mind, wouldn't I have killed Sue Ellen? She was obviously willing to reveal it. And Tony had kept it a secret all these years."

"True. But it wouldn't accomplish anything to kill Sue Ellen if you didn't know who her informant was, since they'd still be able to repeat it."

"Oh, Lucy," she sighed, leaning back against the cushions of the sofa. "I simply didn't care that much about my marriage to be upset about any of it. I sometimes considered turning him out of the house, even before I found out the letters were coming from him. That's one of the reasons I wanted to go through his desk the night I discovered the newspaper cuttings. I was looking for his business records to see how much money I could get from him if I kicked him out."

Lucy stared at her friend, thinking that there were depths to this woman she had not even begun to realize. But it all fit, both factually and with what she was learning about Jane's personality.

"I'm sorry if I sounded accusatory. But I wanted to clear up your involvement so I can move on to the others who I'm beginning to think might be responsible for all of this."

Showing no curiosity about what this indicated, Jane only said, "If you talk to Sue Ellen, be sure to tell her I'll see her for my next appointment."

"You're continuing to use her services?"

"Of course. She's very good at what she does, and I need her help. A woman I used once washed my hair with ammonia and water. It shined nicely, but almost fried my scalp." A mischievous smile lighted her eyes. "I've prepared a list of topics we can discuss that are very far from personal. That should allow us to reestablish our old comfort level with one another."

Lucy smiled down at Jane. "Don't bother to get up. I'll see myself out."

Lucy's timing was perfect. Just as she was hesitating at the end of the alley leading to Sue Ellen's shop, a woman exited, climbed into a black rig parked on the street and was driven away by a man at the reins. Quickly knocking on the door, Lucy hoped Sue Ellen would think it her customer returning for something. Toward this end, she stood off to the side so that she was hidden from view if Sue Ellen pulled back the curtain of the window.

The door opened slowly. When she was seen by Sue Ellen, she half expected the door to slam in her face. Instead, Lucy's arm was grabbed by a strong hand and she was pulled inside.

"Oh, Lucy, thank God it's you. I was wondering how I could get you here without anyone knowing."

"Why?"

In answer, Sue Ellen hurried to a small desk in the far corner and across from the screened wash stand area. Taking a piece of paper from the desk blotter, she handed it to Lucy, saying, "I found this in the middle drawer this morning. I've never seen it before, and I'm sure I've been in that drawer many times over the last couple of weeks."

Dated in April of that year, it read: *Mrs. Green, I know what you did in Groveland before coming here, and why you had to leave there. You did not pay then, but you will now to me. We both know it was no heart attack. Leave $10 the first of every month under the black rock on the grave in the far corner of the cemetery up the hill from Cedar Ravine. If you do not, the whole town will know what you did. – T. Leon"*

"Who's Mrs. Green?"

"I am." She moved to her chair at the work table and Lucy sat across from her. "That was my married name before I married Gabe. I was a widow when I met him. The note isn't referring to that, although by knowing my legal last name back then, it's an indication that the sender knows more about me than many do." She looked at Lucy with a puzzled frown. "Why on earth did he sign it? Don't blackmailers usually want their identify hidden?"

"Yes, unless signing it served a purpose. You're right in thinking this is a very odd note. What's the thing he threatened to reveal? Can you trust me enough to tell me?"

"It doesn't have anything to do with what's happened here."

"The note obviously indicates that it's something that you wouldn't want spread around. Otherwise, you wouldn't be asked to pay over blackmail money."

Sue Ellen buried her face in her hands for a moment before looking up at Lucy. "A woman died while I was washing her hair. The coroner said she died of a heart attack. A doctor even said he was treating her for a bad heart. But that didn't stop tongues from wagging."

"Oh, dear."

"Yes. A rumor got around that I had somehow allowed her to choke when her head was back being washed, and that I didn't do anything to help her." Her face flushed with anger. "How stupid do they think I am? Did they think I wouldn't know a choking woman if she was right in front of me?" She shrugged. "Of course, there were many who didn't think ill of me."

"Oh, Sue Ellen, it must have been a terrible time for you."

"I felt so sorry for the woman's family, losing her so suddenly like that. So I did feel guilty, even though I knew I wasn't at fault." She wiped at a tear rolling down from the corner of an eye. "She just made a little gasp and was still. At first, I thought nothing of it. Women make all kinds of noises when their hair is being washed if I pull at a knot or they get water in their ear. Then I realized she wasn't breathing. I toweled her off, and tried to revive her, but she was gone. I hurried to the sheriff's office and the doctor, too. A deputy showed up, and then went for her husband. Then the undertaker and his sexton showed up, and they carried her out to his wagon, and oh, it was just horrible."

Lucy got up and put her arm around Sue Ellen's shoulders, letting her weep. But it was short lived. Handing her a hanky from a stack on the table, Lucy asked, "Why did you want to show me this letter?"

"Because it gives me a reason to want to kill Tony, of course. But I didn't. And I'm sure that letter was not in my desk until ... well, I don't know when. I know it wasn't there several days ago, because I was looking for a bill I'd lost and I went through everything in the desk looking for it."

"Then someone put it there who has been in here with you over the last few days. Can you make me a list of who those people were?"

"Easily. I have my appointment book here. But why?" She reached for her book as Lucy pulled a small tablet from her purse and prepared to write down the names.

"Because I don't think this note was written by Tony. I think someone is preparing to fabricate circumstances so others will think you're the one who killed Tony."

"Why?" she wailed. "No one dislikes me, as far as I know. Certainly no one hates me enough to do such a thing to me!"

"You might just be a convenient scapegoat."

Sue Ellen gave her the names of the four women customers she had worked on over the last two days, all of whom were known to Lucy, at least casually. The only one of them who made her pulse speed up was *Jane Leon*.

"Did anyone else come here who was not a customer? Like a delivery person, or a visitor?"

"Oh, yes. The boys who bring fresh water to my barrel every morning. One of the clerks from the post office stopped by with a package for me, and to buy hair wash for his wife. The twice weekly girl came to wash the floor and so forth. Melanie St. John and Dolly Robbins came to buy some salve for their hands, like what I used on you. Just as they were leaving, the woman who launders the towels came to bring me fresh laundry."

"When was that?"

"Yesterday morning. I get fresh towels delivered twice a week on the same days the girl comes to clean. Those are the two days that I don't have appointments, so sometimes those who know my routine stop by to purchase things."

"That's a lot of people in and out. More than I thought, what with your privacy policy."

"It is after all a business."

"Sue Ellen, you're not going to like this next question."

Looking startled, she asked, "What?"

"You mentioned those people who knew your routine, but who among all those people knew what happened to you in Groveland?"

Sue Ellen stared at her with her mouth agape. "No! She wouldn't do anything to hurt me. Why should she want me arrested for Mr. Leon's murder?"

"So that someone else *isn't* arrested." Ignoring how shocked Sue Ellen was, Lucy looked around while biting her lip. "Can I take this note with me and add it to my file?"

"Yes, I suppose so."

"I promise no one else will see it. But I want to compare it with Tony's handwriting that I have in a book I purchased that I believe once belonged to him."

"Then of course you must take it with you."

Just as Lucy reached the door, Sue Ellen called out, "Oh, I just remembered. Dolly came back later that day to see if I had an extra nail buffer she could purchase. She'd misplaced her own. I had to rummage around in the boxes under the wash stand, but I found her one. I told her she could have it, but she insisted on paying me for it."

"How long was she here?"

"Oh, just a few minutes." Sue Ellen cocked her head to one side, anticipating what Lucy was thinking. "But she had no opportunity to get into my desk any more than anyone else did."

"Probably not." But in her mind, she could picture Sue Ellen on her knees with her back turned to the room as she rummaged through a box under the wash stand for at least a minute. A whole, long minute.

CHAPTER 12

"The sins ye do by two and two
ye must pay for one by one."
Kipling

Tuesday, June 24 – Thursday, June 26

Two days passed with little progress made on what Lucy called her *investigations*. Lucy and Jim spent most of their time visiting and dining with friends, painting rooms of the new house, and completing numerous other tasks related to the eventual move. They even helped an elderly lady, soon to be one of their neighbors, pick the ripening fruit on her trees. And on one morning they had lingered in bed until what Jim teasingly called the obscene hour of eight o'clock.

For the whole of Roger's young life, he had observed his parents' romantic behavior, and had taken it for granted that there were times he would be excluded from their activities. Thinking that such a close bond must be common to all marriages, he of course grew up thinking that someday he would have the same for himself. Of course, with maturity and experience out in the world, he would eventually realize the great differences in relationships, but it would never leave him that with enough compromise and real affection that marriage could be something very special.

With Jim napping beneath a newspaper while sprawled on the bed, Lucy saw her notes lying on the table partially hidden by the book Jim had been reading earlier. Anger welled up in her throat, because that was easier to feel than her rising resentment. However, she had to admit that if she had been neglecting her investigations, it was not Jim's fault. Since his arrival, it had been her choice to focus on what she felt were her own selfish enjoyments. Still, Jim was a distraction as she acquiesced to whatever he wanted to do. She pulled her notes from beneath his book and several pieces of correspondence that he had brought with him from Jamestown for her attention. She had not answered any of it, and petulantly refused to do so now.

At that moment Jim sat up with a start and pushed the newspaper aside as he slid off the bed. Looking over Lucy's shoulder, he asked, "What's that?"

"It's my notes on the investigation. More than that, it's also my suspicions and conclusions."

Making no comment, Jim walked to the mirror over the dresser and combed his hair. "What would you like to do this afternoon?"

It was too good an opening to let pass. "Jim, I feel very close to the solution of these murders. I have several ideas that are almost coming together, but I can't concentrate." It was difficult for her to admit, but she said, "I've been keeping busy so I don't have to face some very unpleasant truths. Besides, Freda and Roger will be here any day now, and I must resolve this before they arrive. They'd be here now if Freda's head cold hadn't delayed their departure."

"I understand." But he still felt a twinge of disappointment, since he was pretty sure he knew where this conversation was headed. It had been a long time since he and Lucy had spent so much of their time together alone with no one else to consider. And he was pretty sure it was their last opportunity. But if Lucy was not going to be fully committed to enjoying that time because of her promise to solve the murders, it was best that she got on with it.

"If I hadn't put forth so much effort," she told him, "and offended so many people in the process, it would be different. But all of that has gotten me very close to knowing what happened, so I just can't stop now."

She turned to face him, and he almost laughed at the appeal written clearly on her face. "I know." He walked over to her and kissed her cheek before looking out the window with a speculative glint in his eyes. "Why don't I spend the next few days doing what I do best? There's a lot of new people in town and a good number of them are probably in the mood for a game. Maybe I should meet them." He grinned at her and she jumped up to throw her arms around his neck. Anticipation now awakened in him, he told her, "I think I'll start at the Oasis Billiard Saloon. It's just a few doors down and they have iced drinks."

After he had put on his jacket and left the room, Lucy was determined to ignore the fact that she was a married woman. She declared herself a person with a job to be done, and she set out to do it. Thinking of Mrs. Helms, she laughed as she told herself, "Just like a man."

She created a fresh time-line with the aid of her notes and put into words the questions she wanted answered. She also forced herself to face the fact that the killer was someone she knew.

Wanting to be sure it couldn't have been other than the few about whom she had a vague suspicion, she tried to think of those people she knew who were so ruthless that they could kill two people. Maybe the better question was, how many people did she know that might be that desperate? She had been talking to women to find out what they knew, but most of these women were connected to men. Zelda Jones had met her away from her house because Joseph didn't want the letters talked about. Why? And why had Zelda not given her the list of names she had promised to give her?

Was there a husband attached to those women whom she had interviewed, or even a brother or father, who was fearful of something being revealed simply because Lucy had talked to *their woman* about the anonymous letters? Were they so frightened that they felt compelled to threaten her, even though people were beginning to realize that the letters had stopped?

Gus knew most of the men in town, and had told her a little about them, including Tony Leon. But what about himself? For some reason she found the idea of suspecting Gus of foul play outright funny, and found herself smiling. He was so open and honest in his character that she couldn't imagine him resorting to murder as a solution to anything. He might punch some man on the nose, or tell off an opinionated woman, but he wouldn't kill them. And especially a woman he felt wasn't even worth his contempt, such as Mrs. Helms.

On the other hand, she didn't want to ignore the fact that Tony might have killed Mrs. Helms. But if so, why would he report his home as having been broken into the same night? And why would he bring the letter-making materials to her room, especially a pair of scissors that could be traced back to Jane? No, Lucy was certain he hadn't killed Mrs. Helms, even if she had hoped to get money from him. Which was probably what they had argued about when he visited her room just before he left on his last pack trip. As to that, Lucy stopped to ask, why would Mrs. Helms expect Tony to pay her anything? Unless, that is, what she was beginning to suspect was true. "I just need proof," she stated out loud.

Lucy decided to put herself in the shoes of the person who had come to Mrs. Helms's room that fateful morning. She sat at the table in the hotel room, her eyes closed.

I knock lightly on the door, not wanting anyone to hear my arrival, but knowing she's expecting me. She's inviting me in, dressed for her day's appointments. I note that it's a nice room, but I'm too focused on my reason for being there to care. She invites me to sit, but I'm too overwrought and I decide to stand, even wandering around the room as we talk. She says something that makes me so angry that my sense of reason deserts me and I want more than anything to hurt her. I grab the nearest heavy thing that looks like it could do damage to her, which is the kerosene lamp. The clear chimney falls to the floor as I grip the base by its hollow stem. As she starts to turn away from me, I smash the heavy lamp into the side of her head and the wick assembly comes out along with a splash of kerosene. She drops to the floor. I am horrified at what I have done, thinking I have killed her. But self-preservation is stronger, and I drop the lamp and run from the room. I run down the stairs while wondering if it will be easy for me to be suspected. Once outside without anyone having paid any attention to me, I can think more clearly. And then I remember the anonymous letter writer, of whose identity I am aware. I go to the Leon home, force the flimsy lock on the French doors, and retrieve what newspapers are on the desk, along with the paste pot. I see scissors on a nearby table and take them, too. I hide the papers under my coat, put the scissors in a pocket and if noticed will only be seen carrying a small stone crock. I quickly return to the hotel room just at the top of the stairs, again thankful that it is so early, and yet amazed that so few people are about in the hotel. I'm feeling that Fate is justifying my actions and feel a surge of power. Thinking Mrs. Helms dead, and having left the door unlocked, I go right in. But I find her sitting up from where she fell earlier, only dazed. I panic, knowing that she will surely tell everyone that I struck her down, and I will be forced to explain why. I grab again the lamp base. This time I strike her with all my strength, and as close to where I hit her previously as I can. In fact, the strike is so hard that her head is now bleeding as she sprawls on the floor at the side of the bed. I know this time she is dead and cannot give me away. I put the things I have brought on the dresser, not seeing that a small piece of newspaper has settled on top of her body.

I run down the stairs and out of the hotel. About the same time as she is found, I realize the scissors I brought there are left-handed ones. Having taken her key, I am able to sneak back into the room to take the scissors away.

As Lucy thought through this scenario, she realized that much of it was pure speculation, but it still fit what was known. It was possible that the killer had left this last time down the back stairs that led onto an alley, cutting down on the odds of being seen now that it was after six o'clock in the morning. For another thing, the kerosene would probably have splashed onto the killer's clothing as it had the rug and the bedspread. And it had been noted that Mrs. Helms's key was missing, so the killer had either taken it earlier or had spotted it on the dresser when they had put the papers there.

How long had all of this taken? Say they had talked for ten minutes before the initial attack. It would only have taken about twenty-five minutes to go to the Leon home on Coloma Street near Main, force the lock on the French doors and take the items needed, and then return; maybe a shorter time if the killer had been a fast walker or even had run part of the way. It would have taken no longer than three minutes to enter the room, find her still alive, strike her again, leave the letter-making items, and get out of the hotel. Forty minutes in all, and without having been noticed. Most townspeople would have been either asleep or indoors preparing for the day. Those on the road through town certainly wouldn't have taken note of any particular person on the always-occupied sidewalk, no matter what they were carrying.

Lucy stared out the window. After all that, the killer had merged back into their normal routine with no one suspecting anything different about them. Had they felt so justified that it hadn't been difficult for them to carry on as usual? How the act of murder would affect someone, and how they would behave afterwards, had not until then been something Lucy had considered. Maybe it would depend on the type of conscience they had, if not overcome by pure panic at what they had done. The only other thing she could think someone might feel was remorse, and she didn't get the impression from anyone she knew that they were preoccupied with a guilty conscience. Of course, it was still possible that the killer was someone she didn't know. Unfortunately, everyone who had been close to Mrs. Helms, she did indeed know.

She picked up the book of Emerson essays, then put it back down. She had finished reading it, which turned her thought to Mrs. Hall and all her books. Maybe if she brought this one to her, she could swap it for one of that lady's books. Lucy made her way to the City Bakery, not wanting to arrive empty-handed. They advertised a dozen cream puffs for thirty cents, so she ordered half a dozen.

While Lucy was paying for her purchase at the bakery, Melanie was attempting to attract the attention of John Crowder, stage driver for the Pioneer Stage Company. When he approached with a tip of his hat to her, she walked to the back of the stagecoach. He followed, sensing correctly that she wanted no one to overhear the conversation to follow.

"Mr. Crowder, would you be willing to do me a big favor?" She held a letter in one hand and in the other more coins than would be necessary for postage. "When you get to San Francisco, will you mail this for me? It must be mailed from there, you understand. Nowhere else."

He looked at the pretty young woman, smiling so sweetly at him. She was obviously attempting to be winsome and appealing, and he was willing to be helpful. "Why, of course, my dear. I'll be happy to do that for you." But regardless of how happy he was to do this favor for the pretty lady, he still took the money she gave him, thinking of the drinks it would get him at his favorite San Francisco watering hole. He tucked the letter into the inside breast pocket of his vest and bid her good day.

Melanie fought a smile all the way down Sacramento Street, reveling in her cleverness. Seeing the spire of St. Patrick's Catholic Church to the south, she felt a momentary twinge of misgiving. But she shook it off, thinking how good it felt to finally be safely free of Vincent. As good-looking as he was, as elegantly as he always dressed, as much money as he always allowed her for whatever she wanted, it had never been enough to overcome everything else she loathed about him.

She felt so elated that when the thought of Lucy entered her mind, she was willing to admit that Lucy was after all a good friend for Dolly. And maybe over time, she too could form some kind of attachment with Lucy now that she had given up the idea of competing with her over the search for the letter writer. Besides, she had always thought Jim a handsome and exciting man, and if something ever happened to Lucy, well, one never knew. But that was fantasy, and there were pressing matters to be considered right then.

Melanie's thoughts wandered back to how clever she had just been. "Vincent should get the letter in about two weeks from San Francisco," she calculated. "If he gets angry over its contents and flies off to that town, he'll have no success in finding me there. He might even realize that I've never been there. But he'll also have no idea where I actually am. His only recourse will be to file for divorce from me on the grounds of desertion." She smiled with satisfaction. "It'll give him a sense of righteousness, but that'll allow him to keep his pride intact." She smiled again, caring not one whit what any of his acquaintances thought of her. She only cared that she was free, and never had to see him again.

So certain was she of this scenario, that it never occurred to her that Vincent might try to find her by hiring someone whose trade it was to track down people. Or that he might tell those with whom he associated that his wife was dead, which would mean there was no divorce. Consequently, if she married and then was found, he could accuse her of bigamy and ruin her life.

No, Melanie had settled on one scenario based on how well she thought she knew her hated husband. She had longed to escape him for years, and now walked with a buoyancy that she had never felt before, seeing her future free of the major obstacle to having her own business. "Most women," she thought, "might at this point be looking around for a new man, but it'll be a cold day in hell before I do that. Well, at least in the near future." A man passing her on the sidewalk wondered why the pretty young woman was smiling so broadly, and even turned around to watch her walk away, admiring the back of her. Melanie had no idea how often she received such looks, or how many men wanted to pursue her. Remaining single might be more of a challenge than she anticipated.

Mrs. Hall opened the door to Lucy, and recognizing her, let her smile show her happiness. "May I come in and visit, Mrs. Hall?"

"Oh, my dear, of course." Her eyes settled on the bakery package in Lucy's hand and she opened the door even wider. When *Dear Billy* came up behind Lucy carrying a tray with a large pot of tea, Mrs. Hall unabashedly clapped her hands with glee. Once everything was placed on the table, Billy departed with a grin and Lucy handed out the eager woman's tea with a cream puff on the cup's saucer.

Lucy allowed a few moments for simple enjoyment, but finally asked, "How are you keeping, Mrs. Hall?"

"Oh, very well. I swapped a few of my books for new ones at the church rummage sale, and I've been enjoying the new ones very much."

"I purchased a couple of books there, too. In fact, I brought one with me that I've finished. I thought I might swap it for one of your travel books."

"Of course." Mrs. Hall looked at the book Lucy placed on the table and nodded her head. "Oh, yes, quite satisfactory. Pick any of the books in that pile over there." She gestured toward a stack on the floor next to her easy chair.

Lucy took the third one down, not even looking at its title. "Thank you. This will do."

Mrs. Hall asked, "Have you made much progress into the death of Mrs. Helms?"

"Yes, some. Have you heard anything about it from those friends you mentioned where you dine occasionally?"

"No. A little time has passed, and people have generally moved on."

Lucy chose not to comment on how quickly people did that, and instead asked, "Have you remembered anything more about what you heard that early morning?"

"No. But I do still remember what I did hear quite well. Nevertheless, while it was clear in my mind, after I talked to you, I wrote it all down so if there would ever be a trial I could refer to those notes."

"Mrs. Hall, you're a marvel. That's so intelligently well thought out." Lucy felt a wave of resentment toward the hotel clerk who had thought Mrs. Hall "a bit batty".

Mrs. Hall made a show of humility as she admitted, "I'm just well organized."

"You're also a compassionate lady. I remember how you called Mrs. Helms a *poor unhappy lady*."

"Oh, no, my dear, I would never have referred to Mrs. Helms as that."

Lucy blinked, clearly recalling those words. "But you did. We were talking about the murder, and the morning it happened, and you called her a poor unhappy lady."

"Oh, I see why you're confused." She took an agonizingly slow sip of her tea. "I was referring to the lady who fought with her that morning. She sounded so upset and angry."

"You didn't tell me that you'd heard a *woman* arguing with Mrs. Helms." A sense of excitement almost overcame Lucy, finally having a fact to back up the theory she was forming. "You're sure?"

Mrs. Hall told her, "I thought you knew it was a woman in with her. I told you the tread on the stair was a light one."

"Yes, you did." Thinking of all the details she *had* asked Mrs. Hall to confirm, yet not having asked for the one clarification that would have been important to pin down, she sat back and laughed.

Mrs. Hall leaned forward and patted Lucy's hand. "Be careful, my dear. People might think you're a bit batty." She winked at Lucy as she poured more tea.

"You know about that?"

Mrs. Hall smiled and picked up her tea cup. "Of course. They're ever so much kinder to me thinking me as *not quite all there*. If they thought of me as sensible and alert, they'd be wary of me and I'd not hear nearly as much good gossip."

Lucy suppressed an urge to laugh, but said instead, "I promise to keep your secret."

"Do you promise to visit me when you finish the book you're taking with you? You don't have to bring me pastries. Your company is enough of a treat."

"I think you're going to see a lot of me over time. And when we get moved into our new house, we'll have you to supper."

"Oh, yes, I heard you've taken the house on Cedar Ravine. I knew the people who used to live there before the ones from whom you purchased it. Such nice people, they were." But she didn't look like she was recalling a happy memory. "I'll tell you about them some time."

"You've certainly made me curious."

"Good," she grinned. "Then you'll return soon."

Lucy stood up and prepared to leave. "I certainly will, but mainly because I find you such a delightful lady."

As she had done the last time she had departed from Mrs. Hall, Lucy left the tea pot almost full and the rest of the bakery goods in the bag. Mrs. Hall settled into her easy chair and opened her new book. She then reached for a cream puff and bit into its sweetness, all the while feeling grateful for good friends.

The next day a stage stopped in front of the Cary House and the door popped open with such a burst of force that it slammed back against the coach. Out jumped a small boy with coal black hair and bright blue eyes who looked around with a degree of trepidation. Spotting his mother, all uncertainty immediately disappeared and he raced forward. He threw his arms around her neck with unabashed relief as she leaned over to receive him into her arms. Lucy, having always thought of herself as not the most maternal of women, was surprised at the depth of her emotions as she hugged Roger.

She had never been a gusher of sentiment, nor had she made over her son in the clucking way so many mothers of her acquaintance. She told him when he made a mistake, made him admit to it, and then always asked him what he was going to do about it. It was a question he sometimes resented, but always answered after giving it considerable thought. When she had once voiced concern to Freda about her lack of what she thought of as maternal devotion, that good woman had scoffed roundly. "I still have the letters you wrote me when you discovered that you were expecting. They were full of happy excitement."

"But," Lucy had countered, "having children was never something that filled my life with longing, or even expectation."

"Given your circumstances growing up, that's not surprising. But that has nothing to do with how good a mother you have been to Roger."

"I guess not." But she still hadn't sounded convinced.

"Lucy," Freda had chastised her, "you have given him consistent guidance, and have fostered his natural talents. You have also taught him the concept of consequences for decisions made. That's one of the most important things any parent can pass on to their child."

"Yes, I am pretty practical," Lucy had admitted.

"But you're also loving, something I don't think you yet recognize in yourself."

Lucy had looked at Freda with a fond smile. "You're still schooling me."

Freda had shrugged off the compliment, as she did all such accolades, by saying, "Well, needs must." And she had hurried from the room before Lucy could see how affected she was.

This conversation flashed through Lucy's mind as she felt Roger pull away from her and she fought the urge to pull him back into her arms. But Jim had walked up and was looking down at his grinning son with a grin of his own. "Hello, Father."

"Have you gotten so much older in such a short time that you feel the need to be so formal with me?" Jim stuck out his lower lip in a display of exaggerated hurt feelings.

Roger laughed and jumped up into his father's arms with no doubt at all that he would be caught and held. After a brief hug, Jim put him down and he turned to Freda. "Hello, Freda. How are you feeling?"

"I'm fine, Jim." She pushed at her bonnet, tucked a stray wisp of hair behind an ear and told him, "I would have traveled even with a cold, but your young gentleman wouldn't hear of it."

Roger leaned into his father as he looked up at him. "There was a big game planned at the hotel in the back room."

Lucy stopped next to Roger, a hand on her hip. "Excuse me! They didn't let you play, did they?"

"No." He let out a grunt of disgust. "I did ask, but they just laughed at me as usual. Well, those who didn't know me did. There's a low window near a big table where the players sit when it's an important game, so I had a clear view of the play. That's my usual perch." He said this with so much pride that no one had the heart to chastise him.

"Who won?" Jim asked. "Anyone from Jamestown?"

"One of the sheriff's deputies. The really tall one."

Knowing who this man was, Jim nodded his head in satisfaction. The deputy was a friend he was going to miss, and he was happy to think of him as a little richer. At least until the next big game.

Jim, with Roger tagging along happily at his heels, made arrangements for the luggage to be brought up to the room set aside for Roger and Freda. The women sat on the sofa in the lobby, catching up with Jamestown news and a description of the trip just concluded.

"I must say," Freda confessed, "that I'm glad to be off that stage. Roger thought it a great adventure, but it was just dusty and uncomfortable for me."

"Yes, I know. But soon you'll be soaking in a hot tub and rested after a good night's sleep."

"I'm looking forward to doing some shopping, too. I'd like to make a new dress."

"Wolf Brothers on Main has French calicos at twenty cents a yard. And they have domestic calico at only twelve and a half cents a yard. But if you'd rather, Caroline Fountain recently purchased the store of Mrs. Irwin of San Francisco, which means she now has ready-mades at what she advertises as New York prices. She's near Wolf Brothers."

Walking over to the two women who were the anchor of his world, Roger waited politely for his mother to stop talking before asking, "How soon are we going to eat?"

His mother looked at him, resisted the urge to grab him up for another hug, and said, "How about now?"

Once seated in the Cary House dining room, the adults took up menus and began looking them over. While they did this, two men at a nearby table were having an animated discussion, and were being none too quiet about it. Roger was paying rapt attention to them, and although Jim and Lucy saw this, they said nothing.

One of the men said, "I read in the local paper that the Secretary of the Navy has ordered the enlistment of run-away slaves into the Navy."

His companion answered, "Yeah, the article said they're being rated as boys at $8 to $10 a month and one ration a day."

The first man shook his head. "The next step will be the Secretary of War ordering our Army officers to enlist them in the Army."

"Well, as long as they can shoot a gun, why not?"

His friend looked at him with a raised brow. "It just seems odd to me."

Roger leaned over so that he was close to the last man who spoke. "Excuse me, sir. Why does that sound odd?"

The man turned to him, surprised at the question, but not offended by the intrusion of a child. He just wasn't used to children asking him such pointed questions. "The country has never had darkies in our Army before."

"If I understand it, the country has never been in a war like this before. If a black gentleman wants to fight, why shouldn't he be allowed to do it?"

The man couldn't hold back a patronizing smirk. "You think escaped slaves are gentlemen?"

"I've been taught to think of all men as gentlemen. Aren't they men?"

"Um, yes, of course." Suddenly uncomfortable with the direction of the questioning, the man turned his back on Roger. He drank the last of the coffee in his cup, jerked his head to his friend who was doing a poor job of hiding his laughter, and the two men left the dining room. As the still chuckling friend passed Roger, he looked down at him and offered a pronounced wink while asking, "Do you know what precocious means?"

"No, sir."

"I bet your parents do." The man hurried after his friend waiting for him in the hotel's lobby, and who was pondering the wisdom of a question asked of him by an innocent child.

Lucy and Jim said nothing, although they both wanted to say a number of things. They didn't want Roger to think that what he had done in questioning an adult was wrong, especially considering the politeness with which he had posed the question. Nevertheless, Lucy made up her mind to discuss the occurrence with Roger later so he would understand a little more about the war going on in the background of their lives. Freda also felt she should say something to Roger, but wasn't sure what it should be. Instead, she took her cue from Lucy and Jim, and remained quiet.

Meanwhile, Roger had turned his attention to the people on the other side of their table, hoping for more interesting conversation. He couldn't hide his disappointment when their words were too low to be overheard. He sat back and looked around at the other people in the room, finding them equally uninteresting. However, as soon as food arrived at the table, he focused on that and his mood returned to its normal happy state.

The next morning, while Jim prepared to take Freda and Roger to see the new house, Lucy informed her family that she had errands to do in town. In actuality, she wanted time to think about her next move. She always thought more clearly when she walked, even if it was in a busy town among people sharing a crowded sidewalk with her.

Not far from the fire station, Lucy saw Gus walking in her direction. Two women pulled their skirts away from him as he passed, but he didn't seem to notice. Lucy stopped and sat down on a bench outside a shop, smiling in his direction but saying nothing.

"Do you mind if I sit a moment with you?" he asked.

"Please do."

Hearing her say this, the two women who had just passed turned around and looked with obvious surprise at Lucy. They gasped when seeing her smile at the "unsuitable creature called Old Gus", as they would refer to him when telling their friends about Mrs. Murphy's behavior. Their judgmental look of disdain was not missed by Lucy or Gus, but when Gus saw that Lucy was ignoring the women, he nodded and sat down. He did, however, sit at the far end of the bench.

Lucy told him, "The only reason I didn't stop you was that I didn't want to impose if you wanted to be alone."

"You surely are an unusual woman. Thank you."

"For what?"

"When we've talked, you haven't told me that I don't have to live the way I do. That I should do this ... or that. Most women do."

Lucy laughed. "You're an intelligent man. I assume that by now you've made the choices you want."

"Yup." He nodded and looked out at the street to watch a passing freight wagon, tightly tarped over to protect what was beneath. The muleskinner was riding one of the two gray horses immediately in front of the wagon while whistling and cracking his whip at the twelve mules in front of him that were pulling the heavy wagon two-up in the traces. It was not an unusual sight, and Lucy wondered why Gus was watching it so closely, then realized he was just hesitant to come to the point. Finally, with his jaw tight, he said, "I knew Tony Leon a long time ago in San Francisco."

Lucy turned toward him, carefully choosing her words so as not to appear as eager as she felt. Casual was always going to be the best attitude around this man. "Did you?"

"Yeah. He said he'd never been out of the country. I told him that's not what I'd heard him say before."

"I thought he had come from Scotland where he had killed a flock of sheep."

"A major lie."

"I always wondered why no one commented on his not having a Scottish accent. But why tell such a story about himself?"

"By making himself look bad, no one ever thought of questioning the story. It's a trick of a good con man. The thing is, when I knew Tony, he had just met Jane and was thinking of marrying her. I told him he shouldn't."

"Oh?"

"Yeah. Once when he was drunk, he told me he was married, but didn't want his wife to know where he was. Later when he was sober, I reminded him about his telling me that, but he denied it."

"Did he still plan to marry Jane? Didn't he know that was illegal?"

"Sure. But he didn't seem to care. Neither did I really. I just didn't want him to marry Jane."

"Interesting."

"Well, she wasn't. Interesting, I mean. Unless you think bossy and manipulative is interesting."

"You could see that in her, even then?"

He looked at Lucy in surprise. "She's your friend and you're not going to argue on her behalf?"

"She's more an acquaintance that I had hoped might become a friend. But I think that's not going to happen now. We're very different women."

"I should say you are!" He chuckled with evident humor. "I'm looking forward to meeting your husband." Lucy tactfully refrained from asking him to explain, and after a few moments, he returned to the original subject. "Tony was always a randy old goat, as they say, and yet he wanted to settle down. He said he missed being taken care of by a woman. He found Jane, who was looking for a husband, having been on the market for some while."

Lucy looked at him with a raised brow. "She would have been in her early twenties."

"That's right. Over twenty and a spinster. She were on the hunt, was that one."

"Well, she sure hooked Tony."

"Which is what got me to thinkin'." When Lucy wisely held her tongue, Gus felt free to continue in his own way. "I don't think Tony much liked women. He used to say pretty disgusting, disrespectful things about them when he'd had a few too many. Made most men I know uncomfortable to hear such filth."

Lucy looked at him with disbelief. "I've heard plenty of colorful complaining about women from men in my life."

"Oh, sure. But this was really foul, even to what he'd like to do to them against their will. Men sometimes have private thoughts about talking a woman into laying with him, even to hearing her say *no* while knowing she doesn't mean it. That kind of thing. But few men would ever think of pushing beyond that and doing what he'd talk about." He was speaking more quickly now, as though he wanted to be rid of what he had to say as quickly as possible. "It got me to wondering if maybe he'd actually done it to some gal, and her man killed him for it."

Lucy said nothing in response. She was not offended by having a man discuss such a thing with her as most women might be. The life she had led had purged her of that propensity. But hearing this about Tony still disturbed her, especially when she thought of Jane and wondered what she might have endured in her marriage. But had that made any difference in his death? Had Jane intentionally misrepresented to Lucy the quality of her marriage?

"Thank you for telling me this, Gus. It paints a picture of a man who would only too willingly send anonymous letters to women if he thought it would upset them. From what you say, that was a relatively mild thing for him to do."

"You'll never know how mild." He got up and walked away without a further word.

When Lucy returned to the hotel, she was surprised to see Jim in the room. "I thought you'd be at the house."

"Roger and Freda are there now cleaning the kitchen. But as I was leaving the hotel with them earlier, I saw an envelope in our box. It was addressed to you, but the clerk hadn't put it there."

"Where is it?"

He reached for it lying on the table and handed it to her without comment. She looked down to see the envelope already open, but before she could say anything about that, Jim said, "It was like that when the clerk took it from the box. I think it was left that way so anyone could see it."

Lucy pulled out the contents. On a piece of cheap paper, and formed with the obviously damaged nib of an ink pen, was written in block letters: STOP NOW OR DIE

"Well, that needs no clarity of meaning," Lucy chuckled.

"This isn't funny." His blue eyes had darkened as they were wont to do when he was suddenly hit with strong anger or fear.

"Of course not. But it shows that I've ruffled someone's feathers very badly."

"I don't like this."

"I'm not pleased about it myself."

"What are you going to do?"

"Just what I've been doing. And, of course, remain alert."

Jim walked up to her and took her hands in his. "You know I've never taken the traditional role with you of the husband who sets down rules for his wife. I'm not sure I'd know how to do that, but..."

Lucy pulled her hands away and sat on the corner of the bed, forcing him to sit in one of the chairs by the table, their knees almost touching. She looked at him with an intensity that told him it would behoove him to listen carefully. "I could never have been married all this time to a man who set rules for me. But that doesn't mean that I don't always consider your feelings, or that of the rest of the family. I always do. It's not just about my safety, but also about what all of you would go through if I did let something happen to me. So, my love, I will always know where my little gun is. And that's close at hand."

Jim sighed heavily and cleared his frown, knowing the issue had been settled between them. He said nothing more and they changed their clothes in preparation of meeting Mrs. Hall for supper. Jim had not as yet met this new friend of Lucy's, but he was looking forward to it. After returning to the hotel with Freda and Roger, and making sure they had plans for a nice supper there at the hotel, Jim and Lucy walked down the street to the Orleans Hotel.

Jim was not disappointed with their evening out, finding Mrs. Hall bright, funny, and a fascinating conversationalist. As they parted after their supper in the Orleans Hotel dining room, he promised to come fetch her often in their rig for visits at their home. He also escorted her to her room where he handed her the extra desert he had ordered with the dinner. As she heard his footsteps retreat down the stairs, she smiled. "Such a nice couple. I'm going to enjoy spending time with them." She smiled to herself the rest of the evening.

CHAPTER 13

"Though this be madness,
Yet there is method in it."

Shakespeare

Friday, June 27 – Sunday, July 6

Lucy sat in Dolly's parlor, waiting for her to return home. The quiet of the empty house was a welcome retreat from the noise and dust of town, and even the comings and goings at the hotel where Jim had been invited to join a private game. She wanted time to think away from all that, and assumed correctly that Dolly and Melanie would be out spending the morning on errands in town, as was becoming their habit on Fridays.

Enjoying the cool comfort of the house, Lucy walked over to the bookcase to see what she might read while waiting. On the fly leaf of a book of poetry was written, *"Dolly, Happy Birthday little girl. Your Pop, L.A."* Lucy smiled, wondering what birthday this had been when Dolly had been a child in Los Angeles before her father had deserted the family. No wonder Dolly had kept the book all these years. That must have been the last time in her life when she had been part of a family.

She looked at the book again. No one signed a *Happy Birthday* dedication with the location of their home. "L.A." had to be her father's initials. Hadn't Dolly mentioned that their last name had been *Anthony?* So, his name had been *L. Anthony.*

A tightness engulfed her chest as she recalled an idea that had occurred to her several days earlier, but then had been pushed to the back of her mind. Probably because it had been too painful to confront. She put the book back on the shelf, but continued to stand where she was for several minutes, staring at the book with her thoughts racing. She finally turned and slowly walked into one of the bedrooms, feeling as though her body was moving forward even while her mind screamed at her not to do so.

Opening the large wardrobe closet, she immediately noticed at the far end a long black coat. But she didn't reach for it, instead removing and inspecting each dress and skirt until she came to a dark burgundy skirt with a detachable bodice. Across the bottom of the skirt was a splatter of crusty brown spots that had slightly bleached out the color of the fabric beneath them. The kerosene used at that time being not as refined as in later years, it had dried and left this damage to the cloth.

"What the hell are you doing in my closet?"

While clutching the skirt to her chest, Lucy swung around to face an irate Melanie. She said the first thing that came into her mind. "I thought you were out shopping with Dolly."

"I came back while she went on to the market."

Lucy's heart pounded as she formed a lie and stammered to get it out. "Dolly told me I could borrow a two-piece dress for a pattern to take to Agnes and Sarah, the seamstresses. You know, the dressmakers over on Main opposite Cedar Ravine. I admired this skirt of yours when I saw you wearing it. But I have a top for it."

Melanie frowned, suddenly uncertain and afraid she had over reacted. Nevertheless, she knew what was on that skirt and that she had to get it away from Lucy. She also knew there was only one morning that she had worn that particular garment since arriving in Placerville.

"You never saw me wearing it." Her voice was low and harsh, edging toward fury.

Lucy laughed shortly, hoping she wasn't betraying her nervousness. "Oh, but I must have, because I remember admiring it."

Melanie, however, knew that she had worn it only once and that was very early on the morning of June 4, two days after her arrival. Through a clenched jaw, she told Lucy, "Put it down."

"I promise I won't harm it." Acting as though she didn't hear the tone of Melanie's words, Lucy began rolling it into a tight ball that protected the stained portion along the bottom edge. She was desperate not to leave it behind where Melanie could destroy it. It was a wonder she had not already done that, but she must have thought herself so safe that she felt no immediate need. Lucy briefly wondered at the conceit that had to underlie such confidence. Now, however, Melanie would know she could no longer refrain from destroying it.

"Put it down," Melanie again demanded. Her fists were clenched at her sides and her face was white with naked rage.

Lucy had for most of her life been able to talk her way out of even the most difficult situations. But if she had to physically fight Melanie, she was prepared to do it. As Lucy wondered how she could avoid this and still get out of the room with the skirt, the front door opened and then slammed shut. "Hello," Dolly called out. "Melanie, are you home?"

"We're in here," Lucy called out, trying to sound cheerily nonchalant.

Dolly stepped into the bedroom. Seeing the strange tableau before her, she looked back and forth between the two women. "What's happening?"

Lucy spoke up loudly and rapidly, accompanying her words with a big smile. "Oh, Dolly, I'm so glad you're here. I seem to have upset Melanie again. I only came to get the skirt I needed for a pattern. Do you remember that I mentioned that to you?" Not waiting for an answer, she hurried on. "I'll just take it and be on my way. I want to get to the Murphy ladies so they can make a pattern from it." She turned to Melanie as she moved toward the door, carefully placing Dolly between herself and a trembling Melanie. "I'll get this back to you tomorrow, Melanie. Thanks for lending it to me." And she practically ran from the house.

Unbeknownst to Lucy, Melanie started to follow her. But Dolly had seen a look on her sister's face unlike anything she had ever seen before and it frightened her. "Melanie, what's the matter?" When Melanie didn't answer, but instead tried to push past, Dolly grabbed her by the arm. "Talk to me!"

Unaware of the confrontation brewing between the sisters, Lucy was only aware that she needed to get away before Melanie could come after her. Just to be on the safe side, she didn't continue down Pacific Street to Sacramento as she usually did, but instead dodged between houses and onto Reservoir Street where she hurried up the hill to Main. She had to fight the urge to lift her skirts and run.

Once on Main, she hurried on, knowing that she had a long walk back to the hotel. But at least she was assured that Melanie wouldn't be following her. On the other hand, it gave Melanie time to reach the hotel ahead of her. That was something she had to seriously consider. The weight of the gun in her pocket was reassuring, but not something she wanted to use.

Cradling the soiled skirt in her arms, Lucy knew she couldn't leave it in the hotel room. Melanie was desperate enough to break in when she and Jim were out, or with a weapon if she thought Lucy alone. Of course, she could take the skirt to Jane, or even Sue Ellen, but they were compromised in several ways already. It then occurred to her that there was one person she could fully trust, and she headed west on the north side of Main Street until she reached her destination.

"Hello, Gus. I'm glad you're home. I need a favor."

"From me?" His eyes danced with humor as he stepped back and let her in, but he chose not to give voice to a number of things crowding into his mind. He had already surprised himself by finding that he liked thinking of this woman as a friend, and he didn't want to jeopardize that with a smart remark she might not appreciate. He erased his smile and asked again, "You need a favor from me?"

"Yes. I need to put this skirt where it won't be damaged or discovered by anyone else. I know I can trust you for that. It's evidence that might be needed later."

He gave her a long, thoughtful look and then slowly nodded. "What's on the skirt? Blood?"

"No. Kerosene."

After another moment's pause, his eyes opened wide. "So it was a woman who killed the suffrage woman?"

"You're quick."

"It helps to keep me alive," he smirked. "Does the woman this belongs to know you have it?"

"Yes. That's why I can't take it back to the hotel with me."

"It also means you're in a lot of danger."

"Most of the time I'm with my husband now that he's in town."

"Well, you'll not be with him when you leave here."

"No, that's true. But I'll be careful."

"Should you tell me who it belongs to in case something does happen to you?"

"You mean, so the police can trace the one most likely to have killed me?" She shrugged, trying to appear unconcerned. "I probably should tell you, but I'm not going to."

"Okay. At least I'll have this as a starting point when I have to help find your killer."

"I wish you'd stop saying that." At first having received his comments with a degree of humor, she now felt it too close to a possibility. "You'd be surprised at some of the things I've done to survive in my life."

He nodded, again flashing one of his rare smiles. "Yeah, I bet." He took the skirt from her, and walked through two rooms to a third at the back. He opened a large trunk and carefully placed the folded skirt inside. Taking an old padlock with a key stuck in it from a drawer in a rolltop desk, he attached it to the trunk, pocketing the key before leading the way back to the kitchen. "Want some coffee?"

"It belongs to Dolly's sister," Lucy blurted out.

Gus swung around to face her. "Oh, hell! That's going to have a lot of sorry repercussions."

"You can say that again! I'll be back for the skirt when I need it."

Gus simply nodded in the all-knowing way that was his manner, and asked nothing further. Lucy respected him even more than she already did, leaving with no further discussion between them. She still felt a little traumatized by not only the confrontation with Melanie, but the knowledge that at some point Dolly would have to know what her beloved sister had done to their mother; and if she wasn't mistaken, also their father. It had flitted through Lucy's mind earlier on that Melanie could be a prime suspect, but she had given the thought no real credence. However, little by little the idea had found a foothold as so many circumstantial facts pointed that way.

Lucy realized her stomach was unsettled and wondered if she had time for a cup of tea in the hotel's dining room before going up to her room. This plan was cast aside when she saw that Melanie was waiting on the sidewalk in front of the hotel. Lucy stopped and pulled herself together with a burst of resolve, then slowly approached. But Melanie turned aside and walked into the alley between the hotel and the Arch Saloon on the west side of the hotel while motioning for Lucy to follow. Lucy moved into the alley, but stopped just off the sidewalk, refusing to move any further than a shout would carry to the foot traffic passing by them.

In a voice just loud enough to be heard, Melanie immediately demanded, "I want my skirt back."

"I don't have it."

Melanie blanched white. "Did you give it to the police?"

"No."

Melanie's eyes widened with hope. "You're going to take pity on me? You know I didn't mean to hurt her." She still couldn't bring herself to call the dead woman *mother*, and *Mrs. Helms* was like a foreign name.

But if she thought Lucy was going to fall easily for her pleading justification, she was wrong. "If you hadn't hit her a second time, I might believe that, but you did mean to kill her that time." Lucy had decided to act as though her assumptions of what had taken place the morning of June 4 were accepted facts.

"But I did it that time simply out of fear that she'd report me for having hit her. I saw her there still on the floor, only stunned, and I panicked. I grabbed up the lamp base and struck out. But I didn't go there initially to kill her."

"You can arrange the facts any way you want, but at some point you wanted her dead, and dead she is. You might have gotten off with attempted manslaughter for hitting her the first time, or even self-defense if you had a clever lawyer, but now it can only be seen as murder. They may not hang you, but you'll spend the rest of your life in prison."

Melanie smiled, cocked her head to the left and looked up under her long, dark lashes at Lucy, an odd little smile playing around her lips. "Don't be too sure about that."

Even more alert, Lucy asked, "Why?"

"I'm just a poor, helpless woman," she whined pitifully. "I over-reacted to an unreasonably strict mother who forced me into a violent marriage, and who had just informed me that she wanted nothing to do with me. How awful it is to be rejected by one's mother!" She wiped away an invisible tear and stuck out her bottom lip in a little girl's pout, breathing in a shaky but dry sob. "Being a naïve young woman who has spent so little time out in the world, I didn't stop to think of consequences when I lashed out. I was just pushed beyond reason by my mean old mother." Simpering prettily, she batted her long lashes up at Lucy.

Lucy rolled her eyes in disgust. "You forget one thing. You also killed Tony Leon. What you don't know is that there was a witness to your conversation with him in the livery."

"What witness?" she snapped. "I don't believe you! You can't prove I did anything to him."

Lucy said nothing in response to that, knowing it was true. Mrs. Holliday's eavesdropping was only something that had helped lead her to Melanie as Tony's killer. The thought suddenly occurred to her that she should get the black coat from Melanie's closet, as there might be on it some evidence of having been in the livery. Rather than mention the coat, however, Lucy said, "There'll be no problem getting the witness to come forward to say they saw you."

"Saw me doing what? It couldn't have been doing anything to him, or they would have gone straight to the police." Her eyes lit up. "They didn't recognize me, did they?"

"Enough so that it could very likely have been you."

"But not well enough to prove it was me, right?" She flashed a cocky smirk at Lucy. "If I do get connected to Tony's death, I'll just tell them how he physically threatened me, and I had to defend myself. I'll tell them how I tried to cover it up because I didn't think anyone would believe me."

"Why would your own father attack you?"

Melanie looked at Lucy with a rueful smile. "Oh, you figured that out, did you?"

"Yes. It was a number of little things. But his being your father answers the main question of why he was arguing with Mrs. Helms in her room. She wanted money from him, didn't she?"

Melanie shook her head with impatience and sighed. "And he did give it to her. She told me about it the first time I saw her. He didn't want Jane or anyone else to find out they were never legally divorced. He should have known that Jane wouldn't have wanted the illegitimacy of their marriage to come out either."

"Evidently he didn't realize that."

"I can't believe my father was such a fool." She looked out at the street and frowned. "He looked so different. I only recognized him in the post office after I heard his voice. I'd not forgotten that. I spoke his real name softly as I stood behind him just to be sure it was him. When he turned around and looked at me, I could see the shock on his face, and I knew for sure. I quickly walked outside before he said anything."

"So you lied about that meeting to Dolly and me."

"Well, of course I did." She leaned against the brick wall of the hotel. "I wasn't ready to admit that he was our father. I told him I'd say nothing and that we could talk again some other time. I thought that was what he wanted to do when he sent me a note saying to meet him at the livery. I didn't know he wanted to confess that he was the letter writer." She made another sound of disgust deep in her throat. "I'd known that since the first

full day I was here. That was when I went to see Jane, after departing from
Sue Ellen, and stopped outside Tony's study when I overheard him arguing
with someone. It was about money owed from a pack trip, nothing special."

"Not the time I saw you there then."

"No. That time I went back to verify the books I thought I recognized.
That's when I realized he was our father."

"How hard do you think a jury will come down on you if they know
you killed both your parents?"

"No one knows he was my father except you, and Dolly if you've told
her. I did tell Sue Ellen. I was in such a dither that I couldn't hold it in."
She pursed her lips as she looked into Lucy's eyes. "Dolly won't testify
against me, and I've made sure Sue Ellen won't either. And Jane won't
admit that Tony hadn't legally severed ties to a marriage before her. If
she does, she'll be open to being accused of knowing her marriage was
bigamous. And no one has reason to believe what you say if Dolly, Jane
and I together deny anything you say."

"You're assuming a lot on Dolly and Jane's part."

"Not really. They won't want that kind of notoriety."

Lucy wanted to keep the argument focused on Tony Leon's murder.
"Whether he was your father or not, you were seen in the livery with him
the morning he was killed. The witness saw the newspapers in Tony's hands
while talking to you."

"I took them away with me, so the police still don't know they were
ever there, no matter what someone else may say. Your witness could easily
be mistaken about what they saw. Any good attorney can get them to
admit that."

Thankful that Melanie was unaware that the witness could not positively
identify the person with Tony that morning as even a woman, Lucy said,
"But you and I know he did bring them."

"Oh, yes." Her face darkened. "As proof that he was the sender of the
letters. He was too stupid to realize that anyone can cut up a few papers.
He said he was sorry for all the unhappiness he had caused people in the
town. He was going to confess to the police so he could turn over a new
leaf." She began to pace back and forth in agitation as she thought back on
their conversation. "He planned to tell everyone that he was our father so
he could be in our life again. What rot!"

"He might have gone to jail for a short while. Maybe as a public nuisance or something. He could then have been a part of your life. If you didn't want that, you could just have told him to stay away."

Her snort of derision was anything but lady-like. "In the first place, he didn't care about what I wanted. He was set on doing what he wanted, as he'd always done. All I could think of right then was that if he confessed, the police would stop thinking that Mother-dear was the letter writer, killed by someone she was blackmailing. It would mean that the investigation into her death would open up again. Then it would come out who she was, and that would lead eventually to me and Dolly."

"You killed him for that?"

"Not exactly. He began talking about wanting to ... let me see, how did he put it? The son-of-a-bitch wanted to 'be the father he always wanted to be'." She sighed with unrestrained exasperation. "It set me off into a fury just like when *she* had taunted me with being a spoiled and ungrateful daughter and wife. I shouted at him that it was too late for him to be a father, and that he could go to hell. He told me not to be disrespectful, as though I was still the child that he had deserted. As he started to walk around me toward the door of the livery, I screamed at him, '*Disrespectful? After you deserted us and forced us into poverty and hardship? And I was forced into a hateful marriage?*'" She took a deep breath to calm herself, but her fists were clenched together at her waist. "He just kept walking toward the door, ignoring me. Ignoring me! Men are always ignoring me! It was as though a red fog enveloped me. I saw the hammer on the anvil and I grabbed it." She cocked her head to the side with a look of puzzlement. "He dropped straight down, without even a sound." She shrugged and smiled with satisfaction as she looked at Lucy. "He wasn't nearly as heavy as I thought he'd be when I dragged him into the stall. I don't know why the stupid horse didn't step on him. Then no one would have thought to question how he died."

Lucy felt her skin turn clammy and she fought a haze of nausea. Melanie had recounted it with such nonchalance that one would think she was telling a story read in a book. *Once upon a time, an angry and twisted daughter killed her father...*

Melanie sensed Lucy's repugnance. "Oh, don't act like you couldn't kill someone if you had to."

Melanie had no way of knowing that this hit much too close to home, and Lucy had to resist the urge to finger the faded scar on her cheek. "You don't act like you're sorry for either killing."

"Why should I be?" She tossed her head in defiance. "My life has been a nightmare and a torture! And it was all because of my damn parents!"

"So, you did kill out of revenge?"

She shrugged. "I didn't meet with either of them with the intention of killing them, but I'd never felt such desire to wreak havoc on someone as I felt when they wouldn't acknowledge what they had done to me." She passed a hand over her mouth before hissing, "They just wouldn't listen to me!" She took a deep breath, and after a moment of thought, posed a fake, simpering pout. "But again, being a woman, I can't be expected to think logically. We women over-react to everything that upsets us, what with so little experience of the world. We're only fit for taking care of the home and having children."

"So that's how you plan to play it?"

"If I even get arrested." She took a step closer to Lucy, a cold, calm determination having settled over her. "It's the rules men have set up for us. I only plan to play by them." She winked at Lucy. "Isn't there something in the Bible about an eye for an eye? Well, after what they put me through, I think we're even."

"What about what you tried to do to Sue Ellen? I know about the fake letter from Tony that you hid at her place."

"That was only insurance in case I needed to pull someone else in as a suspect in his murder."

"Some friend you turned out to be." Lucy came close to slapping this venomous woman, but fought back the urge. "Sue Ellen has never been anything but a loyal friend to you."

"Oh, please," she scoffed. "She's as expendable as anyone else."

"That doesn't exactly make you a helpless little woman then, does it? It makes you a vengeful virago out to save yourself no matter who you have to take down to do it."

"Don't pass judgment on me, you interfering bitch! If you think anyone will believe you if you repeat what I've just said, I can deny it all and be believed. Especially when I tell them what I know about you."

Lucy felt her mouth go dry. "And what is that supposed to be?"

"Oh, how you say you were *only* a cook in the brothel where Dolly worked, but were really more than that."

"But I *was* only a cook!" In that moment Lucy understood how easily someone could be provoked into reaching out to throttle another person. But she also recognized that part of herself that was sufficiently repelled by the idea, which kept her from following through. It was that part of most people's character that would always stop them before going too far. But then there were those like Melanie, so wrapped up in themselves and so far removed from the feelings of others, that they felt justified in whatever they chose to do.

"And what about your marriage?" Melanie continued. "Why else would you have married a gambler? No decent man would want you, given what you'd been."

"Doesn't that cast aspersions upon your sister, too?"

"I don't care, as long as it throws you into disrepute. And, of course, I'm sure your boy will enjoy having these innuendos to deal with after he starts school. You know how boys like to tease and repeat what they overhear from adults."

"You really are a hateful shrew!" Lucy took a deep breath and fought to bring reason back into the conversation. "Dolly knows the truth of all this and won't let it go unchallenged."

"Who do you think Dolly will back up? You? Or me, her dear little sister?" Her lip quivered in mock helplessness, then an idea occurred to her and she looked at Lucy with a sly smile. "Especially if she thinks I might hang?" She didn't wait for an answer, but simply turned and walked down the alley away from Main Street. Her derisive laughter went with her, lingering in the alley like a jeering echo that ridiculed any response Lucy could have devised.

It took her several moments to recover her self-possession, but when she did, Lucy went immediately to the law offices where she asked to speak to Officer Reynolds. She was told he was off duty that day, so she walked back to Pacific Street not far from Cedar Ravine, where she knew he had a small house. He greeted her at the door with surprise.

"We need to talk," she told him. "I know everything now."

He immediately invited her in, but then realized that he was in his stockinged feet and a shirt open at the neck and not tucked in. He excused himself for a moment and returned dressed more appropriately for receiving a woman into his home. Noting how pale Lucy was, he led her to the sofa and asked, "Would you like a sherry? Or something stronger?"

"How about a whiskey with a splash of soda water, if you have any."

"I do."

"Where's your wife? I'd like to meet her one of these days."

"She's visiting with a friend in Diamond Springs."

He handed the drink to her and sat in a nearby chair. After she had taken a large swallow, he asked, "Okay, now what's happened?"

She told him everything, excluding only Melanie's threats to her. She felt an odd degree of gratification when J.J. exclaimed, "Her father! Wow!"

"I have the skirt that she was wearing when she killed Mrs. Helms. It's safely at Old Gus's place."

"Oh, bully! Good thinking."

"It shows the kerosene that splashed onto it. Unfortunately, I have no tangible proof that she killed Tony Leon. Even Mrs. Holliday won't be able to say for certain it was Melanie she saw through the window of the livery that morning, even though a coat like the one she described is, or was, among Melanie's clothing. It's also probably the one she wore when she was passing the note along to Mrs. Helms to set the early morning meeting on June 4th. Anyway, I doubt Mrs. Holliday will admit to having eavesdropped on a private conversation."

"You're right. No woman wants the reputation of being an eavesdropper. And Melanie is right in saying that your conversation with her in the alley won't be admissible. Even if a judge allowed you to tell about it, she can always say you're lying for some reason." He rubbed his hands over his face before looking down at Lucy. "And for most people it will sound like a preposterous, made up tale. Few people will believe that a young, naïve woman such as Melanie appears to be, would kill her mother."

"And she has it all worked out how she'll besmirch my character." She gave way and told him what Melanie had threatened her with, glad that he didn't question how much truth there was in it.

"All I can do is tell all of this to the District Attorney and see if he wants to bring suit against her for the murders."

As it turned out, he did. But only for the attack on Mrs. Helms, since there was some evidence of that. There were also several people who could be called to testify as to Melanie's involvement with Mrs. Helms. The deciding factor was when Dolly told Mr. Hume that she had discovered the key to Mrs. Helms's hotel room among Melanie's things. And she was willing to say so in court.

Even more surprising to everyone involved was that when Officer Reynolds and the sheriff came to arrest Melanie, she confessed freely to having bashed Mrs. Helms on the head with the lamp. She then shocked them by boldly declaring that Mrs. Helms was her long-lost mother. Of course, all of this was said with tearful intervals interspersed with tales of how desperately difficult her life had been since she turned fifteen and had been forced to marry an older, violent man. At which point Melanie informed them of the attorney she had hired to represent her. It was at this point that Mr. Hume knew this case was going to be a challenge to his expertise when they got into the courtroom. The attorney chosen by Melanie had at one time been a partner with Mr. Hume in a law practice, and they hadn't parted well. On the other hand, few men were better at preparing a prosecution than John Hume.

Melanie was escorted to the jail portion of the courthouse, and put in a cell guarded by Mrs. Barnes, an old crone of a woman hired specifically to be of assistance to Melanie. The necessity of housing a woman of quality had not been anticipated when the jail had been built, so the sheriff went out of his way to accommodate this unexpected circumstance. Melanie was brought food from a restaurant, and given books to read. There was already a chair next to a small table in the cell. It was beneath the one high window, so she was able to read during daylight hours. The willingness to indulge Melanie's needs didn't extend to putting a kerosene lamp in with any prisoner.

Nevertheless, Mrs. Barnes talked the jailer into allowing her to bring in a mirror on a silver stand, along with Melanie's hair brushes. Mrs. Barnes also ushered her charge to and from the facilities, and after the second day she was let into the cell so the two women could play cards.

Melanie had only one visitor during her stay in jail while she awaited her trial. On the third day, the door to the cells opened and Sue Ellen stepped into the corridor outside the line of three cells. Currently, only the one housing Melanie was in use. Mrs. Barnes, having gone out for her noon dinner, was not present and Melanie suddenly felt her absence keenly.

"How nice of you to come and see me," Melanie smiled, her face a mask of innocence.

"Don't try to bullshit me, you two-timing bitch!" Even Melanie was shocked at such words coming from someone thought to be so mild and placid. "No one's here that you have to play to. It's just you and me, honey, and we both know what conniving trash you are."

Melanie dropped all pretense and took a step closer to the iron bars between them. "Yes, I am. It's taken years of molding me into that by a selfish mother and a nightmare of a husband. I am the product of their actions."

"Oh, for crying out loud!" Sue Ellen felt like screaming. She was full to overflowing with the frustrated desire to have Melanie realize the point she wanted to make. "You act like you had no choice in any of the things you've done your whole life. You were not a puppet dancing on their strings. You're in the situation you are now because of your own choices. No one else caused this for you!"

Melanie folded her arms across her chest and glared at Sue Ellen. "Maybe so. But no one blames a dog for biting the hand that rises up to hit it. And yet here I am in jail."

"The dog can't reason! People can." Sue Ellen took a deep breath. "But I only have one question for you, and that's why I came here. Why did you put a fake letter in my salon from Tony Leon? Just explain that."

"I really am sorry about having done that. I'm glad I didn't have to make use of it."

"Use of it?"

"If I had been backed into a corner that I didn't think I could get out of, I was going to say you told me that you had killed Tony."

"Why would I do that?"

"Because he had proof that you had let that woman die in your salon over in Groveland."

"There is no proof!" Sue Ellen shouted. "Because that's not what happened. It *was* a heart attack."

"I know that," Melanie told Sue Ellen, as though she was a somewhat stupid child. "But the suggestion would be out there that Tony had proof of something different. By the time the whole thing would have been settled by telegrams sent to Groveland and back, I would have had time to get out of town."

"But I would have been in danger of being arrested for negligent behavior, or worse."

"Oh, don't be silly. There wouldn't have been any proof. You would have been cleared eventually."

"My business hinges on my reputation and that would have been in shambles. Some people would always think I had gotten away with something."

Melanie shrugged and looked down at a recently filed fingernail. "That couldn't have been helped. I needed you as insurance."

"I would call you a few colorful names we've all heard freighters call their mules, but I can tell you wouldn't care." Sue Ellen turned and walked to the door. But before opening it, she turned back to the woman she once thought her friend. "I hope you hang!"

Like water off a duck's back, Sue Ellen's parting shot rolled right off of Melanie's conscience. Some while later, however, it did occur to her to wonder why she had not been visited by Dolly. She had assumed that she was not allowed visitors, but now knew differently. Could she have miscalculated Dolly's loyalty? A tiny knot of anxiety began to form in her mind, and when Mrs. Barnes returned with a plate of food for her, she found she had no appetite for it.

It bothered Lucy how Melanie had masterminded all the little extras allowed her while in jail. She told Jim she was starting to think that Melanie just might be able to convince the jury that her attack on Mrs. Helms was the result of temporary insanity, or was even justifiable. Unaware that his tone edged on patronizing, Jim reassured her that the men on the jury would be intelligent enough to see through any of Melanie's *feminine* wiles. This got him a severe lecture on *masculine* deceitfulness and double-dealing in business and politics.

The trial, being only a week away, Lucy spent a number of hours with Mr. Hume in his office. She shared with him all the interviews, the lists, and her conclusions along the way. During this process, he realized he was having to readjust his conclusions about the intelligence and reasoning ability of women. Before the case was over, he would also change his ideas about the ruthlessness of the so-called gentler sex.

Although Lucy found it difficult to accept that Tony Leon's murder was going to be left unsolved, Jane was jubilant with relief, assuming that it would now not come out that Tony was the anonymous letter writer. She had gotten past caring if people would always wonder why the letters had stopped being written or if they might start up again. She knew that many would always think it was Mrs. Helms who had written them, because it was easier than thinking that the sender still lived among them. Some might even suspect that it was Tony, since they stopped about the time he died, but eventually even that idea would fade out. Jane thought about getting Lucy to promise to let the whole thing drop, but on second thought she was pretty sure there was no need of that. Lucy was, she reminded herself, a kind-hearted woman.

Lucy was of course aware of how people would react, and it may have bothered her more if Freda and Roger had not filled so much of her time. They were all swept up in preparing the new house for their occupation, and Lucy surprised herself by finding that she enjoyed decorating the rooms. She and Freda had not spent so much time sharing a project in years, and that was much of the enjoyment for her.

When not helping with various projects at the house, Jim and Roger spent time in a number of gambling rooms. Of course, Roger was not allowed to play, but in a few games consisting of local men, they delighted in watching "the kid" shuffle the cards for them, and they even occasionally let him deal.

Martha Hume gave a luncheon for Lucy and Freda, and although she would have liked to have invited Dolly also, Martha thought it not politically wise, considering the trial that was soon to take place. Martha did invite Mary Morrill, since Lucy had met her at the dinner party several weeks previous, and Martha remembered the women as liking one another. It was a pleasant couple of hours of eating good food and drinking even better wine.

While Lucy and Mary followed Martha through the garden to see what was blooming, Freda stayed behind in conversation with Nancy Hershel, the Hume housemaid. Freda had met Nancy on a previous visit to Placerville while out shopping with Lucy, before Nancy had been hired on at the Hume household. Mrs. Hume generously gave Nancy permission to visit with Freda in the kitchen. By the time the other ladies had returned from the garden, there was awaiting them in the parlor slices of cake and a large pot of tea.

Nancy Hershel and Mrs. Butler had been keenly appreciative of Freda's offer to whip the cream for the cake. When Freda eagerly fell in with helping to bring the cake slices into the parlor without even being asked, Nancy was impressed. When she discovered that Freda had made the attractive but simple dress she was wearing, Nancy decided she would introduce Freda to her brother, Randal Hershel. For some time, she had thought that her nice, mild-mannered brother needed a practical woman in his life who knew how to run a house and was a good cook. He had been a widower for ten years, and too many of the women Nancy saw setting their caps to land him had not met her high standards. They might have been prettier than Freda, but she was not unattractive and she had real character.

Soon Freda and Randal, or as she referred to him, my *Randy*, began a regular routine of outings, dinners, and walking out together in the evening. His offer of help during the move was gratefully appreciated, as he was quite strong, being a builder and bricklayer. Soon his presence in their life became an accepted fact, and Lucy prepared herself to hear that he and Freda would be getting married. It would mean Freda moving out, although knowing Freda, it did not mean that she would stop caring for Roger whenever she and Jim wanted time away.

Not long after the move was completed, and Lucy had somewhat wistfully said farewell to the Cary House, she settled with her family into a daily routine. During the first few days in the house, a number of women came to call, bringing pastries, baskets of fried chicken, or loaves of bread. All of this was not only in recognition of how much effort went into setting up a new home, but also to judge how neighborly the Murphy family was going to be.

Lucy and Freda made all their visitors welcome with pots of coffee, tea or hot chocolate, and served them using the best china, crystal and silver. Charming conversation that fit the social protocol was shared, along with homemade scones or cookies. Freda and Lucy also made sure to inquire about local charities that might welcome some extra help. The women were introduced to Roger, who charmed them with his smile and politeness. Men usually stopped by after supper so they could sit with Jim on the front porch, sipping his whiskey and smoking one of his cigars. In the end, each visitor left satisfied that the Murphy family was a good addition to Placerville society.

During this time, Lucy had not spoken with Dolly, although she had several times thought about going to her. But since Dolly had not come to visit her at the new house, Lucy wasn't even sure Dolly wanted to see her. Now, with both of them awaiting the trial to begin two days later, Lucy felt she could no longer put off knowing how things stood between herself and Dolly. As her hand lifted the brass knocker on the front door of the Robbins home, her heart beat heavily, not knowing how she might be received.

"Lucy! I almost didn't hear you." Dolly stood back so Lucy could enter. She was smiling, but it no longer sparkled as it had in the past, and Lucy was saddened by this.

"I wasn't sure I would be welcome," Lucy told her, surprised at how shy she felt.

"Oh, don't be silly." Dolly led the way to the kitchen table and poured them each a mug of coffee from the enamel pot on the stove. If she had served her in the parlor using fine china cups and saucers, Lucy would have known there was a rift between them. But now Lucy took her mug to the kitchen table and relaxed as she realized how deep was her bond with Dolly after all. Her appreciation of this almost choked her throat, and it took her a moment to resist throwing her arms around her friend.

Instead, she poured in cream from the white china pitcher Dolly set in front of her and told Dolly, "I feel like I should apologize to you."

The tension of the last week bubbled to the surface, and Dolly took a moment to collect herself. Ever since Melanie's arrest, she had been fighting the urge to throw herself onto the bed and weep. But being a woman of the world, she kept telling herself that this would solve nothing. "Lucy, I'm the one who brought you here. Of course, it was to find out about the awful letters, not to find the killer of some stupid suffrage woman."

"Who turned out to be your mother."

"You should have seen the look on Robert's face when I told him that. But it was nothing compared to when I told him who Tony Leon really was." Dolly shook her head and reached for the handkerchief in her pocket.

"Just think. If Tony Leon had not been such a bitter soul, and had not written that first letter, you wouldn't have sent for me."

"And you wouldn't have been here when Mother was killed. But what happened between her and Melanie would have happened whether or not anonymous letters had been going around." She looked down at her coffee cup. "Melanie would just have covered up her deed in a different way. She was always very clever."

"You mean good at manipulating people? Because that's what she's going to do to the jury. It's an all-male jury, of course. She, at least, is glad women don't have the right to serve on a jury."

"Looking back, I think she always was a bit devious. But she was also sweet and kind and compassionate." She grimaced and rolled her eyes. "Well, all of that has disappeared." She breathed out a heavy sigh, and with it let go of any naïve hope that Melanie would ever return to the generous and kind girl Dolly had known as a child. "What led you to believe it was Melanie who killed Mother?"

"And Tony."

"Yes. Sue Ellen recently admitted knowing who he was, but wouldn't tell me how she knew. It was from Melanie, wasn't it?"

"Yes, it was. When I knew Melanie had killed Mrs. Helms, and having already made up my mind that the two killings were connected, I had to ask why Melanie might kill Tony. What was the connection between Mrs. Helms and Tony? It occurred to me that if Mrs. Helms had changed her name, so maybe had Tony. Later, when I saw that the books in his study were gone, and then saw them at the rummage sale with the dedications inside of *L.A.* in them, I thought of Los Angeles.

"I had already thought about Jim once mentioning how people often call him Murphy, his last name, but that some people might think he was being called by his first name. It occurred to me when he said that, that L. A. could be Leon Anthony, which was the reversal of Anthony Leon. But that meant that Tony had not divorced your mother, and if Jane had known this, she could have killed him out of anger or fear of it becoming known. I hadn't gotten any further than that at that point. But later, when I saw a book given to you by *L.A.* in your book case, that clinched the connection to you and therefore Melanie. And there was one book that was signed *V*, which I had thought was the Roman numeral for five. But I then realized it was for *Vespacia*, your mother's name."

"But Anthony wasn't his first name."

"Tony is the nickname for Anthony."

"Oh, so it is." Dolly stared into the distance. "Just think, for a short time my mother and father were both here, and I didn't know it. And all these years Tony never knew one of his daughters was in the same town with him." She still could not think of him as anyone other than Tony Leon.

"It's not that much of a coincidence, really," Lucy explained. "Your mother was here because Placerville is the County Seat of El Dorado County, and a place with a growing female population. She told Vincent that she was going to be here, and after Melanie read that, she too came here. She wasn't trying to avoid your mother. She wanted to confront her. But your mother only remonstrated with Melanie and took no responsibility for Melanie's years of unhappiness as Melanie wanted her to do."

"I sensed a lot of turmoil in Melanie the minute she got here. I just didn't realize how much of it was suppressed anger."

"I think it was mixed up with a deep hurt that had festered like a boil for years," Lucy explained. "Then it turned into rage and overcame her in the moment she first struck out at the mother who offered no remorse or solace. Society paints a picture of women as either fragile, delicate creatures needing to be coddled and protected, or as strong pioneer stock that maintains hearth and home in the face of any adversity. But we're human, complex creatures. Even if we're not allowed to show our deep feelings of displeasure or unhappiness, it doesn't mean they're not present."

"Yes, and sometimes only needing a trigger to explode into inappropriate action. Which as we know, women are only too capable of inflicting on others." Dolly moved to the stove and poured them more coffee. "Either that or we keep our feelings inside eating away until it shows forth in failing health. I've seen both more than once."

"I guess it could be seen as a coincidence that your father was here. But after all, this is a popular supply town for those going over the Sierra, and a lot of miners in the nearby hills and ravines need supplies packed in to them. That was true even when he came here in '56, to a town that was desperate for anyone's help in rebuilding. I also don't think Tony was so much a man with a roving eye for young girls, as he was always hoping he would recognize one of his daughters." She frowned and added, "Although his nasty comments about women might explain why he wrote the anonymous letters."

"I don't think I ever came across him face to face," Dolly mused.

"No. But he did see Melanie in the post office. And regardless of what she told us, she and Tony did talk. At that point, she knew he was the letter writer, and told him so."

"Oh, surely Melanie would have at least told me that he was our father."

Lucy looked at Dolly with a crooked smile. "You really think so, given what she had done to your mother?"

"No, I guess not." It was another sad moment of realization for Dolly.

"When Tony decided to give himself up, it wasn't that unusual that he asked to see her alone. Or that he chose the livery stable for the meeting, since he kept his mules in the corrals out back. He probably thought he was doing a noble thing to admit to being the letter writer, although bringing the cut-up newspapers with him was a bit melodramatic."

"He was like that. As kids, when he gave us gifts, they'd be handed over as though he was performing an act of benevolence." Dolly shrugged. "Maybe he just wanted to reassure Melanie that he hadn't killed Mother."

"Could be. But what he didn't know was that his confessing to the police about the letters would cause them to take a closer look at the Helms murder. They had concluded that she had been killed by a letter recipient that she was blackmailing."

Dolly caught onto Lucy's line of reasoning. "Oh, I see. If they knew Mother wasn't the letter writer after all, they'd begin to look for another reason that she had been killed. And they would wonder why the newspapers were in her room to make it look like she *was* the writer, because they'd know after Tony's confession that the newspapers had to have been brought there from Tony's house. Tony wouldn't have done that, so the question would become *who did?*"

"That's right. The police would question those who might know who the real letter writer was, because the killer had known where to go for the newspapers, paste and scissors. Melanie was afraid of any attention in her direction. Besides that, she hated the father that had deserted the family when she was just a child. All of this resulted in her lashing out at him to stop him leaving the livery."

"No doubt part of her rage did stem back to his deserting our family right after we got to California. I know I still resent it, even though he's dead. Maybe I just wish I'd had the opportunity to tell him off."

Lucy said no more, knowing that Dolly had to resolve the whole thing in her mind in any way that allowed her to be able to live with it. When Dolly stood up suddenly and walked into the parlor to stand at the front window, Lucy followed her. Dolly looked out at a view she had enjoyed for years. The distant sun was sinking low over the Sierra and cast shadows over the houses of her neighbors, drawing their inhabitants out onto their porches to enjoy the cooling air.

Standing behind her friend, Dolly's voice as she spoke was so low that Lucy could barely hear her. "Robert is asking around if anyone wants to buy his livery."

"Why?" Lucy was alarmed not only by such a drastic idea, but especially by the sadness in Dolly's voice.

Dolly turned back to Lucy, a tear running down her cheek. "We can't continue to live here after Melanie is sent to prison for murder. The people here have tolerated me well, but now I'll be the ex-prostitute with the sister who murdered her mother. It won't be any different if by some chance she gets off. Over time, the details won't matter. People will just remember those two facts."

"But you love it here."

"Yes. And I was looking forward to our being neighbors, enjoying all the town events together. But even if I could rise above the talk, I can't put Robert through what we both know society will do to us. It's not fair to him. He's had offers from the other liveries as well as the wagon shop for his stock, but no one seems to want the old building. Maybe they'll tear it down and use the wood elsewhere, like has so often happened to other old barns." She produced a rueful smile. "It'll make it easier to forget we were ever here."

Lucy swallowed the lump in her throat and asked, "Where do you plan to go?"

"I don't know yet. Just far away, where no one knows our past and won't ask about it. We've talked about going to Virginia City. Robert doesn't want to do any mining, but there's a demand for men who can work with horses and mules, and run a forge. And I hear more women are arriving, and some even run rooming houses or restaurants. Or..."

She stopped because Lucy had encased her in her arms, recognizing someone desperately trying to put forth a positive picture of an uncertain future. She held Dolly as long as her weeping continued, then led her to the sofa. After bringing Dolly a glass of water and making her drink it, Lucy sat next to her dearest friend while resting a reassuring hand on her arm. And herself trying not to weep.

"I want so much to forgive Melanie," Dolly gasped. "And our parents, too. I can't spend the rest of my life focusing on their selfishness. Robert said they should have known better, but they couldn't be more than they were." Dolly sighed with resolve. "Maybe we'll move to the Owens Valley." Lucy looked at Dolly in shocked surprise, which was immediately engulfed in the spontaneity of their laughter, the moment lightened by the absurdity of such an idea.

"They're having terrible Indian troubles, you know," Lucy pointed out unnecessarily. Everyone along the Sierra was aware of the Owens Valley Indian War, as the newspapers were calling it.

"Yes, I know. But that won't last. We heard lately that a Colonel Evans has started from Fort Latham. That's between Los Angeles and Santa Monica. He has 157 men with him, part of the Second California Cavalry."

Lucy and Dolly sat back so that their shoulders touched, the friends needing nothing more to calm them and bring them a few moments of quiet peace.

They didn't know it then, but the Cavalry would arrive in the Owens Valley in a few days from then, where the soldiers would set up camp on Oak Creek. Being July 4th, after raising a 50-foot flagstaff topped by the American flag, they would fire salutes, give three times three cheers, and consider themselves established. After digging primitive caves into the side of a wide and deep ravine that ran north and south through the area, they would begin building rude cabins. The soldiers would name the site *Camp Independence*, and eventually would build more permanent buildings to be used until abandoning the fort in 1877.

A century and a half later, all traces of the fort would be long gone, the wood of its buildings used to enlarge a nearby town that the citizens named *Independence*, in honor of the brave soldiers and the fort that had once protected them. Amazingly, still at the original site of the first encampment, would be the ravine that had given the soldiers their first protected habitation.

CHAPTER 14

"A truth that's told with bad intent
Beats all the lies you can invent."
Wm. Blake

Monday, July 7

The trial started on the first Monday in July. Seen from the street, the courthouse built in 1857 was a simple, rectangular building made of red brick, with two narrow entrance doors that opened off the sidewalk. Giving the building a prestigious appearance was a raised section of shingles in the center of the roof that slanted up to a modest bell tower. Across the front of the second story ran a roofed, white-railed veranda that at the same time created a covered walkway below. The second floor was reached by a stairway that cut into the center of the building off the sidewalk, giving access to the courtroom, judge's chamber, and attorney offices.

Citizens regularly scanned the two message boards nailed to the outside wall along the sidewalk where court schedules and other messages were posted. A basement storage area was accessed by a narrow flight of stairs at the rear of the first floor, and from outside at the bottom of the slope upon which the courthouse was built. In this basement was housed the town's historic records belonging to the Recorder, Auditor, Assessor, Surveyor, District Attorney, and Superior Court -- all of which would be lost in a fire in 1910.

Facing south, the front of the building caught much of the morning sun, which was beneficial in winter but not comfortable in summer. Consequently, canvas shades were provided that could be let down from the outer edge of the veranda above. This had the additional advantage of blocking from sight anyone on the sidewalk entering to stand trial. Most people were grateful for the privacy of this, but Melanie was not. She wanted as many people as possible to see her, thinking of her arrival as the opening act of what was to follow.

On this day, a jury of twelve men were seated and ready to pass judgment on the accused, one Melanie St. John. She was a stranger to all of them, and they were eager to see this female who was accused of killing the suffrage woman. They had heard the rumor that the District Attorney had wanted to charge her with second degree murder, but had been convinced by others that he could more easily get a conviction on a first degree manslaughter charge because of the type of provocation involved. It was this "provocation" that heightened the jurors' curiosity, almost replacing their disappointment that it meant that no matter the outcome of the trial, they were not going to witness a hanging. What would these men have thought if they had been told that 54 years in the future, there would be seated a jury composed of all women?

The jury members had also heard that a second blow had killed Mrs. Helms, with a first one having only stunned her. They wanted to know how this was to be proved. Coroners' medical examinations, not yet considered absolutely scientific, when used in court cases were often discounted as opinion.

No charge had been made against Melanie, or anyone else, related to Tony Leon's death. It had been officially classified as a robbery gone bad. Consequently, with no one having stepped forward with information to make that conclusion invalid, it would stand.

The rumor mill had gotten it around that Tony Leon might have been the writer of the anonymous letters, but it was mixed with other rumors that had the letters coming from Mrs. Helms. The fact that they had stopped being sent seemed to confirm to many people that it had been one or the other of these murdered persons. A few imaginative people surmised that the letters had been sent by someone smart enough to know that if they stopped sending them at this time, these would be the general assumptions and they would be safe from discovery. Whatever the reason, everyone was just thankful that they had stopped arriving.

Melanie was ushered into the courtroom by Constable Adam Simonton and seated at one of two small, pine tables. Her view forward was the judge sitting at a large, highly polished and imposing mahogany table. He was reading the case notes and didn't look up. Consequently, she couldn't catch his eye as she had planned. To his right was a chair for a witness while they were testifying, and beyond that two rows of chairs filled with local men serving as jurors who faced into the room. To the left of the judge sat his clerk, Thomas B. Patten, at a table holding a Bible, a jar of pencils, an ink well and pen, and a stack of writing paper.

Behind the two tables set up to face the judge, one for the defense and one for the prosecution, were long benches with no backs that seated about thirty spectators. For this trial, the benches were filled with curious and excited townspeople who had gotten in line early that morning, along with those people to be called as a witness. There was also the unusual sight of people standing around outside on the sidewalk awaiting word of what was taking place inside.

The gentlemen of the press, not allowed inside, were hovering next to the door, determined to maintain their places by force if necessary. In this way, they would be the first to have the opportunity to talk to those exiting. The trial promised to be a headline-maker, considering how seldom a woman of quality was put on trial.

The presiding judge was Justice James Johnson, who had served in Placerville since 1852. He was a stoic man in his late forties, clean-shaven, with a broad nose and full lips usually pursed in disgust or dubious approval. He also had what some called a stubborn chin, a window into a large part of his character. His prominent, high cheekbones accented eyes that seemed in a perpetual glare because of straight, over-hanging brows, while his head was crowned by a hairline well receded to the back of his head into a ruff of short hair turning gray. Looking at his dour countenance, it was the first time Melanie had qualms about walking out a free woman.

The prosecution, sitting at a table to Melanie's right, was represented by District Attorney John Hume, well known and trusted by every man sitting on the jury. Her attorney, sitting next to her on her left, was Mr. S. W. Sanderson, whose office was on the second floor of the Douglass Building next to the Cary House, and well-known to Mr. Hume. Middle-aged but not yet gray, he was almost as well-known as his esteemed colleague, and his general reputation was a good one. Adding to the anticipation of the jury was the knowledge that Sanderson and Hume had several years earlier come to blows during a trial. However, if any of the men on the jury had arrived at a preconceived conclusion, they didn't show it. Everything for a fair trial was set in place.

Melanie sat up straight, eyes forward and hands folded demurely in her lap. Although the eyes of the jury focused on her, she avoided eye contact with them. She was dressed in a simple, high-necked gray dress lined with only one petticoat, a simple crocheted collar, and no flounces across the front. And yet it somehow flattered her. The dark plainness of it allowed for a stark contrast with her pale face that now hinted at smudgy shadows beneath her eyes that gave her the appearance of a forlorn waif. Lucy was sure it had been artfully applied from soot.

Throughout the trial Melanie kept her eyes piously cast down, except when they were raised to meet the eyes of a juryman, and then her pleading gaze was quickly averted. It was, after all, what a proper lady should do.

Sitting one row back to Melanie's right, Lucy watched Melanie's adroit, well-rehearsed performance with grudging admiration. Whether or not it was good enough to set her free was anyone's guess. Dolly sat to Lucy's right, stiff and upright, and terrified.

After Melanie had risen and declared herself "not guilty", the testimony for the prosecution began with the County Coroner, Mr. Eichelroth. He, as well as every witness who followed him, swore on the Bible to tell the truth. He began by verifying that the marks on the skirt held out to him as Exhibit 1 were made by kerosene that had splashed onto the skirt. He also testified that it was his opinion that Mrs. Helms had died of two strikes to her left temple by the same object, wielded by a right-handed person, and one strike a little later than the other.

"Can you explain how you can tell all that?" Mr. Hume made sure he didn't block the coroner from the jurors' view.

"It has to do with the degree of bruising between the two places where she was hit. The second hit was not exactly on top of the first, so I could see the two places well enough."

Mr. Hume asked, "Can you tell anything about the weapon used?"

"Yes. The object was a heavy glass lamp base." It was shown to the jury and entered as Exhibit 2. The coroner then declared, "The first strike would not have caused death. However, a second blow was struck the deceased with such force that it definitely caused death. This indicates a well- developed arm, such as a prominently right-handed person would have. And the second strike, the deathblow, was struck anywhere between fifteen minutes to an hour after the first one."

"What was the main difference between the two?"

"The first one didn't break the skin, but the second one did. It also crushed the skull. She died almost immediately after that."

The judge leaned toward the witness and asked if he could tell *exactly* how long a time there had been between the two blows.

"Not exactly, any more than I can tell you whether those two blows were struck by the same person. It's not my job to decide that," Mr. Eichelroth piously added as he glanced toward the jury.

Mr. Hume then got the coroner to admit, "Yes, it's just as true that the two wounds *could* have been made by the same person. The timing of the two blows is, however, more certain."

"Would a right-handed person using the same weapon a second time tend to strike the same place on their victim's head?"

"Possibly, especially if they wanted people to think the victim had been hit only once. Also, the fact that the weapon used was already familiar to them and readily at hand, might count for something. But the second strike was applied in a more downward direction, as would be done if the deceased was sitting on the floor, possibly still recovering from the first blow. The first one was more lateral in application."

Mr. Hume returned to his chair and Mr. Sanderson rubbed his chin thoughtfully as he approached the Coroner. "If a person much taller than Mrs. Helms had hit her the second time while she was standing, wouldn't this have looked the same as a short person hitting her while she was on the floor?"

"The strike would have been the same, but she wouldn't have fallen exactly onto the same spot. She was found where the accused's statement said she had left her." Lucy glanced at Melanie and saw her jaw tighten. Was she regretting having been so specific in her statement?

Attorney Sanderson, not pleased with this added comment, asked, "Now, Mr. Eichelroth, isn't it true that much of what you have just said is pure speculation on your part?"

The Coroner puffed up with indignation. "Not at all. It is my job to know these things. I wouldn't attempt to question your knowledge of the law, and I find it very displeasing that you would presume to question my forensic knowledge." He turned to the jury. "That is, how the human body reacts to physical forces upon it."

"I beg your pardon, I'm sure," Mr. Sanderson said, not wanting to appear unnecessarily argumentative. "I merely wanted to be sure of the scientific validity of your statements."

"Well, you can be assured of them," the Coroner huffed.

Several men on the jury were seen to display their impatience with this exchange. Accurately interpreting this, Mr. Sanderson excused the coroner.

Mrs. Hall came next to say what it was that she had heard the morning of Mrs. Helms's death. She was very clear about the time of the morning involved, and that she had heard two arrivals and departures. Mrs. Hall glowed with contented enjoyment throughout her testimony, clearly untouched by the seriousness of the occasion, and simply enjoying the unusual adjunct to her normal routine.

"How much time would you say elapsed between the first arrival and the second one?"

"Almost half an hour, maybe a few minutes more."

When asked by Mr. Hume if she had ever heard any arguments or raised voices emanating from Mrs. Helms's room, she lit up. "Oh, yes, several times."

"Do you remember when they occurred?"

"Yes. One was a man about two weeks before she died, and another was with a woman the night she gave her big speech."

"Was there another time?"

"Well, of course there were raised voices on the morning she was killed. But they didn't last long."

"Was it a man or a woman who was with her that fateful morning?" Mr. Hume asked her.

"Oh, a woman. Very definitely a woman." Several people in the audience gasped and she looked at the jurors as if seeking approval. She was, however, met with stony stares. Her smile didn't falter, and she turned her attention back to Mr. Hume.

Her chipper attitude didn't change even when Mr. Sanderson, on cross examination, got her to admit that she couldn't swear if it was the same person she heard come and go twice that morning. She shrugged and asked, "What difference does it make?" She was immediately excused. On her way out of the room she looked around, spotted Lucy, and waved in her direction. Lucy couldn't help but smile back, but she resisted waving.

The next to be called was Dolly, since she had found the body. The judge had to tell her twice to speak up, for which she apologized before continuing in only a slightly louder voice. She described her reason for going to Mrs. Helms's room the morning of June 4, what she saw while there, and how she screamed before running down to the clerk.

Mr. Hume asked, "Did you have any personal relationship to the deceased?"

With obvious reticence, but forcing her voice louder, Dolly said, "Mrs. Helms was my mother."

Most of the people present had not been aware of this, and Judge Johnson had to shush the spectators with a stern rebuke in order for the trial to continue.

"Was this the first time you had gone to her room?"

"No. I was the visitor to her room the night of the speech, the one Mrs. Hall heard talking to her that evening. When I attended her speech, it was the first time I had seen the Mrs. Helms everyone had been talking about. She had shown no recognition of me when I arrived for the speech, so I wanted to know if it had been because she hadn't recognized me, or didn't want it known who I was. So, I went to her room after the speech to talk to her."

"Had she recognized you when you entered the Orleans Hotel meeting room?"

"Yes, but she didn't want it known that she had ties to anyone in town."

"Why was that, Mrs. Robbins?"

"She didn't want to be seen in a maternal role, but only as a champion of worthy causes, such as women's rights and the abolishment of slavery."

There was a buzz of comment, mostly of approval, but also some of distinct disapproval. Lucy wondered if Mr. Sanderson might think this would influence the jurors in some way, no doubt knowing the men and which way they leaned regarding the war, as well as the women's rights issue. The judge struck his gavel, not bothering to use words along with it, and everyone immediately stopped talking. It was the only time Lucy saw him look pleased throughout the trial.

"How did you feel about her choices?"

"I could see her point, and I really wasn't that interested in pursuing a relationship with her anyway."

"But there was an occasion during your visit that Mrs. Hall could have heard raised voices?"

"Yes. It was when Mother said she was glad I had come to her so she could see me one last time. I was okay with that, but then she said she didn't want to see Melanie. That upset me."

"Did you ask her why she didn't want to see your sister?"

"Yes. She said Melanie would only whine about her life and try to blame her for it. I told her that I could blame her, too, for leaving me to make a distasteful choice in order to survive during the rush. She only laughed and said I was too level-headed to believe that."

"Mrs. Robbins, when you were in the room upon the occasion of having discovered her body, did you see anything lying on top of her?"

"Yes. I saw a piece of scrap newspaper."

"Was it a torn scrap?"

"No. It had clearly been cut from a newspaper, having straight edges."

Mr. Hume showed Dolly a scrap of newspaper, which she identified as the one she had seen, or at least one just like it. It was entered into evidence as Exhibit 3.

"Had you always been aware of Vincent St. John's harsh treatment of your sister?"

"Yes. She had confided in me from almost the beginning of her marriage."

"Was your mother aware of it?"

"Yes. Melanie told me she complained to her several times before Mother moved away."

"Did you or your mother ever try to do anything about his treatment of her?"

"I wasn't in a position to try, and I don't know if Mother ever said anything to him or not."

"When you first saw your mother at the Orleans Hotel upon your entering the meeting room, did she greet you with enthusiasm?"

"No."

"Did she acknowledge that she even knew you?"

"No."

"Did that rejection remind you of that which you received from her that forced you into an unhappy profession during the rush?"

"No. I made the choice I did after having made several others. Unfortunately, those jobs didn't provide enough money to support myself."

"Were you angry at your mother for rejecting you at such a crucial point in your career choices?" Mr. Hume knew he was cutting into questions he was sure Sanderson would be asking. But by asking them himself first, he could get the subject out of the way in a manner not antagonistic to the witness. And maybe he would disconcert Sanderson, throwing him off his stride as he took his turn at cross-examination.

"I wasn't angry with Mother, but I was a little hurt. On the other hand, she had moved far away and I assumed she didn't have extra money to share with me. I simply took charge of my life and did what I had to do."

"As we all did during the rush," he reminded everyone. He then turned her over to the defense.

Mr. Sanderson immediately snapped at her, "Were you angry at your mother for not claiming you as her daughter when she saw you at the suffrage meeting?"

"No. She even hugged me when I arrived at her room. She had chosen a difficult path in her life, that of working for the rights of others. I realized that she had to continue down that path unburdened by a maternal image. After all, my sister and I are adults, and we no longer *need* a mother."

"Your anger was on behalf of your sister?"

"I had no anger," she answered, her composure still intact, but impatience now creeping into her tone. "When she expressed her opinion about Melanie, I raised my voice in exasperation and she raised hers to emphasize her position. It wasn't more than a sentence on both our parts, but we at least understood the other's position. I didn't stay much longer with her after that, but we parted pleasantly."

This seemed to frustrate the attorney, having been unable to ruffle Dolly's aplomb, or insinuate that Mrs. Helms had prompted rage in her. He dismissed her with a curt, "Thank you," before abruptly turning his back to her and walking to his table.

The judge informed her with surprising kindness, "You may return to your seat now, Mrs. Robbins."

The hotel clerk next testified as to the accuracy of what Dolly had said to him, as well as her white-faced look of terror upon approaching the counter. He hadn't heard her scream as she had stated in her testimony, but he declared positively that the time between Dolly arriving at his desk and returning to it had only been a couple of minutes. Considering the length of time he said that it took ladies to cross the lobby, climb the steep stairs and come back down them, he estimated that Mrs. Robbins would have been in the room less than a minute. There was no doubt left in anyone's mind that there had been insufficient time for Dolly to have done what the clerk saw when he went to the room. He then described this in gory if somewhat unnecessary detail.

Officer J. J. Reynolds and his partner, Officer John Van Eaton, testified as to how they had been summoned by messenger and arrived at the scene. They too described the room as they had found it, which only confirmed what the jury had so far heard. They also described how, upon leaving the deceased's room, they had locked the room with the key given them by the clerk. Officer Reynolds said they could not find the key that should have been in the possession of Mrs. Helms.

Mr. Hume asked him, "Did you find anyone who was an eye witness to the murder?"

"No."

"Did you find anyone who would come forward to say they heard someone coming and going from the room on the morning of June 4?"

"Not immediately. But eventually I talked to Mrs. Hall and she told me the same thing that she testified to in court." He carefully didn't say that Lucy had told him to go talk to Mrs. Hall.

Mr. Sanderson addressed Officer Reynolds. "Mrs. Hall testified about what she *heard*. Did you find anyone who *saw* anything?"

"No."

"Did you find anyone who said they saw someone in the hotel who didn't belong there?"

"No." It was an admission that still bothered him.

"Did you interview anyone other than Mrs. Hall who even *heard* someone come and go from the deceased's room?"

"No. But the room next to Mrs. Helms had been unoccupied."

Mr. Sanderson had not known that and his frown showed his pique. Glaring at Officer Reynolds, he snapped out, "No further questions!"

The judge turned to Mr. Hume. "Please call your next witness."

Mr. Hume called young Billy Dooris to the stand to relate how he and an as yet unnamed man had transferred a note to Mrs. Helms the day before she was killed. "A man stopped me after school and said some woman in a long black coat came up to him and said she'd give him two bits to hand a note to some kid he could trust. Then she handed the note to him and gave him a nickel to give to the kid." He turned to the spectators and grinned. "That was me. I bought a big bag of candy for me, and a cookie for my ma." The audience smiled back, and even a few of the men on the jury cracked a smile.

Mr. Hume cleared his throat and Billy relinquished the admiration of the crowd to return his attention to his questioner. "Did the man who gave you the note and the nickel know the woman who gave these things to him?"

"He said he didn't. I was curious and asked him."

"Did he say what she looked like?"

"Just that she was wearing a long black coat and a head scarf that hid part of her face. Lots of ladies do that when it gets real windy, like it was that day."

"Do you see anyone in the courtroom that looks like the man who gave you the note?"

Billy slowly looked around the room and then shook his head, saying, "No, sir."

When Billy was turned over to Mr. Sanderson, he asked Billy if he had read the note. Billy made clear his exasperation. "Of course not! My pa would skin me proper if I ever opened someone's mail!"

Billy was told to step down and he reluctantly returned to his seat at the back of the room. However, he was met by his mother, who marched him out of the adult arena of a murder trial.

Officer Reynolds, for cross-examination, was recalled to the stand by Mr. Hume and had to admit that such a note had not been found. Nor had they found any man who admitted to giving a note to Billy. The note was therefore not proven to have had anything to do with Melanie, or even Mrs. Helms's death. The assumption, however, lingered that the note had most likely brought about the meeting that took place the next morning.

To help cement this impression, Mr. Hume asked, "Officer Reynolds, did you search for a long black coat in Mrs. St. John's closet after her arrest?"

"Yes, I did."

"Did you find one there?"

"Yes. It was at the extreme left side of the wardrobe closet."

Walking to his table, Mr. Hume unwrapped a paper parcel sitting there and returned to the stand carrying a black wool coat. "Is this the coat?"

J.J. reached for the collar and fingered it. "Yes. I recognize the label and the bit of rice powder rubbed into it."

"Thank you." He turned to the clerk and told him to enter it as Exhibit 4.

Mr. Sanderson declined to cross-examine on this point. Lucy was then called and asked to describe how she had come into possession of Melanie's skirt. She did this in detail, including her reasoning as to why she had gone to Melanie's closet. When Mr. Hume asked if she had also seen a long black coat in the back of Melanie's closet, she answered, "Yes, I did." Of course, she wanted to say that the person facing Tony Leon the morning he had been killed had also worn a long black coat, but she was unable to do that.

Mr. Sanderson decided to let her testimony about the skirt stand without questioning, since Melanie had not denied hitting Mrs. Helms with the lamp and therefore having gotten kerosene on her skirt. The coat was entered as Exhibit 5.

Mr. Hume recalled Dolly to the stand to tell how she had found the key to Mrs. Helms's hotel room in a drawer of Melanie's dresser. That caused a few gasps from the spectators. It was impossible to tell if it was due to the fact of the key being there, or that Melanie's sister was testifying against her. They could not know how strenuously Dolly had argued against it, but had eventually realized that it was her duty to do so. The key was entered into evidence as Exhibit 6.

When Melanie was finally called to the stand, something she had forced her attorney to allow, she maintained her pitiable demeanor. In fact, Mr. Sanderson assisted her to the witness chair as he might help an invalid. Mr. Hume took his cue from this and began his examination by gently asking her a few mundane questions. She admitted that her name was Melanie St. John, that she was married to Vincent St. John, that her permanent residence was in Los Angeles, and that her temporary residence was in the home of her sister, Dolly Robbins.

"What was your relationship to the deceased known as Vespacia Helms?" Mr. Hume asked.

Melanie looked him in the eyes, saying loudly and clearly, "She was my mother."

If she wanted a reaction from the spectators, she got one. Lucy found this odd, since Dolly had already admitted that Mrs. Helms was her mother. Surely, she thought, they realized that *sisters* meant they had the same mother. Then it occurred to her that the murmurs and gasps might be due to the full realization that this woman before them was accused of killing her own mother. Lucy snorted to herself, "If they knew that she also killed her father, they'd go crazy."

Judge Johnson also seemed surprised at their reaction, but in addition, he was irritated at the disruption. "If there's another outbreak like this, I'll clear the courtroom." That was enough to encourage them to keep still, as no one wanted to miss what came next.

"How long had it been," Mr. Hume asked, "since you had seen your mother prior to seeing her in Placerville?"

"About three years."

"Had you no communication with her during that time?"

"No."

"But you did know where she was and that she was coming to Placerville, did you not?"

"Yes. She occasionally wrote to my husband."

"Is that how you knew of her whereabouts, from those letters?" he insisted.

"Only if Vincent would allow me to read them, or if I retrieved them from the trash when he would not."

This ruler-of-the-roost control was getting too close to what he knew the defense would be bringing out, so Mr. Hume told her, "Just answer yes or no, please. Did you know Mrs. Helms was going to be in Placerville in the month of June?"

"Yes."

"Did you *have* to be here at that time?"

"No. But..."

"I heard your answer, which was *no*. Did you arrange for a meeting to be held in her room on the morning of Wednesday, June 4?"

"Yes."

"Did you expect your meeting with her to be a pleasant one?"

"Not particularly." Melanie couldn't hide a flush of irritation at being verbally restrained.

"Did you think the meeting with your mother might become confrontational?"

"I had no way of knowing."

"But you knew it was a possibility?"

"I suppose so."

"Could you have avoided any unpleasantness or confrontation with her just by not going to her room?"

"Obviously."

"Yes or no will be sufficient."

"Yes."

Mr. Hume switched the topic. "How long have you been married to Vincent St. John?"

Melanie's head jerked back as though she had been struck across the face. "Since I was fifteen, which was nine years ago."

"Was he a wealthy man at the time of your marriage?"

"Yes."

"Have you always had nice clothes to wear?"

"Yes."

"Do you have as part of your wardrobe a long black coat?"

"Yes, as do many people."

"Is the home you share with your husband a comfortable and substantial one?"

"Yes."

"Have you ever known want of funds for fashionable clothing or good food?"

"No." Before he could stop her, she quickly added, "Just want of love and tenderness."

Mr. Hume frowned, but chose to ignore this in case some of the jury members had not heard her. "Are you aware that there are many women who cannot claim advantages such as has been yours?"

"Yes, but..."

"On the morning of June 4 when you were in Mrs. Helms's room, and you felt yourself becoming angry, did she bar the door?"

"I beg your pardon?"

"Did she get in front of the door to her room so that you couldn't get out?"

"Oh." Melanie pinched her lips together and then forced them into a sorrowful little smile. "She did not."

"Then you could have simply left if you didn't like the conversation?"

"Yes, but..."

Mr. Hume stood back and announced to the judge, "No more questions."

Mr. Sanderson approached his client, who was showing heightened color and obvious irritation brought on by the restrictions of Mr. Hume's questioning. She no longer looked pitiable and Mr. Sanderson was well aware of this. "Mrs. St. John, it is obvious that you did not lack the trappings of what might appear to others as an advantageous marriage. But we all know there is much more to a marital relationship than food on the table and clothes on one's back. Were you ever afraid of your husband?"

"Oh, yes."

"Did he ever physically hurt you?"

"Yes, often."

"In what way?"

She swallowed with difficulty and Lucy felt that for this part Melanie did not have to act. "He beat me if I didn't do as he wanted, or if I displeased him in some way, or if I refused to...do certain things of a private nature."

"Did other people see the damage you sustained from this mistreatment?"

"No. My husband made sure he hit me where it wouldn't show. If he slapped my face, I wasn't allowed outside until the red imprint of his hand disappeared." She swallowed with an effort. "I seldom went outside the house."

"Didn't you have friends who might question your isolation or any bruising they may have noted?"

"No. He wouldn't allow me to make women friends. And if we were out in public on the rare occasions when he had me accompany him somewhere, I was forbidden to talk to a man. I couldn't even talk with a woman beyond his hearing."

"Did you feel it was important for you to come to Placerville, where you could stay with your sister, at just this time?"

"Yes."

"Why was that?"

"Vincent's temper was escalating, and I was terrified of him even more than I had been before."

"After you discovered that your mother was going to be here in Placerville in June, couldn't you have delayed your trip?"

"I had already made my plans to run away from him and come here. I was afraid that if I delayed, not knowing how long the delay would have to be, I might miss my opportunity to get away safely."

"Why was this particular time one of safety for doing that?"

"Vincent was going to San Diego for a few days on business. He had given me tasks to do that he calculated would take me all of that time, so if they were not completed upon his return, he would know I had not stayed home all the time he was gone." She looked down at her lap and up again at Mr. Sanderson. "I know that doesn't make sense, but that's the kind of thing he did."

"Nevertheless, once you were here, you didn't have to go to your mother's room to visit with her, did you?"

"I didn't *have to*, no. But I decided to do it on the spur of the moment the day I arrived, even before going to my sister's home. The letter to my husband had mentioned the hotel where she planned to stay."

"How did that conversation with Mrs. Helms turn out?" Mr. Sanderson preferred to refer to the dead woman as Melanie's mother as little as possible. Melanie, however, wanted everyone to remember this in order that they might pass harsh judgment on how terrible a mother Mrs. Helms had been.

"Our meeting was disappointing. She told me she didn't want anyone to know she was my mother. It didn't suit her purpose for being in town."

"Did she tell you that she had spoken with your sister?"

"No." Her lips pursed as she remembered that Dolly had not informed her of this either.

"Did you and Mrs. Helms have heated words?"

"I told her she needn't worry, since I didn't want to be known as *her* daughter. I hoped she might feel the sting of such words, but she was unmoved, and I left."

Several of the women spectators shook their heads, showing their empathy with how they imagined Melanie must have felt at such a rejection. A few even exchanged sympathetic glances among themselves. Lucy saw this, and was instantly worried.

"If you had agreed to her demand," Mr. Sanderson asked, "why did you go back to see her on the morning of June 4th?"

"I had received a note from her, delivered when Dolly was not at home, asking me to come to her room just before dawn when she knew people wouldn't be about." When Dolly gasped at the falsity of this statement, Lucy reached over and gripped one of her gloved hands, knowing that it was only the beginning of the various ways Melanie was going to twist the truth. This was brought home when Melanie added, "Since she wanted to see me, I hoped that we were going to have a reasonable visit after all. I still wanted her to understand the kind of marriage she had forced me into."

"Did you send her a note in reply?"

"Yes. I paid two people to pass on my note of acceptance, disguising my appearance while doing it. She didn't want me connected with her in any way, and I had promised to go along with that."

"Wasn't that a rather elaborate way to go about it?"

Melanie shrugged. "Maybe."

Mr. Sanderson asked, "When you got to her room, what time was it?"

"I don't know. It wasn't yet light out."

"How were you received by Mrs. Helms?"

"Coldly." Melanie pulled a handkerchief from a skirt pocket and pressed it to an eye before continuing. "She said she wasn't convinced by our last conversation that I wasn't going to claim her as my mother, and wanted my solemn promise that I would keep my word. She even offered me money to stay away from her."

"How did you feel about that?"

"I was insulted!" She quickly changed her angry face to one of disregard. "Then again, having been apart for so long, she didn't know me or my quality of character. I'm a person of integrity and honor."

Lucy fought the urge to snort with derision. To stop herself, she bit her lip and reached out again to Dolly's hand. Dolly glanced at her, but was too stunned by all that Melanie was saying to wonder at the gesture.

Mr. Sanderson took a step closer to Melanie, and faced the jury. With a tone of sympathy that he had practiced before his mirror at home, he asked, "What did she say that brought you to the point of rage?"

"When I tried to tell her how terribly I had been treated in my marriage, she made it clear that she didn't care. She accused me of being spoiled and ungrateful for what I had. She wouldn't listen to me. She said it was all 'tales of woe whined by an ungrateful wife'. She said I should return to my husband and beg his forgiveness, then obey him as I had promised to do in my marriage vows."

Lucy looked at the men on the jury. Four of them were nodding their heads, probably without even knowing they were doing it. The rest were frowning, but Lucy couldn't decide what this meant. For herself, she couldn't believe that Mrs. Helms would ever give a woman such marital advice. Any woman in attendance at the Orleans Hotel meeting would doubt it too, but Lucy figured that the men on the jury would have no way of knowing that.

However, aware that women at that meeting might have talked about it to their husbands, some of whom might be on the jury, Mr. Sanderson asked, "Were you surprised that she of all people would tell you to obey a man?"

"I certainly was." Melanie managed to look appropriately indignant. "I called her a hypocrite. I told her she had finer feelings for women who were strangers than she had for her own daughter."

"How did she respond to that?"

"She told me I was incapable of seeing the broader picture, that it was all of woman-kind that mattered, and not just one spoiled child."

Mr. Sanderson paused a moment to let the callousness of such a statement from a mother sink in with the jury. "Did you explain to your mother about the physical abuse?"

"Yes. She walked up to me, got in my face, and said that it was my problem and not hers." She looked down at her hands tightly clasped in her lap, then back up at Mr. Sanderson. The room was hushed and still, everyone aware that this was the critical moment in her testimony. "It was then that it fully dawned on me that I would never get any sympathy or acknowledgement from her. To her, I was no better than dirt under her feet, and I felt crushed by the irrevocable certainty that there was nothing

I could say or do to change her opinion. I heard a ringing in my ears, and although I knew I wasn't screaming, I heard screaming filling my head. I remember little of what came next, certainly no reasoning on my part. I only vaguely remember reaching out for the lamp next to where I was standing and striking out at her with it as she turned away from me."

She stopped talking and placed a trembling hand over her mouth, giving the appearance of someone who couldn't believe they had just said such a thing. Mr. Sanderson gently prodded her. "What did you do then?"

"When I saw her on the floor, I panicked and ran from the room in horror. I almost fell down the stairs in my rush to escape from what I had done. I'm still surprised that I got out of the hotel without being seen."

"Did you think you had killed her?"

She looked up at him, wide-eyed with surprise. "Oh, no. I knew she was still alive because she was sitting up with her hand to her head."

Lucy fought the urge to yelp in protest. So here was the beginning of the completely fictional portion of Melanie's testimony, contrived to set her free. Beside her, Dolly choked back a sob. Several women nearby heard, and gave her a sympathetic glance. Lucy, knowing this would get around town among other women, had a surge of hope that Dolly would be able to survive her sister's scandal.

Mr. Sanderson asked, "Did you return to Mrs. Helms's room later to see if she was okay?"

"No. I was so horrified at what I had done that I never wanted to see her again."

"When you were in her room, did you see newspapers on the dresser?"

"Yes. As I walked around while we were talking, I noticed those and a paste pot next to them. On top of the papers was a pair of long scissors."

"How did you come into possession of Mrs. Helms's room key?"

"Oh, that." Melanie managed to look as though the subject was of the merest trifle. "While I was wandering around the room, and she had her back turned to me while looking out the window, I picked up the brass tag attached to the key to look at it. I must have slipped it into my pocket without even thinking when she then began yelling vile, hurtful things at me. It wasn't until later that I found the key in the pocket of my coat when I hung it in the closet. I just tossed the key into a drawer."

Mr. Sanderson announced that he was finished, for the moment, with his examination of the witness. Mr. Hume rose up from behind his table and approached Melanie with a thoughtful air.

"Why didn't you return the key to the hotel?"

She shrugged. "I forgot all about having it."

"Did you think you might want to go back to the room later that day?"

"No!"

"Could that be why you kept the key, so you could go back some time after your attack on your mother?"

"No."

"Maybe you wanted to be sure she was not going to report your attack on her?"

Mr. Sanderson stood up. "Objection, Your Honor. He's trying to put suggestions into the jurors' minds, and hounding the witness in the process. She already said she had forgotten about the key."

"Sustained," the judge proclaimed, not allowing Melanie to answer.

Mr. Hume brushed that moment aside, having made his point to the jury. "So, Mrs. St. John, you claim you didn't intend to see your mother again, even to apologize for hitting her. But someone did see her, not long after you admit to being there. She was in fact struck a blow with the same lamp with which you admit hitting her. This second blow killed her." After a hesitation just long enough that Melanie began to fidget, he looked at her and smiled. "You said she was sitting up when you left her. Is that correct?"

"Yes."

"Exactly what was her location when you left?"

"She was on the floor, sitting about at the midpoint of the bed."

"When she first fell, before sitting up, where did that place her head?"

"At the corner of the bed."

"Which, in fact, was how she was lying when found by your sister. Does this surprise you?"

"Should it?" she snapped at him.

"Don't you think it shows that she didn't get up after you say you left her? Like she would have if she hadn't been knocked unconscious?"

"I don't know." But Melanie was breathing harder, suddenly seeing a point that might cause the jurors to question her version of what had happened.

"When your mother was found, there was a piece of newspaper scrap on top of her. It was later determined to have been cut from the newspaper on top of the few stacked on her dresser. Wouldn't you say this indicates that the newspapers were in the room *away* from the dresser *after* she was lying prone on the floor?"

"I couldn't say."

"How could Mrs. Helms have picked up the newspapers after being hit and, as you claim, sitting stunned on the floor? So stunned, in fact, that she was still in the same position on the floor when she was hit a second time?" He carefully didn't conclude that sentence with "...by someone else", because he wanted to retain the idea that the second strike was by Melanie herself.

She took a deep breath to calm herself. "I don't know."

"Alternatively, why would someone enter her room, pick up the lamp base and hit her almost in the same place that you had hit her earlier, then remove that particular newspaper from the dresser and walk over to her while holding it in such a way that a scrap of newspaper could fall onto her?"

She gave him a bland look of indifference. "I couldn't say."

"Does this scenario seem unlikely to you?"

"I don't know."

"But you did see the newspapers on the dresser?"

"I've already said so."

"Did your mother or you touch the papers at any time while you were talking?"

"No." But she had hesitated before answering, as though she wasn't sure which answer would be the least incriminating, whether it was true or not. The judge was frowning even more than previously.

"Let me help you," Mr. Hume smiled. "Could it have been that the stack of newspapers, along with the paste and scissors, were brought into the room *after* Mrs. Helms was lying on the floor? Wouldn't that account for a piece of them on *top* of her?"

She tossed her head and stared at him with stubborn resolve. "They were there when I first got to the room!"

Mr. Sanderson rose up with a purposefully loud sigh. "Your honor, this is bordering on badgering of the witness. She obviously knows nothing about the newspapers brought to Mrs. Helms's room."

Mr. Hume countered with, "Mr. Sanderson is presenting conclusions on behalf of his client. She should be the one to offer her conclusions, not him."

"Gentlemen!" The judge scowled at the two men. "Mr. Hume, if you have other questions to ask the witness, please do so. Mr. Sanderson, please let your client or any witness, answer for themselves. Now, Mr. Hume, continue if you have more questions or stand down."

"Yes, Your Honor. I do have a few more questions."

"Then proceed with them."

Mr. Hume turned to Melanie. "The way the newspapers in her room were cut up, and what accompanied them in the way of paste and scissors, seems to indicate that Mrs. Helms was the anonymous letter writer that had been plaguing the town. And that she was making those letters in the privacy of her hotel room. Do you agree?"

"It certainly seems like it to me. Even the police concluded that." Melanie smiled, the questioning finally going in the direction she had hoped. "I think she was very definitely the letter writer! She had always been a nosey type, and also vindictive."

Mr. Hume ignored this last comment. "Mrs. Helms had lived nowhere else in town, so she would have had to create the anonymous letters in her room at the Orleans Hotel. Correct?"

"Of course." But she frowned, unsure where his questioning was going, and feeling at a distinct disadvantage.

"When you saw the newspapers, paste pot and scissors in her room, did you think that something was missing?"

Lucy's heart beat faster. This was a point she had brought to Mr. Hume's attention that had forced from him a laugh, it being a point that he hadn't immediately seen for himself. It had been the thing about the room that had haunted Lucy from the beginning, and she was embarrassed that it had taken her so long to figure it out.

Melanie, not seeing the point of Mr. Hume's question, scowled at him, then quickly recovered her composure. "Not knowing what was usually on her dresser, I couldn't be expected to know what was missing from it. Of course, there was also a pitcher and bowl for washing up."

"Have you ever seen one of the anonymous letters received by someone?"

"Yes." But the word had been wrenched from her.

"Whose letters were they?"

"My sister and brother-in-law."

"Did you not notice that the cut-out newspaper words or phrases used to form the text of the letters were mounted on something?"

Melanie's eyes opened large and she swallowed with an effort. "Oh, you mean white drawing paper."

"Yes. Did you see any of that in Mrs. Helms's room?"

"No." Thinking quickly, she added, "It must have been in one of the dresser drawers."

"In fact, it was not." Mr. Hume's wolfish grin of tolerance fooled no one. "There wasn't anything of the kind in the room anywhere. Did the letter you had once seen arrive in an envelope?"

"Yes."

"Did you see envelopes or postage on the dresser?"

Melanie hesitated a moment before murmuring, "No."

"Did you notice that the paste pot had no paddle with which to apply the paste?"

"I didn't notice."

"Would your elegant, fastidious mother have used her fingers?"

"I don't know." But she was beet red and her breathing had noticeably increased. Her glare at the District Attorney was one of pure loathing.

As prosecutor, Mr. Hume was determined to remind everyone that in spite of her attitude toward her children, Mrs. Helms had still been Melanie's mother. It was society that had cast women in the sanctified role of mother, even using that as a reason to deny them more rights, and he wasn't beyond using that fact now.

"Don't you find it strange that your obviously intelligent mother had only *some* of the supplies needed to create the letters, but not the most basic items needed?"

Melanie reverted to her earlier safe reply. "I couldn't say."

Lucy knew Melanie must not have looked inside Tony's desk drawers, simply grabbing up what was within sight and thinking this was enough to implicate someone as the maker of the letters. If Melanie had thought beyond that, she would have searched the desk and seen the envelopes in the right-hand drawer, even with the drawing paper locked in the left one.

"So, if the paste was not normally in use in your mother's room, and therefore had been brought there that morning, might not the newspapers too have been brought there at the same time? And after she was thought to be dead?"

Melanie knew she couldn't very well deny this in face of the logic just presented, so she stubbornly repeated her original lie. "I don't know what was brought there after she was dead, but I know that I saw those three items on top of the dresser when I got there."

"Did you see any newspaper in her waste basket?"

"I don't remember."

Mr. Hume practically crossed his fingers in the hope Mr. Sanderson wouldn't stop him with an objection as he continued. "There was in fact no newspaper scrap anywhere in her room. Her wastebasket was empty. In fact, the chambermaids said they had never seen newspaper scrap in her room. If she was making the anonymous letters, how could this be possible?"

"Maybe she took the scraps away in her purse and disposed of them elsewhere."

Titters and guffaws rippled among the spectators, but although some of the jurors smirked, they didn't make a sound. The judge reached for his gavel, and the spectators seeing this, silenced themselves.

"Obviously," Mr. Hume stated, "the person who brought the newspapers, paste and scissors to her room knew where they had gotten these things. Could the killer have obtained them from the actual anonymous letter creator?"

"I suppose so."

"Did you ever visit with Mr. and Mrs. Tony Leon on Coloma Street?"

Lucy had never seen anyone go white and then red in such rapid succession, and she hoped the jurors had also seen this. Melanie glanced in Lucy's direction before replying. "Yes."

"Did you ever look through the French doors behind Tony Leon's desk and see newspapers, paste and scissors on his desk?"

She looked again in Lucy and Dolly's direction, knowing that if she didn't answer truthfully, Lucy could testify having seen her there. Dolly might even testify that she had heard Melanie talk about being there. She looked boldly at the prosecutor. "Yes, I did look through those doors once.

He did have a newspaper spread out, and there may have been paste and scissors there, but I didn't see them. I only thought he had been interrupted while reading a newspaper, because I heard raised voices beyond the screen around his desk."

"Is that the only time you looked into the Leon home and saw such items on Mr. Leon's desk?"

She hesitated, aware that she could have been seen the first time she had been there the day after arriving in town, when she really had gone there to visit with Jane, and had seen the letter making items. The time Lucy saw her, she had gone there to see the books on the shelf that she had in retrospect realized were familiar to her. But she decided to risk a lie. "I only went there once. Mrs. Murphy saw me there. I only stayed a brief moment because I heard voices raised in anger."

Not to be deterred from the point he was making, he asked, "Did you happen to see white writing paper in the left drawer of the desk?"

She just stared at him. Obvious to Lucy and Dolly was that Melanie was realizing where her mistake had been in not also bringing blank paper to the murder room. Before Melanie could dredge up an appropriate answer to Mr. Hume's question, he asked another one.

"You stated that the first visit you had with your mother upon entering town was a disappointing one?"

She was flustered at the sudden change of subject, but answered quickly enough. "Yes."

"Were there no heated moments of expressed anger during that first meeting?"

"No. That's why I didn't hesitate to go back when she wrote me a note asking me to come to her room the morning of June 4."

"Are you aware that your conversation during your first meeting with her, the one when you had just arrived in town, was overheard by chambermaids on duty. They described the conversation as a loud argument."

"A few impassioned words said in a raised voice might be interpreted by an eavesdropper as an angry exchange, but it wasn't."

"There were also angry words overheard when you admit to having been in her room on the morning of June 4. However, there were no words spoken at all when someone went to her room a half hour after you say you left her sitting up holding her head. When entering, that person didn't knock, but walked right in, the door either unlocked or the visitor having a key. Whichever, they spoke not a word."

Mr. Sanderson bounced out of his chair. "Your honor, is the District Attorney testifying, or is there a question looming?"

The judge simply looked at Mr. Hume, awaiting his reply. "Yes, Your Honor, I do indeed have a question based on what I was summarizing before interrupted."

The judge nodded his acceptance and sat back in his chair, Mr. Sanderson sat down with a thump, and Mr. Hume turned back to Melanie. "Are you aware that within only a few minutes of that second exit from Mrs. Helms's room, your sister, Dolly Robbins, arrived at the room? And that she found Mrs. Helms dead and bleeding from the same part of her head where you admit to striking her earlier? So that Mrs. Robbins barely missed seeing the killer leave the hotel?"

"Yes, I'm aware of all that. But it wasn't me." Melanie looked him directly in the eyes and declared, "I never returned to her room." She knew Dolly had not seen her. Mr. Hume knew this too, and therefore didn't bother to recall Dolly to the stand.

And, Lucy thought, there isn't any way to prove she's lying. There was only inuendo and suggestion supported by common sense that could be put into the minds of the jurors. But that didn't change the fact that it was all circumstantial evidence. A sudden shudder passed through her, and Lucy briefly closed her eyes. In the private sanctuary of her thoughts, she opined with unladylike candor, "The heartless shrew is going to get away with it!"

"Mrs. St. John," Mr. Hume asked, "did you return after the murder of your mother was discovered, use the key to the room that you had retained, let yourself in, and take away the scissors that the police had left on top of the stack of newspapers?"

Reacting to the implied criticism, Officers Reynolds and Van Eaton shifted uneasily in their seats, unable to explain that it had not been their idea to leave anything in the way of possible evidence in the room.

"Why should I remove the scissors? They were nothing to me."

"Was your mother right-handed or left-handed?"

After a quick glance at Dolly, she said, "Right-handed."

"Did you at some time become aware that the scissors were made to be used by a left-handed person? And, therefore, they couldn't have been used by your mother?"

Melanie looked up at him, a slight smile showing. "I have no idea what you're talking about."

"It didn't occur to you that if the police realized they were not Mrs. Helms's scissors, then they might change their opinion about her being the anonymous letter writer?"

"That never occurred to me."

"Oh? If you don't know what I'm talking about, why did anything about the scissors occur to you?"

Melanie glared at him with such venom that he took a step back from her. "I meant it didn't occur to me because I was unaware the scissors had gone missing."

Mr. Hume looked at her without asking anything for so long that not only did Melanie show her discomfort, but so did the judge. He was about to say something when Mr. Hume announced, "No further questions, Your Honor."

Melanie was dismissed, and she returned to her seat while trying not to show how rattled she was. She sat stiffly erect, staring straight before her with a total absence of expression on her face. There was nothing more she could do. All power was now with the jury, and all control of those men rested with two attorneys. And there was not one man among them for whom she had the least respect.

CHAPTER 15

*"Nothing except a battle lost can be half
so melancholy as a battle won."*
Duke of Wellington, 1815

Monday, July 7 – Friday, August 1

There being no other people to be called by Mr. Hume, he rested his case. Mr. Sanderson had no one he could call, either as a witness to prove Melanie couldn't have returned a second time, or even to testify to her good character. Dolly had steadfastly refused his request in this regard. Consequently, closing arguments were briefly made by both attorneys.

Mr. Sanderson emphasized the extent of provocation from an uncaring, overbearing mother and the fact that Melanie had not meant to kill Mrs. Helms. He declared positively that Mrs. Helms had been alive when Melanie had run from the room. He threw in phrases such as *in the heat of passion, possible temporary insanity brought on by extreme mental cruelty, maternal rejection, years of sustained physical and emotional abuse,* and basically tried to show that Melanie was the true victim. He also made it clear that there was no physical evidence against Melanie St. John. He enjoyed pointing out that there was no witness that could swear it was Melanie they had heard inside Mrs. Helms's room talking, or even that she had been outside in the corridor on the morning of June 4, although Melanie fully admitted she had been there once.

"And," Sanderson declared dramatically, "isn't that an indicator that she has taken responsibility for what she actually did and is suffering remorse? But all she did was wound her mother; she did not kill her." After a brief buzz of spectator reaction, Mr. Sanderson ended with, "No one can say for certain that Melanie St. John returned a second time to the room of Mrs. Helms. The most that she might be accused of doing is striking her mother in anger, after terrible provocation, causing slight bodily injury. But she is not accused of that. Nor is she accused of murder. She is accused of the involuntary manslaughter of Mrs. Helms, and even of that there is no real proof because the death occurred after she fled the room after only slightly wounding her mother." He resumed his seat, displaying a self-satisfaction that made the judge's low brows even lower as he showed his disapproval.

Mr. Hume then stood up and approached the jurors. With calm and deliberate phrasing, he restated the progression of events and occurrences that had led up to the death of Mrs. Helms, with Melanie being central to all of them. He carefully linked her *directly* to as many of them as was incontestable. He ridiculed the way in which Melanie had sent a note to Mrs. Helms the day before the death, indicating that it was not to accept an invitation but rather to instigate a meeting. For the rest, he insinuated that her actions perfectly fit the circumstances, and that she was the only person involved who had any substantial motive.

Sensing the jury's intensity of focus on what he was saying, he suggested that someone who was unhinged enough to strike out once, could do so a second time, especially if it was to cover up the discovery that she had seriously injured her own mother. "If discovered, it would make her unwelcome in a town where she was determined to stay in order to hide from an abusive husband. It also opened her up to being charged with causing bodily harm to another, one who was her mother."

It was at this point that Melanie looked the most frightened. Watching her, Lucy realized that Melanie was afraid that word of the trial might reach Los Angeles. If she was found guilty, the trial would be reported in newspapers near and far. However, if she was declared NOT guilty, the whole incident might not seem important enough for the press in other towns.

Mr. Hume reminded the jury that Melanie had kept the key. He claimed this was not a mindless act of slipping it into a pocket, but a deliberate act with the intent to have the ability to return, if need be. He claimed she had in fact done this in order to put the letter making materials in the room. He reminded the jury that, having previously seen Tony Leon's desk, Melanie had known where to obtain the newspapers and paste, and once inside the Leon home that fateful morning, had also seen Jane Leon's scissors and had taken them, too. And later, when she realized they were for a left-handed person, she had returned to the hotel room to steal them.

Mr. Hume declared that all of these deliberate acts of misdirection proved that Melanie had an *awareness of guilt*, and that they had been done because she thought Mrs. Helms was dead after the first time she had hit her, when in fact she was only stunned. He looked directly at the jury and said, "The second attack, after she returned with the letter making items, was when she made sure her mother's death was the reality." He then emphasized to the jury that Melanie must have been the one who killed Mrs. Helms, there never having been anyone else found to even come close to filling that role.

"How likely is it," he pleaded to the jury, "that someone would come to Mrs. Helms's room shortly after Melanie St. John left, and without conversation immediately hit her with the same item and in the same place as the accused had done? Especially considering that this mysterious person would have to pick up the lamp base from the floor? If they were hell-bent on killing Mrs. Helms, why wouldn't they have used the very pointed, sharp scissors lying in plain view on the dresser? Isn't it more likely that the person that had already struck down her mother, upon returning and finding her still alive, would hit her a second time with what was a familiar weapon? And in doing so, attempt to hit the same spot on the head so it would be thought there had been only one visit to the room? Only Melanie St. John, who had hit her mother there once before, would know where that injured spot was. Especially since there was no blood there to show an injury. Only the second blow split the skin."

He allowed for the murmur of voices to quiet before continuing. "Did this so-called second person come there, see the newspapers, paste and scissors on the dresser, where the accused claims they were, but not kill Mrs. Helms with the long, sharp scissors? All after finding her already wounded and unable to escape him? Or did the accused return to the room carrying the newspapers, paste and scissors, being the second light tread on the stairs heard by Mrs. Hall? I offer to you that she then entered without knocking because she thought her mother dead, only to find that *her mother* was only stunned. She had only to put the paste pot on the floor, or clutch it in her left arm, before quickly approaching *her mother*. The scissors were probably in her pocket and the newspapers under her coat, so it would have been a simple matter for her to pick up the lamp base and strike her mother with it, again. Only this time much harder. But she didn't notice the scrap of newspaper that fell out onto her mother. She then only had to put the paste, newspapers and scissors on the dresser and run from the room, most likely using the back stairs to avoid being seen." It was obvious that he was driving home the fact that it was a *mother* who had been killed, and not merely some unfamiliar suffrage woman.

"I beg you, gentlemen, to apply your reason and common sense to the matter at hand, and realize that there was only one person in that room with Mrs. Helms before her death on the morning of June 4, and that was the accused. Therefore, this demands a verdict of *guilty* of first-degree manslaughter against Melanie St. John."

He didn't have to remind anyone in the courtroom that far less evidence had gotten a number of men, and at least one woman, hanged during the gold rush only a few years earlier. Everyone living in gold rush country would always be aware of this, as it was part of that area's unique and infamous history.

It was obvious that the jury's decision would be based on whether or not they believed that Melanie had returned a second time, and that the light tread on the stairs heard by Mrs. Hall had belonged to her. They would then have to believe that when she returned, she brought with her the letter making items in order to incriminate Mrs. Helms as the sender of the letters, only to find her still alive. But the crucial thing they would have to accept was that Melanie was brutal enough to have picked up the lamp base to hit her mother again with the same weapon, while being cold-bloodedly calculating enough to try and hit the same spot.

The case was turned over to the jury immediately following the closing arguments. For whatever reason, Judge Johnson made only a few remarks to the jury. He informed them that they knew what to do and to please do it in a timely manner, as was only seemly.

The jury of twelve men marched out just at half past one, to be served sandwiches, coffee and beer while they deliberated. The spectators left to hurry through their own meals, after which they returned without delay, expecting the verdict to either be awaiting them or at least declared soon after their arrival. However, by late afternoon, there was still no verdict. Most of those still present left in disappointment, having businesses or families demanding their attention.

Just at five o'clock, the judge came into the room. Melanie was led in at the same time that Mr. Sanderson and Mr. Hume hurried into the room, all three of them taking their seats with beating hearts and dry mouths.

Lucy and Dolly were now sitting at the very back of the courtroom near the door, behind a scattering of die-hard observers. Melanie was pale and stiff with tension as she awaited her fate.

When asked for their conclusions, the jury foreman stood up and cleared his throat with self-conscious uneasiness. "We considered carefully all the factors presented by the prosecution and the defense. We agree that there was malice aforethought in Mrs. St. John's act of striking out with the lamp, which she admits to doing and for which there is after all some evidence. But this trial is about murder intended, even if called manslaughter, and we feel that there's insufficient evidence to prove that Mrs. St. John came into Mrs. Helms's room a second time and struck her a killing blow. We have therefore decided that we must declare Melanie St. John *not guilty*."

There was a moment of hesitation before the judge turned to the room, his frown more pronounced than was usual even for him. "In that case, I declare this trial over." Just as the murmur of voices began, the judge's voice stopped everyone. "However," he practically shouted, "this case will not be closed, since evidently the killer of Mrs. Helms has not been brought to justice. If *any* further evidence comes to light regarding who murdered her, the case can be opened again for prosecution." The judge looked directly at Melanie, took his gavel in hand and struck its wooden plate with a decisive blow. "The defendant is free to go." He looked like there was more he wanted to say, but he simply closed the file in front of him, rose and left the room. The spectators stood and prepared to leave while talking among themselves in low voices, all of which showed a degree of surprise and even dissatisfaction.

Melanie, however, looking worried instead of relieved, turned her gaze upon the jury. So did Lucy and Dolly. As the men slowly stood up, six of them looked pleased if not smug, three appeared to be a little embarrassed, and three looked as if they wanted to object to something but had left it too late. They all seemed discomfited by the judge's added remarks, and no one was left to wonder why the jury had taken so long to deliberate.

Just as Lucy slipped from the room, Melanie turned around and rushed toward her sister, several people moving out of the way as though avoiding a carrier of disease. Dolly allowed herself to be embraced by her sister only briefly before pushing her away, showing no joy but considerable embarrassment. Melanie acted as though she hadn't noticed, saying, "Come sister, take my arm and see me home."

As Melanie and Dolly walked past Lucy standing in the corridor just outside the courtroom door, Melanie's lips twisted into a sly smile. But she wasn't foolish enough to look directly at Lucy or say anything to her. She had won, and that was all she needed right then.

The mild warmth of June had changed into the stultifying heat of July, even reaching into the mountains and the towns along the old gold rush trail. Women did their most strenuous chores as early in the day as possible, such as beating rugs, scrubbing floors, churning butter, baking bread or ironing. Men did such things as chopping wood, mucking out stalls, laying bricks or other construction work, also in the early morning. Consequently, it meant that mornings were busy times and visiting was put off until late afternoon or early evening when cooling mountain breezes pushed aside the heat. Then, nary a porch, chair beneath a tree, or bench along Main Street sidewalks was empty. Children came out to play, and their dogs to romp along with them, while kitchen doors and windows were thrown wide open as supper was placed on tables.

Lucy, Freda, Jim, and even Roger before school, were no different. They started their days with each having tasks to perform while looking forward to getting through them as quickly as possible. After that, while waiting for the cooling, they played cards, wrote letters, mended clothes, and read books. The Murphys were fortunate in that they were able to enjoy their front porch a little earlier in the day than some because it faced east, and thus caught the shade in late afternoon.

For those who enjoyed reading newspapers, it was fortunate for some and a disappointment for others, that the newspapers had finally ceased mention of the trial. Lucy sat alone on the porch late one evening enjoying the darkness lit only by a quarter moon, a sky thick with stars, and a lantern turned down to a weak glow. She ignored the several local papers on her lap while listening to laughter from an upstairs window to the room where Freda was putting Roger to bed. Jim was writing a letter to a friend in Jamestown, every once in awhile swearing as his new ink pen released a drop too much ink. Still, Lucy was thankful for the solitude so she could think. Gnawing at her was not, as some might have supposed, the memory of the trial and its dissatisfactory outcome. Rather, it was Jim's frequent reference to the war.

In September of the year just past, Senator Edward Baker from Oregon had gone to Philadelphia to command a brigade in the name of California. It had been known as the *California Brigade* and was composed of the 1st, 2nd, 3rd, and 5th California Infantries. Now in the summer of 1862, some of the Eastern-born citizens living in California wanted to fight in the war anywhere in the east that they could be of benefit. A group of 100 cavalrymen had organized themselves and had contacted Massachusetts Governor John Andrew. He had accepted their offer to join him, but only if they provided their own uniforms and equipment, and paid their own way. The men had agreed and were now journeying east.

History would show that three more companies of Californians would join the war effort, and altogether these westerners would become known as the *California Battalion*. They would spend their first year of the war battling guerilla bands, but in 1864 would join Phil Sheridan's Army of the Shenandoah, to be active in the Shenandoah Valley campaign. They would also take part in the largest cavalry charge of the Civil War at the Third Battle of Winchester. Their participation would continue in the Union counter-attack at the Battle of Cedar Creek, as well as in the protection of "the Angle" during Pickett's Charge.

Jim, as well as many other men, were torn between their duties at home and the urge to be part of what was happening to their country. After the *California 100* had gathered and left, local men could no longer claim that the war was too far away for them to be able to participate. This fact only added to their self-reproach and indecision.

Nevertheless, the town found a way to be of service to the war effort. There was a warehouse situated where Washington met Main Street at Spanish Ravine, at the east end of town. Built of thick stone walls only the year before for Wilcox and Brown as extra storage for their grocery store, it was now used as an armory and storehouse for supplies that would eventually be shipped east to aid in the war. Children were no longer allowed to climb the old cottonwood tree that shaded its peaked roof, and those passing viewed the small stone building with patriotic respect.

Jim and Lucy sat on the porch love seat one cooling evening a few days later, taking advantage of a rare moment alone to enjoy the relative quiet of evening. There was just enough activity around them to invade their peace and keep them from feeling totally isolated. An open wagon carrying home five miners rumbled past, several children shrieked in the distance, two dogs barked while chasing a cat up a tree where it defiantly cleaned its face, hummingbirds came near to feast on the pots of red flowers on the porch, and nearby crickets began to creep out to make themselves heard.

After several minutes with nothing said between them, Jim spoke up. "I had a beer with William Cary today. He admired the gold stick pin you gave me and we got to talking. I told him how much you had enjoyed your stay at his hotel."

"Did you?" She was content to remain nestled in the crook of his arm without talking, but she sensed he had something to say worth hearing.

"He said he'd heard about you."

She didn't have to look up at him to know he was smiling. "Did he mean that as just a comment, or was there censure in it?"

"I'm not sure, but he didn't sound overly judgmental." She sat up and waited for him to add more. "Well, he did say it's gotten around that you helped Mr. Hume with his case."

Lucy decided not to probe more deeply, only too aware of the judgmental nature of comments aimed at her during her investigations. Some of that criticism lingered, of course, only now it was mostly from those who knew she was a close friend of Dolly's. To many people Dolly was the sister of the woman who had killed her mother and "gotten away with it". And they thought Lucy should discontinue any contact with "such women". For the two women who had had the audacity to put such a thought into words, Lucy had expressed a few thoughts of her own. Thinking that she could write them off as ever talking to her again, she smiled in satisfaction.

After a moment, Lucy said, "I only saw Mr. Elstner's old El Dorado Hotel, where the Cary House now sits. It was back in '54 when I was passing through the area. Too bad it burned in the '56 fire. Had you been inside it?"

"It's where I stayed when I was hunting for you back then."

"Yes, that's when I saw it, although not from inside." She sighed gently. "If only I'd stayed there and not moved on."

His arm tightened around her shoulders. The silence was filled with such tender memories of what they had suffered when he had been desperately trying to find her seven years earlier, that neither of them dared put any of it into words. Jim cleared his throat and said, "For Bill Cary, his losses during the '56 fire were devastating, as they were for so many. But what he has now on the Old El Dorado Hotel lot is so much better, and he claims the Cary House is fireproof, being of brick."

"Humph," was the only sound she made, expressing her doubt that any hotel surrounded by buildings of wood could claim such a thing.

Pushing through the busy traffic on Main Street the next day, one of the stages of the Pioneer Line pulled up in front of the Cary House. It carried five men, two of whom were miners up from the Southern Mines around Angels Camp, two who were young men returning home from having spent a month with grandparents in Mariposa, and one tall man in a fine business suit accompanied by a large suitcase.

This last man had spent several days transferring from one stage line to another since leaving Los Angeles a number of tiring, dusty days before. While the other men had passed their time on the road visiting and recounting experiences when mining or with family, this man had remained aloof. The only time he had joined in the conversation was when the subject had been that of the flood and its impact on the state.

As soon as the stage arrived in Placerville, everyone took charge of their luggage from the boot of the stage. The miners headed to the nearest saloon, the young men hurried home to their parents, and the lone gentleman checked into the Cary House. He spent some time bathing, after which he donned a clean shirt, brushed down his suit and polished his boots. He put on his coat, something no man of refinement would be seen in public not wearing, and reached for his hat.

He stood before the mirror and for a rare, self-assessing moment, wondered how he was viewed by others. Did they see the few strands of gray in his still thick brown hair? Did they see a coldness in his brown eyes, such as he had more than once been accused of using to intimidate? Did he have a hard mouth, not often seen smiling? Maybe all of this was true now, but it had not always been the hallmark of his appearance. On the other hand, he didn't remember ever having been as angry as he felt right then.

However, as he arrived at the bottom of the stairs into the lobby, he didn't look angry. There were no red patches on his cheeks, his jaw was not clenched, and in all likelihood his blood pressure was not even elevated. He had been holding onto a festering ire for so long now that he could barely remember what it felt like to carry any better emotion in his heart. His was a tamped-down, slow burning wrath fed by an embittered disillusionment that had been with him for a long time. Consequently, his thinking was clear, and there was no challenge to his reason. He knew exactly what he wanted, and what he was willing to do to get it.

He entered the dining room for a bite to eat and a perusal of several back issues of the *Mountain Democrat* and the *Placerville Daily News*, for which he had paid handsomely to one of the chambermaids. These local papers, for the few days following the trial, had been full of its details. It had rocked the town's complacency, had caused many a man to treat his wife or daughter more solicitously, and had sparked several spurious legal debates in the saloons; all of which had been given voice in newspaper articles and editorials. The stranger found it all very interesting indeed.

There had been several interviews with members of the jury, although most had shunned the spotlight. One who had not, stated that throughout the trial he just couldn't imagine such a fine specimen of womanhood being shut away in a prison cell. Another complained that he thought justice had gotten a black eye, but evidence had been pretty circumstantial and he had needed better proof. Yet another juror had answered with such a stream of invective that not only couldn't it be published in any newspaper, the reporter hadn't been sure what meaning the juror had attached to his words.

The desk clerk at the Orleans Hotel had told the reporter, who had approached him with a coin in his hand, that he now thought he recalled hearing a "scream of terror" from Mrs. Robbins when she had found the body. He had added a few lurid details about seeing Mrs. Helms's bloody head and how he had felt at the time, which of course he had not. But it earned him a few free beers in his favorite saloon when he retold it there to the titillation of his friends.

Even young Billy Dooris had been approached, and succumbed to the temptation of a bag of candy. He repeated the story of how he took the note to the hotel, but he refused to enhance any of his story, no matter how hard the dogged reporter had pressed him to do so.

When Mrs. Hall had answered a knock on her door, she had been bluntly asked, "What does it feel like to live across from the room where a murder took place?" She told the reporter, "Young man, you're rude!" She had then slammed the door in his face.

Coroner Eichelroth had been stopped by two reporters on his way to supper with his wife the night of the trial. Responding to their persistence, he had told them, "A little decorum, gentlemen, please. This is neither the time nor place for such a discussion." This verbal but tactful snub was nothing compared to the look of contempt cast upon the reporters by *Mrs.* Eichelroth. The reporters, being young and new to the job, had apologized and promptly hurried away.

Officer J. J. Reynolds had responded the same to all inquiries. "I am not at liberty to discuss the trial or an open investigation." One newspaper concluded from this that the police had focused on someone in particular as the *real killer.* At the same time, another paper drew the conclusion that this meant the law had already put on trial who they thought was the *guilty party*, and weren't looking further. Both of these conclusions generated several paragraphs about the fickleness of jurors and how easily they could be influenced.

Officer Van Eaton was willing to describe the murder scene, since he figured it had been described during the trial. He had kept firm control on his imagination, however, and drew no conclusions from what he had seen. Even so, some women who read his interview thought him too liberal with his description of the room and the body. However, they didn't dare complain to their husbands for fear they would no longer be allowed access to newspapers. This had been the consequence for some of them after voicing an opinion about a news article that had been in opposition to their husband's views.

All of the newspapers pointed out that the authorities were still wanting to talk to the man who had passed the note to Billy, as well as anyone else who might now remember something pertinent. More than one person commented on how strange it was that no one had seen Melanie or anyone else come and go twice from Mrs. Helms's room the morning of June 4. Those who believed Melanie's story agreed that she had only come there once and that was very early, so it wasn't all that unusual. Those who didn't believe her story agreed that the second time she came there that she must have left by the back stairs. But no one denied that luck had played a part for those who had come and gone from that room that fateful morning.

It must be noted that no one tried to interview Melanie, much to her chagrin. Several reporters did try to interview Dolly and Robert, but they simply refused to say anything, and soon it was understood that they weren't going to give in to any amount of beseeching, badgering, or offers of financial remuneration.

Lucy Murphy, considered a *prime catch* by every newspaper, was approached on numerous occasions. She either turned her back and walked away before a question could be asked, or said, "I have nothing to say." In one instance, she turned on the importunate reporter with a raised palm practically in his face, and had barked a sharp, "No!" Soon after that, requests for an interview ceased.

For someone just arriving in town, all of this was informative and interesting reading, as it had been for those townspeople who had not been inside the courtroom. What with so much news of the war and its various battles, not to mention local political events, the trial had not been considered important enough to be mentioned in the newspapers in San Francisco, Sacramento or Los Angeles. Although the newly arrived stranger found the details of the trial interesting, and the various responses of the besieged townspeople produced a bemused smile, none of it was what had brought him to Placerville. Nor did it dissuade him from following through with his reason for being there.

Leaving the hotel, he visited a barber shop for a shave, as he preferred a cleanshaven appearance even if not considered the fashion for men. While there, the voluble barbers caught him up with the local gossip, whether he wanted it or not. They were still talking about the trial of the sister of a local woman, and consequently it only took casual questioning to learn where that local woman lived. The stranger left the barber shop humming to himself and was soon walking east on Pacific Street, where he stopped on the street in front of the Robbins home.

For a few moments before being noticed, he watched two women drinking lemonade while seated in the shade of the covered front porch. They weren't talking, and sat well apart. In fact, he thought they didn't look all that comfortable in one another's company, which showed that he was a perceptive man. When at last one of them noticed him at the edge of the road, she stood up, screamed loudly, and rushed inside, slamming the door behind her. The other woman stood up and walked with purpose toward the man.

"You're not welcome here," she declared.

"Hello, Dolly. I didn't expect to be welcomed. I came to see Melanie." His voice was deep and just this side of having a rasp to it, which kept it from being overly authoritative. The steadiness of his gaze, however, made it difficult for Dolly to look away while he was talking.

On the other hand, she gave no indication that she was intimidated by him. Her anger didn't allow for it. "Go away, Vincent! She doesn't want to see you. If necessary, I'll get a complaint sworn out against you so you're not allowed near her."

He stared at her for a long moment. "We'll see about that." He smiled and calmly, almost nonchalantly, stated, "She is my wife, after all. And she has abandoned our home. I have my rights."

"So does she!" That wasn't exactly true and Dolly knew it, so she added, "Maybe not legal ones, but she has the moral right not to be harassed by even her husband."

"It's a shame your mother didn't get to know you as an adult. You have a lot in common with her."

Dolly wanted to argue the point, but instead asked, "How did you know Melanie was here, anyway?"

"She was stupid enough to mail me a letter from here."

"No, she didn't. She... Oh." Realizing that the stage driver must have decided not to wait until he was in San Francisco to mail Melanie's letter, she said instead, "Everyone in town knows how poorly you've treated her over the years. You won't find yourself welcomed here once it becomes known who you are."

Vincent made a wry face that Dolly couldn't interpret, but which was followed by several slow nods. "Yes, I imagine she feels pretty much in control now that she's pulled the wool over the eyes of a jury, and therefore the town. She's good at that."

"If she has hardened over the years, only you can be blamed for that. Yes, she's lied to a lot of people. But in order to survive her marriage to you, she's had to learn how to lie and be manipulative."

Vincent's sardonic chuckle surprised Dolly, as did the cheerless smile that followed it. But it was the sudden sadness in his eyes that surprised her. "Dear, sweet, naïve Dolly. She has never been anything else. If you had lived with us instead of choosing to stay in Nevada City, you might have helped her find a better way, but the time has passed for that."

Dolly almost choked as she struggled to form an objection to such a statement. "It was your choice not to let me live with you and Melanie, not mine!" Dolly fought a rising urge to reach out and slap him across the face.

Seeing how upset she was, he took a step back, the sadness in his voice even more pronounced. But there was now also a tinge of resignation in it as he told her, "I see she has fooled you, too. I doubt there's anything I can say now that will change your mind, so I'll be on my way. If you want to talk, I'm staying at the Cary House." He started to turn away, but then turned back, saying, "I'm sorry."

Dolly was startled by that, because she wasn't sure to what the apology referred. She concluded that he was simply sorry for the whole sad situation in which they all found themselves. She sure felt that way.

He didn't explain further, but instead turned and walked the way he had come. As Dolly watched him walk down Pacific Street, she realized that Vincent was wearing a side arm, an 1847 Colt Walker single-action revolver. Although appreciated because it had the power of a rifle, it also had a reputation of sometimes blowing up in the user's hands. But when accuracy from a distance was required, it was a very handy weapon.

More than the presence of the gun, Dolly had been bothered by Vincent's overall attitude throughout their exchange. He had not been threatening, as she had expected him to be, but more in the way of heavy-hearted and resigned. Maybe this was why, as she entered the house, some of his words rang like a clanging bell in her mind. She decided that for a change she was going to face what his words indicated, and not pretend that they couldn't be true. Too much had happened over the last two months to allow for that now.

In a mood of determination such as she had seldom felt before, Dolly went in search of Melanie. She found her sister locked in her room, and it took some considerable persuasion to get her to open the door.

"He's gone, Melanie. I threatened him with trouble from the law if he didn't leave you alone."

"Oh, thank you, Dolly." Melanie opened the door like a frightened mouse unsure if its bolt-hole was really free of the coyote's lurking presence. She moved into the parlor and collapsed onto the sofa, her hand to her throat. "How on earth did he find me? I had the stage driver mail my letter to him from San Francisco."

"The driver didn't wait until then to mail it." Seeing the look of fury that quickly crossed Melanie's face, for the first time in her relationship with her sister, Dolly didn't dissemble. "Vincent made an interesting comment."

"Oh?"

"He indicated that you were good at pulling the wool over people's eyes. I certainly saw evidence of that at your trial." She sat across from her sister, looking at her with keen interest and a degree of speculation. "Were you telling the truth about his abusing you? Did he really cause bruises?"

"Of course, he did." She leaned back and smiled, then shrugged with indifference to what she had just claimed. "Well, maybe not as much as I let on. But he did slap me once and I didn't dare go outside until the mark of it went away. I hated him so much, right from the day I met him. He was so sure of himself, with all his money and respect from others. So kind and generous. Patronizing bastard! I hated every moment of my life with him."

It took Dolly a moment to absorb this. "Did Mother know you hated him? Before you were married, I mean."

"She knew I wasn't in love with him." She shrugged again, but avoided looking at Dolly by turning toward the front window. "But he was a better bet than the young men my age who *maybe* bathed once a week, and who thought two bits spent was a big night out. Vincent was good-looking and wealthy, and I figured I could accumulate some of that money for myself. I certainly wasn't going to get money any other way, not in a town where women were either a servant or only slightly better than that because of a marriage contract. Unfortunately, it was more difficult than I thought, getting it away from him."

"You mean Mother didn't really *force* you to marry him?"

"Well, she certainly wanted me married and out of the house. Only when I was married would she be able to get away and go back east again, but she didn't *make* me get married. In fact, when she realized I'd married him for his money, she told me she thought me heartless and grasping to have suckered him into a loveless marriage simply out of greed." She made a face and muttered, "Stupid cow!" Looking directly at Dolly, she added, "She also said that I should never let him know how I really felt because he might turn violent. That gave me the idea how to proceed." She smiled more with teeth than humor. "Then she moved away, and for a long time I didn't know where she was. But then I realized that Vincent was writing to her in New York, and she to him."

"Did he indeed turn violent when he figured out why you had married him? Did he ever beat you? The truth now!"

Melanie started to protest, but then sighed with resignation. "Well, no, not actually. I tripped and fell on the back steps, and when someone saw the bruising on my cheek and hands, I suggested it might have been from such treatment. Their reaction was all I could have hoped it would be. Of course, his closest men friends didn't buy into it, but their wives did."

Dolly had to force herself to ask, "Did he force you to have relations or treat you roughly in that regard?"

Melanie's laugh was full of contempt. "After the first six months, he never wanted relations with me, rough or otherwise. I think he has a *favorite lady* in one of the better brothels in town." She curled her lip in scorn. "Let her kind deal with that. If I knew who she was, I'd send her a thank you note."

Dolly closed her eyes and let all these shocking revelations slowly overcome her natural inclination to avoid unpleasantness. Instead, she opened her eyes and stared at Melanie, finally accepting what her sister had become. As a result, she pushed into the past the young girl with whom she had grown up, and decided to consider that sister now dead.

Melanie lay back against the sofa cushions with closed eyes and a complacent smile. While watching her sister luxuriate in her self-satisfied stupor of invulnerability, Dolly recalled the grizzly moment she had looked down on their mother's dead body. She also recalled the lighthearted way Melanie had walked up to her after the trial, and how those nearby had seen Melanie's smirk of satisfaction as she had embraced Dolly. They had also heard Melanie's flippant request to be escorted home.

"But," Dolly reminded herself, "I was the only one, later that night, who heard Melanie in her room singing and laughing in celebration of having fooled twelve men good and true." And then something else occurred to Dolly.

"Look at me!" The sharpness of Dolly's words startled Melanie into sitting up, alert to something different in Dolly's attitude. "Tell me truthfully! After my husband died and I wanted to move in with you and Vincent, was it really Vincent who didn't want me to join you in your home?"

Melanie offered a dispassionate laugh. "You hadn't figured that out before now? It was my idea, of course. The last thing I wanted was another woman in the house."

Dolly leaned back in her chair, wishing Melanie would go away so she could sit there and have a good cry. The weight of what this last admission meant almost overwhelmed her. There had after all been an alternative to a year of having strange men paw at her body, most of them drunk and many far from gentle. She tried to settle for the positive thought that she wouldn't have met Robert if she had not been in Nevada City back then. "To be his wife now," she told herself, "I would gladly have gone through what I did." But her feelings were in a turmoil, not the least of which was her sense of betrayal by a sister who she had also considered her close friend.

Dolly stood up and announced. "I'm going out."

"Are you going to tell Robert about this?"

"It's none of your business what I do, is it?" She took a deep breath. "But no. For now, I'll leave him a few delusions about who you really are. Besides, I'm sure if I did tell him, you'd find a way to talk yourself back into his good graces with more lies."

As Dolly turned toward the door, it flashed through her mind all the men she had been forced to service while working in a brothel. She turned back and took a step toward Melanie, looking down on her with eyes merciless and hard. "I'll tell you the real reason why you didn't want me in your house. You were afraid your husband might see how a woman with a soul behaves."

Dolly didn't wait for a response, but left the house and headed straight to the livery stable. More than anything else in the world right then, she wanted to be with her husband. Ignoring Piney Paul leaning against the livery's door frame, she walked directly to Robert as he was closing a stall door. He took one look at the anguish on his wife's face and held out his arms, wrapping them around her without inquiry. But such reticence didn't stop him from wanting to somehow fix the problem, even without knowing what it was. Nevertheless, sensing that right then what she really needed was simply his reassurance, all he said was, "I'm here."

Paul glanced in their direction and discretely slipped away, quietly closing the big double doors and flipping the sign to *closed*. He liked Robert and his missus, and knew they were going through a tough time. He had on more than one occasion stood up to someone's caustic remark about them. The men with whom he regularly drank already knew better than to criticize Robert, or say anything snide about Dolly's past. He did, however, think it odd that men no longer made comments about Lucy Murphy being a nosey busybody. Maybe, he surmised, they respected the fact that she had chosen to expose the truth, when she could have chosen to cover it up to protect her friends.

Robert led Dolly to a bench at the back of the livery near an open window funneling in fresh air. "Now, did you finally have enough of your sister?"

"You knew I would?"

"Eventually. What finally brought things to a head?"

When she finished telling him of Vincent's arrival and her conversation with him, Robert let out a breath mixed with several swear words. Then, although Dolly had told Melanie she wasn't going to tell Robert about their conversation, she decided to do it anyway. "After all", Dolly told herself, "lies and promises seem to be nothing to Melanie."

After hearing what had transpired between the sisters, Robert said, "It's like peeling an onion; one deception after another, layer by layer." He picked up one of Dolly's hands. "I don't care where she goes, but I want her out of the house."

"Yes, that's necessary, isn't it?"

"You're not going to argue with me? Your soft heart isn't going to feel sorry for her?"

"No, my heart has hardened against her." She looked into the distance, and although she tried very hard to firm her chin with resolve, it still quivered.

Seeing this, Robert asked, "Have you told all of this to Lucy?"

"No. I came straight here. I just wanted to be with you."

Ignoring how pleased this made him, he told her, "I think you need to tell Lucy."

Dolly turned to him and smiled. "You think that if I need some spine-strengthening about kicking Melanie out, I'll get it from Lucy, don't you?"

Robert laughed, feeling like a kid caught with his hand in the candy jar. "It couldn't hurt."

Robert put a side-saddle on one of his horses and helped Dolly into the seat. Avoiding Pacific Street, which would have been quicker but would have brought her past their house, she instead made her way through the traffic on Main Street. As she turned right onto Cedar Ravine, she cast an admiring look at the imposing brick edifice of the Methodist Episcopal Church, only a year old, on the corner. The small wooden church first used during the rush was at the back, but would someday be moved over onto Thomson Way and restored.

Dolly dismounted in back of Lucy's house next to the barn, slipped off the horse's bridle with bit and reins, and exchanged it with a simple halter and long lead rope. Satisfied that the horse was securely tied to the hitching post, she watched it begin to graze the long grass around the watering trough. Suddenly aware of good smells emanating from the house, Dolly hurried up the back steps and into the kitchen.

Lucy was preparing that night's supper and had just put a pot of vegetable soup on to simmer, while fresh bread baked in the oven. Roger sat nearby at the kitchen table playing cards with an imaginary rival, talking to *him* as though a real person was sitting there. He was waiting for Freda to return from her walk into town with Mr. Hershel so he could have a real person to play against. But his only display of impatience was one dangling foot lightly kicking a leg of his chair. Then he remembered that his father had once told him this was "a gambler's tell", and he immediately stopped.

As soon as Dolly entered through the back door without knocking, and Lucy saw her face, she told Roger, "Why don't you work on the list of spelling words your teacher gave you? You can do that in your room."

Roger sighed, not fooled that he was being sent from the room so the adults could talk. But after also seeing the strained look on Dolly's face, he said, "Okay. I hope you get happy again soon, Aunt Dolly."

Lucy turned to Dolly, who was looking surprised as she watched Roger leave the room. "He doesn't miss much," Lucy commented. "Now, sit down at the table and tell me what's wrong? Is living with Melanie beginning to pall?"

"Oh, heavens, yes. But several new things have turned up. For one thing, Vincent is in town."

Lucy sat down across from her friend with a graceless, unladylike movement. "No!"

"I talked to him briefly. He was very calm. Maybe too calm." She described the gun he had boldly carried in a holster for anyone to see. "I got Melanie talking after I sent him away, and now I'm thinking that much of what she has claimed about him wasn't even true."

Lucy's eyes grew large, but then she let out her breath and found herself nodding. "I guess we really shouldn't be too surprised."

Dolly proceeded to tell Lucy some of what had been said between herself and Melanie. "I guess he wasn't the most pleasant man to be married to, especially if she didn't love him and he came to realize it soon after their marriage. Still, he wasn't as awful as she described him to us, as well as to the whole town during the trial."

"What do you think he'll do now?"

"He wants to see her. I don't know if that's because he wants to allow for a divorce, or if he plans to drag her back home."

"If the latter, I think she'd be able to get legal help in resisting that. But not if he's able to convince a judge that she lied on the stand. That's perjury."

"That's against the law, right?"

"Yes, because her lies directly impacted the subject of the trial and it's outcome. If she had lied about her age, or something not related to the charges against her, it wouldn't be perjury."

"You'll have to tell me someday how you know that, but right now all I can think about is that she's been lying to me ever since she married Vincent."

"What about?"

"You mean other than why she married him and about his treatment of her?" she scoffed. "How about the fact that it was *Melanie* that didn't want me to live with them after my husband died?"

Realizing immediately what impact this had made on Dolly's life, Lucy felt herself choke up. She was furious with Melanie, yes, but also incredibly saddened by the waste of Dolly's potential happiness that had been cast aside like seed spilled upon the ground. Lucy listened intently as Dolly told her how she had parted from Melanie.

Although picturing in her mind her hands grabbing chunks of Melanie's hair and pulling them out, Lucy instead did her best to comfort Dolly. She even offered to return to the house with her if she wanted someone to be with her when she threw Melanie out. Watching that might at least give some satisfaction.

"Thank you, Lucy." Dolly couldn't help but laugh. "I appreciate your readiness to corner the lioness in her den, but I need to return the horse to Robert. Then we'll go home together and tell Melanie what we've decided."

"Where will she go?"

"I'd like to say I don't care, but I do." After a moment's thought, she said, "I guess we'll give her enough money for a couple of nights in a cheap rooming house, although I think she has a lot more money with her than she's let on, even after paying Mr. Sanderson. I'm sure she has at least enough for stage fare. She'll want to get away from Vincent as soon as she can. She has a friend in San Francisco, and it's a big enough city that it will be difficult for Vincent to find her there."

After Dolly left, Lucy sat in her cozy kitchen thinking about the wonderful smells with which it was filled. She also thought about her family, her new house, and all that she had survived in her life to get to that moment. She was filled with such an overwhelming sense of gratitude that a tear ran down her cheek. When Jim walked in and saw this, the startled look on his face forced from her a burst of laughter.

He sat next to her and said, "Tell me." And she did. He listened without comment and then made them both a drink. Sitting at the table and watching Lucy move gracefully around the kitchen, Jim thought of many things. Not least of his random thoughts was wondering what Robert must be going through. Dolly had Lucy with whom to share her thoughts and feelings, but he wasn't sure Robert had anyone he felt comfortable enough with to say what was really on his mind.

"How much time before supper?" he asked aloud.

"A couple of hours at least."

"I think I'll go into town for an hour or so."

Lucy watched him go into the barn, soon coming out riding his horse. She knew this meant that he was going further than a short block away, but was puzzled that he hadn't been more specific as to his destination. However, as he passed her standing on the back porch, he said, "I want Robert to check the back, left shoe."

Lucy said nothing, but was pretty sure she understood why Jim was going to see his friend. It got her to thinking that maybe she should go see a friend, too. She quickly changed into the split skirt of her riding outfit as she noted the warmth of the day, and boldly refused to add a light jacket or shawl over her waist. Once her horse was saddled, she rode down Pacific to Sacramento, and over to Coloma Street.

"Lucy! Come in. It's nice to see you."

As Jane guided Lucy into the parlor, Lucy told her, "You're looking well."

"Thank you."

Lucy started to say something else, but was immediately struck with the change to the room. Gone was the screen around Tony's desk, and in fact so was the desk.

Jane, watching Lucy look around, said, "I'd have gotten rid of the bookcase next to where his desk used to be, but it's built into the wall."

Hearing the ironic humor in Jane's voice, Lucy didn't bother to hide her laughter. "Well, the small gate-legged table you put there is very nice and so are the flowers in the vase. The whole room seems so much lighter."

"It should. That's a new rug, with new drapes, and the paintings on the walls are ones I had stored away because Tony didn't like them."

"Well, it's all lovely."

"Would you like a cup of tea?"

"No, thank you. I actually came to invite you to join us for supper tonight. Jim can come fetch you with the rig. I thought you might enjoy being with a rowdy family for a bit."

"That would have been nice, but I already have plans."

"Oh, well, maybe some other time."

"You came all this way on horseback just to ask me to supper for tonight?"

"It was a somewhat spontaneous gesture, I realize. But I got to thinking about how I've been concerned about Dolly and even Robert, and how they must be feeling. I wanted to be sure that you didn't think that I was neglecting you."

"It's not your responsibility to see to my happiness," she responded somewhat sharply. "Are you feeling a little guilty about your involvement in all that has happened?"

"No, not at all." Lucy didn't hide her surprise. "I just thought you might be reeling a little from all that you've gone through lately."

"I assure you, Lucy, that I'm not that fragile. I can handle any down-the-nose looks I get, or any snubs in the shops. I don't need your protection, or your pity."

"I don't pity you," Lucy objected. "I was just trying to be a supportive friend."

Jane walked further into the parlor, leaving Lucy by the front door. Lucy wondered if she should stay or not, but she didn't want to leave with an obvious awkwardness between them.

"I had another reason for coming to see you." Lucy held out her hand and Jane then saw that Lucy was carrying a pair of long scissors.

"Mine?"

"Yes. Dolly found them in the back of a kitchen drawer where Melanie must have hidden them. No one during the trial seemed to think it was necessary to question where they had gotten to; just that they had disappeared from Mrs. Helms's room. Dolly gave them to me to get them out of her house."

Jane reached out and took hold of them, looking at them as though she was seeing again an old friend. "Thank you. I've missed them."

"Jane, I'm sorry if I gave you the impression that I thought you incapable of taking care of yourself. I know what a strong and capable woman you are."

Jane turned to face Lucy. "I haven't done anything wrong! I shouldn't have to bear the burden of what my husband did. That damn trial!"

"How can people blame you for anything he did?"

"Just having a husband who was killed under suspicious circumstances had been enough to garner sly looks when I was in town. But now that they know he was the letter writer, it's worse."

"Oh, dear. I'm so sorry to hear that."

"No one seems to care about my feelings."

"But that's why I came here this afternoon to see you," Lucy tried to reason.

"To laud it over me that you have a wonderful family and I have no one? That I never had a good marriage, but that you do?"

"Jane! How can you think such a thing?"

"Well, that's the way your invitation has made me feel." She turned her back on Lucy and folded her arms across her chest.

"That may be the way you feel," Lucy told her, near to tears in her frustration, "but I didn't *make* you feel it. It's your choice to interpret my act of kindness that way, and not even give me the benefit of the doubt that I meant well."

Lucy stalked out of the house, then hesitated as she heard through the open window that Jane was weeping. Nevertheless, she didn't turn back, but instead mounted her horse and started for home. She was so upset that she didn't even notice the curious looks from those who saw that Mrs. Murphy was riding astride, wasn't wearing anything over her waist, and was muttering to herself as she headed east through town.

Two men on the sidewalk in front of the soda works watched her ride past and took note of all this. One of them, a man who had several times lost a big hand to Jim, said, "Wonder if something's up." Noting how Lucy's horse was holding up its head with its ears alertly pitched forward, he added, "Her horse seems to think so."

"Yeah," the other man nodded, "it looks about ready to salute. She's that kind of woman."

The men shared a good laugh and headed into the nearest saloon to share their witty exchange with those who had so often commented on Mrs. Murphy's unorthodox behavior. One of those who heard the retelling, asked, "Ain't she a friend of the gal who whanged her ma and kilt her?"

"Naw," another answered, "she's friends with the sister. Fact is, the Murphy woman had a big hand in gettin' the killer woman arrested."

"Yeah, but the jury didn't send her up."

Such was the conversation on more than one occasion following a sighting of those involved in the trial and what had led up to it.

Late that night, as Lucy fought the onset of insomnia, she began thinking about cause and effect, and what starts a cascade of repercussions that can follow one ill-considered decision. She questioned all that had happened to Dolly and Melanie, and those closely associated with them. Would any of it have taken place if Leon Anthony had not decided to abandon his family and change his name to Tony Leon? Would his wife have married off her children so young, just so she could more quickly have a fulfilling life for herself? Had her passion for women's rights been fed by her bitterness at having been deserted by *Mr. Anthony*? Would Dolly have been forced to choose prostitution in order to survive? Would Melanie have chosen to marry for love rather than out of greed, and therefore avoid becoming a heartless shrew? But most of all, she wondered if cold-bloodedly manipulating the lives of others would have occurred to any of them as a solution to their problems.

CHAPTER 16

"Patience – and shuffle the cards."
Don Quixote

August and September, 1862

Dolly was about ready to pull her hair out. She had been listening to Melanie pacing in her room since before dawn. Robert had left for work, irritated beyond endurance and declaring that he would get breakfast in one of the restaurants in town. Consequently, Dolly was left feeling as though she had shirked one of her wifely duties, and was torn between wanting to shed a few tears, or grabbing Melanie to shake her insensible. She rejected both of those feelings, and decided to simply review the situation calmly and logically.

She had taken her stand with Melanie the day before, insisting to Robert that she needed to have the final confrontation with Melanie by herself. After later listening to Dolly's description of what had transpired between the sisters, where Dolly had informed Melanie that she would have to leave the house *as soon as possible*, Robert declared that she should have said *immediately*. Dolly had to admit that although her words had been clear, her delivery of them had been somewhat hesitant, possibly leaving Melanie with the impression that there was some wiggle room about when she had to leave. As Dolly drank coffee in the kitchen while listening to Melanie moving about in her room, she thought back on their conversation.

Melanie had immediately turned to her old trick of manipulation, playing on Dolly's finer feelings. "You're the only family I have left in the world and you're abandoning me?"

Dolly blushed to recall how her throat had tightened with sympathy before recovering herself to bark back, "If I'm all that's left of family, it's because you removed our parents."

"Yes, but they needed removing."

"Oh, Melanie, how can you?" Dolly had turned away in disgust, fighting so many emotions that her stomach had churned.

"Oh, don't go all uppity on me!" Melanie had snarled, all innocent pretense gone. "You resented them, too."

"Maybe I did. But it never occurred to me to kill them."

"Nevertheless, if you turn me out, I'll be in danger of being killed by my violent husband."

"That's bull and you know it!"

"Maybe," she had smirked, "but that's what everyone will think, and that you callously put me in danger of him."

Dolly had faced Melanie, finally prepared to confront and not back down. "Do I need to remind you that you already admitted that you made up all that violent history guff?"

"Oh, right." Dolly recalled how Melanie had then flounced over to the parlor fireplace to stare down at its clean and swept interior, her arms crossed and her lips pouting.

Dolly had not been fooled, sure that Melanie was simply marking time until she could think of some new approach that might change Dolly's mind. Before that could happen, however, Dolly asked, "Have you told so many lies that you can't keep them straight?"

"Oh, Dolly, give me some peace. My head aches, and I have to think things through. Just give me until Saturday. I'll pack my things and get a ticket out on that day's stage to San Francisco."

Melanie had then retreated to her room, and had stayed there ever since. There had been some noise in the kitchen during the night, so she knew Melanie wasn't starving herself. Dolly poured herself another cup of coffee, suddenly aware that there were no sounds coming from Melanie's room. This continued for the rest of the day. Melanie even refused to come out for supper that evening, which was a relief to Robert.

Now that morning had dawned, and with Robert gone, Dolly figured Melanie had to be very hungry and knocked on the bedroom door. "Would you like me to fix you some eggs?"

"No! Go away!"

With a reply such as this, Dolly didn't ask a second time. She sliced some bread from yesterday's loaf, slathered it with butter and jam, and chewed it thoughtfully while guzzling her third cup of coffee. When finished, she put her plate in the sink and walked rapidly to the Murphy residence.

She immediately realized that Lucy was enjoying her favorite pastime of reading a book while resting on the sofa in the parlor. Lucy explained that she was taking advantage of everyone being out of the house; Jim playing in a game with some local businessmen, Freda out shopping, and Roger in school. Realizing that she had intruded upon Lucy, Dolly immediately felt guilty. But that was such a common emotion of late, and she was so deeply disturbed, that the feeling quickly passed.

Knowing Dolly might feel this way, Lucy was doubly enthusiastic in her greeting, and soon they were sipping tea and eating coffeecake. After hearing Dolly's latest tale of woe, Lucy told her, "I don't know what you can do. Melanie is obviously trying to work something out in herself. Maybe she's finally facing what she's done, and is at war with her conscience."

Dolly sighed. "I hope so. I've talked to Reverend Ross, the Pastor at the Methodist Church. He says we must be patient with her, since he insists that she must have a tormented soul right now."

Lucy resisted the temptation to scoff at the good reverend's generous if somewhat pious judgment. It was Lucy's opinion that Melanie was one lost lamb that not only didn't know how to find her way to salvation, but who didn't want to try. But she merely said, "If that's the case, it will be interesting to see what happens next."

That day's next event introduced itself right then by the banging of the heavy iron knocker on the front door. Whoever was using it was putting it to persistent use, and Lucy hurried to open the door. Finding herself facing an obviously agitated Sue Ellen, she stepped back so the woman could enter.

"Come into the parlor," Lucy invited. "I'll get another cup. You look like you need some refreshment."

While doing this, she heard Dolly greet Sue Ellen with concern. "Are you well? You look ashen!"

"I don't know when I've been this upset."

Placing a cup in front of Sue Ellen, Lucy filled it with the steaming amber liquid from the pot. "Now, tell us what's happened."

Sue Ellen put the cup down, afraid she was going to spill, as her hands were shaking so badly. "I was doing my weekly inventory, to see what I need to order, and I found a bottle missing."

"What was in it?"

"Laudanum tablets. A new, full bottle."

She didn't have to explain why she would have it in her salon. Women used it for cramps, diarrhea, bladder problems, and the after-effects of child birth; anything they might be more comfortable talking to Sue Ellen about than even a doctor, who would of course be a man. The amount of arsenic in each tablet was very small, but as Mrs. Butterick had known, too much of it could end a life.

"Do you know when it was taken?" Lucy asked her.

"I have no idea."

Sue Ellen was twisting one of Lucy's good linen napkins into a tortured knot, and Lucy fought the urge to take it from her. Instead, she asked, "When was the last time you gave it to someone?"

"Several days ago. I give it so seldom, and very sparingly at that, and only to women who are regular customers. But I think it was stolen night before last. I came in yesterday morning and found the door unlocked. I thought I had locked it the night before, but since nothing looked disturbed, I figured I had after all left it unlocked. Then later yesterday I realized the front window next to the door was unlocked. I do believe that was my fault. I had closed but not locked it the day before."

"So maybe someone came in through the window, but went out through the door," Lucy suggested.

"Yes. But not having a key to the door, they wouldn't be able to lock it after them."

"Have you reported the theft to the police?"

"No. I just discovered it, and what can they do anyway? It's not like it's illegal to possess it."

"That doesn't mean it can't be misused," Dolly commented.

"I know, and two bits can get four ounces of it from any drug store. But some women don't want to be seen buying it. A lot of husbands have no idea their wives take it as often as they do. Unfortunately, it was a large bottle. Telling the police would just draw attention to why I had so much of it in my salon, and they might want the names of my customers."

While the three friends at Lucy's house were trying to puzzle out what to do next, Melanie was standing very still in the center of her room. There was nothing of indecision about her, just as there hadn't been the night before last when she had snuck into town and back. In fact, right then she looked very much like a woman who had made up her mind about something, and was exceedingly proud of her decision. It wasn't like her to be hesitant and while staring at herself in the mirror of the dressing table, she sternly rebuked herself for her current reluctance. After several minutes of this, she said a silent prayer of thanks to the memory of Mrs. Butterick, and declared to herself that she was desperate enough to be willing to do anything in order to avoid a future not of her own choosing.

Melanie sat down at the small writing desk in the parlor, and after half an hour of repeated attempts to word a note just right, she stuffed it in an envelope and printed a name on the outside of it. She walked into town and to the Cary House, where she determined that the recipient of the note was still in the hotel. She then handed the clerk the envelope, giving him very specific instruction that it should be delivered to the addressee immediately. From the hotel, she went directly to the nearby Neptune Restaurant, where she took a table in the furthest, most shadowed corner.

Sitting with her back to the wall so she could see those entering, Melanie ordered a pot of hot chocolate. When the tall china pot arrived, hand painted with elegant red and yellow roses against a light green background as was common with such pots, she poured some chocolate into her cup. After tasting it, she opened the lid and poured in sugar to sweeten it, stirring the contents until it was properly mixed. She then pulled out a gold pocket watch from her small beaded purse, checked the time, and sat back to wait.

Although her stiff, upright posture was dictated by the training of years and the knowledge of being on public view, the tightness around her eyes and jaw told of displeasure bordering on repugnance. This would scream out to women, practiced as they were in hiding their emotions, but would be unnoticed by men who never had to bother with such artifice.

Back at Lucy's house, Lucy turned to her friends and announced, "I'm hungry. Why don't you both join me for luncheon. It's a little early for a big dinner, but I think we could all use some food." She turned to Dolly. "You'll be fixing a large supper in a few hours, so let me treat us to this."

"Why don't you go on?" Dolly told her friends. "I think I need to spend some time with my husband, and he'll be home any time now. He's been through a lot because of me and my family."

After Dolly bid her friends good-bye, Sue Ellen and Lucy walked down Pacific Street to Sacramento, and then up to Main Street where they practically ran into Jane Leon.

"Hello, Jane," Lucy greeted her, somewhat hesitantly. She hadn't forgotten how they had last parted and was unsure if Jane was friend or foe. "You know Sue Ellen, of course. Why don't you join us for a bite to eat?"

Jane hesitated, then smiled warmly if a bit shyly. She held out her hand to Lucy, who gripped it firmly and smiled back. "I'd like that very much." Lucy's heart soared and she led the way with a renewed bounce in her step.

The three women entered the Neptune Restaurant just behind a large family, taking a seat next to a small retaining wall that broke the sightline between themselves and the nearest table west of them in the corner. They didn't become aware of Melanie at that table until they heard her add ginger biscuits to her order. Obviously, Melanie had not seen them. To maintain this state of anonymity, Lucy set the large menu upright on the table so that it even more completely blocked a view of their table. Still, the three women realized that they could be heard, so after an exchange of glances full of curiosity and caution, they all remained quiet.

They had an unobstructed view of the entrance, and soon saw Vincent enter, recognizing him from Dolly's description. He found Melanie immediately upon entering, having deduced that she would be waiting in the most unobtrusive portion of the room.

As Vincent walked past their table, the waiter approached Lucy and her friends for their order. She put a finger to her lips, pointed to the listing of soup and held up three fingers. The waiter, being Young Tom and familiar by now with Mrs. Murphy's eccentricities, caught on to what the women were doing when he saw Jane glance over at Melanie at the next table. He simply nodded and walked away.

Vincent's deep voice was subdued. "I must say I'm surprised you sent me a note to meet you. I was under the impression that you were going to go out of your way to avoid me."

Melanie's answer was delivered in an even tone of forced casualness. "I've thought it over and I realize that I am, as much as I wish I was not, still legally your wife. The only way that circumstance can change is if I talk to you face to face."

"But in a public place," he noted with a tight jaw. "Is this to reinforce what you've led people to believe? That you'd face physical harm if alone with me?"

Melanie ignored this and came to the point. "I want a divorce, Vincent. I'm not the right wife for you. If you're not attached to me, you can find a woman who will treat you well."

"I don't believe in divorce. You know that." His tone was severe as he crossed his arms across his chest in a pose of stubborn refusal.

"Yes, well, we all change," she shrugged. "Circumstances do that to us. You'll never be happy if you force us to stay married. Because I'll not live with you. I'll take you to court if I have to. I've looked into it, and I know how to do it."

"Go ahead. I know better than you how to work within the legal system."

"You don't love me," Melanie declared, her frustration rising as she forced herself to keep her voice low. "You only want me back because my leaving you is a hit to your pride."

"Don't be ridiculous." Vincent sat back and looked at her with scorn.

She continued as though he hadn't spoken, her argument carefully worked out and not to be denied its airing. "You just can't accept that you're not going to have your life the way you want it. You're getting older and you're facing all the things that are changing in your life. Losing me is just one of those things you're afraid you're losing control over."

Their conversation was too far from the other tables to be clearly overheard, except for the table they couldn't see that held Lucy's party. For the rest of the room their words were more like sounds of combative felines; hisses and gasps, whines and growls.

"Control? You dare talk to me of control?" His face was dangerously red. "Isn't that why you killed Vespacia? She left you in control of your own life when we married, and you chose to trick and lie to everyone around you. What do you have now because of that? A husband who despises you, everyone you know aware that you're capable of murder, and a town who has rejected you far more than Vespacia ever did. And all because *you* wanted my money and to be in control of your life without consideration of anyone else. You never paid any attention to my advice, or appreciated what I tried to do for you."

Melanie offered no further argument. "I guess we're at an impasse then." She leaned forward and picked up the tall chocolate pot. "Here, let me pour you some chocolate. I know how much you like it and I ordered it specially. And you might try one of the ginger biscuits."

She filled his cup with the rich, fragrant drink, and then sat back with an almost angelic smile. When she made no move to drink from her cup, he asked, "Aren't you having some?"

"I already did." She poured more chocolate into her cup and picked it up, taking a swallow. "Very nice. A bit strong, perhaps, but nice."

Vincent picked up his cup. Before he could drink, however, Lucy stood up and shouted, "Stop! Don't drink that, Vincent."

Sue Ellen and Jane, along with everyone else in the restaurant, looked at her in shock. Melanie stood up and yelled at her, "You stupid, interfering bitch! Mind your own business, damn you!"

Vincent shot up out of his chair and stood looking at Lucy as though he thought her insane. The diners looked on as though watching a stage show they thought somewhat unseemly. No one touched their food, and some even considered whether or not they should leave. But no one did. The waiters rushed from the kitchen, Young Tom hurrying to Lucy's side. "Is something amiss, Mrs. Murphy?"

"Yes. I think the chocolate in that pot is poisoned." When the room buzzed with alarm, she turned on them with impatience showing. "Oh, not by the restaurant." She stretched out her arm and pointed at Melanie, even while knowing it was a melodramatic gesture. "By her. So that Vincent will die and she'll be free of him. It's very dangerous to reward bad behavior, like the jury did with her."

Vincent looked at the white face of his wife and felt his legs give way, knowing that what Lucy had said was true. He groped for his chair and sat down while staring at the woman to whom he had been insisting he remain tied to for life.

"You lie!" Melanie shouted at Lucy. "You lie!"

Vincent looked at her, then at Lucy. "But she drank some of the chocolate herself. I watched her."

"Most of what she drank was poured before she doctored the pot. What little she added she could drink without any ill effects. As many women do, she's been ingesting arsenic sparingly as part of her beauty regimen for a long time. Her porcelain complexion and slick hair comes at a price. She stole a large amount of laudanum from a shop in town, and along with what she already had in her possession, I'm certain that she put a lethal quantity of it in the chocolate before you got here."

Young Tom said, "There's one way to find out. We just caught a rat out back of the restaurant in the alley. One of the waiters was going to bring it home for his cat, but we can feed it some of what's in the pot and see what happens." Without waiting for anyone to say anything, he picked up the pot and retired to the kitchen.

Two of the other waiters took up a stand behind Melanie, who had started to move away from the table. Sue Ellen then moved to block Melanie's way to the door, telling her, "Try to get past me, and I'll lay you out." Melanie recoiled from her, only too aware of how she had betrayed and used her one-time friend. She stood stiff and quiet, but her eyes darted continually as she looked for any opportunity to escape.

Lucy told Sue Ellen, "Maybe you should check her pockets and her purse for a container that might have a bit of the drug still in it."

But after a thorough search, no paper was found. With Melanie smirking her triumph, one of the waiters standing behind her said, "Wait a minute. What's that under the table?"

Looking down, Sue Ellen saw what he was pointing at, and picked it up. It was a small envelope, and inside was a tiny bit of white powder residue, the tablets having been crushed to aid in dissolving quickly. Sue Ellen carefully wrapped the paper in a linen napkin and brought it to Lucy, who put it in her purse.

While searching Melanie's purse, Sue Ellen had removed something she had found there. Holding out her hand to Lucy, she displayed the gold pocket watch. "That's mine!" Melanie screamed.

Lucy took it and showed it to a surprised Jane, who nodded and said, "Tony told me it had belonged to his father, whose name he said was Victor."

"No," Lucy told her gently. She turned it over and exposed the engraving on the back while reading aloud, "*Golden promises. V.*" She put a hand on Jane's arm. "It's Tony's watch alright, but given to him by Vespacia, and taken from his dead body by his killer."

Jane and Sue Ellen turned to stare at Melanie, then sat back in their chairs, too emotionally exhausted to find appropriate words for further conversation. One of the waiters behind Melanie put a hand on her shoulder and pushed her down onto her chair. After half an hour of tense waiting, Young Tom came back into the dining room. His voice subdued, he told Vincent, "The rat died."

Melanie jumped up from her chair and leaped toward the door, but the two waiters grabbed her arms. Tom said, "I'll get the police."

A voice from the far opposite corner was heard to say, "You don't have to do that." Everyone turned to see Officer J. J. Reynolds standing up. Even Lucy hadn't seen him, so quiet had he remained after seeing Melanie enter and then Lucy with her friends. He now walked forward, preparing to use a large napkin rolled lengthwise to tie Melanie's wrists behind her back.

But she didn't submit easily. While struggling against his efforts, she let loose with a stream of invective so coarse that it brought a cavalcade of protests from a number of women in the room. They were immediately led from the restaurant by their escorts before the ladies' sensibilities could be further tainted by such odious language. This seemed to anger Melanie even more. "It's a lie! You're all set against me. You men are all alike. You always get away with everything. I'll make you pay for this!"

Officer Reynolds finally got her hands bound behind her. "I suggest you stop talking and just come with me."

She turned on him with lips curled back and eyes bulging. "Go to hell! I made my father pay and I'll make you pay! I'll smash your skull in too, you sonofabitch!"

As Melanie was led away amid the shocked silence of those in the room, Vincent looked up at Lucy still standing beside his chair. "Her father? I thought he died during the gold rush. Who is her father, then?"

Loud enough for all to hear, she said, "It *was* Tony Leon."

Those in the room who had not realized what it meant that Melanie had Tony's watch, reacted with gasps and murmured comment. But it was a sound behind Lucy that caught her attention. It was Jane, crumpling onto the floor in a faint. But she hadn't completely passed out, and as soon as she was helped back onto her chair, she grabbed Lucy's hand. "Then Dolly is his daughter, too?"

"Yes, of course."

In a voice filled with the shock of the revelation, but also a degree of gratification, she said, "All this time I've been her stepmother. I know that doesn't mean much, really, but I've always liked Dolly. In an odd sort of way, I feel like I've just found a long-lost family member."

Sue Ellen, none too gently, said, "Yes, but that also means one part of that family killed her father, your husband."

Jane looked at her with the fullness of what this meant dawning on her, but it was a struggle for her to accept the idea. "Well, yes, of course." She then formed the words that everyone in the room was thinking. "Melanie killed Tony. It wasn't just a robbery gone bad, or done by someone who knew he was the letter writer." She looked over at the door through which Melanie had just exited, and finally comprehended the horrid entirety of what had happened. "His daughter killed him." A large tear rolled down Jane's check as most of the diners still there realized they were too upset to finish their meal and rose to leave. Only a few men remained.

Lucy felt sorry for the owners of the restaurant and left more money on the table than would cover just the cost of their three meals. While Jane and Sue Ellen clasped hands and composed themselves, Lucy went into the kitchen and asked Young Tom to pour the chocolate in the pot into a clean, lidded crock and take it to the police. "Leave it with Officer Reynolds and no one else, please."

As Lucy left with Jane and Sue Ellen, she wanted nothing more than to go home and hug those she loved. The other women also desired time to themselves to sort out what they had just witnessed, each in their own way having been impacted by the morning's events. With a glance shared between them that conveyed they understood one another, the women parted without further words.

Late the next afternoon Officer Reynolds arrived at the Murphy home, finding Lucy and Jim sitting on the front porch. After accepting a cold glass of water, he took a seat and told them what had happened over the last twenty-four hours.

"I had them perform a Marsh test on the chocolate. It was full of arsenic."

Jim raised a brow. "What's a Marsh test?"

"It's a way of detecting the presence of arsenic in something. Been around for over twenty years. Marsh was a French chemist that figured out how to do it because in France arsenic had become known as 'inheritance powder'. The symptoms are not unlike cholera."

Jim leaned forward eagerly. "How does the test work?"

"You put some of the liquid, or body tissue if a dead body is involved, in a glass vessel with zinc and acid, and it produces arsine gas if arsenic is present. If you ignite the gas mixture, it'll oxidize any arsine present into arsenic and water vapor."

Although Lucy found this interesting, she was more concerned about what this meant for Melanie. Officer Reynolds told them, "Because I heard her confess to killing Tony Leon when she was screaming in the restaurant, as did you and many others, she can't deny that she was his killer. And she obviously tried to kill her husband. The judge told her that if she pleads guilty, and doesn't demand a trial, he'll send her to prison for twenty years, and not hand down the death penalty. She didn't like it, but she did it."

Lucy swallowed with difficulty. "Where will she go to prison?"

"She'll be taken by stage to San Francisco, and then transferred to a prison coach that'll take her north about seventeen miles to San Quinton Prison."

He stopped talking when Lucy rose up and walked into the house, trying to balance what she understood of justice with her compassion for the waste of a young woman's life. Try as she might, even considering what Melanie had done, she found that she wanted to sit down alone some place away from everyone and have a good cry.

All she could think about was how much unhappiness had been wrought in one family. How Dolly had managed to retain a character so different from her parents and sister was almost a miracle. Society had denigrated Dolly for her choice to work in a brothel, but it was her socially acceptable family where corrupt morals had truly resided. She then thought of Mrs. Helms and her diatribes about how callous and awful men were for denying women more rights, but it was a woman who had manipulated and betrayed her friends — and who had murdered her parents.

Such irony of Biblical proportion tempted Lucy to mix laughter with her tears, even while knowing that such action was too close to a form of hysteria to be allowed. Deciding that she needed more time alone, she didn't return to the porch.

Jim understood Lucy's need to be by herself. He remained where he was, glad that she was not present as J. J. told him what the conditions would be like at the prison. "After some while," he concluded, "she might wish she had opted for the death penalty."

The prison had been built ten years before by prisoners held on a prison ship off Angel Island near San Francisco. Built of red brick and rock quarried by the prisoners, it consisted of long rows of cramped eight by nine foot cells, each with a high arched ceiling, but side walls only five feet tall. A solid iron door fronted each cell, with a small slit in the center for the passing of food trays and intrusive, regular inspections.

It was an era preceding prison reform at San Quentin, including the women's section. Men wore baggy pants covered by long, loose shirts, both patterned with horizontal black and white stripes. In order to obscure any individual character, they wore only a number to identify them.

Women wore plain black or brown dresses made of coarse linsey-woolsey, with one thin petticoat beneath. And, of course, their assigned number was prominently displayed on their chest. Only when working outside their cells did they add a white apron to their bland apparel. Crowning this drab outfit was a white stuff cap such as servants might wear.

But in one sense, they *were* servants. They served the time of their sentence (usually the full length of it), the warden (at this time, the Lt. Governor) and their jailors (most of whom were men). The frequency with which they were allowed to bathe was always a matter of contention between the inmates and the guards. These guards were known to occasionally take some of the women with them to local saloons for drinking and *other* activities. This eventually would be forbidden in the early 1870's, but only because rumor of it had reached the public's notice and the State had taken control of the prison.

When let out of their cells, the women either marched around the open yard for exercise or sat shoulder to shoulder on long wooden benches where they sewed, knitted or mended whatever was given them. What items that didn't stay in the prison for their own use, went out to the poor-farms.

Punishment for real or fabricated misbehavior, or refusal to cooperate with a guard's personal request, might be the withholding of food, or sitting alone in a dark cell with no window and nothing to occupy their time. Although mostly known to be used on male prisoners, in some cases corporal punishment could be dealt them; until this too was abolished in the early 1870's.

By the time J.J.Reynolds had gotten this far in his recital, Jim wanted to yell at him to stop. But, of course, he didn't want to be perceived as *soft*, so he said, "I get the picture, John. But maybe that's enough of the picture, in case Lucy might hear. I think the fact that she's been instrumental in sending someone to such a place is starting to settle in, and it's bothering her."

"I guess I think of Mrs. Murphy as a tough lady who can handle whatever life dishes out."

"She is and she has. But she's still a woman, and maybe has a tendency to more sensitive emotions than she wants to admit."

Officer Reynolds nodded slowly. "I'll have to remember that about women. Even strong women."

Jim smiled at him. "It would probably serve you well if you do."

"Oh," J.J. added as an afterthought, "I ushered Vincent St. John to the stage depot yesterday. He was eager to leave, but I told him that although he might think of himself as a victim, he still wasn't any too popular here. He assured me he had no desire to ever return to this town."

As August ended, the heat settled in and Lucy was longing for the cool reaches of the forests north of town. Dolly felt the same, and consequently she and Lucy, along with Jane at Dolly's suggestion, rented horses from the Pioneer Livery for a day's outing. Robert's livery didn't rent out horses, being much smaller than the Pioneer. Wearing acceptable riding dresses of split skirt and long jacket over a white waist, leather gloves and boots, and a small bonnet with their hair twisted up beneath, they were ready to depart.

As Mr. Bennett approached them with the horses and began to saddle them with the standard lady's sidesaddle, Lucy looked at her friends and recognized their frowns for what they were. She caught Dolly's eye, who laughed and nudged Jane, who in her turn shrugged. "Oh, why not?"

Lucy stepped forward, willing to accept disapproval for the request she was about to make. "Excuse me, but we would like to ride astride." When the man's brows lifted to his hairline, she added, "We'll be riding over some uneven ground as well as over some steep hills, and we'll be safer that way. Especially as we don't know these animals."

"I assure you, Mrs. Murphy, these are very gentle mares."

As Lucy hesitated, Jane told him, "Then maybe you should give us horses with a little more spirit and regular saddles."

Pursing his lips, he did just that. The women didn't miss the glint in his eyes and before mounting, led their horses in a wide circle. As soon as the horses relaxed and let out the air they had inhaled, the women tightened their own loose saddles and handily mounted without asking for assistance. Only Jane's horse considered it might challenge its rider, but she immediately corrected its bad behavior, and horse and rider together settled down to a cooperative relationship. Mr. Bennett unbent and showed a degree of admiration as he watched them ride off.

The women chose the road to the town of Coloma, passing first down the narrow alley of Center Street just beyond the Plaza, past the hay yard and feed barn, then through a small neighborhood. None of them commented as they passed Jane's house, each with memories flooding through their minds, about which they didn't want to give voice. Outside of town, the road became more winding and several times they encountered freight wagons and other riders on the narrow road. They ignored the curious and sometimes judgmental looks cast in their direction, and continued to enjoy their ride.

Dolly eventually led them down a side path into a heavily forested area that had somehow escaped the lumbermen's axe. They dismounted next to a trickling stream where the ground was covered in grasses and the remains of wildflowers now wilting in the summer's heat. They spread a blanket on the ground while the horses slurped from the stream. As they unpacked their lunches from saddlebags, their conversation was at first sporadic while they eagerly drank from their canteens. However, once they began eating their sandwiches and fruit, their conversation flowed easily.

When they were sated and nibbling cookies, Dolly turned to Lucy. "Thank you for standing up to Mr. Bennett so we could have a decent ride. I hate sidesaddles. I feel twisted in the mid-section for days after."

"Maybe someday," Jane said, "it will be fully acceptable for women to ride astride."

"I know women who call it riding *clothespin style*," Lucy told them. The others laughed, having also heard this term.

Dolly sobered quickly, looking down at her lap as she brushed crumbs from her skirt. "Jane and I have something to tell you, Lucy."

Lucy stiffened, hearing a seriousness and anxiety in Dolly's voice that made her wary of what was to follow. When Jane turned red and looked away, Lucy knew for certain something important was about to be forthcoming. "Go ahead. What is it?"

"Robert and I have decided that we must leave Placerville."

"Oh, Dolly..."

"No, Lucy, please. You don't see the little looks I get or the way women move away from me in the shops, as though getting too close would soil them. Or how those I used to call *friend* exclude me from all their social events."

"Has Robert experienced any of this?"

Dolly sighed heavily. "Some. Not from men who like his livery and his work. But in the saloons, he's noticed a change. Some men seem uncomfortable around him. You know, awkward."

"Don't you think that will pass off in time?"

"For Robert, yes." She picked a blade of grass and ran its length between her fingers. "Women don't forgive breaches of society's rules, such as having a sister in prison for murdering her parents and trying to murder her husband." Lucy couldn't help smile at Dolly's sarcasm, even though the principle of it was true. "They forgave me what choice I had to make in order to survive during the rush, but they're not about to ignore this."

There was no convincing way to argue the point, and Lucy didn't try. Feeling her throat tighten, she asked, "When do you propose to leave?"

"Oh, not for some time yet."

"Where will you go?"

"We haven't decided that. But I'm pretty sure it will be over the mountain."

Jane reached over to Lucy and placed a hand on her wrist. "And I'm going with them."

Lucy blinked, her thought the natural one of, "I'm to lose another friend?" But realizing this wasn't about her, she told Jane, "I do realize that you'll be much happier some place away from here."

"I haven't had women refuse to stand near me," Jane admitted, "but I have had several backs turned to me. I am after all the woman married to the man who sent out nasty, anonymous letters. And then he had the bad taste to get himself murdered. When one's spouse does something hideous, there's always a little associated thought that you somehow failed to keep them from it."

Dolly nodded in agreement. "Or that whatever tainted one sister's character must have also tainted the other. They may think both of us have the same propensity to kill whoever stands in our way."

"Oh, dear," Lucy blinked. "Assuredly, you've seen into the worst of human nature. But we mustn't forget that it's not the *whole* of human nature." Lucy wanted so much to say something more that could mitigate the truth of what they all knew, but there was no denying the harshness of what they were experiencing. Lucy knew the rules of society too well, having herself suffered its decrees throughout her life.

It was a mostly silent ride back to town, although still an enjoyable one given the beauty of the route and a cooling breeze that had started up. The horses behaved perfectly even when a road runner crossed their path as comic relief. It was as though Life had given them a perfect afternoon as consolation for what they were experiencing.

The next few weeks were too busy for the ladies to plan outings or even visits among them. Fall would come early to this mountain community, and everyone had begun preparations for it, as well as the winter to follow. Trees were felled and the wood packed into sheds, water tanks were filled, hay bales stacked in barns, roofs inspected and repaired, ice houses swept out and lined with fresh straw, culverts cleared of weeds, and so many other tasks necessary in advance of whatever type of winter might come to the area. After the last one, when so much rain fell, no one was taking anything for granted.

Jim came home and walked in the front door late one afternoon in September, his stride showing purpose. Lucy knew he was eager to tell her something startling, although the grin he was wearing bordered on jubilation.

Hearing Roger enter the kitchen from the rear yard and head upstairs, Lucy told him, "Okay, husband, out with it. What's happened?"

He helped himself to a whiskey from the sideboard and casually walked to his chair, propping his feet up on the ottoman. Lucy sat in her chair on the other side of the table between them and waited for him to begin. He took a slow sip of his drink, relentlessly toying with his wife's rampant curiosity.

"Jim, for heaven's sake."

Laughing, he told her, "I met someone interesting today. He heard someone use my name and asked if I was by any chance Lucy Murphy's husband. When I admitted to that privilege, he let out a guffaw that brought other eyes to stare at us."

"Where were you?"

"In Goldie's saloon. I must say you have made some rather unusual friends in this town before I got here. This one certainly had much admiration for you, 'considering her a woman and all.'"

Lucy clapped her hands together. "Gus?"

"Yep. He thought you uncommonly courageous and intelligent, again 'for a woman'. I gathered from such comments that he hasn't had much regard for women in general. But he seems to think you're an exception."

"What a sweet man."

"Hmmm. I wouldn't think many women would call him that, especially if they got close to him. His odor is more of the stable."

"But he's a perfect example of not judging a person by appearance. He's intelligent, well read, and very savvy."

"I did enjoy talking to him. He has a wide knowledge of many things and can express himself well when he wants to."

Lucy thought a moment. "He was usually pretty taciturn with me."

"We were having a very interesting and somewhat animated discussion about the war, his knowledge of the battles so far as up-to-date as they can be. Then a few other men joined us at our table. Without being invited, I might add. All of a sudden Gus changed. He became sullen, his words few and clipped. The other men didn't stay long, and as soon as they were out of earshot, Gus was once again voluble and open with his opinions."

"What a compliment to you! He's very choosey about those with whom he'll spend his time."

"I assume he accepted me because he likes you so much."

"Not necessarily. That might have gotten you through the introduction, but he's very intuitive about people and forms his opinions quickly, I think."

"Well, I know he liked Roger."

"What?" Jim chuckled at her surprise, enjoying her reaction.

"I was walking home after my visit with Gus, and I realized it was time for Roger to get out of school, so I met him coming home. Gus was still in town and coming out of a shop, so I called to him. I then introduced him to Roger."

A mother's protective instinct came to the fore, and no matter how much she liked Gus, she recalled how gruff he could sometimes act. "How did Gus react to Roger?"

Jim laughed. "You'd think he had been around children all his life. He treated Roger like a young man and asked him how he liked school. Roger looked him right in the eyes and told him he learned more from reading books on his own, but that the school mistress was nice and he liked his schoolmates."

Lucy smiled with pride. "A very commendable response."

"I could tell Gus approved. He told Roger that he had a lot of books and he was welcome to come look through them and borrow what he wanted."

"Did Roger thank him?"

"Of course," Jim rejoined, feigning indignation. "Our son has been properly raised."

Lucy looked at Jim and smiled. "Yes, he has very fine manners, just like his father."

"Roger went on to inform Gus that there had been a public library in New Hampshire since 1833, and he thought Placerville should have one as well. And not just books in a room over the fire station. Gus agreed and told him that there had been a free lending library in the Colonies in the late 1600's. That got Roger all excited and he told Gus he should come for supper Saturday night so they could talk some more. I told him I thought that a great idea."

"What did Gus think?"

"He accepted."

"That's tomorrow night. Oh, dear."

Noticing her consternation, he hastened to reassure her. "It certainly doesn't have to be anything fancy, not for him."

"Oh, no, it's not that." Lucy bit at a fingernail. "It's Freda. Even when we were in the gold fields together during the rush, she wouldn't stand for coarseness from the men we fed."

"She may have plans with Randy Hershel and won't even be here."

"He's out of town until Monday. She'll be here. Not that she's like so many of the women in town who treat Gus with contempt. But he is a bit, um, disheveled in appearance."

"His exterior may be rough, not to mention his manners, but any fair-minded individual can soon look beyond that."

"And Freda is certainly that. Well, we'll just have to let happen what will."

As it turned out, it was Freda who opened the door to Gus, Lucy being in the kitchen and Jim upstairs with Roger. Lucy rushed into the parlor as soon as she realized what was happening, just as Freda was showing their guest into the parlor. She was offering him a drink, which he was gratefully accepting. Gus had learned long ago that it's always easier to get established in a social situation with something in one's hand.

Gus had his profile to Lucy and was unaware of her entrance, so he didn't see her gawking at him. Gus had obviously spent some coin at the barber and bath house, and possibly at the Round Tent Store's men's suit department. His beard was neatly trimmed, his cheeks stubble-free and he smelled of bay rum. For the first time in anyone's memory, when he removed his hat, his hair was combed smooth. His only stamp of individuality had been his refusal to wear a tie, although his new white shirt was buttoned at the neck as was only acceptable. Lucy looked down at his feet and saw that he wore his regular pair of dusty boots, and for some reason she was glad of that. He may have tried hard to please his new friends, being grateful for their invite, but he was not willing to forsake who he preferred to be.

"Gus!" Lucy called out, watching him turn around and able now to view all that he had done to himself. She tactfully did not call attention to this change, for which Gus was gratefully relieved. "How delightful to see you again," she told him. "Come have a seat. Supper will be ready soon."

There was a slight blush on his unusually smooth cheeks as he smiled at her. "Thank you for having me to supper. I just met the wonderful Freda you've so often spoken about."

Freda laughed. "She talks about me behind my back, does she?"

Even though he knew Freda had meant this in jest, Gus said, "Oh, but only extolling your virtues, and the impact you've had on her life."

To rescue the moment from embarrassment, Lucy broke in. "It's our pleasure to have you visit, I assure you. Here's Jim now."

The men shook hands and sat on the sofa just as Roger bounced down the stairs and made directly for Gus with a book in his hands. "Hi, Gus. I have that book I told you about. The one I found on my mother's book shelf." He handed his new friend a book called *Smith's Modern and Ancient*

Geography that was accompanied by a large atlas. "It has a bunch of great colored maps." He looked over at the adults in the room and turned back to Gus. "I'll show them to you after supper if you want."

"I think that would be fine. It's a truly wonderful book."

"Mother said I could keep it in my room." He hugged the book and scurried out.

Gus told Lucy, "You've chosen educational books for him that will give him a knowledge of the world. That's such a good idea."

"I'd like to take credit for that, but he really did find it on the book shelves among those left behind by the last owners." She gestured toward a tall book shelf on the wall next to the fireplace. "He picked it out for himself. He has a very curious mind. I'm glad, because he spends a good portion of his time practicing a number of card games." She glanced at Jim, but he merely smiled back, the picture of innocence.

"He has a talent for numbers," Jim added modestly.

Freda laughed and threw up her hands in mock exasperation. "Oh, for heaven's sake, people. Let's face it, he's a genius child with unending talents and will probably rule the world by the time he's twenty." Everyone laughed, and they moved on to other topics of general interest.

But Lucy had received great pleasure from seeing her son and Gus together, talking as though they were long-time friends, for that was the way she felt about Gus. In fact, as she sat watching those people for whom she cared so deeply, she felt such an inner radiance of joy that it brought a lump to her throat. She glanced at Jim and found him watching her. He too looked pleased, but she knew it was because he enjoyed seeing her so happy.

Her moods always colored his own. Lucy's awareness of this caused her to sometimes hide any despondency or worry she might feel. Although this could have caused either of them to feel resentment for the responsibility, it did not. For them it was what marriage should be; a mutual effort that put the other person first in their consideration, which action would establish harmony in the home for everyone. There was no sense of sacrifice in this, but only recognition of a mutually supportive partnership. So, for the moment, they could bask in the comfort of their home, surrounded by those most beloved to them.

But Life doesn't often allow such moments of uplift to linger long. The next morning Lucy walked to Dolly's house and as she lifted her hand to the iron knocker, she found an envelope stuck behind it with her name on it. Sitting in one of the white wicker porch chairs, she read the letter Dolly had written her.

"My dearest Lucy,   *September, 1862*

When you find this letter, we will be gone, and Jane with us. It is no doubt the coward's way, but I have already shed more tears than Robert thinks good for me. I don't think he can tolerate more of them. And I cannot abide the thought of the moment I would have to let you go from our final embrace. So I apologize for this method of departure, although I know you will understand and even realize that it is for the best.

I don't know where we will end up. But as soon as I can, I will write to you so you know that we are well. And if we have found a new home. At least that way we can remain a part of one another's lives.

Jane sends her love and apologies too, and has left behind her spinning wheel for you. She says you should go get it if you wish to have it, before the people to whom she sold the house can move in at the end of the month. I find it a great comfort having her with us. We have a complicated connection, I freely admit. Most important, both of us have things in our recent past that no one will be aware of wherever we decide to put down roots.

I will tell you this much. We are heading east over the mountain. We have talked about Carson City, Genoa, and Virginia City. Each offers us something attractive. I, myself, would like to try Genoa, as there is a fort there if we should need protection. I suppose it is nice to have so many options from which to choose, but it does nothing to allay the sense of uncertainty that underlies all thoughts of the future.

For now, my sweet friend, let this be just a small space of time between us. We will fill it with adventures and challenges and anecdotes that will soon fill our letters. Give my fondest regards to Jim and Freda. And give Roger a big hug from his Aunt Dolly. Oh, to hear him call me that one more time! But God willing, that too will be in our future.

Your loving friend forever, Dolly

Lucy sat on the porch for the next half hour trying to absorb the impact of her two best friends departing so suddenly from her life. For until she received a letter telling her not only where they had settled, but also that they had all arrived there safely, she would not be at peace in her mind. She had experienced so many losses of valued people from her life over the length of her twenty-seven years, and in that moment there in Placerville it was as though all of them merged with the loss of Dolly. She felt the collective weight of them crash down on her, and she knew it would be hopeless to try and stem the flow of tears cascading down her cheeks.

After half an hour, she got up and walked to the back of Dolly and Robert's house, now radiating a profound emptiness. She stood where Dolly had so often done the laundry, the tubs gone and probably packed full in the back of their wagon. She then looked over to the wicker chairs where she had listened to Dolly describe growing up in Los Angeles. She could almost taste the lemonade that had refreshed them. It was at this point that Lucy realized she was slipping into a maudlin state that would not serve her well. She quickly turned her back on the house and walked home with her head high and a determination to simply carry on.

As she approached the house, she saw Jim standing on the front porch with a letter in his hands. "It's from Robert. It was brought here by Piney Paul."

Standing at the bottom of the steps up to the porch, Lucy removed Dolly's letter from her skirt pocket. "This letter from Dolly was waiting for me under their door knocker."

Jim clenched his jaw tight and his eyes gleamed bright as he held out his arms to Lucy. For a moment she thought of denying her need for such comfort, but then gave in to reality. Lifting her skirts, she bounded up the steps and into his arms. Feeling the comfort of them close around her, she burrowed into him and surprised herself when she found that she had not after all released all her tears.

When she had purged herself of her initial grief, she pulled back and accepted the offer of his handkerchief. "Now we have to tell Roger. He's going to be so upset."

"We still have to do it." Jim's practicality strengthened Lucy, and she gave her face a good mopping.

At that moment the subject of their concern came out onto the porch, having been standing just the other side of the door listening to his mother's weeping. He was pale and tense as he stepped forward. "What's wrong, Mom? Are you ill?"

"Oh, no, dear." She sat on one of the porch chairs and motioned for him to approach. Taking his hands in hers, she told him, "I have received some sad news. Robert and Dolly have moved away, and I don't know yet where they'll be living."

"But I didn't get to say good-bye." His frown was pronounced as he tried to understand this sudden change to his world.

"Neither did we. But they thought this best, to save us having to say good-bye face-to-face. They thought it would be too wrenching."

Roger thought a moment. "I'm not sure I agree with that." Then his face brightened and he turned to his father. "Can we go see Gus and talk to him about this?"

Jim, envying the resiliency of youth, asked Lucy, "Would you mind if we leave you for a little while?"

"No, not at all." Her smile was a bit wobbly, but her voice was steady. "I'll go tell Freda what's happened, and we'll spend time in the kitchen baking something."

Jim smiled at this feminine response, thinking the creative productivity of it more practical than what he was going to be doing for the next hour or so. However, as he had done so many times over the years, he gave thanks that Lucy still had Freda in her life.

After an hour of watching a stimulating conversation between his son and Gus, covering a number of topics, Jim exclaimed that it was time they left Gus so he could get on with his day. He ignored the disappointment on Gus's face, and turned to the door.

As Roger got up from the table, he asked Gus, "Do you think I'm precocious?"

Gus fought back an urge to laugh, running a hand over his mouth and beard. "Well, yes. Why do you ask?"

"A man once asked me if I knew what it meant? I wasn't sure, so I looked it up. I know what it means now, but I'm not sure why the man asked me that."

Gus glanced at Jim, who shrugged and looked out the window. Gus took a moment to formulate his words. "I think, as far as you're concerned, that it means you're clever and smart. And that you're maybe a little more mature than most boys your age."

Roger nodded thoughtfully. "I can shuffle cards better than any of the boys at school, that's for sure. Even the older ones. But they're not interested in card games like I am." He let out a sigh of resignation, then stood up straight and grinned. "I've even bested some adults when we lived in Jamestown." He added quickly, "But not playing for money." He looked over at his father. "He won't let me get into a real game with adults." No one could have missed the annoyance in his voice.

Jim turned back to the room. "Come on, Roger. It's time we return home."

As they opened the door and Roger prepared to precede his father, Gus called to him. "You won't always be this age, Roger. Enjoy what you can of it. That's something to remember, no matter what age you are."

Roger smiled, nodded, and walked into the alley with his father close behind him. Gus sat back in his chair, looked around his cabin, and decided that maybe it was time he did some cleaning of it. Maybe even some new paint on the walls. It had been some time since he had thought of his home's appearance. But, well, if he was going to have unexpected company from time to time, maybe it was something he needed to think about. And maybe he should buy a new shirt. He looked down at his old boots, but then thought, "Naw, not yet."

Leaving the shadows of the alley and breaking into the sunlight on Main Street, father and son blinked as their eyes adjusted. Roger felt his father's hand on his shoulder and looked up at him.

Jim was looking down at his son, thinking about how life itself was a high-stake gamble, and how much he had won in that particular game. But there had also been times when he had lost, and had once come close to losing it all. Yes, he thought, every day is a fragile gift that needs to be treasured and handled gently. And maybe sometimes its rules can be set aside as long as it hurts no one.

He then surprised Roger by saying, "You're not only more mature than boys your age, but you're also taller. If not told, I think most men would think you twice your age."

"Is that significant?"

Jim raised a brow. "Is that a new word you've learned?"

Roger grinned. "Yeah. I've been waiting for the right time to use it."

"Well, yes, that is a *significant* point. Because I've been invited to play poker with a few friends who I think might be open to letting you sit in, at least for a hand or two. Would you like that?" Roger, being speechless with excitement, only nodded. Jim laughed and pushed his son in the direction of Goldie's saloon, where they walked straight through the bar area and into a back room. The four men at the table looked up at Jim's entrance, but their eyes quickly focused on the boy with him.

"Gentlemen, some of you know my son, Roger. Hal, you haven't met this young man, but he loves poker and is more adept at it than you might suppose."

"Hi, kid," Hal mumbled. "You want to watch us?"

"Uh, no," Jim corrected. "He would like to play with us. Not for long, of course, but maybe a couple of hands. If it's okay with everyone."

The men were actually very okay with it, thinking it a great lark and a good story to tell later. One of those present was Piney Paul, who had heard about Roger from Robert, so he tried not to look cagey as he suggested that maybe Roger should shuffle the cards and even deal. When the other players saw what a graceful and thorough job young Roger did of this, they almost had second thoughts about having agreed to let him play. But he was just a kid, so how good could he be at a complicated game like poker?

Lucy and Freda, having placed their pies in the oven, were cooling off on the front porch with cold water in their glasses when they saw Jim and Roger walking down the road from the direction of Main Street. Roger was swinging his arms and taking big strides, and Jim looked about ready to burst with laughter.

"Mom! Aunt Freda! I won three out of four hands!"

"Hands of what?" Freda asked, moving aside so Roger could sit next to her on the wicker loveseat.

Lucy immediately knew what had taken place. "Oh, Jim, you didn't!"

"I did." A grin cut his face, unabashed pride beneath it. "I let him sit in on a game in Goldie's back room."

Before Freda could object, Lucy asked, "And the other men were okay with that?"

"Yep." His blue eyes danced with mirth as he removed his hat and ran his fingers through his long black hair. "But after he won three out of four hands, they suggested that maybe that was enough of a kid playing an adult game."

Roger watched his parents laughing, felt Freda's hug, and remembered Gus's last words to him. Yes, he was indeed enjoying that moment in his life. But he wondered if maybe Gus had also been trying to tell him that there would be a lot of moments in his future that he could look forward to enjoying. Roger liked the thought of that, because he often fantasized about what his future would be like.

Of course, life doesn't have set rules like a game of cards, and a child's imagination cannot fathom the twists and turns that the game of Life can deal out. He would someday look back on this particular moment with fondness, and remember that particular truth only too well. But for the moment, he felt that life was grand; and that the first time he had played poker with adults was, for him, somehow going to be very *significant*.

ACKNOWLEDGMENT

Some of the people in this fictional novel were real people who lived in Placerville in 1862. Their jobs and locations in the town, if mentioned, are real; however, it must be noted that their actions and conversations are not, and that any emotions or actions displayed by them in the novel are purely a writer's device to bring realism to the story. Below is a list of those individuals who lived in Placerville in 1862.

Bill Baldwin, waiter at Cary House
Ann & Henry Banta, divorcing in 1862
Fredrick Barss, jeweler, Main St. between Coloma and Plaza
Caroline Beck, laundress and divorcing Peter
William Bennett, proprietor, Pioneer Livery and Feed Stable
Leo Bernathowitz, barber, lived at Cary House
Mike Borowsky, owner Post Office Exchange, and City Alderman
Sara Burns, owner of Main St. cigar store near Cedar Ravine
W. R. Chapman, Deputy Sheriff
John Crowder, stage driver for Pioneer Stage Lines
James Derham, porter at Cary House
W. M. Donahue, liquor dealer
Mrs. Dooris, fruit dealer, Upper Placerville
Nancy Edward, laundry on Cary Alley
Mr. W. Eichelroth, County Coroner
Caroline Fountain, milliner and women's clothing
G. Francis, clothing store owner, Main on the Plaza
Lizzie Gordon, entertainer
Tereise Guidici, boarding house on Reservoir St.
Tuck Hing, Chinese merchant and community leader
Bill Hooper, steward at Orleans Hotel
James B. Hume, Deputy Collector, City Marshal
John B. Hume, City Attorney and Law Office of Hume & Sloss
Martha Hume, wife of John Hume, house east side of Bedford Ave.
Alex Hunter, County Sheriff & Fire Dept. Board of Delegates

William Hyman, waiter at Orleans Hotel

Mrs. Irwin, millinery

James Johnson, Judge, County Court, Court of Sessions & Probate

Louis Landecker, grocer on corner Main and Sacramento streets

Sarah Landecker, wife of Louis, house on Main St. above Mill St.

Josephine and George Landers, divorced in 1862

W. H. Lowell, steward at Cary House

Mary Mahon, chambermaid at Cary House

Mr. McClure, desk clerk at Cary House

Henry Morey, Placerville Iron Foundry

George P. Morrill, druggist north side Main St. on the Plaza

Mrs. Mary Morrill, living with George south side Washington St.

Agnes and Sarah Murphy, dressmakers (no relation to Lucy)

William Norris, driver for Pioneer Stage Co.

Mary Nary, laundress at the Cary House

W. P. Packard, clerk at Orleans Hotel

Thomas B. Patton, Clerk of the Court

Maria Piarein, laundry on Cedar Ravine

Maria Price, laundry

Anne Radigne, saloon worker

Henry Rehl, clerk for Mr. Landecker

J. J. Reynolds, City Police officer

Reverend Ross, pastor, Methodist Church

Mr. Roy, furniture dealer and sometime undertaker

Mr. S. W. Sanderson, Esq., Attorney

J. W. Seeley, jeweler rooming at Cary House

George Shaw, telegraph operator

Adam Simonton, constable

Henry Sloss, law partner with Mr. Hume

Ollie Sprague, stage agent, boards at Orleans Hotel

Ben Turk, laborer

John D. VanEaton, City Police officer

Mr. Williamson, clerk for Mr. Landecker